RECKLESS SOULS

SAINTS ACADEMY

1

KC KEAN

Reckless Souls
Saints Academy #1

Cover Designer: Covers by Christian
Editor: SCW Editing Services
Proofing: Sassi's Edits
Interior Formatting & Design: Wild Elegance Formatting

Reckless Souls/KC Kean – 1st ed.
ISBN-13 -

To Laura,

For listening to my inspiration for this story, and envisioning it just as I did. For teaching me pinterest, and making everything so damn pretty as always!

You're a queen, thank you!

Whatever the cost. Whatever the pain. We shall prevail.

PROLOGUE

Rage.

Destruction.

War.

Darkness attempts to overwhelm the bright sky as chaos continues to swirl through the air. The chill that follows the blackness, sends shivers through our bones.

Despair consumes us, forcing our survival instincts to the forefront. We must protect ourselves, by any means necessary. And we will.

We have the power to build an army.

But simple human soldiers will not do.

We are Gods, kings among men, and in our wake we'll ensure we are immortalized within story books and tales of lore.

Angels.

Demons.

Vampires.

Shifters.

We will rule the world, protecting ourselves from the evil that is the Goddess Nyx, the ruler of the night, just as Zeus proclaimed we will.

We won't settle until her force is gone.

We won't settle until the threat on our lives has been eliminated.

We won't settle until we are the supreme leaders.

This time shall be marked in history as evolution. Young and old supernaturals working together as the world has never seen before to create a safer future.

Whatever the cost.

Whatever the pain.

We shall prevail.

"Dead. She's dead!" The cries of glee sound distorted and distant, but I know them to be true all the same.

The sun has barely risen as I step out onto my balcony, looking down at the town square below as people dance and sing together. Rejoicing that the evil that consumed us all has been vanquished from this world.

Two hundred years.

For two hundred long years, we've been creating our armies, fighting this battle, and searching for the evil that is Nyx.

I grip the railing, my knuckles turning white as I look around the streets.

High rise buildings frame the cobbled square below. Little cafes, shops, and bistros line the pavement, with tables and chairs scattered around waiting for guests to take a seat, but they're long forgotten now in favor of a more energetic celebration.

I've never seen so many people dance before. Not in public, and certainly not in the town square. But I guess these extraordinary times mean people will temporarily lose their inhibition.

The huge billboard attached to the building across from me flickers, the pixels quickly forming as Zeus appears on the screen.

Our *hero*.

Our *leader*.

His smile fills the screen as the camera slowly zooms out, capturing the God from head to toe for us all to worship. With his almost white hair swept back off his face, and his pearly white teeth on full display as his blue eyes sparkle, he looks every inch the almighty God you'd expect him to be.

Impeccable. Personable. Our savior.

Adjusting the cuffs of his tailored shirt, he slowly lowers his hands into the pockets of his dark gray trousers, before he finally speaks. The noise from below is silenced as we all wait with bated breath for our idol to address us.

"I'm sure you've heard the news," he starts, pausing for dramatic effect before he continues. "The. War. Is. Over," his voice booms, ricocheting off every wall as cheers erupt from below again. It's almost like he's standing right here in front of us, hearing the joy as he glances around and waits for the noise to settle before he speaks again. "With my bare hands…" He raises them up in the air like they're his weapon before slowly lowering them into his pockets. "I brought Nyx to her knees in the early hours of the morning, and there's nothing else to say, but the rest… is history."

"It's over! It's all over!" I hear someone below cry out, raw emotion in their voice as they chant the words on everyone's minds.

"In the coming days, arrangements will be made to make our lives much more comfortable going forward. I have plans for how we can work as one, united and triumphant, in the aftermath of this war," he says, his smile infectious as he reassures everyone that the worst is behind us. "We all deserve harmony, peace, and structure moving forward. Simple things we've not had for so long. Now is our time, with Nyx and her entire bloodline gone, no evil will *ever* hurt our world again!" he booms, certainty in his eyes as he pulls his hands from his pockets and splays them out wide, almost like he's embracing his people.

I wet my lips, stepping back from the railing as his smile widens even further. "The Hexagon, a joining of all kinds, will oversee the new laws to protect and serve you. Always. I can't wait to lead us to greatness."

Moments later, the screen goes black and the cheers pick up again. The magic in my chest swirls, excited, giddy, and desperate to unleash with the knowledge we will no longer suffer.

Whatever the future may hold, it can only end with light and happiness now.

ONE

RHEA

Rage courses through my body as I march down the sidewalk. Fire burns under my skin as the red shiny target of my emotional chaos comes into view.

That motherfucker.

That damn motherfucking cuntish… cunt.

"Rhea. Fuck. wait, Rhea!" he calls out from behind me, likely stepping out of his house with nothing but a sheet wrapped around his waist, but I don't bother to turn around to confirm.

He can choke on a bag of dicks, while he stays as far away from me as possible.

My pulse pounds in my ears as my palms sweat from the desire to give him a physical response instead of a verbal one. I reach into my jeans pocket to retrieve my house key. Slowing my steps, determination takes over as I look down at my hand to find my mini Stanley knife keyring.

Dante, that motherfucking asshole, bought it for me when we started dating ten months ago. He's going to regret that by the time I'm done.

"You mean everything to me, Rhea. I need you to be safe at all times."

Ha. Those were the words he'd uttered as he handed it over so long ago.

What a whole heap of bullshit that is. Or maybe he should have been more specific with what he actually meant.

"I want you safe at all times, especially while you're working so I can fuck my neighbor."

I fucking hate how mad it makes me because I let my walls down for this guy. Well, I considered it, offered him nothing but my body, but there's no respect in this. Not an ounce, and I, at least, respected *him*. Our embarrassment of a relationship, if that's what you could even call it, is a complete shambles after what I just saw.

"Rhea," Dante hollers again, his voice getting closer as I stop beside his most prized possession; a shiny, red Porsche. I'm sure those obsessed with cars would scoff at my simple description of the vehicle, but that's all it is to me.

Turning to face the asshole shuffling toward me, with his gray sheet wrapped around his waist like a greek god, I almost chuckle at the absurdity.

If only he was a God. Then I could have him wipe this shit from my mind or something.

But we're not in Paradise Heights where the supernaturals live their best life. No, we're down here in Phoenix Valley among the rest of the mundane humans.

The way his brown hair is ruffled, the dark stubble on his jawline taunting me, I want to reach out to him. This is, *was,* my favorite version of Dante; after sex. But that can't count when it's someone else who's been running their fingers through his soft hair. Now the thought makes me recoil and I mentally slap myself for even *wanting* to touch him. I hate feeling weak because that's not the type of woman I am.

His gray eyes plead with mine, desperate for me to understand that he magically slipped, his dick falling inside her by accident, leaving him just as shocked as I am.

No second chances.

No forgiveness.

No disappointment.

I've lived by those rules for twenty-two years. I'm not about to change them for him.

Not now.

Not on my fucking birthday.

But even if it wasn't, I still wouldn't bend my words-to-live-by and disrespect myself in the process. That ship set sail long ago.

I run my tongue over my teeth, keeping my face neutral

as I stare at him with eyes void of emotion. I can feel people watching us, but I don't tear my gaze from him. It probably includes the woman he was just fucking, wanting a front row seat to the drama she just caused.

Whoreish… whore.

Twirling the mini blade in my hand, I flick the switch over as I turn to look at his shiny, red, fucking Porsche.

"Please, Rhea, let me—"

He doesn't utter another word as I lean forward, tracing my fingertips along the top of the hood, down the fender with the blade in hand, making it look like I'm about to key his car. But instead, I slightly crouch and swing out to my left, piercing the sharp edge into the front right tire.

I want him to taste a touch, even a pinch, of my anger, and this will at least release some pent up rage inside me. Before he's really caught up with the situation, I'm taking a step back, and repeating the motion again, relishing in the symphonic hissing sound that surrounds me.

"Fuck, Rhea, stop! What are you doing to my girl?" he growls, storming toward me, one hand around the sheet and the other clenched at his side, but I slip around the back of the car, repeating the same motion once more on the back left tire, before finally stepping away and looking at my handiwork, a satisfied grin appearing on my lips. "Rhea!"

Now he's angry.

Good.

Always leave the last tire, Rhea. Don't let this fucker get away with not paying anything because of insurance.

Standing tall, I meet his gaze over the roof of the car, outrage shining in his eyes as he gapes at the mess I've just made of his *precious girl.*

You and me both, asshole.

I crack my neck, making sure to keep the raw anger off my face, my eyes uncaring, before pointing the blade at him. "I don't ever, *ever*, want to see you again." The sharp bite is noticeable in my tone, but he doesn't respond, still gaping like a fish out of water, his eyes bouncing from me to the car.

Finally looking away from him, I take in the row of small, cookie cutter houses, his fucking side piece hanging out of the upstairs window as her mouth drops at the scene I just made.

Fuck her.

I offer a two fingered salute with a manic smile as my heart thumps wildly in my chest.

It's times like these I wish I knew someone with powers, someone to make all of this go away. By death or just wiping my memories, right now I'd consider either, but that's not the case.

Instead, I stand here, as broken as ever on the inside.

My eyes fall closed as I take a deep breath, letting the usual feeling of bitterness and disappointment wash over me, basking in it, before I blink my eyes open again.

"Rh—"

"Ever," I interrupt, not letting Dante mutter another fucking syllable of my name.

Turning on my heels, I cut across the quiet street, the sound of a horn ringing out as a car almost hits me, but I don't pause my stride because I'm past caring.

I used the last of the cash I had on me to take the bus over here. It's not everyday I get to leave early, but since it's my birthday, Vinny took pity on me, letting me go without closing the diner like I was supposed to tonight. A complete surprise, nothing in comparison to what just took place before me, but a shock all the same.

The thought of birthday sex had me climbing on the bus with an extra bounce in my step, but apparently Dante was already celebrating, with someone else.

Fun, with a capital F.

Swiping a hand down my face, I pull my old, worn earphones out of my pocket, wiping them off before slipping them in, plugging the cord into my phone and pressing play on my latest *moody* playlist.

I've got a forty minute walk home so I may as well entertain myself on the way.

Pulling the hair tie from my wrist, I run my fingers through my long brown hair that falls to the middle of my back, scooping it up into a messy bun on top of my head. The hot sun beats down on me in my uniform; jeans and a blue and white striped shirt. It's not exactly hot weather friendly.

I don't look back, leaving the more affluent part of Phoenix Valley behind as I cut through the small rundown portion of town.

Apparently this place was beautiful once upon a time; you wouldn't know looking at it. And now? It's just… sad.

Battered. Beaten. Tainted. Forever bruised.

A bit like me, I think with a sigh.

The year I was born was the year the war ended. Thank the Gods. I already suffered enough in the remnants of the chaos to have to live through the war too. I dread to imagine being in the middle of it all. I was clearly the outcome of some sexual celebrations, only to be tossed aside, more like *abandoned*, by my parents. I became another lost soul of the orphanage in town from the day I was born.

Sometimes I wish they had just ended the misery for me then. Instead, I've had to survive in Phoenix Valley, a world that still looks nothing like they promised to restore it to. *They* being the Gods and other supernaturals that ruined the world for humans in a bid to end a greater evil. Repairing their own lives, while leaving us to rot.

Whatever.

They've clearly never had to live a day in our shoes. The shiny high-rise buildings that once offered a stunning landscape continue to stand half-demolished, ruined, and uninhabitable. Making everyone move out to smaller areas of Phoenix Valley.

As I pass the bus stop, I take the next right, getting

closer to the older part of town and my shoebox apartment. We've taken back what we could as a collective, almost like evolving from cavemen to modern men again, but instead of thousands of years to do it, we've had twenty-two.

Paradise Heights is worlds apart from the mess and rubble that still lines the streets of Phoenix Valley. It's visible if you look up at the sky and tilt your head to the left, offering you a glimpse at what could be. After the war, the supernaturals decided to save the land that was the most salvageable, suspending it in the air, and making it exclusively for them.

Fuck us neanderthals, right?

Gods created armies of angels, demons, vampires, and fucking werewolves, then gave them a safe haven, while leaving us with nothing. Nothing but misery, despair, and hopelessness.

When I was younger, I would imagine what it would be like to live such a lavish life. Looking down at the humans like ants, inconsequential, and a constant visual view of hell to them. Seeing glimpses on the television, and hearing stories sent my mind into overdrive.

I would dream I had powers, skills, and anything that could be used to possibly make my life a little better. Which wouldn't have been hard considering I only had a metal bed frame with a lumpy mattress I slept on at night, and shared a room with five other girls. Watching as they were adopted, one by one, but not me. *Never* me.

A shiver rattles its way through my body at the

helplessness I felt growing up. Fuck, I need a stiff drink and a movie. Something fun. Something to distract me from my reality. Something to pull me out of this funk I've slipped into because of Dante being a cheating scumbag.

Dante was more of a friends with benefits situation than a relationship, but fuck, he was at least a constant in my life. The *only* one, a clear reminder to rely on no one but myself. Screw everyone else.

My favorite Chinese restaurant, Peacock, comes into view on the corner of my street, and the thought of dipping into my measly savings to splurge on a chicken lo mein fills me with a little bit of joy. It's a birthday treat, break up fix, and overall happiness gift to myself, and I deserve it. But before I can indulge and spoil myself a little, I need to run home and raid my savings jar.

I smile at the old guy that lives across the street, sitting in his rocking chair out front without a care in the world. Always a story to tell and a smile on his face. He's in his late seventies now. You'd expect him to be as miserable as the rest of us, since he lived through the dreaded war, but I don't think I actually know a happier person. The slight tingling of warmth spreads through my chest at the realization.

I can sense words on the tip of his tongue, and quickly pull my earphones out.

"Happy birthday, child," he sings from across the street, making my steps stutter, but I manage to cover the mishap as I grin at him.

"Thank you, Al," I reply, stunned that he knows it's my birthday, but I must have mentioned it before. I've lived here ever since I was kicked out of the orphanage at eighteen, four years ago, and I don't recall him saying it before, but I shrug it off, offering a wave as I turn to my front door.

The wooden boards that replaced the glass are a stark reminder of how deteriorated the building is. Updating infrastructure in the lower income areas was never a priority.

Entering the pin into the dated locking system at the door, I step inside, the damp, moldy scent instantly hitting my nose, making me cringe. You'd think I would have become immune to the smell after all this time, but if anything, it gets worse every day. I wonder if any of my neighbors feel the same? Doesn't matter though because nothing will be done about it anyway.

The building holds six individual apartments, but none of the other residents are around. Thank the Gods. I don't need a fake, meaningless conversation right now. As tough as I'm trying to be, I'm still disappointed, *hurt*, by today's revelations, and talking about the weather is only going to irritate me. Which will only make me a snippy bitch, and none of us want that today.

The elevator has never worked, and of course I'm on the top floor. So, I take a deep breath, ready to trudge up the dirty green carpeted stairs, but an envelope peeking out of my mailbox makes me pause.

Mail?

I don't ever get mail unless it's an overdue bill, and I've been on top of that lately. What the fuck could it be?

Frowning, I detour to the wall of mailboxes, pulling my key from my pocket to open it, only to find another envelope inside too. Well fuck.

Worry crinkles my eyes as I reach for them both, tucking them under my arm before racing up the three flights of stairs. Sweat trickles down my spine from the movement and heat combining, and there's no reprieve when I step inside my apartment since the air conditioning is broken.

I'm met with a blast of humidity, the heavy air causing a bit of tightness in my lungs. I take a look around my tiny apartment. The front door opens to reveal the mini kitchen to my right, with my sofa set up to the left, which pulls out as my bed, leaving the door to the left as my bathroom. The windows straight ahead offer a pitiful view since I'm overlooking the back of the property, staring at the brick wall of the neighboring building. Natural sunlight isn't really a privilege for me in here, that's a fact.

Moving to the small refrigerator in my kitchen, I swing the freezer door open and stick my head in the cold space for a second to cool down. A shiver runs through me at the drastic change in temperature, my lungs protesting at the cool air. Taking one final gulp, I take a step back, glancing down at the letters in my hand.

When they don't magically reveal their contents, no pun intended, I open the top white one first, a birthday card slipping out. A pretty purple butterfly decorates the front page, *Happy Birthday*, written intricately along the top, but when I open it, there's no indication of who or where it came from. It simply reads,

To Rhea
Happy 22nd Birthday
Best of luck

Uhh… thanks, Mr. Invisible?

I stand it up on the laminate countertop, the only card I have, before moving onto the other letter. The envelope is almost gold compared to the first, the quality feeling thicker, pricier. Sliding open the flap, my frown deepens when an official document falls out.

My eyes scan over the words as I unfold the paper, making my heart gallop in my chest. I try to swallow past the lump in my throat as my fingers tremble ever so slightly.

Miss Rhea Harrington
As your twenty-second birthday has arrived, you are cordially invited to attend a testing at the Town Hall on Monday, October 2nd at four p.m.
The testing will confirm if you have any supernatural abilities

as required by law.

Failure to attend will result in The Hexagon taking matters into their own hands.

Kind Regards,

Hex

TWO

RHEA

I swipe my hair back off my face as I glance at the clock, internally screaming at the time. Irritation burrows deep in my chest, anxiety coiling tightly around my throat as I wrap the last set of cutlery and add it to the pile, ready for the evening rush that'll come later.

Not that I'll be here for most of it, but it's my way of contributing.

My brain has been stuck on four p.m. since the second I opened my eyes this morning. Fuck, let's be honest, ever since I opened the damn letter.

Now it's three thirty, and if I want to make it across town in time, I need to head out.

The quicker I get there, the quicker I can get back, and the less money I'll lose for the day. With a resigned sigh, I run my hands down my apron, before untying it and folding it neatly on the server station.

"Vinny, I need to go," I holler, looking toward the open window that gives everyone a direct view into the kitchen, and a moment later he makes an appearance.

"You know I can't pay you, girly," he grumbles, and I roll my eyes.

"I know, Vin, you've mentioned it a time or two," I reply. More like a million times. He's like a broken record. "I'll go there, do what I need to do, and be back as fast as possible," I add, forcing a smile to my lips as he tosses a dish towel over his shoulder, shaking his head and waving me off.

He knows it's mandatory for me to go, something I'd completely forgotten about in my disaster of a day with Dante, but it still inconveniences him and ultimately that's all he cares about.

Now to just put one foot in front of the other and actually leave the comfort of the diner.

Making sure I have my phone and keys in my jeans pocket, along with my small wallet, I'm ready to go. I step into the main hustle and bustle of the room. Large wooden tables fill every inch of the floor, cramming the space full. With only a few customers in at the moment, I wave at the other servers still working before I step out into the sunshine, letting the door fall shut behind me. The smell of grease still lingers on my skin.

I shield my eyes slightly, tilting my head up at the sky

for a moment as I take a deep, calming breath, letting the fresh air fill my lungs. Wetting my lips, I huff, before turning in the direction of Phoenix Valley's Town Hall. If I hurry, I should make it there with a few minutes to spare. I can take the stupid test and it will all be over. Then I can continue on with my life as if this was nothing but a blip.

The nerves I'm feeling don't seem to shake off so I dig out my earphones, immediately tucking them into my ears before pressing play on another angsty playlist. The sun's not helping. It's too fucking warm. That must be why I feel like I'm overheating and sweating like a pig.

Tightening my ponytail, I swipe the beads of sweat from my temple as I make my way through the streets. At this time of day, people are either working, picking up their children from school, or doing anything else that keeps the center of town quiet. There's only ever minimal people out, the mad rush will start again in the next two hours. Then it will be like this sense of calm never existed.

I don't usually have a reason to come over to this side of town, ever, and the further away from my comfort zone I get, the more my anxious thoughts threaten to consume me.

Get in, get out, get back to work. I repeat the thought over and over, with each step I take.

Although, what would it be like if the outcome was different from the reality?

What if I was… *supernatural… gifted… powerful*?

What would that feel like? Physically, emotionally?

My eyes instantly tilt to the sky and search out Paradise Heights, far off in the distance, casting a permanent shadow beneath it.

To live a different life, to have an ability, *any* ability that makes you unique, makes you important, makes you visible.

An audible scoff falls from my lips as I shake my head. Flying under the radar is all I've known, all I'm comfortable with.

Get a fucking grip, Rhea.

I don't know why they even bother with these tests. Surely they must know before someone turns twenty-two if they have any supernatural skills and abilities. It doesn't make any sense, but I've always begrudged supernaturals, and the pretty, appealing life they get to live. I've never been eager to learn more about them, other than their general existence. They stay perched high on their pedestal in the sky, while we survive on the minimums down here.

I've seen a vampire or two, hovering on the edge of the dodgy parts of the city, but I've always run as far away as possible, because they're not there for a casual good time. Even from a distance you can sense their aura of danger. They're either there for blood, money, or both, and it's something I *never* wanted to get caught up in. Not when I've seen so many of the girls from the orphanage caught up in all of that trouble.

Just thinking about it sends a shudder down my spine.

But you could tell what they were the second they extended their fangs and their eyes glowed blood red. Their leering, aggressive body language made it clear that they are the hunters and we are the hunted.

Everything else I know about supernaturals, I've seen or heard on tv, but I've never seen a demon, nor have I heard the murmurs of an incubus or succubus, luring you in with their desires and appeal. They've been nothing short of a myth to me.

I've never knowingly seen a shifter of any kind, in their animal form at least, but I've seen the people behind them on the television before.

Angels look almost like me, from the television too, but I can't explain the difference. It's almost like they're… lighter, freer, glowing.

Then there are the Gods. The biggest assholes ever to grace the world. Better than the rest of us and quite happy to remind you of it.

Fucking… fuckers.

Taking the next right turn, I glance at my phone. I have five minutes to get there on time, so I increase my pace as I brush the wispy hair back off my face.

It really is too fucking warm. I glare up at the sun, not a single cloud in the sky, hoping the supernatural in charge of controlling the weather feels my pain and suffering.

Since the war, that's all they've done; control every inch of our human lives, right down to the damn weather. The mythical four seasons no longer exist. We have sun all day, and it rains in the darkness of the night between one and four in the morning. Every. Fucking. Day.

I've seen snow in old movies, but it's not something I'll ever get to witness first hand, since they deemed it an unnecessary weather condition. I appreciate the fact that there's no more disasters caused by Mother Nature, but this is just… boring. We may get the occasional gust of wind, or a gentle breeze, but otherwise, the Hex seem to think they're doing us a favor by keeping us in the hot weather.

My phone vibrates in my pocket, pausing the music in my ears, but when I look at the screen, my nostrils flare with irritation.

Dante.

He can fuck all the way off.

For the last five days he's called me non-stop, swamping me with voicemails and texts. I haven't given in and answered a single time, not once, but he still continues, relentless in his approach. I don't need nor want his apology or bullshit. I don't think we knew each other very well to begin with. It was a heavy case of fucking that went on too long because we got comfortable. I can detach myself from the reality of our relationship. He needs to as well.

Good dick won't make me crawl back.

Ever.

Hitting the red button, I pocket my phone again as I turn

right into the huge square where the Town Hall stands tall and imposing.

Large stone steps lead up to a column-framed building, with a sloped roof and cream coloring. It reminds me of the type of building they had in the old Greek movies about Gods, legends, and all of the myths. Only here, there are armed guards standing in front of each pillar, in full black uniform, with the haunting Hex symbol hanging on flags.

I come to a stop, considering whether I should turn and run back to the diner, but the reminder in the letter of what would happen if I didn't show, has me putting one foot in front of the other.

The Hex are… judge, jury, and executioner, in both the human and the supernatural worlds. I've never researched them, apart from the few times Zeus himself has addressed us on television and thankfully I've never had any other kind of interaction. The other members seem quite happy to let him reap all the glory, be the face of Hex, while they stay hidden in the background running the show.

Short for *Hexagon*, the group is made up of six members, each representing their *kind*, to create a united front for everyone after the devastating war.

A God. An angel. A vampire. A shifter. A demon. And a human.

They're the politicians of the new world who have a much heavier footing in the supernatural city than the human one. Likely because it's prettier up there, more luxurious. No one wants to have to make do down here. Not even the most affluent areas of Phoenix Valley compare to the images I've seen of Paradise Heights.

As I near, the Hex symbol looms above me, its presence a reminder of who controls who. A black background with what look like six white slashes mark the material. One for each member of the Hex. Short, simple, and fearsome, with three words written among the image.

Veni, vidi, vici.

I have no idea what it means, but I'm more than happy to continue with my naivete rather than try to find out. The less I know, the better off I am.

I startle when a large, calloused hand is waved in front of my face, making me blink up at them as I quickly pull my earphones out. "Are you going to move, Miss, or am I going to have you escorted off the property?"

I stare in surprise at the guard, who has stepped away from his post to glare down at me. I'm frozen to the spot at the bottom of the steps that lead up to the entrance of the Town Hall.

Fuck.

I hadn't even realized I'd stopped walking.

"No, I'm moving," I murmur, hastily stepping around him to rush up the stairs, stuffing my earphones into my pocket as I go.

Thankfully he doesn't say another word, but the

glare I feel on my back screams a thousand words of how much I inconvenienced him. I rush inside without any further interruptions.

My heart thunders in my chest, and I'm not too sure if it's because of the way the guard just startled me, or what I'm actually doing here, but either way, I don't like how fucking unsettled I am.

Taking a deep breath or five, I wet my lips and glance around the open space. It feels eerie, echoey, and overbearing. I'm surprised to see there's no foyer, just a queue of people lined up around the exterior of the huge room, while the center is taken up by what must be the testing area.

There's no privacy, no separation, the whole process is just done out here in the open for everyone to watch.

Great.

Like my life hasn't gone to shit already, I now have all of these people watching me be reminded just how *not* special I am. Joining the back of the line, I watch the center like a hawk, trying to figure out exactly what happens from start to finish.

There are two women and two guards standing up on the simple wooden platform, with something in front of them, but from this angle I can't see anything but their backs.

One by one, someone takes a step forward, declares their name and day of birth, and the advisors tell them what to do. It seems like they've collated everyone with birthdays in the past week or so. They talk quietly, so you can't hear what the directions are, and as I move to the side, hoping to catch a glimpse, I realize there's a mahogany wooden wall up, shielding whatever they're doing from the rest of us.

With a sigh, I try to distract myself with the details of the room, but when I scan every inch around me, I realize there's nothing but more Hex flags. No posters, no leaflets, nothing at all. It's just… bare. Just as forgotten as every single one of us in here. Well, except on our twenty-second birthday. Apparently, that's when we matter most.

We come in, they test us, we don't change magically before their eyes, so they send us on our merry way, discarding us once again. Rinse. Repeat.

I'm the one not getting paid, and completely inconvenienced right now, not them.

It doesn't take long until I'm facing the podium head on, nerves tingling my fingers as the advisors come into view, but they're too busy, focused on the person directly in front of them to pay anyone else any mind. I'm unsure why they even bother doing this. Sure I've heard of a few people who test and are confirmed supernatural —no one I know personally— but the ratio is slim to none. I remember hearing the caretakers at the orphanage once say it was because all the celebratory sex for winning the war was orchestrated by the demons, more specifically the incubi and succubi, so they could regenerate their magic or something. But this then led to supernaturals and humans *socializing* together, and nine months later, there was a baby boom.

Looking around the room, it dawns on me that everyone here has just turned twenty-two, the same as me, and we're all the product of orgies.

What a way to enter the world.

A grin tips the corner of my mouth up as I amuse myself, and I'm so lost in thought that I almost miss the woman calling next. Meeting her gaze, I realize I'm next in line, and I take a tentative step forward.

"Hurry now, name and date of birth," she calls, fixing the thin-framed glasses on the bridge of her nose, her lips twisted tight as she waits impatiently.

Clearing my throat, I move toward the small wooden steps leading up to the platform, placing one heavy foot in front of the other as I make my way to the top, wishing there was an extra step or two to delay my arrival. I can sense the two women and two guards staring at me expectantly, waiting for my answer, but my eyes are fixed on the object that sits on the table before them.

I can feel my jaw slacken as I stare, in complete and utter awe of how majestic it looks. At first glance, it just seems like a small box, but the way it captivates you, almost hypnotizing, tells you that there's more to it than meets the eyes. It's a mixture of blues, greens, and all of the shades in between depending on how the light hits it, but even more interestingly, there's carvings and images ingrained into the sides.

It's like nothing I've ever seen before.

"Name and date of birth," one of the women calls out again, but I can't take my eyes off the box before me.

"Rhea Harrington, September twenty-seventh—"

I don't get to finish when the guard interrupts. "Here," he murmurs, seemingly marking me off from a register on the tablet in his hand as he pulls my attention away from the little glimmer of magic before me.

"Miss Harrington, if you could please dip your hand into Pandora's Box, that would be all you need to do to complete the test," the lady closest to me says, and I flick my gaze to her. She has her blonde hair pulled into an eccentric beehive on top of her head, wearing a quirky orange dress-suit, with intricate flower detailing running along the hem. There's nothing mundane about this woman. Fuck, even her eyes are yellow. Yellow. If that doesn't tell me she's not human, I don't know what would. She's definitely supernatural.

Clearing her throat as she runs her hands down the front of her blazer, she lifts her eyebrow, and I fumble forward, looking down at what she called *Pandora's Box.*

All I can see inside is darkness, a black hole, which instantly sets me on edge, but I find my fingers moving forward of their own accord. Before I even realize it, my fingertips are stroking along the rim of the intricate box.

I expect them to hurry and nudge me along, but if they do, I don't hear them as an almighty scream rings in my ears.

Pain. Fear. Misery. Death.

I can't breathe.

I can't see.

I can only seem to *feel*, and what I'm feeling is utter torture.

The scream continues, ringing and ringing in my ears uncontrollably as I feel my eyes pinch shut even tighter. My body is locked in place, a mixture of dread and trepidation tainting me as I will the noise to stop.

"Miss Harrington! Miss Harrington!"

The sudden calling of my name breaks the hold I seem to be in, as if it unlocks me from the screams attempting to devour me, and I fall. In a heap on the floor, a tangle of limbs, a whimper escapes from my lips as I sigh in relief, the screaming no longer there consuming my mind, body, and soul.

I can hear the sound of scuffling shoes around me as I try to pry my eyes open and figure out what the hell is going on, when a hand on my shoulder suddenly makes my eyes pop open.

Face to face with the eccentric lady with yellow eyes, I watch as her mouth moves, but I can't process what she's actually saying. My brows knit together in confusion, and I shake my head trying to communicate what I can't seem to verbalize. She must sense I'm not registering a word she's saying because she rolls her eyes, taking a deep breath before she lifts her hand to my temple.

"Better?"

What the fuck?

It's her voice, but her lips aren't moving.

"You can hear me then?"

Nope. Mouth still not moving.

Is she… talking directly into my mind?

"Yes, I am, Miss Harrington. You seem to be in a little bit of shock, and actually talking to you isn't registering right now, so here we are. Me talking to you in your mind."

She replies to my thought.

To. My. Fucking. Thought.

I try to nudge back, but she simply widens her eyes at me, freezing me in place as my heart pounds wildly in my chest.

What on earth is going on? Who the hell was screaming?

"The Box, Pandora's Box, or I assume, at least, because no one out here has made a noise let alone a scream," she states, continuing in my mind as I stare at her with wide eyes. "Are you able to stand? We have much to do," she adds, making my frown deepen.

Much to do? I need to get to work, I think, and the woman before me shakes her head. Her yellow eyes lighten as she looks at me with sympathy.

"I think not, Miss Harrington. Pandora's Box called to *you*."

Called to me?

She must be mistaken, this entire thing is a fraud. I need

to lie down because this conversation can't still be going on in my head like this. That's ridiculous.

"It's *not* ridiculous. Do you know what this means, when the Box calls to you like that?" she asks, her voice almost gentler, even in my mind.

I shake my head slightly in response, at a complete loss for words and thoughts. This is probably the first time in my life where I've ever been shocked into speechlessness.

"It means there's more to you than meets the eye, Miss Harrington. Pandora's Box only calls to those with supernatural powers. Although I must admit, I've never seen it happen to someone who simply touched the rim," she explains, and I feel the blood drain from my face, leaving my brain empty, void of any rational thought.

"What does that mean for me?" I find myself asking out loud, and she drops her hand from my head, rising to her feet as she looks down at me with what almost looks like genuine pity in her eyes. Who would have thought, a supernatural pitying a human?

The noise in the Town Hall slowly tries to creep in and bring me back to reality, but my eyes cling to her lips, waiting for them to move, but when they do, the words spoken make no sense at all.

"It means you'll be spending the next three years at Saints Academy."

THREE

RHEA

I run my fingers through my hair, looking down at the contents in my small, rundown suitcase. It's been through a lot with me, from leaving the orphanage, to storing my clothes here, and now. Here we are, about to go on another unknown adventure.

What the ever-loving fuck is going on?

And how in the fucking fuck did this become my life?

Honestly, I don't know, but I feel like someone somewhere must be able to answer the questions swirling around in my head. I was escorted home in a daze, the reminder of the douchey guard in my mind has me looking over my shoulder at the front door to my apartment.

They're on the other side, waiting for me to get my belongings before we leave.

Leave.

It doesn't make any fucking sense to me at all.

There's clearly been some kind of mistake somewhere because I can't be supernatural. Not even a little bit. I would know if I was, I'm sure of it. I would bet my life on me being human.

Apparently, Saints Academy awaits since Pandora's Box said I'm gifted, and I'm expected to leave right away. For Paradise Heights.

Paradise. Fucking. Heights.

My brain keeps short circuiting because… just what the *fuck*?

A hard knock sounds from my door, and I release a huff, flipping the lid of my suitcase over before zipping it up. The temptation to flip them off is strong but at this rate, who knows if they can see through my door? "I'm coming," I grouch, still confused why the change had to happen today, this very instant. Can't I be given a moment to process any of this?

What happened back there was… That sound, that *scream*, I don't ever want to hear anything like it again for as long as I live. I shake my head, trying to remove every inch of the memory from my mind.

I would have told the lady with the yellow eyes she was truly mistaken if she hadn't proceeded to pull out a dagger from the box, dipped in gold, with my name engraved into the handle.

Rhea Harrington.

Any other time or place and I would have said it was a

parlor trick, but it seems my life is taking a whole different path. Not that I understand what any of this actually means, but fuck, it's mine now apparently.

Taking one final look around my apartment, my home, my sanctuary, I lift the suitcase, upset that all I have to bring with me fits comfortably inside. I've written a note and left it on the kitchen counter, advising my landlord I'll be gone for a while, or forever? On the way home, my brain went into overdrive, worrying about all of the things that needed to be arranged, all the bills I can suddenly no longer pay, and I even had to send Vinny an email to explain I wasn't coming back to work. There's no way in hell I had the words to explain it over the phone, with actual complete sentences, so an email had to do.

Once someone speaks to me about the situation, then maybe I'll have words to consider using to provide a coherent explanation. This better not be a fucking hoax because *they're* upending my life and I'll have nothing to come back to if it turns out this isn't real.

"Let's go," the guard calls out impatiently from the other side of the door, another heavy knock quickly following, and I roll my eyes.

In leggings and a white blouse with my nicest pair of sandals, I move toward the door, leaving my greasy uniform behind.

I've thrown up in the toilet, screamed into my pillow,

and downed the largest mug of coffee I've ever made, and still I find myself as tense as earlier. Only this time there's the added worry of what the fuck actually comes next. I hate not knowing what lies in store for me because it feels like I no longer have control over my life, once again.

Opening the door, the bulky guard stands with his arms firmly folded over his chest as he glares down at me. My snarky comment freezes on the tip of my tongue. As much as I want to lay into him, he's also dictating what I'm supposed to do, and I don't want to piss him off. Just by his gruff appearance alone, he looks like he could make my life a living hell. So when he turns on the spot, heading for the stairs, I don't miss a beat and I follow after him. A subdued little girl I'm definitely not, but I'm okay to admit that I'm *not* okay right now and letting him take the lead seems like the most logical choice I can make.

The walk down the stairway feels daunting, knowing I won't be able to come back here any time soon. I've always dreamed of a better place than here, but at twenty-two, I was also highly aware of my reality. I know I'm going to miss this place. It's home. It is mine. And now, it seems I'm *theirs*.

I tried to tell the yellow-eyed lady that I was happy where I was, being who I am, a human, but that apparently wasn't taken into consideration and Pandora's Box is *never* wrong.

Stepping out into the street, the guard is polite enough to hold the door for me. I offer a tight smile which he doesn't return. Dick.

I look around for a car that doesn't look like the rest, screaming it belongs in Paradise Heights, but I don't see a single one.

Confused, I take another step toward the road, glancing up and down, when I hear Al call my name from across the street. "Miss Harrington, are you going somewhere?" I meet his questioning gaze, an easy smile on his lips as always, and it's frightening how much I think I'll miss him too.

"Uh, I am, Al," I respond lamely, pointing down at my suitcase, not really sure what else to say.

Against my will?

Save me?

"Well, it was good knowing you. Take care of yourself up there," he adds with a short wave, before pulling his cap down over his eyes and dozing off in his chair as if the conversation didn't happen.

What did he just say? Up there? Where did that come from? I mean it's true, but how the hell does he know?

The guard, he must be able to tell by the damn guard.

Turning to face him, he nods for me to follow him to the right, and I fall into step beside him. The streets are a little busier now than they were earlier, the after work rush hour upon us, but the guard side steps everyone effortlessly, me hot on his heels, before turning right off the main road, and down the sketchy alleyway at the back of my building.

"Where are we going?" I ask, my brows crinkling in confusion as I look for a vehicle, but still nothing.

"To the Academy of course," he grumbles like I'm a stupid human, and I glare at the side of his head, but sadly no magic power of being able to burn him with laser vision comes to fruition.

The thought of magic has my hand heating on the handle of my suitcase, a reminder of the dagger inside confirming my place in the supernatural world.

When he continues toward the graffiti covered wall at the far end, I finally stop, refusing to follow him blindly anymore. This motherfucker is going to walk me to my impending death. "Well, that's a dead end, so maybe we need to go in another direction, hmm?" I gripe, pointing over my shoulder with my free hand, watching as he shakes his head at me, slightly exasperated by my questions.

"Miss Harrington, it seems you're forgetting where we're actually going," he says mockingly as he glances back over his shoulder at me.

My response is cut short when he turns back around, swirling his arm slowly clockwise in front of him toward the wall, where a sudden gust of black smoke forms before him.

What. The. Actual. Fuck?

They seem to be the only four words sitting strongly in my vocabulary right now, but seriously, what the actual fuck?

"W-what is that?" I ask, unmoving from my spot

as I watch the smoke swarm out until it sits in the shape of a rectangle against the wall.

"A portal," he replies in a bored tone. I gape in surprise, my feet suddenly carrying me toward the contained smoke.

Coming to a stop next to him, it's my turn to shake my head. "I'm not going through that," I state, standing taller, confident with my decision, but the guard beside me scoffs.

"Let me remind you, Miss Harrington, you don't have a choice in the matter," he retorts, before placing his hand between my shoulder blades and pushing me into the smoke.

I brace for impact, hand out to catch myself before my head smashes into the wall, but to my surprise there's no impact. The ability to breathe becomes tighter for a split second, before a bright light glares ahead.

Fuck. Am I dead? I never thought I'd be stepping, no, stumbling, into the white light before I made it to Paradise Heights.

It all happens so fast, I'm still toppling forward from his push when my palm hits the ground.

Gulping a huge breath, I stare down at the grass beneath me, just avoiding the faceplant I was so close to.

Grass.

Perfectly cut, greener than green grass.

Those four words of complete mindfuckery threaten to infiltrate my mind, but it's clear I have no clue what's going on. Asking myself again isn't going to change that. But for real…

What. The. Actual. Fuck?

With my suitcase still firmly in my grasp, I take a couple of breaths before I tilt my head up to see where the hell I am, only to find a poised woman towering over me.

"You must be Rhea Harrington. Come, you're late, and there's much to do." Can she not at least give me a second to stand? "Oh, and my apologies, welcome to Saints Academy."

FOUR

RHEA

Saints Academy?

How the fuck did I just get here that fast?

Dusting off my knees as I rise to my feet, I glance around us, blinking a few times, a deep frown on my face as I confirm her words.

Before me, stand tall wrought iron gates, attached to a high brick wall which outlines the perimeter for the property on the other side. A huge sign just to the left, in granite and gold lettering confirms where we are. 'Saints Academy'.

Not sure I'm fully believing what I see, I tuck my hands behind my back and pinch my forearm. Much to my surprise, I wince with the sharp pain, and everything remains the same. Nope, not delusional. Thank fuck for that.

Which means I'm officially in Paradise Heights, when

mere moments ago I was in the back alleyway of my apartment in Phoenix Valley. The reminder has me glancing over my shoulder, expecting to see the perfectly shaped black fog, but there's nothing there at all, not even the guard. Just the outline of a forest in the distance. Talk about a mindfuck.

"How did I get here?" I find myself asking before I realize it, and the lady turns to me, offering a sympathetic smile as she presses her thumb against an entry pad beside the gate. A hint of excitement courses through my already anxious body, adding a slight tremble to my fingertips.

"Portal, dear," she replies casually, like that makes any sense to me as the gates slowly begin to open. I expect to hear a creak as it moves, but to my surprise, there's no sound at all. Just an eerie silence.

As she takes a step toward the opening, clearly just expecting me to follow without another word, something in the air makes me pause. Squinting at the sky above the gates, I watch as a ripple effect captures my attention. It reminds me of when I was a child at the orphanage on my birthday. If you had been good, and not a problem child for the last twelve months, then you got a small tube of blowing bubbles.

The way the sky shimmers so slightly, a tinge of colors mixing like a kaleidoscope, it reminds me of a bubble, floating above me majestically like a dome, luring me in with the desperate need to pop it.

"What's that?" I ask, a finger reaching out toward the

bubble in the sky, just like when I was a child as I put one foot in front of the other and follow after the woman. "And what's your name?" I add, a hint of guilt at the fact that I haven't asked already, but this is all a lot right now, and my basic human 101 manners are still down in Phoenix Valley.

"My name is Noreen, I'm a receptionist at the school and your guide for this evening. While that up there is a ward." She waves her hand out in front of her, encouraging me to catch up as she steps through the open gates, and I rush to fall into line with her. At least she's not being an asshole like the guard was. She seems to understand my confusion, my curiosity, my disbelief and is willing to help. I don't want to piss her off and have her shut me out. I need as many allies as I can find.

The bubble dazzles before my eyes, and I walk through it, just like Noreen, prepared for a distinct pop sound to come, but it never does. Instead, it's almost like the sound of a finger snap claps around us, a jolt of electricity zaps through me as I look up at the ward.

It almost seems brighter, shinier, thicker from this side. How strange.

"What is it for?" I murmur, realizing it's as if we're inside the semi-bubble now.

"Do you always ask so many questions?" she replies, answering my question with a question. I expect her to respond with a certain tone but there's no snark, no anger, and no disinterest. If anything, her voice has a hint of teasing to it, prompting a ghost of a smile to reach my lips.

"I can't say I've ever been in a position where I've needed to," I answer truthfully, my steps slowing as she turns to face me. The insecurity I'm feeling begins to peck at my nerves and that emotion is something I'm not used to experiencing.

I'm eager for her response, desperate to understand *everything*, but I can't help but stare at the grass around us. It looks like fields and fields of the lush green stuff, but nothing else. Literally nothing else. As far as my eyes can see, there's no Academy here which makes me a little suspicious.

"It's to protect the Academy. A glamor and defense bubble all in one. The snap sound you heard was the imprint or pulse of your magic linking to the ward, adding in another layer of defense to protect what is sacred to us," Noreen explains, my eyebrows reaching my hairline as she speaks, but I'm far too speechless to respond.

Magic.

My magic?

I can't stop my gaze from lifting up to the sky again, the buzz of electricity that seemed to jolt through me earlier runs through my body again as a reminder, leaving me in utter disbelief.

"Where is—"

"Give it a moment, the ward is adjusting to you being here, and once it does the glamor will drop," she interrupts, apparently knowing what I was going to say before even I truly did.

I squeeze my eyes shut as I try to adapt to the feelings coursing through me. The sensation, what must be my magic, is like nothing I've ever felt before. I had been hoping I would have recognized the feeling before today but it's completely foreign, before it's suddenly gone.

She stands, tapping her right foot on the ground as she folds her arms over her chest, waiting expectantly, and I take the moment to look the woman over, now that I'm not completely bewildered by where I am.

In a brown pencil skirt, with matching blazer, and a silk white blouse beneath, she gives off the air of being part of the administration, or even a librarian, but there's a sparkle in her brown eyes that tells me she's much wiser than she first appears. Her comfy small heeled leather shoes don't disturb the soil beneath her feet, and her brown hair is pulled back into a ponytail. Guessing her age would be like guessing how long the sun has burned for, but I would assume she's maybe ten years older than me.

When my eyes meet hers, I find her staring at me just as I am her, clearly sizing me up. Curiosity swirls in her irises, possibly even a hint of judgment. I clear my throat uncomfortably at being caught, when another crackle rings out around us.

"Perfect," she mutters, turning on the spot, and I take the extra step to come to a stop at her side.

In slow motion, I watch as an invisible curtain is slowly lifted in front of me, inch by agonizing inch, until I'm left gaping at the scene before me, my knees ready to give out in a mixture of shock and awe.

I have been rendered speechless, again, and that shit doesn't happen very often.

Black, gray, and onyx tones color the huge building before me. Intricate patterns, delicate window frames, and archways decorate the gothic cathedral. Or that's what it reminds me of at least. Super tall and splatterings of stained glass finish off the overall appearance, leaving me in awe.

The sudden sound of birds chirping in the distance makes me startle out of the visual overload of Saints Academy, but what catches me by surprise even more, are the people strolling around in groups, going about their day, like I wasn't just standing here staring at nothing moments ago.

Holy. Fuck.

Could they see me standing there acting like a toddler being introduced to candy for the first time? Not like I give a shit about my reputation but still.

"Come," Noreen orders, heading for the grand steps straight ahead that lead up to a huge double-doored wooden archway.

I scramble to keep up with her, wetting my dry lips as I tighten the grip on my shambles of a suitcase. "Are you sure this is all correct? I mean, I'm twenty-two years old, done with school and all of the learning crap. I think Pandora's Box may have gotten it wrong," I state, staring at the fact everyone here is wearing a uniform, but before I can take in anything else, Noreen turns around and stops right in my path, forcing me to a stop directly in front of her.

"Pandora's Box *never* gets it wrong," her tone is sharp, nostrils flared and hands clenched at her side. Well, fuck. That's me being told.

I nod once, which she seems to accept and interpret that I'm going to keep my mouth shut as she marches up the steps, leaving me to chase after her. Again.

The huge double doors slowly swing open, revealing cream marble flooring and a grand staircase in front of me. Gold framed photos adorn the walls, with baroque patterns trailing the rim, all unique and beautiful, with what looks like random people inside the images. I'm sure they hold some importance, but I don't recognize a single face.

"Miss Harrington," I hear, and my gaze flicks back to Noreen where she stands to the left of the staircase, waiting for me to get a grip and catch up again. I avoid colliding with anyone as I approach, no one paying me any mind as I fall into step with her. "You've missed the start of the school semester, so you'll have to get caught up on all of your studies," she advises as we make our way down the wide hallway, lined with at least a dozen doors, each as ornate as the rest of the building.

Why does she make that sound like it's my fault? I

don't even want to be here and she clearly doesn't understand that I was forced to go for testing. I mean, let's be real, I was quite happy with my boring mundane life, rather than facing the unknown.

Better the devil you know.

"Maybe I should just *not* be here," I mumble, my eyes trying to take every inch of the place in, yet seeing nothing at all in my shock. Being non-observant is unlike me because I need to be able to protect myself from the unexpected.

"Don't be ridiculous. When your powers grow, Miss Harrington, which they will, you're going to want all the guidance you can get. Let's not forget the fact you added to the ward as you entered the property, before the Academy revealed itself. If you were simply human, as you seem adamant on believing, then those things wouldn't have happened."

My cheeks blush a little at her blunt statement of facts as she takes a left at the end of the hall, revealing more wooden doors at the end. It's like a fucking labyrinth. I keep in step with her, a million questions running through my mind, but none of them forming to actually ask out loud.

"Is anyone going to explain to me what I'm actually supposed to do here?" I ask, finally forming a question as the crowds of people thin out in this part of the hallway.

Noreen nods in response. "You'll pick things up along the way, and I have an information booklet for you to read which will cover the basics. It's been quite some time since we've had an earthling among us, so, please be patient," she says with a smile.

Earthling? Is that supposed to be me?

And patience? I'll give them every drop of it, as long as they have some in return for me.

"Okay," is all I manage to respond as we step through the wooden doorway, only to come face to face with another cloud of black smoke.

"Nope. No. Nada. Not again," I ramble, looking back over my shoulder for a clear escape route, but even I know it's pointless deep down.

"You're going to be here for three years, Miss Harrington, there's a lot to take in. But I'm going to be honest with you now, portals are a thing here, you're going to need to get used to them," she states, a hint of a smile on her lips as she quirks her eyebrow at me.

"It's Rhea," I mumble, swiping my brown hair back off my face as her smile softens.

"Rhea," she repeats, before walking to the table set up beside the billowing black smoke. She grabs a small suitcase and a clipboard up off the table before turning back to me. "The portals in the Academy, like this one, are forever in place. Created by the Goddess Hecate before her demise in the war, may she rest in peace," she adds, clearing her throat. "The ones at the Academy are modified compared to standard portals. For example, this one will take you to the hall the Academy believes your magic will be best suited for. It's been spelled so they can somehow read your magic's strengths and weaknesses, even when you yourself cannot."

I continue to stand, gaping at her as she speaks, no words rising to the surface as I simply nod along like what she's saying makes *total* sense.

But now that I think about it, I literally just learned I have magic hidden within me so how would I even know what my strengths and weaknesses are? Fuck. My brain cells hurt.

"They're a common mode of transport around the Academy, with stronger ones made by Hecate that will determine the best classes for you also." She looks down at the clipboard in her hand before she continues. "Your Saints Academy uniform will be available to you when you arrive at your room, the wardrobe filled and ready. Please remember to read the booklet I have for you, and the emails too. The information is of utmost importance and there's no leniency on this," she adds, looking up at me, including a 'you better do as I say or else' look on her face. Although I know this is all serious stuff, I bite the inside of my cheek to contain a smirk at being chastised, but it doesn't settle my nerves.

"Sure," I manage to mutter, completely lost in the swirl of information. I wouldn't be surprised if my brain starts short circuiting.

"You'll spend this next year figuring out the origins of your magic, and unlike others, who know their family background, you'll be navigating a little blind and with a wider range of options, but you'll know the answers before the end of the academic year. Your second year will be devoted to learning your skills, understanding the art of your gift, before your full strength kicks in by the age of twenty-four. Then you'll find your role in this world."

"Err, what? I'm not really taking any of this in," I blurt out, admitting the truth, nibbling my lip in embarrassment, and the smile she offers tells me she already knows that.

"It's all in the booklet, dear. But for now, I shall just let you know that the dining hall is back here in the main building. There's a portal in each hall of dorms that will take you there effortlessly. Your schedule will be in one of the emails, along with details on the Dean, house leaders, and your professors. The only thing left for you to organize is the linking of your thumbprint to the monetary system." When her eyes meet mine once more, she shakes her head, likely at my paling face and round eyes. I'm not sure I can handle any more explanations since I can already feel my ship sinking so there's no use denying the inevitable. The reality is, I'm in way over my head.

"You have my email address?"

What a stupid fucking idiot. As if that's the only question I had to offer right now.

"Oh, yes. This is for you," she says, placing the suitcase down on its wheels and rolling it toward me. I tentatively take the handle as she continues. "You will find Academy assigned technology along with a few other pieces to get you settled." I nod numbly, not really sure what else to say as she glances at her watch. "It's almost seven in the evening now. I'll arrange a meeting with the Dean for you tomorrow at eight, right before classes, but I do believe there may be an assembly first too. I'll make sure to send over all the updated information."

"Right," I murmur, watching as she steps aside so I can access the portal, but I can't seem to move my feet.

"When you're ready, Rhea, the portal will assign you to your chosen hall."

I rub my lips together, tiptoeing forward as my mind battles with my body and heart. As much as I may not want it to be, this seems like it's my only option. A reminder of the little I've left behind has me snapping my head up high as I take a few more confident steps until I'm right in front of the smoke.

This is it.

This is my future.

"Thank you," I mumble to Noreen, but I don't turn, the portal holding my attention as I release one last breath and step forward with my suitcases.

This one feels different. Almost like I'm suspended in time, the portal deciding where I should go, running over every inch of my skin and leaving goosebumps in its wake, yet when my feet touch the floor, I don't think a second even passed by.

Blinking at the change in lighting, I try to adjust to my new surroundings, but the boom of a deep voice interrupts me.

"Who the fuck are you?"

FIVE

RHEA

"*Who the fuck are you?*"

I blink, and blink again, snapping out of my haze as the angry guy standing before me remains firmly in place.

He could almost be a figment of my imagination. He's that beautiful.

It should be illegal for someone to look like him.

Jet-black hair falls messily over his head, past his eyebrows and almost touching his piercing green eyes that hold me captive. He's easily over six feet tall, with broad shoulders and a cold, detached air around him.

My gaze slowly rakes over him from head to toe, from his fitted black sweatpants, to his long sleeve white t-shirt, he looks mesmerizing. When my eyes finally meet his again, I find him staring at me expectantly, with a quirked eyebrow, making me audibly gulp as I scramble to remember what he actually said to me.

"I said, who the fuck are you?" His tone is even colder than earlier, a chill running down my spine as I continue to gawk at him like he's asking me if I want to sell my soul to the devil. When I still don't respond, he shakes his head dismissively at me as he glances at his watch. "I don't have time for this," he grouches, placing one hand on his hip as his emerald green eyes bore into my simple blue ones. "Look, whoever you are, you know you can't be in here, right?" He waves his hand in dismissal.

"I, uh, didn't know that. I just stepped through the portal like Noreen said. I—"

"Noreen?" he interjects, frowning as he drags his eyes over me like he's finally seeing me for the first time, and I watch as he acknowledges both suitcases, before sighing. "I get you wanting to rank in one of the higher halls, I mean who doesn't? But if your name isn't on the board then you can't be here. It's clear you must be a little dense, but it really is that simple."

The pretentious motherfucker. How fucking dare he speak to me that way.

With an exasperated roll of his eyes, the sinful dickhead takes a step to my right, and points to the wall. For the first time I see something else here that isn't him. A wooden plaque is fixed to the wall. *AGION* is written in large gold letters on the dark mahogany wood, followed by a listing of rooms from one to six. All of them have a name written next to them, except number four, but as I scan the board, looking for what clue he's trying to give me, a gasp falls from my lips as gold writing suddenly begins to carve into the wood.

I can sense the stranger glaring at me, still waiting for me to talk, but again, words seem to fail me and my gasp must've drawn his attention to the board. More specifically, the name being etched into the wood beside the number four. *My name.*

There, before my very eyes, *Rhea Harrington.*

Mic drop, motherfucker.

Glancing back at the dark and mysterious guy, I clear my throat, finally finding a hint of my attitude as I push my shoulders back and cock an eyebrow at him. I can feel a smirk grace my lips too because I won. "It would appear that I *am* on the board after all," I purr, pleased with myself as he glances between me and the plaque once more.

"Rhea Harrington," he mutters, almost to himself, rolling my name across his tongue in a caress as I shudder.

Sensing sudden movement from behind me breaks the stare off between us, followed swiftly by the sound of a girl's voice. "Hey, asshat, have you seen a new girl anywhere? I'm supposed to... oh, *you're* new," she babbles, coming to a stop beside me, searching my face, before widening her smile. "Rhea?"

"That's me," I respond with a tight smile, swiping the loose hair back off my face as I look her over. Her hair is pure white, right down to her hips, and her eyes are a stunning shade of pink. Almost a baby pink shade, but a little darker, and it leaves me completely surprised. We're about the same height, but instead of jeans and a shirt like me, she's in a cute mint green summer dress.

"Perfect, my name is Harmonia. I'm assuming he's being an asshole like always," she states, not even questioning it. "Let's go before that escalates, shall we? I can already sense it won't end well for him," she adds, her gaze flicking from me to the hot guy scowling down at me. His jaw is so tight that there's a high chance it may snap or maybe break some teeth, but he doesn't utter a word. Fine by me since he was hotter when his mouth wasn't spewing bullshit.

As much as I'm curious about him, I've dealt with far too much today to be on the receiving end of his misdirected wrath too. With that in mind, I offer Harmonia a slight nod, before wheeling my suitcase around him, my personal one firmly in my grasp still as I follow her lead toward the staircase straight ahead.

Approaching the staircase, I take the six steps up before it turns to the right, and another flight of stairs comes into view. I can't stop myself from glancing back over my shoulder, needing one last glimpse at the arrogant mystery guy, but to my dismay, he's already gone.

Dammit.

I should have paid more attention to the board. If that's where the names of the people staying in this building are listed, I would have been able to try and guess who he is.

That's a sleuthing job for another day, this evening I just need to get to my room and hide away. Forever.

Or at least until morning.

Rubbing my lips together, I try to replay the past few minutes of my new supernatural-esque Academy life, and something catches me off guard. "How did you know you were looking for me if I didn't know where I was going when I stepped into the portal?" I ask, struggling to wrap my head around it all, around all of the *magic*, but she thankfully offers me a reassuring smile as she points ahead for us to walk down the hallway.

"When your name etches on the board to confirm your hall, it also etches on the official documentation back at the Academy. Noreen sent an email through, just as I was heading back from dinner. She was shocked by your assignment to say the least, but I was already here so no issues," she states, tucking her hair behind her ear as she slows in front of the door labeled *four.*

"Shocked?" I ask, unable to form many words apparently, but she nods, cringing a little as she runs her hand down her dress.

"Yeah, uh, I guess because you're an earthling and

you've walked into the most elite hall at Saints Academy, but I'm not really sure," she rambles, making my brows knit together in confusion.

None of this makes any sense. The more I keep repeating that sentence, the more I realize just how much my *human* upbringing and culture makes it hard to accept this new way of thinking.

I need to sleep, and wake up in my own bed, in my mundane life, before everything gets twisted any further upside down.

"I didn't realize there was a name for us," I say, looking the wooden door over for a handle or key or anything at all, but then it dawns on me and I'm trying hard not to panic because of how much I'm craving space. "How am I supposed to get in here? Noreen didn't give me a key or any instructions."

"Oh, uh, sorry. Here in Paradise Heights, the word human was dismissed as *boring* a long time ago, and someone deemed earthlings more fitting," she advises, making me roll my eyes. Of course, there the supernaturals go again, acting like they're better than we are and making decisions for us without our input. Assholes. "And to answer your question about the door, when you stepped through the portal, it ran a scan over your body. If you place your palm flat on the wood, the door will open for you."

"Oh."

Yup, locked down to just two letter words now. Great,

Rhea, that's just great. What a way to make a fucking impression. No wonder humans have a bad rep, it's because of people like me who can't form a full sentence.

"I'm in room three," she says with a smile, pointing to the room across the hall from me. "The house leader of Agion is Sky. Just Sky, since she's a Goddess. She stays on the ground floor, otherwise it's just the four Elite assholes of Saints Academy in the building," she adds with a huff.

Just Sky because she's a… Goddess? What?

I can only assume the guy downstairs was one of the Elite assholes, but four? Holy crap. I will legit die if they're all as gorgeous as the first. "Thank you," I murmur, referring to her explanation, and her smile widens.

"No worries at all. I was told to remind you to check your emails, and that you need to set up a link for finances before your meeting with the Dean tomorrow." I nod along, appreciating the reminder as she takes a step back. "You are going to have a lot to catch up on, classes have been in full swing for almost three months," she states, making a lump lodge in my throat. "I can meet you in the morning, show you around if you'd like?" she offers, and it feels like a weight is lifted off my shoulders at her kindness.

"Fuck, for real? That would be awesome. Thank you," I reply, making her chuckle.

"Thank the Gods for that. I was worried you were limited to a few words and not a big talker. That still might be the case, but if you can drop an *f bomb* as casually as that, then I think we're going to get along just fine."

My own smile grows as I release the handle of the suitcase to place my palm against the wood, and a moment later a lock clicks and the door unlocks.

Holy fuck. It worked!

"See you tomorrow?"

"Yeah, I'll see you tomorrow. Thanks again for this," I reply, offering a short wave before stepping into my room with my cases.

I waste no time at all closing the door behind me, using it as a leaning post to prop me up for a moment as I inhale deeply and take in my surroundings.

My new home for the next few years.

With gray walls, navy silk curtains and a geometric patterned comforter spread across the bed, it feels even homier than my own home did. A door immediately to my left looks like it leads to an attached bathroom, while a double bed is central to the room, the headboard right underneath the window with a nightstand on either side. A desk is to my right with an oversized comfy chair tucked in, while a chest of drawers, with a television on top, are nestled against the left wall beside the attached walk-in wardrobe.

The room is… everything.

Pushing up off the door, I cut the distance to the bed, flopping down on it as I release my hold on the cases. It takes a moment for my hands to relax so I shake them out, trying to relieve some of the tension. I need to get settled and sleep, before my brain melts into a million pieces.

I pull my phone from my pocket, but it flashes with no service, so I place it on the nightstand, jumping back to my feet to find my favorite oversized t-shirt to sleep in. Eyeing both of the cases, I decide to open the newer one, leaving the dagger in my old and ratty suitcase, a stark reminder of the overall day.

Lifting it up onto the bed, I quickly unzip the bag to find a laptop, a tablet, a phone, and a Saints Academy binder of information packed inside. This is crazy. My mind screams for me to slam the lid shut, and pretend none of these things actually exist in my life, but the knowledge of having an early start tomorrow has me pulling out the phone. The second I press the button to light up the screen, it shows I have ten emails already. Fuck my life At least it seems to work the same as my old one, just on a different network or something? Who the fuck knows.

The entire thing overwhelms me as I read the subject lines.

Meeting confirmed with the Dean. 8:10. Accept?

Meeting with financial aid confirmed at 7:50. Accept?

First year assembly confirmed for 8:30. Mandatory

attendance required.

Welcome to Saints Academy, Miss Rhea Harrington. Please find your schedule attached.

I quickly accept the two meeting appointments and add them to my calendar, before dropping the phone on my bed, ignoring the rest of the messages for now.

Carefully moving the case to the floor, I opt to open my own where I placed it, quickly pulling the purple tee out and stripping out of my clothes, before climbing into bed with a huff. A glance at my phone tells me it's nearly eight in the evening, which is early for me, but fuck it.

This morning I woke up in my own bed, living my usual life, doing my usual job, before all of… this. I deserve an early night, a fresh reset.

I have no idea what tomorrow holds for me, but either way, I hope I get some answers to what is going on. The one word that keeps running around in my head, overruling everything else, has my eyes slamming shut as I let sleep finally consume me.

Magic.

I have fucking magic.

SIX

RHEA

An alarm wakes me from the deep sleep I'm in. My body feels groggy as I swipe at my tired eyes, searching for where the noise is coming from.

My new, spiffy school issued phone.

I quickly hit the snooze button, frowning at the fact it was even set, when a notification pops up on the screen.

Alarm settings confirmed for two hours prior to first calendar entry. Do you wish to proceed with this setting?

It takes a second for me to process, all of the events from yesterday flooding my memory, ending with the emails I read just before I crashed.

I have a meeting with financial aid this morning at 7:50, so the new Academy supplied phone automatically set an alarm this morning for 5:50. Without me setting it up. That's crazy.

Deciding I like the feature for now, I click *yes*, before flopping back down on the bed. My stomach growls, a stark reminder that I haven't eaten since lunch yesterday, and I need to rectify that as soon as possible. Which means I'm going to need to get a move on if I have any hopes of getting ready and finding where I can actually eat before my meetings and the assembly.

I stretch my arms above my head, the orgasmic feeling of an excellent stretch runs through my body, before I swing my legs over the side of the bed, letting the sun rays peeking through the gap in the curtains caress my skin. My eyes instantly fall to the two opened suitcases on the floor, and I make a mental note to unpack properly later. Then I can go through everything the school has supplied, *if* I'm staying.

That sounds weird on my tongue. Yesterday was an entire whirlwind of madness, and another option was never given. Not one. Part of me questions whether I should just accept this as my fate, or push back? But the lingering worry of all this being true, and me needing help, is the motivation I need to get to my feet and shuffle over to the walk-in closet.

I gape in surprise, the reminder of what Noreen had said yesterday flashing in my mind as I look over the rack of uniforms. Five hangers, five full sets of clothes, with two pairs of black shoes to choose from sitting beneath them to the right. There's a pair of sneakers to the bottom left, beside a brown leather satchel, but otherwise, there's a medium size safe that sits central on the floor and nothing else.

There's no combination or lock on it, which makes me wonder how it even works, then the memory of how I got into my room yesterday replays in my mind. A hint of nerves tingle my fingertips as I reach my hand out and place my palm against the metal. I almost think I'm being ridiculous, ready to lift my hand when the sound of a soft click registers in my ears, and the door unlocks.

That's cool as fuck.

Is it too soon to say I'm enjoying the perks of magic?

Opening it the rest of the way, there's a lot of space inside, and before I even realize what I'm doing, I rise to my feet, flip the lid on my old suitcase, and lift the dagger out of it. Even with the minimal light peeking in through the curtains, it still shimmers like the sun in my hand. There are gems in the handle, which look like real jewels, an array of colors that twinkle with the gold

I just can't wrap my head around why Pandora's Box gave it to *me*.

With a shake of my head, I move back to the walk-in closet, and set the dagger down inside the safe, closing it shut afterward. Placing my old suitcase on top of the safe, and wheeling the newer one in from the Academy, I make sure to take the electronics out, and grab the satchel, along with a pair of black pumps and a full uniform set.

Placing it all down on the bed, I stare at the tech spread

out for a moment, trying to remember what I would usually be doing right now. The thought of scrambling to get up and across town to work, compared to where I am right now, feels bizarre. But I don't have time to sit and dwell on it. I slept like the dead last night, swirling in dreams of possibilities, and now I need to get ready.

I grab my new phone, and quickly download my favorite music app, signing in and turning the volume to little more than a hum. The heavy bass thrums in my veins immediately, almost calming my soul with its familiarity.

Now I just need to shower and hit today hard.

Moving toward the bathroom door, I notice it's shut, which is a little confusing because I don't remember touching it last night. I frown at it for a moment, expecting the inanimate object to just give me an explanation or jog something in my memory, before I roll my eyes, wrap my hand around the handle and swing the door open.

Steam billows out around me just as I'm about to step in but the graphic scene playing in technicolor freezes me to the spot. Noise infiltrates my ears all at once as the sound of the shower running and a guy grunting falls in sync with what I'm seeing through the glass walls of the shower. I blink a few times then pinch myself to make sure I'm not stuck in a dream.

Fingers splayed out on the tiled wall, head flopped forward as wet blond hair hangs over his forehead. Tight coiled muscles hunch over as his other hand tightens around his cock, working his length.

I need to move.

I can't just stand here and watch this guy jerk off.

I can't.

Or I shouldn't at least. But everything about his physical appearance is just… *mesmerizing*.

As if sensing my presence, he tilts his head, and his eyes immediately find mine. A grin spreads over his face as his eyes darken, but he doesn't stop what he's doing. If anything, he squeezes tighter, tugs faster, groans a little louder. This asshole is clearly putting on a show.

I know because I'm watching it all unravel before me as my core tightens with desire at the pure sex appeal of this guy.

His tongue sweeps over his bottom lip, capturing a droplet of water from the shower, before he pushes off the tiled wall and turns to face me, his cock aimed in my direction.

Once. Twice. "Fuckkkk," he grinds, eyes remaining locked on mine as he finds his release, shooting it over the glass that stands between us.

A heavy silence hangs over us as I remain in the doorway, in just my oversized purple tee that hits mid-thigh and my rosy cheeks.

"I didn't realize I was going to be getting an audience this morning," he says, his voice almost a purr, and I shiver at the thought of voyeurism.

Finally finding my tongue, I fold my arms over my

chest. “I didn’t realize this is a shared bathroom,” I mumble pathetically, annoyed that my snarky side hasn’t risen to the surface quicker. But even more frustrated with myself that I didn’t check the bathroom out last night and realize it was a jack and jill setup.

“Surprise,” he sings with a grin, grabbing the shower head from the wall and washing the remnants of his orgasm down the drain, before striding from the shower in absolutely nothing. Fuck. I’m not sure if that’s a blessing or a curse.

His cock swings, still semi-hard and hypnotizing, and it takes everything in me to force my gaze away. I’ve never been dickmatized before but here I am.

I clear my throat, wetting my lips as he comes to stand in front of me. “I thought shutting the door would be enough, but it seems I was wrong,” he murmurs, dragging his eyes over every inch of me, sizing me up as his gaze caresses my skin.

“Maybe lock it next time,” I retort, a smile of my own gracing my lips as I attempt to portray sweet and innocent, but the way he smirks, lifting his hand to tilt my chin back, I know he sees *right* through me.

Leaning forward so we’re face to face, our noses almost brushing, his smirk turns into a smug ass grin. “Baby, I’m a fucking incubus, I *want* an audience,” he advises, his breath blowing against my lips one second, and in the next, he’s gone.

I stand frozen in place, blinking rapidly as I try to figure out what the hell just happened here, but there’s no explanation for it. I pinch myself once more just in case the first time was a fluke.

Incubus? In real life?

Why the hell do I want to find out more?

♅

I stand in front of the floor length mirror, running my fingers over the foreign clothing I'm wearing, and I sigh.

A uniform. A fucking uniform that involves a damn skirt.

I didn't even have to dress in one when I actually went to school, so it's bullshit that I have to start now. I'm twenty-two years old, I know how to dress myself but here I am, wearing a silk white shirt, navy tie, with a navy skirt and blazer that has gray stitching embroidered around the hem. Finished off with the black pumps and my hair pulled back into a ponytail on top of my head, I'm ready to go.

I'm not sure whether I should have put some make-up on, but at the last second I thought better of it. That would only set an expectation for me to wear it all the time, and that's far more effort than I'm willing to commit to.

Grabbing the satchel from my bed, which I've stuffed with the gadgets in case I need them, I head for the door. The vision of the hot fucking Adonis from earlier still flits in my brain, urging me to find my own release, but that's going to have to be paused until tonight. At least I won't have to go searching for material to help.

It's bizarre as hell that there's a handle on this side of the door and not the other, but I swing it open and let it fall shut quietly behind me as I hold my phone in my other hand.

I make my way quietly down the corridor, back to the staircase I came up with Harmonia yesterday. Scanning through the emails I received yesterday, I look for the one I remember having portals in the heading. Making a mental note to go through the pamphlet I got too at some point. I don't want to have Noreen breathing down my neck for not following orders.

There's so much for me to read through. I'm really going to need to make a plan of action tonight, along with getting settled in, but for now, I need to figure out how I get back to the main building.

Reaching the bottom of the stairs, I'm not watching where I'm going when I walk straight into a hard chest, stumbling backward, before a hand grabs my arm and stops me from falling.

I gape up in surprise, caught off guard again this morning for the second time, only to come face to face with the dark haired and green eyed asshole from yesterday. Before I can truly appreciate his chiseled jawline and piercing eyes, made all the brighter by his long black hair framing them, he unfortunately decides to open his mouth.

"Watch where you're fucking going," he hisses, eyes

glaring at me as he releases his grip and storms up the stairs without another word.

"Asshole," I mutter under my breath in agitation as I straighten the sleeve of my blazer, and focus my attention back on my phone, finding exactly what I was looking for.

Portals

To access many points of the Academy, you will be required to use the portals situated throughout campus. There are numerous types of portals on site, required for different purposes.

The main one in your dormitory halls will be located on the ground floor, and will give direct access to the main Academy building.

I stop reading, saving the rest for later since I now have the information I need. I didn't want to step back into this thing without confirmation that I wouldn't be lost forever in some version of a supernatural purgatory.

Moving toward the black mist that stands against the wall like a door, I gulp, hoping I'll get used to this sooner rather than later.

Before I can think any more of it, I grip my phone and satchel tightly, before extending my right foot into the darkness, followed quickly by the rest of me. I haven't even finished blinking when I find myself at the foyer to the main building I was in yesterday.

Huh, so the portal didn't bring me out exactly where I entered last time. Noted.

There are a few people around, a couple stepping out of other portals around the room, but overall everyone seems to be heading in the same direction, toward the smell of food. My stomach grumbles again as my phone pings in my hand.

Financial Aid meeting rescheduled for 7:30, confirm?

Fuck, that's like, right now.

Food will have to wait, although it might be better to get the financial aid stuff out of the way first so I can understand how it all works anyway because I have no clue how I can pay for Saints Academy.

I click *accept*, taking another step out into the open space at the bottom of the grand staircase, trying to figure out where I should go next, when I notice the plaque on the wall to my left.

Arrows point in every direction, floors labeled next to different rooms, and I scan through it all to find where to go for the Financial Aid, but it's not listed.

Fuck.

What am I supposed to do?

Brushing a loose tendril of hair back off my face, I open my phone and press to the meeting invite again.

Financial Aid meeting confirmed for 7:30

It doesn't state where, but when I scroll down the notes section, I catch sight of the button labeled 'directions'. Jabbing the screen quickly, I expect it to tell me which room to go to, instead it turns into a little GPS on my phone, telling me to head in the same direction as Noreen took me yesterday. Thank the Gods for technology.

Moving to the left of the staircase, no one pays me any mind as I walk by, the few people hovering around lost in their own world as I follow the blue arrow on my phone. It leads me to the door next to where I was yesterday.

The door is slightly ajar, and as I lift my hand to knock, the woman on the other side meets my gaze. "Oh, come on in. You must be, Rhea, Rhea Harrington? I'm Beverly," she says, rising to her feet as I push the door all the way open.

Ginger curls frame her face as she fixes the glasses on the bridge of her nose. In a pair of black pants, and a thin white sweater, she looks artsy compared to everyone else who have been all business and well put together. When I say all, I mean the guard and Noreen. They're the only two people I've actually seen apart from other students. Well, and the people back at the Town Hall.

Which was only yesterday.

Only. Yesterday.

"Hi, yes, I'm Rhea Harrington. I'm here for a 7:30 am

appointment," I finally reply, extending my hand as we meet in the middle of what seems to be her office, and she offers me a warm smile.

"Pleasure to meet you, Rhea. I'm sure this whole thing is quite a shock. I mean it is for us so I can imagine it is for you too, but we've made sure to put everything necessary in place for you. It's just a matter of your finances that requires our attention," she states, getting straight to the point as she guides me to the seat in front of her desk, and I like her approach.

I'd prefer her not to flower everything up and beat around the bush when there's so much to learn. I just need to know everything, and I need to know it now, or preferably yesterday.

"What financial information do you need?" I ask, placing my satchel at my feet as I smooth my skirt down and take a seat. My new attire is going to take a minute to get used to.

"Well, to pay for anything on-site at Saints Academy, we use thumbprints, linked to accounts that are held by the families of the pupils attending. Like a parent, grandparent, that sort of thing, but we have little information coming through on your family background." Her tone is gentle, like she knows she may be touching on a difficult topic, but has to ask nonetheless, and I appreciate it.

"I never knew my parents, all of my memories are from the orphanage. I was always told I was left on their doorstep as a baby," I explain, clearing my throat as sympathy shines in her eyes. I'm so fucking glad it's not pity because I can't handle that.

"I'm so sorry to hear of your challenging upbringing," she murmurs, and I offer a tight smile in response. I can tell she's sincere but it doesn't make the situation any better. "Don't take this the wrong way, Rhea, but I'm going to assume that living in Phoenix Valley hasn't lined your pockets the way things are expected up here."

I hear what she's not saying, and I nod, nibbling on my bottom lip as embarrassment threatens to take over. "I live paycheck to paycheck," I say, but her smile doesn't change, and I don't feel small or inadequate. If anything, my statement seems to spring her into action.

"That's usually the case on the rare occasion that earthlings join us," she says, rising to her feet and moving around to sit on her desk in front of me, her ginger curls bouncing as she moves. "In that instance, we reach out to the human representative for the Hex, and they provide the assistance required to help with finances," she says with a smile, lifting a tablet to tap away, and I balk at what she's saying.

"I don't want someone else to—"

My words are cut short as she lifts a finger, pausing me as she aims it at the table to my right, the sound of a call ringing. But what has my attention is the blue lighting that suddenly appears on the circular silver disc on the floor. I hadn't noticed it before. What the fuck is it?

"Hello?"

A gruff voice comes through the phone, familiarity ringing in my ears as Beverly starts to ramble, and I feel my breaths getting shallower with each passing second. "Mr. James, I'm sorry to bother you at such an early time, but I have a new entry into Saints Academy from Phoenix Valley, and we need to arrange linking them to your accounts."

The guy clears his throat, a sigh barely audible, followed by some shuffling. "Just a moment," he states as Beverly smiles down at me, nodding toward the blue lighting, when the back of a man's head appears, followed quickly by the rest of him.

My heart lodges in my throat. Reason number one, the fact a holographic version of someone has just randomly appeared in front of me, and two, I fucking detest the person looking back at me with wide eyes. Now so more than I ever had before.

Motherfucking cunt.

"Rhea," he breathes, surprise etched in his features, before he coughs, and looks to Beverly. "Beverly, a moment please," he advises, short and curt, and she happily obliges, squeezing my shoulder before stepping out of the room and shutting the door behind her. "What the fuck, Rhea?"

I scoff at the audacity of this man. "Fuck you, Dante," I bite, my hands clenching in my lap as I glare at the man before me. "Or should I call you, *Mr. James*?"

"What are you doing there?"

"What am I doing here? What do you think I'm doing here? How about you explain to me the fact you're Mr. fucking James, the human representative for the Hex, not Dante Paul, the IT guy for the local news," I hiss, completely in shock at the fact that he lied about who he was, on top of fucking cheating.

Did I really date this pathological liar?

He sighs, a hint of disappointment in his gray eyes as he looks at me. "We need to talk, Rhea," he states, and I shake my head.

"Like fuck we do," I retort, even more angry at myself for letting this, *him*, affect me.

"You ruined the tires on my car," he states, like that's what's important here right now. I bark out a sarcastic laugh because is this guy for fucking real?

"I'm dealing with bigger shit than you and your goddamn car, asshole," I grind out, rising to my feet and pointing my finger in his direction.

He should be lucky he's not here, because I would fucking throttle him right now.

"Could you let me explain, Rhea? I never—"

Taking a deep breath, I get a handle on my emotions and raise my hand, and to my surprise he stops. "Honestly, I don't give a shit, Dante. I didn't love you, we just fucked, not enough apparently, but really, we were never more than that. I'm hurt by the disrespect, nothing else." My words are true and honest, and he must see it because he doesn't snark back at me. "Now do you want to explain how you are… you?"

"The Hex doesn't really mean anything down here in Phoenix Valley, Rhea, so no one knows who I am or what I do. Things are a little different up in Paradise Heights. What's more intriguing right now is the fact that you're sitting in Saints Academy and enrolled as a student." He pauses for a moment, likely running over the bit of information on my past I offered to him, before he sighs, a sympathetic smile on his lips. "Are you okay?"

The question catches me off guard, stunning me silent for a moment since I haven't had time to think about it, before I nod once in a non-committal response. "I'll be fine."

My tone is cold, distant, and completely void of any emotion. I watch as he swipes a hand down his face, before pinching the bridge of his nose, likely trying to find his patience.

"I'll get the financial aid taken care of immediately." I open my mouth to argue, but he continues before I can even try. "It's not an option. It's protocol. The Academy has my details set up in case of an instance like this involving earthlings."

I hate that god awful nickname on his lips too, and it makes me hate him even more because of how he degrades us… them.

"I don't want to have to speak with you ever again. Ever," I reply, somber in acceptance.

"For what it's worth, I *am* sorry," he states, his voice

earnest, but it means nothing to me now. Apparently, this fucker was living more than a double life, thinking he was a God walking among men on earth. Shame on me for buying into it.

"Yeah, me too."

Dante must end the call from his side because he disappears before my eyes in an instant. Beverly is suddenly rushing back into the room.

"All sorted?" she asks, a wide smile on her face, and I offer a short nod.

I'm expecting her to ask how he knew my name, but she's not as nosey as I assumed. Taking her seat again, I grab my satchel off the floor and turn to face her.

"Is that everything you need from me?" I want to get out of here, the sooner the better. I need to clear my mind a bit after the truth I just learned about my ex.

"Let me grab your thumbprint and you're good to go. Zellus has advised that your meeting isn't required as he will see you in the assembly this morning instead, since it's starting now."

"Zellus?" I ask, confused as she scans my thumb, but she just looks up at me with her glasses slipping down her nose.

"Yes, the Dean."

SEVEN

RHEA

Beverly leads me to the hall where the assembly is taking place, leaving me at the open double doors near the entry into the main building, before quickly disappearing as I stand and gape at the room before me.

Reds, oranges, blues, and greens stain the glass that fills the arched windows around the room, counterbalancing the dark and gothic walls and intricate carvings around the edge of the ceiling. It feels like a cathedral in here, the ones in the movies that were demolished in the war all those years ago.

I have to pick my jaw up off the floor as I focus back on the people in the room and the layout. Rows upon rows of pews are to the left and right, facing the large podium at the front. Dark mahogany wood is everywhere, and not a light hanging anywhere with the glass-domed ceiling, letting the sun shine in.

Students enter the hall around me, as well as through a few entry points toward the front too, and when I'm nudged one too many times, I join them. Moving with the sea of the crowd, I put one foot in front of the other, holding my satchel close to me as I fumble over where I'm supposed to sit.

I notice the end of the pews have different words engraved.

Gi.

Fotia.

Aeras.

Nero.

Agion.

Earth. Fire. Air. Water. Saint.

Agion? That's what it said at the top of the board yesterday, when my name was inscribed on the wood by my room number. But more importantly, how the fuck do I know what it means? I wasn't aware I'd suddenly learned to read a foreign language. What even is it?

I glance around again to see if I recognize any faces, more specifically Harmonia, but I come up blank among the uniform-clad students everywhere.

"Rhea, hey." The sound of someone calling my name fills me with a mixture of relief and tension, but when I look over my right shoulder, I find Harmonia rushing toward me, weaving her way through the crowd, with a bright smile on her face.

My shoulders sag, my body relaxing as she comes to a stop before me. Her white hair sweeps over her shoulder, and she holds something out between us.

"I didn't see you in the dining hall, so I grabbed you a protein bar, just in case," she states, and my stomach grumbles at her words. She's officially my hero.

"You're a lifesaver, thank you so much," I murmur, taking the chocolatey snack from her hand and opening it immediately. "I didn't eat yesterday, and then by the time my meeting ended this morning, Beverly brought me straight here," I admit, glancing around me. "And now I have no idea where I'm supposed to sit."

Harmonia chuckles, linking her arm through mine as she pulls me to the very front. That was not where I expected to be dragged to sit but since she's the only student I know, I'll just roll with it. "The names on the end of the rows are for each house, and ours is the front row to the right since there's not many of us compared to other houses," she explains, and I nod like it all makes total sense to me because of course it does… not.

I take the lead, walking all the way to the far end of the pew since no one else is here yet, and not actually wanting to sit so central in front of everyone. Being a new student is bad enough. I don't want to draw any more attention than necessary. Harmonia is right behind me as I quickly eat the protein bar.

For the first time since I've arrived, I can sense eyes

on me. People unfamiliar with my presence, and their curiosity getting the better of them.

Placing my satchel on the wooden seat to my right, I take my spot, Harmonia doing the same. As soon as I get comfortable, I look to my left, around Harmonia, to find the people sitting on the other side of the front row glaring at me like I've got five heads.

Excellent.

The girl sitting on the end, with wide blue eyes and perfectly styled blonde hair is drilling holes in my head with her glare alone.

Harmonia must sense where my attention has drifted, and follows my line of sight, before scoffing. "Don't pay Selene any mind. She's a class A bitch through and through, to literally everyone. She thinks she's our *queen*, it's so ridiculous. When she didn't get placed in Agion with *the guys,* she was pissed. She thinks they're her men, no one else's."

Men? Plural. Huh.

"So she's going to hate me even more for being placed in the fourth room then," I reply, not even bothering to ask for confirmation, just making the obvious statement as I pull my attention back to Harmonia who rolls her eyes.

"Yeah, but something tells me you can hold your own, Rhea. Considering this is your first full day here, you seem to be taking this all in your stride, and honestly, the uniform looks good on you," she says with a grin and wink, which I return.

“Seriously, a uniform though? I didn’t even have to wear one when I was younger and in school, but here I am at twenty-two taking a step back in time, or that’s what it feels like at least,” I respond, curving the compliment on me as a person and lightening the conversation.

“I can’t even imagine, Rhea. It must be crazy not knowing who or what you are,” she says, a hint of concern in her pink eyes as her lips twist to the side. I guess my joking around came across more serious than I thought.

“You know what you are?” I ask, trying to redirect the questions. Although, it feels rather personal, and I cringe internally at myself, but thankfully, Harmonia doesn’t seem to mind.

“Yeah, both of my parents are angels, so it’s presumed I am too. Pandora’s Box can only confirm there is magic within me, but for now, assumptions are what everyone else here is riding on,” she explains, and I nod, absorbing her words.

So everyone here has to have a little meeting with the Box of screams, huh? I wonder if they heard what I heard? I almost consider asking Harmonia, but I refrain, not wanting to divulge or relive my experience just yet. And since I already have a target on my back from just living in the same building as four guys, I’d rather not give them any more ammunition.

My response lodges in my throat as my eyes fall on the four guys walking into the room from the front left. The entire hall pauses, watching them as intently as I am. I feel like I can’t breathe.

I instantly recognize the hot adonis from this morning, his blazer long forgotten with his shirt sleeves rolled up and his blond hair swept behind his ear as he practically floats across the room. Images of his long, thick cock flash in my mind, making me blush and my thighs rub together in response.

Beside him is the asshat from yesterday, his black hair a mess as it falls over his face, with his sharp green eyes flashing beneath it. He seems to emit a cool, standoffish tension without even trying, but whatever the blond guy beside him says, has the briefest touch of a grin appear on his lips. I don't even blink and it's gone, like a figment of my imagination.

Slightly behind them are two other guys who I haven't seen before, but my gut just knows they're from the same hall as me. Side by side, they're almost like yin and yang; complete opposites of one another.

The tallest of the two is easily over six feet tall, with short, brown, untamed hair and tense brown eyes. His frame is huge, his broad shoulders magnified with the tightness of his uniform. He seems quiet, not really paying attention to what his friends are saying as he observes the room, his eyes scanning repeatedly around him.

The guy next to him is a good couple of inches shorter, with mousy blond hair, and mystical hazel eyes that shift from brown to green as he glances around. Unlike the others, he seems… calm, relaxed, and peaceful. A casual smile on his lips as he strokes his neck, brings my attention to the fact that his top two buttons are undone and his tie is hanging much lower than you would usually wear it.

"Oh snap, girl's got her heart shaped eyes on. Turn them off, my friend, they're a bag of douches," Harmonia sings beside me, nudging my shoulder with hers, and a genuine grin takes over my face for the first time since I stepped foot on Paradise Heights.

"I don't need a good dick to be attached to a good man, Harmonia," I reply with a wink, and she throws her head back with a laugh, drawing attention our way.

My eyes flick back to the guys as they make their way into the pew, Mr. Cock from this morning offering me a knowing wink as he takes the seat beside Harmonia. The asshat with the mesmerizing green eyes glares at me as he drops down beside him, while the two new guys observe me with a hint of curiosity in their expressions, dropping into their seats a moment later.

Likely they know there's someone new in their hall from their friends and possibly gossip, but still want to feast their eyes on me and make their own judgment on the little *earthling*. Well, they can fuck off right along with everyone else.

I force myself to face forward as a man walks in, flanked by two women, one of whom I recognize as Noreen, and the energy instantly changes around us. Without having to question it, his mere presence, and the deafening silence that follows his entrance means that he can only be one person.

Zellus.

Dressed in a deep gray pinstripe suit, with his black and white peppered hair combed back off his face, he looks regal, god-like as he looks out at us, but what is startling, is that his eyes are black, or they at least look that way from here. Like a never ending vortex.

I wet my lips, swallowing nervously. As much as I didn't want to meet him this morning, being here, in such a public setting without having done so leaves me a little off-center, and I can't say I like it.

The thought instantly leaves me wanting to run for the hills, but in all honesty, what would I be running back to? Realistically, being here is nothing more or nothing less than where I already was, but the niggling fact that I may be able to unearth some of my past, where I come from, has me planted firmly in my seat.

I taught myself for far too long to not care, to be numb to everything and everyone around me, always leaving my emotions at the door, but the reality of my situation has only shown me that I was masking it all at best. And now I'm here, with the prospect of a different future on the horizon, I can't turn my back on it.

Even in this damn uniform, it just might be worth it.

"Thank you for gathering here this morning," Zellus begins, standing tall and proud at the center of the podium, his voice echoing around me with a boom even though there's no microphone in front of him.

Nobody mutters a response as Noreen stands just to the side of the podium in front of me. Her eyes briefly meet mine in acknowledgment, before she quickly taps away on her tablet.

"The main reason for calling an early assembly this morning is to advise of the confirmed plans for this academic year's Solstice event. It will be taking place the week before Easter. Further details will follow, but Noreen and other staff members are going to be working around the clock to make it a *magical* event." A sly grin graces his face as he waits for his audience to praise him with laughter. Zellus is clearly an attention whore who expects, no, *demands*, the spotlight. Arrogant dick.

A light chuckle at his pun sounds out around me, but I remain silent, frozen in place, observing his every move. Why would an assembly be called now for it? We're in October, it's ages away. My intuition senses something isn't right and my stomach tightens with knots, my throat becoming dry.

As if sensing my question, his dark eyes reach mine, his smile spreading wide as he claps his hands in front of him. "But while I have you all here, there's another announcement I'd like to make."

When his gaze doesn't leave me, I feel all eyes in the room follow his direction, my body burning under all of the watchful stares. But it makes sense now, starting with the solstice event, which is months away, was just an excuse to get everyone here and tell them about… me, the fucking human. The *earthling*.

"We have a late arrival at the Academy, as of yesterday evening. Miss Rhea Harrington was confirmed by Pandora's Box after spending twenty-two years in Phoenix Valley, completely unaware of her magic." Light murmurs begin to spread around me, but instead of sinking deeper into my seat, I force myself to remain tall, my shoulders pulled back as I continue to meet the Dean's stare head on. I refuse to let him get to me. "No current origins or heritage known, so I do hope everyone here will join me in offering Rhea a warm welcome, and wishing her luck in finding out who she really is."

My pulse rings in my ears as my teeth sink into my bottom lip. I don't care if they offer me a warm welcome or wish me luck. Not one bit. Why would he go about introducing me so publicly? There's an underlying agenda but I'm not sure what his end-game is.

Asshole.

"With no known background, Rhea may be required to flit between classes, enabling her to come to terms with all walks of life compared to how she has previously lived as an earthling." It's official, I *really* fucking hate that nickname now. He can fuck all the way off too. His black eyes hold mine for a moment longer, an almost challenge floating in them, waiting to see my response. I'm not stupid though, I've played these games growing up. He claps his hands once more. "Assembly dismissed."

With that, he turns and heads out of the exact door he

came in through, Noreen and the other woman hot on his heels.

That's it.

That was all.

Gather everyone under the false pretense of announcing the solstice event, point out the nobody, then fuck off again.

Excellent.

"He just put a huge fucking target on your head, Rhea," Harmonia whispers beside me, and I give her a pointed look, implying *thanks captain obvious*, as the noise around us gets louder.

Rising to my feet, I shake my head and run my hands over my skirt. "I've handled bullies before. Just because he's the Dean doesn't make him any different. I know how to take care of myself," I reply dismissively, but when she stands beside me, the empathetic look in her eyes tells me I'm missing the message.

"Oh, no, not like that. As in, the guys are going to be tripping all over you," she states, lifting her satchel over her shoulder as I frown in confusion.

"Why?" I ask, scrunching my nose in distaste, but before Harmonia can respond, someone taps their finger on my shoulder.

Whipping my head around, I come face to face with a guy I've never met before. With greasy brown hair slicked back off his face, mud brown eyes, and his shirt untucked, he looks like he woke up like this. There's no denying it, the guy is repulsive.

"Fuck, you're actually pretty too, this could definitely work," he says with a grin, but before I can ask what on earth he's talking about, he's leaning forward. His eyes are half mast as his face nears mine, and I suddenly realize what he's doing.

Before this motherfucker can touch his lips to mine, I reach my hand out and wrap my fingers around his throat, applying enough pressure to let him know he's crossed a line, which pauses his descent.

"What. The. Fuck do you think you're doing?" I bite, feeling everyone around us look our way, but I'll be damned if this idiot thinks he can just kiss me, especially without my permission.

"Claiming you," he manages to squeeze out hoarsely with my grip getting tighter on his neck. His hand rises to wrap around my wrist, squeezing my pressure point, but I don't drop my hold.

"Fuck. Off," I growl, anger turning my face red as I shove him away from me, and he stumbles back into the pew, looking up at me with utter disgust in his gaze. I smirk at the red handprint that's very visible on his neck.

Before anything else can happen, Harmonia links her arm through mine to pull me down the aisle so we can get out of here to prevent any other douchebags from *claiming* me, but I don't even take two steps before we're stopping again, the four guys from our hall blocking the path. I roll my eyes as I wait for them to make a move.

Fucking great.

I meet each of their gazes, ready to stand my ground another four times if necessary, but to my surprise, Mr. Cock takes a step back, and his friends all fall into sync too, clearing a path for us to edge out around them. It's almost like they're protecting me? The whiplash I'm already experiencing with my housemates is frustrating.

Harmonia keeps her grip on me as I keep my gaze locked straight ahead so I don't have to look at any of them as I pass, but the second I'm out of the aisle fully, Mr. Cock calls my name, and I turn to glance back over my shoulder.

"I'll be seeing you, Rhea," he murmurs huskily with a wink, sending a shiver down my spine. My eyes lock on his, the promise becoming a threat in his words, but Harmonia pulls me harder, forcing me to drop his gaze and head for the exit with her.

Selene, the class A bitch is glaring at me still, but I have bigger issues to be dealing with than her cattiness right now.

"Don't let Adonis get under your skin, Rhea. Incubi are literal sex on legs, and he's a manwhore," Harmonia grumbles as we step out of the hall and down a passageway with a portal at the bottom, only this one has a deep purple coloring as opposed to all black.

"Wait, the hot adonis is actually named Adonis?" I ask, mouth wide as I stare at my newly claimed friend, and she nods with a grimace.

"Yup, and you bet your ass he knows it too," she replies, which doesn't surprise me at all, not after his dick show this morning, though I'm not complaining about the dick show. "Ready for class?" she adds, and my eyebrows raise.

I haven't even looked at my schedule yet, so my answer to that is a firm no.

But it'll be a cold fucking day in hell before I let anyone see that I'm sinking. I'll go down fighting; it's all I've ever known, and it's all I'll ever be. A survivor.

EIGHT

RHEA

My first lesson of the day goes by in a complete blur. Harmonia synced my schedule to her phone, and vice versa, and thankfully we both had History together. I almost cringed and rolled my eyes when I saw the lesson, but I guess going forward it will be a good way for me to learn about this whole new world. Just not on my first day, when I'm completely overwhelmed and lost with every word, so not a single one stuck in my brain.

She could have been talking about pigs falling from the sky, and dinosaurs roaming the earth, and I was nodding along, absorbing nothing.

I need to figure my shit out though, because Harmonia and Noreen mentioned the students had all been here for months now, and I had a lot of catching up to do.

"What do you mean we have Combat next?" I question, nose wrinkling as I look at Harmonia who *almost* offers me a sympathetic grin. "What does that involve exactly?" I add, following her lead as she heads toward the portal at the end of the hall.

"It's exactly as you assume. It's all about our strength, skills, abilities, and all things fighting if I'm honest," she explains, flicking her white hair over her shoulder with a grin.

Huh, I can actually get down with that. I've never had fighting lessons before, but growing up in the orphanage definitely helped me steel my spine and learn to defend myself. There's only one problem. "I'm really not dressed to be fighting," I murmur, glancing down at my uniform, and Harmonia chuckles because she's wearing the exact same outfit.

"This portal will take us back to Agion where we can change," she states, before stepping through the portal with me hot on her heels. I blink my eyes a few times as I slowly step into the hallway of my dorm, and the people walking behind us have suddenly disappeared, going to their own halls instead.

Weird. How does the portal know where we should go?

The feeling of stepping through the billowing smoke isn't as bad as it first was, but it's still not my favorite mode of transport.

"Do we come back and change every time before Combat class?" I ask as we climb the stairs, and just as we reach the top, I hear the sound of four deep masculine voices filter from down the hall, making me pause a step, before I remember to keep walking.

"It's for our first year mainly, because when our powers come to light at the end of the year, most people can then change clothing with a snap of their fingers. So this is apparently one of their lessons, to not get lazy before that happens," she says casually, like she's telling me the weather. I nod along, acting like this is common knowledge, when she actually just blew my fucking mind with the 'snap, crackle and pop, I've got a new athletic uniform on' knowledge drop. I mean, that's convenient as hell. "Meet you back here in two?" she offers, and I smile in response, still at a loss for words as I lift my hand to my dorm door.

It unlocks under my touch, and I quickly shuffle inside, shutting the door behind me and dropping my satchel on the bed.

I kick my shoes off, and open the closet doors to find the sneakers inside that I noticed yesterday, but there's no alternative clothes hung up that aren't the fancy uniform.

Stepping back out, I move over to the dresser and open the top drawer to find *Saints Academy* branded t-shirts and shorts, and I quickly grab one of each before slamming the drawer shut and shaking out of my blazer.

I kick my shoes off, unbuttoning my shirt, and just as I let it slip down my arms, a voice behind me makes me freeze.

"I am *really* going to have to get used to you being on

the other side of my bathroom now," Adonis practically purrs, my skin prickling under his attention, making a blush desperate to color my cheeks.

Looking back over my shoulder to meet his gaze, I find him trailing his eyes over every inch of me like a soft caress, his tongue running slowly over his bottom lip as I remember I'm only in my skirt and bra. If we all had our powers already, I'd say this must be his incubus vibes coming out to play by taunting me and creating an atmosphere laced with sexual tension. But so far, we only have the knowledge that magic lives within us, our powers aren't activated yet, so this is all him.

"Get the fuck out, asshole," I hiss, turning to glare at him with my hands on my hips.

A satisfied smirk forms on his lips as his eyes widen slightly, like he was expecting me to hide myself, folding my arms over my chest like I assume most girls would. But I'm not most girls, and I'm not embarrassed by my body.

When his eyes finally meet mine, I see the hint of a challenge burning beneath the surface, but I hold my ground, glaring at the fucker until he reluctantly sighs. Checkmate, asshole. Anybody else and I would be over there and shoving him back through the door he just walked in from, but I know I might falter in closer proximity, so I keep my distance.

"I think you're going to be a lot of fun, *Rhea*," he breathes, but before I can question what he means, he's gone.

I gape for a moment or two, at the space he occupied

before rushing over to the door that's still slightly open and slamming it shut, turning the ironically standard lock in place to keep the asshole out while I finish getting ready. It's clear he thinks the jack and jill is convenient, and maybe in another life I wouldn't have rejected the idea entirely, but for now, I'm keeping my door locked.

Sighing, I look over to grab the athletic uniform. The shorts and t-shirt are navy, with gray stripes down the side, and the sneakers are gray with *Saints* written on the side in navy. Quickly dressing, I grab my satchel, and head back out to find Harmonia waiting for me.

"Are you ready to go?" she asks, and my eyes fall to the door I know Adonis is behind and I wet my lips.

"Yeah, get me out of here," I mumble, trying not to sound desperate for a reprieve from Adonis.

We don't bump into anyone in the hall as we head to Combat, which requires going through the portal to the main building, and taking another out to what is known as the Training Center.

Stepping through the entryway to the center, it looks like a stadium. The building itself runs around the exterior, while the central area is all open. It's huge. Split into four sections depending on what is on the ground. There's grass to my right, sand to my left, water to the far right, and what looks like burned foliage to the top left.

I squint in confusion as I follow Harmonia's lead toward

the rest of the students gathered here. Thankfully we're on the grass, which I'm familiar with and feels safe. I really have a lot to fucking learn, even in combat training.

I notice Selene, whom I've officially named the supreme bitch, surrounded by a group of girls as she glares at me, and I internally groan. Fuck, is glaring all she knows how to do? Her tough, mean girl attitude isn't scaring me; it's more annoying than anything. This bitch is going to have to give me a minute. I have too much going on already to deal with her petty *glares* as well. We thankfully come to a stop on the other side of the group, standing around who looks to be the professor. He's standing up front with a tablet in his hands, ignoring us as he waits for everyone to arrive.

The wind seems to change, my breath catching in my throat as a chill runs down my spine, and as ridiculous as it sounds, I know *they've* arrived. Every cell in my body wants me to turn around and face them, but I clench my hands at my side, biting my tongue as I force myself to stay focused ahead.

A guy suddenly stops in front of me, a leering grin on his face, with his blond hair cut short and his gray eyes searching mine. Fuck. Not again. Although he's a distraction from the guys I feel walking behind me, it's still an inconvenience, especially when he opens his mouth.

"Rhea, right? I've heard a lot about you. If you want an origin, a heritage, you can share mine," he says with a wink, reaching out to pinch a loose tendril of hair around my face. It takes extreme control on my part not to overreact like I did back in the pews with the last dickhead who just wanted to kiss me.

"Fuck off, Hector. Give the girl a chance to breathe," the professor booms, making my eyes round in surprise. "I know how appealing *nothing* may be to you, but even I want to kick you in the dick right now," he states, and to my surprise, *Hector,* fucks all the way off without a backward glance. But my brain is still caught on a single word he said. *Nothing.* What the hell does that mean? Is he saying *I'm* nothing?

I search the professor's gaze for an inkling, but he simply stares back with his black hair pulled back into a bun on top of his head, his matching dark eyes feel like they're peering into my soul as he wipes at his sharp nose.

He lowers his tablet to his side as he addresses the class. "The next two hours will be focused on drills and circuits so I can see how your stamina compares to when you first arrived, or get a feel for your skills if you're new," he states, flicking his soulless gaze to mine, and I feel everyone else do the same.

Kill me now. How much longer is this going to go on for? It was already announced at the assembly this morning that I'm new, so why do they need to keep rehashing the obvious? It's infuriating already and old fucking news.

"We'll start off with five laps on the grass. Go," he says dismissively, and everyone immediately moves into action without complaint. Following everyone, I happily slip into the middle of the bodies running, wanting to take my time and pace myself if we've got five laps to do.

I immediately spot the four guys who seem to make my body react against my will, by simply breathing, as they race off to lead the group.

Thankfully, Harmonia falls into sync with me. I wet my lips considering whether I should ask, but then I scoff at myself, and blurt out what I want to know. "Can you please explain the target on my head that's attracting sleazy assholes?"

Harmonia chuckles, glancing at me out of the corner of her eye before she responds. "It's hard to explain, and I'm probably going to bombard you with far too much information, but bear with me. If at the end you still don't understand what I'm saying, I will explain it to you in a few short sentences," she says, and I sigh in relief. The deep release of air has thrown my inhale in, exhale out cadence out of whack.

"I'm already overwhelmed, what's a little more?" I respond with a grin, brushing my hair back off my face as we run.

"It all comes down to the family unit. There are more men than women in the supernatural world, so it is more than common for there to be multiple men committed to one woman." She side eyes me, watching for my reaction as I gape a little in surprise.

"Well, uh, that's different," I murmur, comparing it to life down in Phoenix Valley, but I guess it makes sense if they want to make lots of supernatural babies. Imagine having a different flavor of cock for every day of the week? I can't see a negative, yet.

"Yeah, so you tend to find that the guys will form their own group first, usually between three and six of them, and then they will find a suitable girl to fit their setup."

"I thought I was going to be able to choose all of the peens, but now you're saying *they* choose *me*?" I clarify with a pout, and she laughs. That process seems pretty ass backwards if the females are the less common gender of the two.

"Pretty much," she says with a shrug. "It sounds worse than it is, but since there are more guys, it's important that they all have a connection with the woman. But, things aren't how they used to be. These days, everything is about status, money, and arrangements. Nobody seals their souls together anymore, as everyone's worried about how the family unit will operate."

I frown, my nose crinkling. I can feel my feet pound against the grass with each step I take, propelling me forward. Looking around, I notice no one has surrounded us, trying to eavesdrop on our conversation so we actually get to talk and run in peace. I cast my gaze over to Harmonia to see if she's joking but the solemn expression on her face confirms she's telling the God's honest truth.

"Yup, information overload. I can't process any of that in one bite," I say with a grin as we jog past a few people in front who have slowed down, entering lap two at a steady pace.

"Sorry. Out of the guys and the woman in the committed

union, the weakest magical member will be the one to stay home and take care of the children. It's not frowned upon in the slightest, but no guy wants to be the one to do that, so they look for girls they deem less powerful than them to complete their unit, so there's no issue of roles."

Ew, gross.

"That's the biggest load of patriarchal, egotistical bullshit I've ever heard," I gripe, my face reddening with anger. "And since I am completely oblivious to all of these things right now, and there's no hint of my background, I'm an easy target. Fucking hell." I look at Harmonia, who nods, confirming every word, and it only adds to the rage I feel building inside me.

You would think if there were less women they would be fucking worshipped, but I guess this is a man's world after all.

"What did you mean when you said sealed souls?" I ask, remembering something else she mentioned, and my new friend smiles. Her response is cut short when something catches on my right foot, and I tumble forward. My hands instinctively reach out in front of me, breaking my fall as I land in a heap of limbs on the grass.

Adrenaline pumps through my veins as my protective instincts kick in, and I glance over my shoulder to see what I tripped over. What I find is Selene's bitchy ass standing above me with her arms folded over her chest, and a wide grin on her face.

Seriously? What in the actual fuck?

Doesn't she have anything else better to do?

I'd been so invested in the conversation I was having with Harmonia, I let my guard down, leaving me open for a petty attack like that.

I hear a few chuckles from those around us as everyone close by stops, forming a half circle, waiting to see how her power play will unfold between us. I've never been one to let an audience down when a bitch needs to be put in her place.

Quickly rising to my feet, a smirk twists my lips because now it's game fucking on. I don't even bother to dust off my hands as I stalk toward her, watching with delight as she takes the smallest step back. It wasn't much, but it was there. It seems she wants to put me in my place, but fuck if that will ever happen. It's always fun proving people wrong when they underestimate me.

I'm less than a step away from her, arms lifting to grab her, when a body collides with mine, blocking me from making the rest of the distance. I grunt as I smack into the hard chest, my pulse ringing in my ears as I glare at the person interjecting.

It's the cool, calm, and relaxed guy who was with Adonis and the others earlier. The anger I was feeling toward Selene has now shifted its focus to him. It continues to rise inside of me, I'm annoyed that he's willing to let her get away with acting the way she is. Before I can growl at or sidestep him, he places his hand on my shoulder, offering a gentle squeeze as he leans forward to murmur in my ear. "Selene Hart is never worthy of your wrath when there are much bigger demons in the world."

His voice… *fuck*, I feel like I'm being hypnotized. His tone lulling me into a sense of calmness as my gaze flicks between his and the bitches behind him.

Clenching my hands at my side, I run my tongue over my teeth as I internally battle with how I want to continue with the situation.

I understand what he's saying, I do, but I have never let anyone push me around. Ever.

"She—"

"Is a fucking bitch," he interjects. I can feel surprise dancing in my eyes at the calm way he even curses. "Don't let her get under that pretty skin of yours," he adds, offering one final squeeze before stepping away.

My chest heaves with each breath I take as I watch him stalk back towards his friends, and by the time I remember myself and my intent, I'm no longer angry enough to beat the hell out of Selene. For today at least. Tomorrow could be a different story entirely.

"I hope I only have to say this once. Stay the fuck away from me," I bite, glaring daggers at her as she remains in place, before I turn on my heel and fall into step with Harmonia.

"Speed up, we haven't got all day," the professor calls, and I do just that, upping my pace that will calm my brain and body just the way I need.

By the time my mind is empty, not focusing on all of the questions that were swarming inside of me earlier, begging to be answered, I've reached the last lap. After we've finished the laps, the professor moves us along to other cardio workouts. Pity really, since the class was called Combat, I was really hoping to beat the fuck out of someone today, especially after Selene's little bitchy show.

Harmonia stays quiet at my side, letting me handle myself, but I can't stop my gaze from occasionally drifting over to the four guys who, for some unknown reason, hold my unwavering attention.

I need to pretend they don't exist, focus on everything else going on around me, but I share a freaking bathroom with one of them, so it's going to be harder than I expect.

"Excellent form there, Miss Harrington," the professor states beside me as I continue my pace through the pistol squats he called out for as a cool down exercise. Sweat is dripping down my temple, my t-shirt clinging to me, and I desperately want this two hour lesson to be over. I don't respond, not feeling the need to thank him for his praise, but he continues to speak. "We have extra curricular sporting activities that take place on campus, if you think you might be interested, let me know."

"Thanks," I reply, panting as I complete my last squat. Trying not to puke from my lack of food intake, I brace my hands on my thighs as I catch my breath.

"No worries. My name is Riva, Eris Riva. If you can't

find me, find Noreen, she always knows where everyone is," he states, his gaze meeting mine as I stand to my full height. I almost frown at how pushy he seems to be with this conversation, but before I can question it, he speaks again. "I was an earthling."

His words are barely more than a mumble, making my head rear back in surprise. That was so *not* what I was expecting to come out of his mouth.

"If you were, then you'd know how offensive that word sounds," I grumble, watching as he swipes a hand down his face. I couldn't guess how old he is, maybe mid-forties.

"You're right, it's a shit word," he replies with a sigh. "But everyone uses it around here, and unfortunately you just unintentionally pick it up." I nod in response, unsure of what he wants me to say next. "Think on the sports," he says, before turning toward the rest of the class and calling time on today's session.

Thank fuck.

I've had enough physical torture for today.

I'm sweaty, starving, dehydrated, and ready for a nap, but there's still one more lesson to go. My first day feels like it's been a fucking eternity.

Harmonia appears at my side, linking her arm through mine as we make our way through the tunnel, back toward where the portal is.

"Remind me why we need this class again?" I say with an exhausted pout, and she grins.

"Girl, I'm calling bullshit. You crushed it out there," she states, pointing behind her, and I roll my eyes.

A bark of laughter behind us catches my attention, and when I look over my shoulder I notice the four guys again.

Shit.

I really need to get a grip on myself and a cold shower. With the door locked

"Why do I get the feeling you're drawn to trouble?" she asks, and a grin covers my lips as I stare back ahead, trying to act like I just hadn't been caught again following the guys' movements.

Wetting my lips, I glance at Harmonia out of the corner of my eye as an overwhelming need to ask my next question takes over. "What does being an incubus actually entail?" I ask, trying to keep my voice low as she chuckles with a shake of her head.

"Girl—"

"You asking questions about me, darling?" His voice sends a jolt of recognition down my spine as my body tenses, and I cringe at the fact that he heard me, but I don't let him see that. Now that he's involved himself in our conversation, I'll just roll with it.

"I am," I reply, forcing myself to keep moving and not glance back over my shoulder, but he quickly moves to stand in front of me, just before we reach the portal.

With the black smoke billowing behind him, it almost

makes him look even more handsome, dangerous, a hint of darkness, and I fucking hate how much I like it.

"We just chew you up and spit you out, princess. Nothing more, nothing less," he purrs, running his tongue over his bottom lip as he watches my throat and I gulp. The fucker can tell how much he affects me. "All we do is take. And you'd just let me, wouldn't you?"

Every syllable hits me straight in the chest, my heart rate increasing with his closeness as I practically pant before him. Just his words, tone, and body language alone have me ready to do whatever he asks.

I can feel his friends circling, but I hold his attention with a smirk, taking a step forward to cut the distance between us as I lift my hand to his chest, rising up on my tiptoes. "But that's all hearsay, right? There's no confirmation yet. Who knows, you could be considered… nothing."

Shock appears in the widening of his eyes almost instantaneously. He didn't expect me to push back, which is clear to see. But before he can offer any kind of response to my question, I slip around him and through the portal, making my escape.

Holy fucking shit.

What have I gotten myself into?

NINE

ADONIS

"*You might just be... nothing.*"

Her words are stuck on repeat, a continuous loop playing around and around in my mind, as I quickly shower the sweat and grime from Combat class off my body.

No one has ever had the audacity to speak to me like that, to degrade me in such a way, especially in front of others, but I saw her insult for what it was. She was using what was being thrown at her, and channeling it my way as a means of escape.

I almost wish I had kept my mouth shut when I leaned in and whispered what being an incubus meant, but everything happens for a reason, and I refuse to ever regret anything in life.

Stepping out of the shower, I quickly dress in my uniform again, ready to head to the dining hall as I run my fingers through my wet hair, sweeping my blond locks back off my face. Slipping my glasses on, I straighten the arms of my blazer before stepping out of my room.

My gaze lingers on her dorm room door for a second longer than I desire, but I can't help it, she's just… captivating, and new. A hint of a sexual toy for me to engage with. Or she was, until she insulted me. It's a shame she doesn't come with the option of having her mouth shut.

Heading down stairs, I find Xander, Khaos, and Zen waiting for me. We wordlessly step through the portal, and head toward the smell of delicious food being cooked. I could make this walk in my sleep now, I've done it that many times since arriving here.

It's one of my favorite times of the day, watching everyone congregate in the same place, wearing the same uniform, yet all being completely different groups of people. There are the nerds, knowing everything and anything with their nose always in a book. There are girls who bitch, slay, and ruin anyone they deem to be beneath them, with Selene perched on their throne. Then there's the people who mind their own business, pretending their body doesn't know when my brothers and I walk in.

That leaves us, the four inseparable guys that have been friends for as long as I can remember. People want to be us, have us, love us, and all we want is for them to… fuck off.

The newly proclaimed Elites of Saints Academy. Tacky,

I know, but I didn't come up with it.

My gaze casts over those who are already sitting as we walk through the tables in the dining room, Khaos by my side, with Xander and Zen behind us. It's our usual formation, for no reason at all, it's just how we've always walked when we're together.

Dropping down onto the bench at our usual table in the center of the room, I click the tablet placed before me, and the menu for today comes to life. Selecting the beef chateaubriand and a sparkling water, the tablet confirms my order, before disappearing.

I sit, my skin prickling as I glance around the dining hall, searching for the girl who's causing my body to react this way. When I find her, she's tucked away off to the far left, sitting across from Harmonia Lovell.

Rhea Harrington.

Fuck.

I regret not encouraging her to her knees this morning and letting her taste my cock on her tongue. She's naturally beautiful without even trying. Her brown hair is smooth and soft, her make-up free blue eyes shining with challenge and pain, and her lithe body is hidden under far too much clothing.

Then she has a sharp tongue, willing to break anyone else before they break her. She wastes no time identifying what could emotionally hurt someone, and when she does, her words hit their target. And as tempting as it is to break her, I know it's not going to happen. Not from my efforts at least, because I won't be trying.

"Stop looking over there," Xander grunts in his seat beside me. My gaze flicks to Khaos across from me who rolls his eyes but says nothing.

"I can't help it. She's a complete fucking enigma; a hot one at that," I state simply, like it should be obvious.

Her words were true earlier. Nothing has been confirmed for me, just like everyone else, but I can feel my body thrumming beneath the surface with a constant need for sexual desire. It's far more intense than any other twenty-two year old around me.

I feel like I need it more than my next breath, like it's the air I breathe, and that's because I'm not a standard, cookie cutter incubus. Nope. One way to determine royalty around here is simply by their surname, or lack thereof.

My name is Adonis. *Just* Adonis.

And that's because both of my parents are Gods.

My Father, Hades, is God of the underworld, and a member of the Hex as a representative for all demons, while my mother, Persephone was once the Goddess of Spring, before she chose a life with my father.

I'm one of one hundred and forty children. It's ridiculous, but what can you do when sex literally sets the soul on fire down there? It's like heaven and torture all at once.

"I've asked a few questions, but it seems the gossip is true. She really is an earthling with no inkling of who she is or where she comes from," Zen murmurs almost whimsically as he too follows my gaze. "She doesn't much like the target placed on her head that has the guys swarming her," he adds, and I hum in agreement. I almost felt bad for Rhea early this morning when she was announced as the new student but after she insulted me, I'm feeling indifferent.

Since Zellus dropped those little facts in assembly this morning, I've watched her have to fight off two attempts already.

"Even I can admit it was hot as fuck in the pews, when she stopped that asshole from leaning in and kissing her by gripping him by the throat," Khaos adds, a slight smirk to his lips at the mention of his favorite body part.

"Only because *you* want to do it to *her* now," Xander retorts, and Khaos glares at him in response, only confirming what was said. "It seems chasing *nothing* is getting to everyone's head."

Khaos' eyes darken as he lifts his fist, likely ready to slam it into the table, but Zen catches it mid-air, stopping him from drawing any unnecessary attention our way. We've got enough of it already.

"She's not nothing," Zen says calmly, slowly lowering Khaos' fist to the table without a sound as the rest of us wait patiently for him to continue with his observation. His eyes trail over to the girl in question, watching for a moment, before he focuses back on the table. "What everyone seems to forget or is simply overlooking, is the fact she was placed in Agion. The hall is literally named Saint. You can't tell me the portal chose for her to be in the most elite hall in the entire school, all for her to be… *nothing*."

There's nothing but silence from myself and the other two as we digest what should be considered an obvious conclusion. His words ring loud and true in my ears, understanding washing over me as I nod.

"That's true," Xander grunts, rubbing his hand over his jaw as annoyance bounces in his eyes. He's the complete opposite to the rest of the guys here. He won't chase someone for being nothing. If anything, he wants our woman to be strong, independent, resilient, and a freak between the sheets.

Taking the *nothing* target off her head only adds to the appeal of her in his eyes.

"So, it's agreed. We pretend she doesn't exist," Khaos declares, and I watch as Zen wets his lips, and Xander tightens his fists on the table.

"As in keep the fuck away from her?" I say, needing confirmation, and he nods once. I twist my lips, looking back at her as she laughs over something with Harmonia, not a care in the world as she sits in her own little bubble.

"So, I can't even—"

"No, asshole, you can't fuck her," Khaos grunts, making a smirk sweep across Zen's cheeks, and Xander clears his throat as he smothers a chuckle.

"Not even—"

"Fuck off, man. The last time you fucked someone when we said not to, she got clingy and hasn't fucking left us alone, and that was four years ago," he grumbles, his gaze flicking toward Selene, and I cringe.

"That was one time, I—"

"There are twenty-eight girls at this fucking Academy, all of whom are thinking they're going to be the woman the Elites claim," Zen says, matter-of-factly, and I stick my finger up at him, just as our food appears in front of us.

"Listen, that's *not* my fault. I told them all it was a one-time thing, they just didn't listen," I bite back as I grab my bottle of water.

"And you really think she's going to be any different? A girl from Phoenix Valley, likely desperate to fit in? She'll cling to anything and everything she can, just like she has with Harmonia," Xander states, reaching for his soda with a grumble, and I pout. Like a bitch.

My eyes flick to her once more, only to find her glancing over her shoulder in my direction. Her tongue peeks out, swiping across her full lips as she unashamedly watches me. But out of the corner of my eye, I see Selene too. A stark reminder of how crazy these bitches get, and I literally have to share a bathroom with the new one for the next three years.

Fuck.

"Fine, I agree. Treat the new girl like she doesn't exist."

The words leave my mouth, even though a part of my

soul doesn't agree, doesn't even listen, but I'll fight against this attraction. I'll do whatever is necessary for my brothers, even if my dick hates the idea.

TEN

RHEA

Gooey macaroni and cheese appears before me, with a glass of soda, and I groan at the sight. I'm starving, and the food here the past few weeks has been nothing short of amazing. Eating the cuisine has been one of my favorite experiences at the Academy. Learning about life here has been a little crazy too, but the food makes it all worthwhile. If we weren't training almost daily, then I would definitely have gained weight, and I wouldn't have been sad about it.

"Oh my Gods, my legs are aching something crazy right now," Harmonia groans after a bite, feverishly digging into her burger and fries as she sits across from me. We're at our usual spot in the corner, alone, with the perfect view of the entire room, while being discreet too.

The noise around us isn't too loud over here, but I

imagine in the center I would be overwhelmed by it all. The hustle and bustle, the clattering of cutlery, the numerous conversations and occasional bark of obnoxious laughter. It would be too much of an audio overload.

"Please tell me this afternoon's class is something that requires me to remain seated with minimal participation?" I add, pulling out my phone to confirm it's the study session, and I sigh with relief.

Professor Cila Orne, might be quiet and timid, but the facts and legends we read about in her classes are freaking epic. The way she can spin stories into such captivating tales is unreal. I think it's become one of my favorite classes over the past few weeks.

Every lesson, Professor Orne is joined by the head of each hall, separating the class into groups dependent on what kind of supernatural they expect you to become. Since I really could be anything at all, I've been floating through them all.

"Girl, never mind that. How do I convince you to come to the party tonight? It's Halloween and you're not allowed to hide away from the world in your dorm room again," Harmonia states, pointing a fry in my direction, and I roll my eyes.

She's asked me almost weekly, but I don't think she understands how much of a nightmare it is being branded *nothing*.

I can't stop myself from glancing around the room, feeling the attention that I seem to automatically attract wherever

I go, simply for existing, and my excuse is already on the tip of my tongue.

Not a single day has gone by where at least two random guys haven't approached me, laying it on thick to try and worm their way into my pants. I don't even give them a second to explain themselves before I'm walking away. It could have fuck all to do with them thinking I might be *nothing,* and everything to do with them just simply thinking I'm hot, but I don't wait around to find out.

Thankfully, no one has just outright tried to kiss me again like the first guy, but if I have to fight someone off again for trying to touch me, I fucking will. Defending and protecting myself is nothing new. I've done it for as long as I can remember.

"Like you haven't seen all the sleezy assholes I've had to bat off every day that ends in y," I reply, sarcasm laced in all of my words while stabbing my fork into my pasta a little more harshly than necessary.

Poor macaroni and cheese does not deserve my wrath.

"But it's a party. You haven't been to a single one yet, and did I mention it's *Halloween*?" she emphasizes, her pink eyes pleading with me to give in.

I nibble on my bottom lip, deep in thought. What she's saying is entirely true. I've spent the past few weeks settling into Academy life, trying to play catch up with the lessons and just find my fucking feet among it all.

It's weird as fuck. I've been out of my comfort zone

before, but shit, not like this.

Like my life literally upended. After spending twenty-two years in Phoenix Valley, you would think I'd have calls or texts from people missing me, but I don't have one. Not a single one. I know, I kept charging my old phone for the first week or so, hoping it would work, before I eventually gave up. The fact I don't really have anyone to look for me, or notice my disappearance, doesn't help. Fuck, Dante was the only one, and he knows where I am, but if he even tries to reach out, I'll hurt the motherfucker.

This is my new life now, and I'm going to embrace it whether I like it or not.

A heavy shadow falls over the table, but I keep my gaze fixed on Harmonia's for a moment, raising my eyebrows at her before the person makes themselves known.

"Hey, Rhea, right? I'm Sh—"

"Wasting your time. You're wasting your time, so fuck off," Harmonia gripes, flicking her hand at him and rolling her eyes before looking at the guy peering down at me. I turn my attention to him, recognizing him from a few classes, but I've never spoken to him before. It's the same old story, just a different guy trying to claim me.

He gapes at Harmonia's outburst, but I simply shrug, watching as he combs his fingers through his brown hair. "What she said," I add, pointing in Harmonia's direction before scooping up the last of my food and finishing my lunch. I watch as Harmonia raises an eyebrow up at the guy, waiting for him to leave since he was clearly dismissed by both of us.

"Bitch," he grunts under his breath, turning and stalking away from the table, and Harmonia chuckles.

"You're too kind!" I holler back to him, making sure he knows I couldn't give a fuck about what he calls me. He's the one that approached me, likely knowing what the outcome would be. Somehow thinking he might get a different response.

"See, I can do that all night long if I have to." She looks down at her nails like she's admiring her handiwork by telling that guy to get fucked, and I can't help but hide a smirk. "Whatever it takes for you to get your ass out and have fun," Harmonia pleads once more, and I swipe a hand down my face.

I do want to have fun, and party, and live my best life, and as I sit here looking around the dining hall, I'm fucking pissed at myself for letting the circumstances, ones that I didn't intentionally create, back me into a corner.

Just as I'm about to turn back to Harmonia, my eyes fall on the center table where the *Elites* of Saints Academy sit. Pretty much the only four guys who have given me a wide berth since I first arrived.

Adonis, Xander Bishop, Khaos Black, and Zen Elias.

Curiosity got the better of me at the end of week one, and when no one was around, I glanced at the wooden plaque in Agion that confirmed the names of each person in the hall. I didn't specifically know who was who out of Adonis' friends, I just knew they were all dark and broody, except for the guy with the mousy blond hair and constant whimsical smile on his lips. I prayed his name was Zen, because it would really fucking suit him.

There's been no sign of Adonis since my first day of classes. Not even a run in while using the bathroom we share. I can't deny they hold my interest, the way they carry themselves and interact with each other. It's like they're a unit in their own little bubble, and we're just all on the outside looking in.

"Rhea?" Harmonia's voice cuts through my thoughts, pulling me back to the table, and I offer her an awkward smile.

"I have nothing to wear," I simply state before taking a sip of my drink, thinking I have made the dumbest excuse ever, and she full-on smirks at me. Busted.

"Girl, it's a *costume* Halloween party, you know I've got you covered," she replies, excitement dancing in her eyes. "Tell me another reason you can't come so I can get over all the hurdles and get you to let your hair down," she adds, and I can't help but grin at her enthusiasm. It's so damn contagious.

Fuck it.

"If you make me dress as a slutty nun I'm not coming."

"Oh, I would never."

♃

A devil.

I'm dressed as a fucking devil.

In a deep red sequin dress that clings to me like a second skin, horns on my head, tail attached at the back, and a pitch fork in my hand, I look absolutely fucking ridiculous.

Harmonia doesn't seem to think so, the girl was excited having a blank canvas to work with. She even went as far as to paint my face with make-up, my lips stained red, and my eyes framed in the same color too, with my hair falling down around my face in waves.

Admittedly, I do feel and look hot as sin in it, but it's also completely wasted on these assholes at Saints Academy. Not one interaction has really been about simple desire, since I caught Adonis working himself over in the shower. Everything else seems to come with an ulterior motive, like *claiming* me, and I'm not here for that. Not at all.

"We're almost there, just on the other side of these trees through the opening," Harmonia states, pointing ahead. Of course she's a fucking angel, just like her namesake says she should be. Her white dress matches her hair, and clings to her body just like mine. But instead of the pitchfork, tail, and horns, she has a halo and a harp.

I can only assume that the party is approved, but not allowed to take place on official Academy grounds. We've been walking for ten minutes east of the main building, reaching the woods that cover this area of the grounds, and moments later, the clearing widens, and the sound of music and laughter starts to fill my ears. The protective bubble still shimmers above us, the safety of the Academy blanketing us as we relax and unwind.

The woods have been sprinkled with tiny lights, offering a dim but manageable glow, while the opening is much brighter, and as I step out into it fully, I notice a lake on the other side of the large open space.

It looks like every member of the Academy is here, there are that many bodies hovering around. Some are dancing to the music booming through the speakers, some sit around a campfire lost in their own worlds, while others remain on the outskirts huddling in their little groups.

I spy the table to the right, where drinks are lined up for people to choose from, and Harmonia instantly pulls me in that direction. For a moment, while we walk around the edge, no one seems to notice us, giving me a moment's peace as I take everyone else in.

There are definitely a few slutty nuns, witches, vampires—which is ironic as fuck—and even a few shirtless werewolves. At least everyone is having fun and the drama seems to be low-key.

"What are you drinking?" Harmonia asks as we approach the table, and I cast my eyes over the options.

"I'll take something with a lid," I mumble, not wanting to risk any of the open containers on the table. Which leaves me with the option of a beer, water, or sealed plastic shot glasses. "Two shots and a water," I confirm, and she grins at my choice.

"I like it," she replies as I grab what I want and she does the same.

Moving away from the table, I hear a few girls call Harmonia's name, and she nods in their direction at the edge of the opening, off to the right toward the lake.

Crossing the distance, drinks in hand, my gaze slips over to the fire burning brightly in the middle of the space, and my breath halts when I see the four guys who intrigue me, standing on the other side. With the fire blazing in front of them, the embers flickering into the sky, I can't help but feel myself be even more drawn to them.

I blame it on my attire. The heat attracting the devil in me to step closer, to challenge temptation, but I don't. The last words I spoke to any of them was Adonis, and that was when I chose the slur of him being *nothing*. Clearly that was a turn off, and his off the cuff flirting quickly vanished right along with him.

"Rhea, this is Cassandra and Thalia," Harmonia says, coming to a stop before two blonde girls. Both dressed as bloodied vampires, it's clear they're identical twins, everything about them is exactly the same except for the color of their eyes. One with blue. The other with green.

"Hey," the girl closer to me says, reaching her bottle of beer out to clink it against my water, and I chuckle.

"Hi," I murmur in response, glad there's no awkwardness.

"How are you settling in?" The girl with green eyes

asks as I place my bottle of water on the rock nearby so I can peel open my shots.

Tilting my head to look at her, I gape for a moment because no one has actually asked me that yet. Harmonia has given me the space to do what I need to do while being a much needed friend among everything, but otherwise, I haven't really interacted with anyone. I'm far too happy in my own presence to want to try and fit in.

"I'm settling," I respond, not really wanting to detail my woes so I don't know what else to say, and she responds with a soft smile. As if she gets what I mean without saying the words out loud.

"If it makes you feel any better, I'm still settling in and I've been here longer," she adds, and her sister nods beside her.

"Thalia is extra antisocial, and from what Harmonia says, you two will get along well, hiding away from having to deal with immature, horny assholes," she says with a grin, and this time I lift my shot glass out to clink with Thalia's, whose green eyes sparkle in understanding as she reaches out for a bottle of water.

"I can drink to that," I say, lifting the drink to my lips and downing the sweet lemon liquor in one go. A shiver runs down my spine as I lick the remnants off my lips. "Although, these are definitely worth showing up for," I say, looking down into the empty cup, making the others grin. I reach over and grab the second one I picked up, doing the same again, tossing my head back as the sweetness drips down my throat, before I shake my head.

We all fall into casual conversation, Cassandra and Harmonia taking the lead, letting Thalia and me nod along happily.

"Have you had any thoughts on what you kind of *hope* you will be?" Thalia asks randomly, as we watch Harmonia and Cassandra slink their way over to the dance area, and my eyes round in surprise at her question.

It seems these sisters like to pull the tough questions out straight away or people are just too scared to ask. I can't deny the fact that I've thought them all through, but I have no idea because I haven't felt or seen anything manifest yet.

God.

Angel.

Vampire.

Demon.

Werewolf.

Five words that hold far more meaning than their simple names. Especially with Gods, Angels, and Demons that come in all unique variations. None of them know their true powers until the time comes. From what I've learned, it could be anything from healing wounds, controlling the weather, to other skills I can't even begin to comprehend.

"I honestly have no idea. I've never really interacted with any supernaturals to be able to understand their traits fully, only what I'm learning in classes like everyone else," I answer, feeling the zing of the shots buzzing lightly beneath the surface. It's on the tip of my tongue to ask what she's *expected* to be, but even with the alcohol running through my veins I still can't decide how rude that is, so I keep my mouth shut.

Although, she must see the question in my eyes because she offers a grin as she meets my gaze. "Vampires."

As simple as that. One word.

I want it to be that easy for me. Having a family background that solidifies the path I should be on here. I can't help but notice the glint of pride in Thalia's eyes. "What are you most excited for?" I ask, and her grin widens.

"All of it really. But I truly love the idea of having all my senses heightened. Sounds, touch, taste. I think it will be alluring and liberating."

My heart beats a little faster from her words, feeling everything she's describing too, as I wet my lips. It really does sound enticing. I'm just scared to get my hopes up for anything. As much as I'm used to disappointment, I want this to feel as magical as it is.

I never in a million years expected this for me, this break, this alternative future I had never considered, and I don't want to regret it.

Sensing my thoughts deepening and heading down a non-party friendly path, I decide I need another drink. Glancing toward Harmonia, I see her and Cassandra making their way toward us.

"I'm going to grab another drink, does anyone else want anything?" I offer, but everyone shakes their head or tilts their almost full drinks in my direction as the music continues to play around us. "Awesome, I won't be long," I add, before turning and heading toward the drinks table.

The next song plays, and I almost start swaying to it, but I need another couple of shots in me before that happens. Liquid courage and all. Stopping at the drinks table, I search through the remaining shot glasses to see if I can find the same flavor, when a hand strokes down my back. The tingles it elicits aren't of desire and need, instead, the hairs on the back of my neck rise as I instinctively get defensive.

I look back over my shoulder to see Hector, the guy who tried to come on to me at the first Combat class I had. I don't have a shield between us now, just me and him. What's more concerning is the way he stumbles slightly on his feet, his eyes blown and a little manic. I can tell he's been hitting the drinks a little harder than me.

Fucking great.

"Hey, beautiful," he purrs, eyes raking over me from head to toe as he squeezes my hip. I immediately lift my palm to his chest, forcing him to take a step back, and his hand thankfully drops from my body.

"I didn't say you could touch me," I state calmly, not wanting to make him flip out, not straight away at least. But I'd love to break his hand or throat punch the arrogant asshole for thinking he has the right to touch me without consent.

"I didn't realize I needed your *permission* to show you how much I appreciate your curves," he says, slowly running his tongue across his bottom lip and I cringe.

So. Gross.

"Well, you do," I respond, turning my attention back to the drinks, hoping he'll get the hint, but unfortunately, he doesn't leave me alone. Instead, he continues to push his luck.

"I can't believe you've been hiding this tight body beneath that uniform of yours," he says, capturing a lock of my brown hair between his finger and thumb, and my hands clench at my sides as I try to contain the irritation starting to thrum through my veins.

It's official. The guys who attend Saints Academy are disrespectful cuntbags.

Looking up at him, I find his gaze locked on the sweetheart neckline of my skin-tight dress, and I instantly hate it. But why should I let this guy dictate to me what I should and shouldn't wear? I'm not asking him to leer at me, or undress me with his eyes. I'm actually pleading him, with my eyes, to fuck all the way off, but it seems he's not interested in doing that.

I lift my arm, knocking it into his so he releases my hair, and the drunken smile on his lips quickly turns into a frown as he glares down at me. He finally realizes that I'm not fucking around and meets my eyes in challenge.

"I'm only going to say this once, so I want to make sure you're listening," I start, taking a step back with my arms extended so he doesn't follow. I wait for a moment to see if there's an ounce of clarity in his gaze before strongly emphasizing my message. "Fuck. Off."

The bite of my tone is harsher than I expected, but I don't care. He couldn't take the hint, so being direct was the only way for him to comprehend in his drunken state. Before he responds, I swipe a few shots off the table, turning on my heels and heading into the woods away from him. When I'm settled in between the trees, the noise not as loud, I glance back over my shoulder to see where he is, and I just about manage to make out his face over by the campfire with his friends.

A sigh of relief sweeps through me as I stop beside a tree stump. The little twinkling lights scattering the trees makes the area feel magical, offering just enough light among the darkness. Being out here alone probably isn't a good idea, but I just need a fucking second to breathe.

Away from leering or glaring eyes, all of the noise, and the constant tension that seeps through me.

Leaning against the tall tree to my left, I let the cool, rough wood texture graze my skin as I press myself into the bark. Without looking down to see what flavor I got, I peel open the first shot, lifting it to my mouth and quickly gulp it down. The zingy taste of green apple coats my lips, and I take a deep breath, slowly exhaling as I try to build up the courage to rejoin the party.

The sudden feeling of someone watching me has me standing a little taller, the hairs on the back of my neck rising as my eyes try to focus on my surroundings. My body tightens, my defensive nature ready to take over.

"I don't think you should be alone in the woods."

The mocking tone comes from behind me, and when I turn around, I'm surprised to find Mr. Asshole standing with his hands in his pockets, dark hair covering his eyes that still sparkle green in the limited light.

Fake blood is smeared on his face and dripping down his ripped white shirt, and I scoff.

"Why? I'm not scared," I reply, my confidence and years of living alone like this coming across as arrogant, but I won't apologize for it, especially not to this guy or any other guy for that matter.

"You should be. There are things out here that go bump in the night," he simply states without elaborating any farther. He slowly walks toward me, each step measured, calculating, as he observes my reaction to him. His eyes remain fixed on mine, not making me feel uncomfortable or like an object as Hector did, and that somehow manages to calm the defensive side of me.

"Is there anything I can help you with? I came here for some fucking quiet. I don't need you patronizing me," I grumble, hand on my hip as I stare at him expectantly, and the smallest of grins touches the corner of his lips.

"I was just wondering what permission I needed to confirm how hot you are with your curves on display," he replies, the words far too similar to what Hector just said, and when my brows knit together in confusion, I realize he must have heard him. Asshole.

"Do you always eavesdrop?"

He doesn't respond until he's almost toe to toe with me, circling around so my back is touching the tree again. The bark bites roughly against my skin, adding to the sensory overload I'm already beginning to experience. My pulse quickens at his closeness, my palms sweating as I grip the two remaining shots in my hand.

Catching the movement, he slowly inches his hand forward, prying one from my grip and opening it. He offers it back to me wordlessly, before taking the other and doing the same, only keeping that one for himself.

When he holds it out for me to clink mine against it, I only assume he's a man of very few words, but decide to roll with it. Almost fucking enjoying it compared to the slimy dickheads who haven't shut up when approaching me.

Touching the rim of my shot glass to his, I quickly swallow it down, a hum of approval slipping from my lips as the lemon taste dances on my tongue. Almost as nice as the apple, but not quite.

I don't realize I've shut my eyes until I pry them back

open to find him glaring down at me, a drastic shift in his cool demeanor from moments before. "You shouldn't be allowed to make sounds like that," he grunts, tossing his empty shot glass on the ground as he takes the final step to evaporate the remaining distance between us.

Instead of raising my hands to hold him back, they fall to my side, almost encouraging him closer by my submissiveness, and my empty shot glass falls to the soil too.

He's all I can feel, all I can see, and it's intoxicating.

"Did your new friend tell you the secret about Vampires and Shifters?" he asks, brushing my curls back over my right shoulder, and without even making contact with my bare skin, I shiver as I shake my head. "She didn't share with you the little known way to predetermine if you will become a Vampire or a Shifter? And here I was thinking you were getting close to my cousins to get under my skin," he retorts.

"Cousins?" I say in confusion, brows raised as I eye him, and he must see the surprise and truth in my eyes because he nods, the darkness ebbing ever so slightly from his gaze. Again, it's like I can see another shift in his behavior based on my reaction.

As if that's all he needed to confirm, he inches closer, his breath on my neck as he runs the tip of his nose over the length of my throat. My body stands stiff, rigid, as I try to predict his next move, but he catches me by complete surprise when he drags the tip of his tongue over the same spot his nose just ran.

"At the age of twenty-two, a vampire's blood already begins to transform, a slight nick, a little taste, that's all you need to know if you will become one. I'd be able to taste it," he murmurs against my skin, causing bumps to prickle the area.

The party is happening so close, but it's like it's just the two of us, completely lost and absorbed in our own bubble. "How do you know the difference?" I find myself asking, too intrigued, too caught up in the moment, and desperate for him to stay this close, his smoky scent intoxicating me.

"One drop of a vampire's blood when in the throes of passion is like being on the biggest high." I swallow at his words, my chest arching into him slightly so my peaked nipples graze against his chest.

In his next move, he runs his teeth over my exposed skin, and I moan, unable to hold it in.

Holy fuck.

What is he doing to me?

My body is reacting to his words before my brain can even play catch up.

Leaning back so he can meet my gaze, our noses almost brushing as his emerald greens meet my sapphires. "You'd like that wouldn't you," he states, not a question, but a fact, and all I can do is gape at him as his large hand touches my thigh at the hem of my skirt, and slowly rises, taking the fabric of my skirt along with him.

Goosebumps rise in his wake, anticipation clawing at

my insides as he flicks his tongue out and drags it across my bottom lip. I feel like a deer caught in the headlights, unable to move, bracing for the impact, but wanting it all the same regardless of the consequences.

"What are you doing to me?" I ask, the words slipping from my lips before I can even process them myself, and he scoffs, stroking a finger down my cheek as he searches my soul through my eyes, intruding on my internal thoughts with little effort.

"I think I'm supposed to be the one asking you that question," he murmurs, his breath fanning across my face, and I don't know who moves first, and frankly, I don't give a fuck, but in the next breath our lips collide.

My fingers instantly reach for his dark hair, scraping my nails along the base of his scalp as his hand on my thigh rises, and his other hand grabs my waist, just below my breast.

His touch makes me feel empowered and small in his grip all at once.

The bark at my back bites into my skin as his thumb drags along the apex of my thigh, a mere breath away from my core, and I arch up into him, letting him take, when someone starts to clap, breaking the moment and pulling our lips apart.

Blinking up at him as he stares down at me with a swirl of emotions brewing in his eyes, I'm sure mine are reflecting the same in response. It takes a moment for us to pull apart, both of us trying to catch our breath.

"Zen, get your fucking ass over here. Khaos broke first. I want my winnings because it wasn't fucking me," Adonis hollers, his voice far louder than it needs to be.

Khaos.

Mr. Asshole is Khaos Black.

He takes a step back, raking his fingers through his hair as he takes a deep breath, eyes still fixed on me, and I turn to my left to glare at Adonis.

"Stop shouting, motherfucker," Khaos grinds out as the two other guys appear behind Adonis.

"You don't get any winnings, idiot, because you're causing a scene," the guy with mousy blond hair says with a sigh as he comes to a stop beside Adonis, flicking his gaze between Khaos and me.

Zen.

The one that literally radiates calm is called Zen. I was right.

That leaves the broody guy who comes to a stop on the other side of Adonis. He's in a pair of jeans with no top on, and fake claw marks covering his chest and abs.

Xander.

"What's going on?" he asks, ruffling his hair as he frowns at me.

"Khaos was nibbling on a snack, weren't you, asshole," Adonis gripes, and I can't tell if he's angry or happy about it.

Either way, I need to get out of here and fucking think

about anything other than his body against mine.

"Adonis, baby, what are you shouting for?" As if conjured by the devil himself, or me in my costume, the supreme bitch appears in all her glory.

Flanked by her two friends that I don't care to know any more about, she struts to the center of us all, dressed as a sexy, bloody nun, and I want to gag. She slowly moves toward Adonis, lifting her hand to his chest as she tries to figure out what the commotion is all about.

I'd rather not be around for the rest of this, but one step from me has a twig snapping and her gaze instantly twists to me.

"You. What are you doing?" she says with a glare, hands on her hips as she looks from Khaos to me and back again. "I warned you not to touch what's mine, I—"

"Shut the fuck up, Selene," Khaos bites, swiping a hand down his face, before storming from the woods without a backward glance.

"Adonis. You can't let him speak to me like that," Selene whines, squeezing his biceps, and I roll my eyes. The sound of her voice is like that of a petulant child and if they want to listen to her, then all the power to them.

Fuck this shit. I'm out of here.

Taking quieter steps, I edge around them, but before I fully escape the group, my eyes lock with Xander's. It's like he can see right through to my bones with the way he eyes me, but what surprises me most of all, is the soft smile he offers me a glimpse of before he turns back to Adonis and the supreme bitch, trying to diffuse the situation.

Going in search of Harmonia, I keep tight lipped on what just happened.

I don't think she'd believe me if I told her anyway.

ELEVEN

RHEA

I spent the rest of the weekend hiding out in my room. A mixture of studying the material that had already been covered before I arrived, the assignments currently set, and finding ecstasy at my own hands as I thought about green eyes and vampire blood. More than once.

Fucking hell.

Khaos fucking Black is going to be the death of me.

I heard Adonis singing in the shower this morning, almost like he was luring me in like a siren, tempting me to step inside and catch him in the act just like last time, but I refrained. Barely.

Friday night was… crazy, and the way he interrupted Khaos and me still leaves me confused, but I refuse to give in and seek him out to understand what he meant when he said

Khaos gave in first.

Now, I'm standing across from Hector in Combat class, with Professor Riva giving out orders of moves we should be making with the long sticks he handed out to each of us.

Two lines of students face each other, which is why I have such an unfortunate view of Hector before me, as Riva explains the weight balance and how that can impact the use of the weapon. Admittedly, it's heavier than it first looked, my arms are taut with tension and I'm sure using it in the right way would cause some damage, but I can't seem to figure out a situation where I would reach for one.

Like where am I going to keep it? My back pocket?

I obviously don't mention a word as I spin it in front of me, before slamming the end into the grass at my feet, just as he's demonstrating. Everyone repeats the movement over and over again until he finally claps, signaling us to stop, and I almost feel like I have a handle on it.

"Excellent, next lesson we may amp it up a little and use them to practice one on one with another student," he explains, and a drop of excitement buzzes through me at the thought of inflicting pain. "Dismissed."

Please, dear Gods, put Hector or Selene across from me. I would take far too much fucking pleasure in rearranging their faces with this pole. A small grin graces my lips, and I shake my head quickly to clear the expression before anyone misinterprets my happiness. Someone would know something is up if they were to see me wearing a big ass cheesy smile with teeth and all.

Brushing my hair back off my face, I instantly find Harmonia in the scattered crowd as everyone moves toward the stand to place their poles away. Thank God it's lunch next, I'm starving.

I meet her at the racks, both placing our poles in the holders. "Do you want to head straight for lunch and get changed for the last class afterward? I'm so hungry, I don't think I can wait," Harmonia says, pleading, pink eyes meeting mine, and my shoulders sag in relief just as my stomach growls.

"Hell yeah, I was just thinking the same," I reply, moving toward where we placed our satchels earlier when the feel of ice water disorientates me for a moment, gushing over my head and trickling down my spine.

I stand frozen in shock, arms out to the side as my shorts and t-shirt stick to me. Mouth wide, I glance around me, the sound of laughter echoing around the space as a smug-faced Selene grins at me from a few feet away.

That bitch.

That motherfucking bitch practically poured a bucket of water over my fucking head.

I can hear Harmonia audibly gasp at the sight, and time pauses momentarily as I try to gauge my reactions to the ridiculous prank.

"What's going on?" I hear the professor call out, before

appearing in front of me, the center of everyone's attention as they stand and stare at me dripping wet. I pinch my t-shirt, pulling it away from my skin because the water is fucking cold. Riva takes one look at me and disappointment colors his eyes. I must look like a drowned rat. "Who did this?" he barks, turning to glance at every student, but I shake my head quickly, and drop my hands to my side. I get he might have a responsibility as a professor to handle the situation, but causing a scene isn't necessary.

"It's fine, it's just water," I say, swiping a hand down my face. I clear the droplets of water that continue to trickle down from my forehead as he turns to look at me again, with concern written all over his face. I don't need his misplaced sympathy.

It takes every ounce of strength that I have to ignore every single person here and focus on Harmonia as I step to her side and talk quietly. "You go to lunch, I'll be right behind you," I state, her brows rising in confusion at dismissing her.

"Hell no, I'll come—"

I wave my hand, interrupting her as I offer a tight smile. "Honestly, it's all good. I need a minute anyway," I say, and with a reluctant nod, she links her arm through mine and we head for the portal.

Everyone's eyes are still on me, including the Elites, but I look at no one as they chuckle, point fingers and gossip like we're back in fucking high school. We quickly step through the portal, and appear in the main academic building, before we part ways.

I keep my shoulders back and head held high as I cut across to the portal that leads to my dorm. A sigh is ready to fall from my lips in relief as it comes into view, my sanctuary is within reach, but just as I'm about to step through, a large hand lands on my shoulder. When my foot hits the ground on the other side of the portal, I instantly see that I'm not in the Agion hall.

Squinting at the blue walls and garish red carpet, I stall for a moment, trying to get my bearings. The hand on my shoulder tightens, and the next second I'm being slammed into the wall to my right. My chest bursts with pain as I heave in a breath, and my hands attempt to brace for impact.

I jolt at the sudden movement, the shock and confusion leaving me defenseless and allowing whoever this is to get the upper hand. Pushing off the wall, I throw my elbow back, hoping to collide with any body part, but there's nothing there.

Whirling around, I come face to face with four motherfuckers wearing white masks covering their faces. The design of black and red markings, the intricate detailing, is almost jarring as I scramble to figure out who is beneath them. I look for clues in their eyes since that's the only part of their face that is visible.

I take a step back, hitting the wall behind me with a thud as I clench and unclench my hands at my side. What the fuck is going on?

My body wants to take another step back and magically retreat through the wall, but as a blessing and a curse, that's just not who I am. I force myself to take a step toward them, watching as they close in on me, effectively blocking me from going anywhere. I tilt my chin higher in outright defiance, refusing to back down to these fuckers who have somehow managed to corner me alone.

Cowards.

I can hear their heavy breaths, see their hands fist as they stare at me, but I can't piece together who the fuck it is, although my gut already has a clue.

I can feel the tension thickening around us. Four against one doesn't seem like good odds for me. I don't need to be able to take them all down, what I need is to fight my way through the ones blocking the portal, then I can get the fuck out of here without taking any damage.

Trying to keep my body as relaxed as possible, I crack my neck as my brain tries to predict how this is going to go down, but there are too many people to cover all angles.

I'm ready for a brawl, my fists ready to go to town on these assholes, but that's my first mistake; these fuckers don't fight like they do down in Phoenix Valley.

The one in the center of the group edges forward, my pulse pounding in my ears as they reach into their pocket and pull out a black silk bag.

Fuck this shit.

I'm not waiting to find out what's in there because obviously whatever the pouch contains, it will only harm me.

Moving to shoulder past the person standing farthest to the left, I manage to make them stumble on their feet by my sudden movement, giving me the leverage I need to move past them. But just as my fingers tangle with the thick black fog of the portal something sharp prods the back of my neck, locking my body in place from head to toe, paralyzing my muscles.

My body screams at me to move, the loss of control wreaking havoc on me as I use every ounce of strength to do *something*, *anything* to get me out of this situation, but nothing happens. The chuckles that surround me only anger me more as I realize I'm unable to move my mouth too.

"Let's get you back where I want you, shall we?" The husky voice of the man who spoke sounds familiar, but I can't quite place a name. Moments later, hands grab at my arms, moving me back to the wall in my frozen state.

I struggle to focus, my vision doubling, possibly tripling and I feel close to passing out. A sob begs to fall from my closed lips, the movement making my chest heave as my eyes search frantically around the four masked people before me.

I want to tell them they're going to regret this.

I want to tell them I'll make them pay tenfold for whatever they do to me.

I want to tell them to sleep with one eye open.

But I can't say a single fucking word.

The person to my right twirls a golden staff in their hand, weighing the object before pointing it in my direction.

"Do you like my gift from Pandora's Box?" a girl's voice asks, far too pleased and proud of the object as she takes a step closer toward me. "It offers temporary paralysis. I've never had a reason to use it before, until *you.*"

Paralysis?

For how long?

Fucking fuck.

The person standing to my left suddenly moves to stand toe to toe with me, before swinging their fist and hitting me square in the face. My grunt is muted from the impact as I almost rock on the spot, my vision becoming spotty. My arm is still stretched out before me and my legs now straight.

I can feel the hot blood instantly drip from my nose.

Motherfucker.

"Filthy fucking earthling," the girl says as she stands back behind everyone, happy to watch the show unfold before her. This bitch doesn't want to get her hands dirty in case there are any repercussions but unfortunately for her, I never forget.

Frustration, anger, and disappointment at the situation burns through every inch of me. And helplessness, fuck do I feel helpless.

Clearly loving having the upper hand, the girl with the slurred insult takes a step toward me with purpose, not stopping until her hand wraps around my throat. Her action catches me off guard as her nails sink into my skin, piercing my flesh as I hiss in my mind.

This bitch is going to fucking pay.

With every ounce that I am, I *will* get my revenge.

It's a promise I intend to keep.

"You're going to learn that you're nothing here, just like you were nothing where you came from," she bites, venom laced in every word she says as my blood chills along with my body.

Only one person would say those words, and I know exactly what they would say them for.

Selene Hart.

This is because of the Halloween party, I know it. How fucking ridiculous and petty.

The overwhelming sensation of the blood from my nose running faster down my face, and into a puddle at my feet, makes my eyes burn as my body begs for me to wipe it away.

It feels completely crazy. Like I'm watching myself in third person, my body unmoving while my brain is fighting with every pound of my pulse to clear my system of the drug.

"Go back to where you fucking came from, earthling bitch. You don't belong at Saints Academy. You don't belong in Agion. You're only prolonging the inevitable by staying."

I want to question her with hows or whys, but it's not possible.

The only other person here who has observed everything

without a word steps forward, knocking the other bitch's hand from my throat, before they crowd my space, placing their palms on the wall on either side of my head.

"You might think you're safe now, whore, but come next spring, when they help awaken the magic inside us, you're going to want to be *exactly* what I tell you to be. Understand?"

I know it's Hector, every ounce of my body knows it, even if I can't prove it.

"Let's go, it's going to wear off soon," one of the girls mumbles, and relief floods me at the confirmation I won't remain like this forever.

I watch as they all move away from me, clearly worried I will rain hell down on them if it wears off now, and it makes me grin, or at least in my mind I do.

Cunts.

The closest two to the portal step through it without a backward glance, while the other two linger for a moment. My toes twitch ever so slightly, and adrenaline begins to course through my body, ready to stand my ground and fight back against these assholes, but it's not quick enough, when one of them lifts their foot and kicks me straight in the stomach.

My muscles react to the pain as it's repeated over and over again, radiating through my body, but this time, the impact makes me fall to the side in agony, my body collapsing in a heap of batteredness.

I take a moment to catch my breath, the retreating

footsteps of my assailants causing me disappointment, but I can't move any quicker to get my revenge before they leave me here.

Selene.

The supremest of supreme bitches.

There's no way this doesn't link back to her, not with those specific words.

When I'm sure no one's around, listening for any little sound, I slowly pry my eyes open to be met with the red carpet and awful blue walls My eyes fix on the plaque that hangs on the wall, just like in Agion, but this one says *Nero*.

I should probably read what names are on the board, but there's more than at Agion, and right now, I just need to get myself to safety.

After I heal, I will find out who lives here.

My body screams as I force myself to my feet, and when I step through the portal, this time, I find myself in Agion.

A sob burst from my lips in relief, I was worried I was going to have to go back to the main building and step out again. As much as I'm managing to move, the remnants of whatever they did to me still makes me feel far more lethargic than I want to be.

I want to keel over, place myself in the fetal position, but I don't. I force myself to put one foot in front of the other, making my way up the stairs to my floor, where I find Harmonia pounding on my door like a crazy woman.

The noise burns my ears, but not as much as the screech does as she sees me and shouts my name at the top of her lungs. “Rhea! Oh my Gods, Rhea! What the fuck happened to you?”

She instantly approaches, blood dripping from my face as I move. “I’m fine, I’ll be okay,” I mumble, my voice croaky as I edge toward my door, which quickly opens under my touch before I step inside, Harmonia hot on my heels.

I can see in her eyes that she wants to help, but has no idea where to touch in case she hurts me, but I’d rather be left alone anyway. I’m used to handling situations by myself, so her hovering over me does nothing to help the anger burning inside.

Flopping down on my bed, I wince at the pain as a deep voice comes from my bathroom door. “What’s with all the fucking wailing?” Adonis grunts. I don’t need to see him look to know he’s caught a glimpse at the state of me, the tone of his next words does it. “Who the fuck did this to you?”

Deep, deadly, and gravelly, it almost doesn’t sound like the same person.

“I don’t know, dickhead,” Harmonia bites. “Hence all the fucking wailing,” she retorts, and I wish I had the ability to laugh at her response, but right this second, everything hurts too much. “She needs to sleep, Adonis, so leave her alone.”

I scoff, my body jolting with the pain. I wish I could sleep right now, but I know there’s no chance in hell I’ll be able to let my guard down for that.

“That’s not going to happen any time soon, but I’ll be

fine," I mumble, my eyes falling closed, but my brain is still running at a mile a minute.

"Girl, you need to sleep, and we need to get you cleaned up," Harmonia says, softer this time.

"Don't let anyone fucking touch me, Harm," I manage to whimper, hissing in pain. I pry my eyes open, my vision blurred, and I manage to see Adonis pass her something, before she moves toward the side of my bed, crouching down next to me. "What—"

Before I can finish my sentence, she lifts her hand to my face, palm up with some kind of powder glistening on her skin, and blows it in my face.

Plummeting into darkness, I see nothing, feel nothing, am nothing.

Just like they wanted from me all along.

TWELVE

RHEA

My mind drifts away from the dream I was consumed in, filled with dark shadows and men hunting me in white, black, and red masks. I wet my cracked lips, stretching my arms out as I rouse from sleep, frowning at where the dream may have stemmed from. A sense of uncertainty washes over me because of the unknown.

The moment my body is pulled tight, muscles aching, especially my stomach area, I blink my eyes open, at the memory of the last thing I remember playing out in my mind. My head is pounding something fierce, my pulse setting the rhythm as pain shoots throughout my skull. Sunlight beams in through my window as I blink up at the ceiling, letting the scene take control of my thoughts.

I stepped through the portal, and the touch of someone's

hand on my shoulder had me transported to Nero hall. I can visualize the ugly red carpets and blue walls like they're right here in front of me causing a chill to seep deep into my veins.

The touch of a staff as it connected with my neck, holding me captive in my own body, makes the ice cold sensation I'm feeling turn into a violent shudder as it runs down my spine.

When I managed to move, the ass kicking over, stumbling my way back to Agion, I remember Harmonia pounding on my door, before she saw my beaten face and weakened body. We'd barely slipped into my room before Adonis appeared from the adjoining bathroom.

His shouting hadn't helped the situation, but I remember him handing something to Harmonia, which she blew in my face, making my world go dark.

I try to control the panic while I try to clear my mind of what happened and focus on the now.

Fumbling for my phone, I thankfully find it on the nightstand, and when I turn the screen on I see it's almost six a.m. the following morning. How the fuck did I sleep for a solid fifteen hours?

I place my phone back down with a sigh, brushing my hair back off my face, when I cringe at the touch against my sensitive skin.

Oh, Gods, how bad does it look?

There's no time like the present to find out, so I swing my legs over the side of the bed and take a second to catch my breath. Moving too quickly, I make myself a little lightheaded, my vision spotting momentarily, but once I have my breathing under control, I confidently plant my feet on the ground and stand up. I bypass the floor-length mirror on the inside of my walk-in closet, opting for the better lighting in the bathroom.

My door is slightly ajar, and when I peek around the wood, I sag in relief when I see there's no naked, masturbating Adonis in sight. His door is slightly open too, but I tiptoe across the tiled floor and quietly close it before I turn my attention to the mirror.

Someone, I'm assuming Harmonia, cleaned up what would have been dried blood and all of the other mess that was on my face, leaving me with clear cuts and bruises. My right eye is slightly discolored and tender with a bit of puffiness. There's a cut on the bridge of my nose, with another small slice on my left cheekbone, but the fact that I don't have two black eyes or a crooked nose tells me it's not broken.

Overall, I look red and blotchy with the mixture of blue and purple bruising on my face. Like an overripe peach left to wilt on a hot summer's day. People will notice, and I'm sure they'll have much to say, but I won't wear makeup to hide it. The limited pieces I have will likely only enhance the damage and make it look worse.

I'm still in my Combat uniform, my t-shirt no longer wet from my run-in with Selene yesterday, but red splodges mark the material. I am grateful that no one tried to undress me while I was in a deep sleep. That would have been a whole different situation to worry about.

But I need to shower. And eat. In that order.

Stepping over to the glass shower stall, I twist the dial to turn the water on, before moving back and stripping slowly as I wait for the temperature to heat. I spot the marble of purples and blues on my waist, and cringe.

I take the fluffy cream towel from the rack and place it at the entry to the shower, before stepping under the spray. I stand, as frozen as I was yesterday, only this time by choice, letting the warm water cascade down my back in a gentle caress. The water doesn't pound against my battered skin causing discomfort, so I consider that a win.

After a few minutes, I reach for the shower gel, lathering the soap in my hands before I rid my body of the grime and blood painting the remainder of my skin.

My fluid movements almost lull me into a sense of calmness, my tense shoulders slowly relaxing as I shampoo and condition my hair. A heavy sigh falls from my lips as I turn the shower off, happy with the new state of myself, before I reach for the towel and wrap it snugly around my body.

Steam billows around me as I move back to the vanity to brush my teeth, impressed with the anti-fog mirror, when my movements freeze at the sound of a voice coming from my right, completely catching me off guard.

"How are you feeling?"

I whirl around in a panic and come face to face with Adonis. He's shirtless, his blond hair swept back off his face like he's run his hands through it a time or two, with a pair of circular glasses on the bridge of his nose. His piercing eyes sear into mine, likely observing my reaction to his intrusion. Adonis' expression is blank, not reacting to my battered face as he expectantly waits for an answer and casually slips his hands into his sweatpants pockets.

Clutching the towel tighter around me, I swallow past the lump in my throat before taking a deep breath. "I could have sworn I locked that door," I state with a frown, completely avoiding his question, and he instantly shrugs.

"You only closed it. I was awake," he replies, like it all makes perfect sense, but it doesn't really explain what he's doing in here when he knows I was in the shower.

"Well, I didn't slip in the shower and fall to my impending death, so you can leave now," I grumble, pulling my gaze from his as I reach for my toothbrush and busy myself, effectively dismissing him.

Minutes tick by as I run through the process of getting ready for the day, but the motherfucker doesn't leave. He just stands there, watching me.

"Are you going to explain what happened yesterday?" he asks when I finish, crossing his arms. I immediately shake my head but regret it as soon as the pounding resumes.

"I don't need you to help me," I say with a sigh, running

my hand over my wet hair as I grip the ends of my towel with the other.

"I didn't say I was, and that was not what I asked you," he retorts quickly, leaning against the door frame with a raised eyebrow, and I roll my eyes.

"Then get the fuck out." I give him a scathing look, before spinning on my heels and taking the decision out of his hands, heading for my own door.

"Rhea, I think—"

"I don't really care what you think. I have enough shit to deal with," I grouch, shaking a hand in front of my face, hinting at the beating I took yesterday. "I don't need you suddenly wanting to swoop in like a fucking hero," I hiss, wrapping my hand around the door handle, and just as I'm ready to slam the door shut behind me, he tilts his head back and barks out a laugh.

"I'm the son of Hades, *earthling,* hero isn't even a word in my vocabulary."

I close my bedroom door behind me, running my fingers down my blazer as Harmonia smiles over at me, and I offer a small one in response.

"Do I need to apologize for knocking you out yesterday?" she asks, a hint of guilt mixed with determination swirling in her eyes, and I shake my head with a sigh.

"No, I clearly needed it, and as much as I was probably resisting at the time, I'm sure my body would have ached much more if you hadn't," I admit, and her smile grows from ear to ear as she links her arm through mine and gently pulls me toward the stairs.

"Good. I had numerous points to say in my favor if you were mad. I can still list them if you want, you know, for reassurance that it was in your best interest. And I didn't take you to a healer, but we could go now if you wanted," she murmurs, the grin on her face dropping and her tone serious. I can see the little brat fighting back the smile desperate to spread across her lips as I give her a direct look of 'don't even go there.' She knows damn well I'm not interested in any of her *points*.

"No, and I think I'll manage without the insight," I grumble in response, adjusting my satchel on my shoulder as we make it downstairs, and my tense posture relaxes a little when we don't come across anyone.

We move seamlessly toward the portal, my teeth sinking into my bottom lip as I take a step through the smoke, and when I appear in the main Academy building, the anxiety threatening to riddle my body seeps away.

If Harmonia notices the adjustment in me, she doesn't mention it as we head toward the first class of the day. Skills. Literally, the first class is Skills. No definition in the name which makes zero sense, maybe someday it will, but the class is broken off into groups, depending on your species.

There's so much hanging between us as an awkward silence descends. I know she likely has a lot of questions about yesterday, but she hasn't uttered a single one. When we get to the Skills hall, I slip my arm from Harmonia's as we step inside.

"Aren't you going to ask what happened?" I mumble, searching her gaze as I wait for her to respond, completely ignoring everyone we walk past.

"Do you *want* to tell me?" she asks, making my eyes widen in surprise because that was not the answer I was expecting. "Only, you don't seem like the type to pass on information you don't actually wish to share, so I thought I would leave it up to you instead of demanding to know," she adds, and my body relaxes in reassurance.

I clearly chose this girl as a friend for a reason.

We move through the open archway, and the Skills room comes into view. Large arched windows, with patterns detailing each one, uniquely frame the room. The stone-slab walls age the entire space as dark wooden furnishings are scattered throughout. Tables are pushed up against the side of the large room today, leaving the concrete floor open for the professors to do some demonstrations.

They don't do them every lesson, but it admittedly makes for a fun class when they do.

Moving with Harmonia to the far left, I place my satchel down beside hers on the floor, watching as others slowly filter into the room. Most will still be coming from the dining hall, but after my run in with Adonis, his words swirling in my head, I snuck to the dining hall and back before most of the Academy was even down there yet.

I need a break from all of the crazy, and to delay the inevitable of people seeing my face. Those are the only conclusions I've come to when considering everything that happened yesterday.

"If you're free, I really could do with some girl time, without all of… this," I explain, glancing around me, and she immediately nods in response, a sense of giddiness floating around her.

"For sure. I actually have dinner with my parents scheduled for tonight, but I can cancel if you want," she offers, which is sweet as hell, but I can wait.

"Maybe this weekend then? Not with parties and shit, but just, no drama."

"Count me in," she replies, and a genuine smile crosses my face as the professor saunters into the room, Adonis, Xander, Khaos, and Zen hot on his heels, and moments later the motherfuckers I'm watching for step in too.

The supreme bitch is flanked by her usual friends, whore one and whore two, and after yesterday, it's no surprise to see Hector beside them too.

Before I can get lost in my anger at them and what I *know* they did to me, even without the proof, Professor Tyler Fury claps his hands, garnering everyone's attention.

"Good morning, everyone, we have a lot to get through today, so if you'd like to form a large circle around the center space, the demonstrations and explanations of the class will begin."

At once, everyone does as he asks, Harmonia and I move to stand with Cassandra and Thalia, who stare at me in shock when they see my face, but they thankfully don't say a word.

As I stand with my hands clenched at my side, I hear the whispers get louder around me when more and more people spot the bruises and cuts on my face. There's nothing worse than being the topic on everyone's lips, especially for something that makes me feel weak.

The only people not gossiping are the Elite four who make their way to join the circle, along with Selene and her cuntish friends. The smug faces of the latter have my teeth grinding together in frustration as I make a vow to myself here and now that I will get those motherfuckers back for sure. One way or another, even if I never have proof, I'll make them weak, vulnerable, and bruised at my hands.

Movement to my left gains my attention as Zen moves to step in-between Thalia and me, and I frown, waiting for him to look at me, but instead he simply stands with his hands linked in front of him, his shoulders relaxed back in a calm stance as he watches the Professor.

My skin prickles in anticipation at his nearness, but

when he continues to practically ignore me, I find my eyes casting back to the remainder of his group who stand a little further to the left in the circle, watching the pair of us.

Screw that.

Turning my attention to the Professor, just as Zen does, I focus on the class at hand. I'm not about to let these assholes distract me. No fucking way.

"Okay, today is going to be about learning the skills and abilities of the artifacts chosen by Pandora's Box for you," Professor Fury begins, and I immediately panic, as do a few others, because I didn't bring the dagger with me, but he quickly waves his hand dismissively as he feels the wave of panic wash over the room. "Don't worry, we won't be working specifically with yours this year, that's more of a second year matter, but for now, we're going to look at the different types you may receive, and learn what they can do. Wielding them expertly is another process entirely, and as much as this is a full on Academy, we're not going to push you *that* far into the deep-end to begin with."

A mixture of nerves and excitement battle inside me at today's lesson. Knowing my dagger is an artifact chosen specifically for *me*, fills me with excitement, but remembering what those fuckers were able to do to with that staff yesterday makes me nervous. Anyone could attack me at any time with their item from Pandora's Box, and there's not much I can do about it if I'm at a disadvantage like I was then.

"There are two types of artifacts you can receive,

but knowing which one you have can be difficult to decipher sometimes, or at least to begin with. You see, it could be defensive or offensive." My interest is piqued, my brain desperate to learn more about my own tool, which I can only assume is offensive since it's a dagger. "Don't be fooled at first glance, what you see isn't always what you get, just like you shouldn't always judge a book by its cover," he states, before pulling a small, golden item from his pocket and holding it out for everyone to see.

"This is my harmonica. Yes, it can carry a tune. No, I don't play it. Yes, it looks like nothing, which is what I thought all along too, until I dropped it one day by accident," he explains, before repeating what he just said and letting the golden object fall to the floor with a clatter.

As soon as it bounces the first time, a bubble forms around the Professor, making a few gasps fill the room as my eyes round in surprise.

Holy shit.

"If someone tries to throw an object or anything at all toward me, it would bounce right off. Of course, a harmonica has no offensive qualities, but it is a rare defensive item," he states, turning to look at Hector. "Throw something." He points toward the harmonica as Hector pats his legs.

"I haven't got anything," he mumbles, coming up empty, but Fury simply shrugs.

"Then kick it."

Hector doesn't need any further encouragement as he

moves toward the device and the bubble surrounding it. He swings his leg back, hitting the barrier with full force, only to recoil with the impact, feet lifting off the ground as he flies across the space, landing in a heap.

The room breaks into a fit of laughter at the scene as Hector quickly scurries to his feet, swiping his hands down his clothes as he glares at Professor Fury who pays him no mind in return.

"Excellent demonstration," he calls out, before clasping the object in his hand as we all watch the bubble disappear before our eyes. "It all began long before the war, when only Gods existed," he explains, moving on completely without another glance toward Hector to check on him. "Pandora's Box, Zeus' Shield, and Poseidon's Trident, were the first three mythical objects to grace the world for a long time, and although Pandora's Box offers gifts to those that are indeed *gifted*, those three items are indeed the most deadly."

I squint as he walks by, observing the harmonica as Zen shuffles slightly beside me, his arm grazing mine, and I shiver at the simple touch. Attempting to glance at him out of the corner of my eye discreetly, proves pointless when I find him already looking at me.

His mousy blond hair looks soft as it practically glows in the sunlight, the earthy scent that naturally seems to float around him reeling me in hard and fast. "I'm sorry someone hurt you," he mumbles, the sound of the Professor drifting away in the distance as Zen holds me in a trance.

"Did *you* hurt me?" I ask, barely able to breathe as my eyes remain transfixed on his hazel orbs.

"I did not," he responds quickly, his brows knitting together in confusion at my question.

"Then don't apologize," I state, desperately wanting to pull my attention back to the class, but it's almost like the staff has wreaked havoc on my body again, only this time, it *is* my body forcing me to remain frozen in place.

He offers a short nod in response, his eyes trailing over every inch of my face like he's ingraining every mark to memory. "You know who did this to you," he states, ever so matter of factly, and before I can think better of it, my gaze shifts to the supreme bitch and the sleazy motherfucker who stands beside her.

It's no surprise to see her watching every second of our interaction, like she wants to be the primary interest of the Elites, or from what I've seen so far, she wants all of Adonis' attention, which just so happens to entail the three other guys too.

Bitch.

When my eyes immediately shift back to his, I know he trailed my vision, his jaw tightening as he turns back to me as well. Has this motherfucker got magic already or something? Because he sure as shit forces me to let my walls down against my better judgment, and it's annoying as fuck.

A pinch to my right side makes me jump ever so slightly,

and I turn to find Harmonia standing with wide eyes, facing the professor, and I follow her line of sight to find Professor Fury staring at me expectantly.

"Care to repeat what I just said, Miss Harrington?" he asks, arms folded over his large chest as he cocks an eyebrow at me, clearly displeased.

Before I can respond, Zen clears his throat beside me. "Apologies, Professor, I was trying to get to the bottom of the injuries Miss Harrington is displaying," he states far too sophisticatedly, all full of wisdom and shit, and it only seems to piss me off more. I don't need to be defended or have someone speak on my behalf.

The professor however, takes a step closer, looking over my face, before he sighs, dropping his arms to his sides. "I understand, but maybe do that on your own time," he replies, before turning his back to us and continuing with the class.

Anger gets the better of me the second the professor's back is turned, and I swing my elbow out to my side, connecting with Zen's abdomen and making him grunt.

"What the fuck, Rhea?" he hisses under his breath. I can feel his eyes on me, glaring daggers at the side of my head, but I don't turn around to face him as I respond.

"I didn't need you when I showed up here three weeks ago, and I definitely don't need you now."

My tone is short and blunt, but I don't care. I told Adonis the exact same.

I have my own back.

Always.

Fuck them.

THIRTEEN

RHEA

The rest of the week dragged by at an excruciating pace, and I've never been more thankful for the weekend to finally be here. Between the endless stream of classes, smug looks from those I know attacked me, and the Elites approaching me a few times more, I've definitely had enough. Concerned or not, I can't decipher their intentions, and it leaves me stressed.

Although the latter eventually got the message, Zen, Khaos, Xander, and Adonis eventually gave me the space they're so good at offering, and I'm grateful. Their attempts at caring were confusing the fuck out of me. I don't like my emotions being played with like that.

Now it's Friday evening, time for the girls' night we planned, which means Harmonia will be here any moment. I'm already dressed to go, in a pair of black leggings and a thin, off the shoulder, mint green tee. I feel completely relaxed, and that's the whole plan for tonight.

While I wait, I sit cross-legged on the bed, the gold dagger in my hands as I look it over from handle to tip. Every night since our Skills class on Tuesday, I've taken my gift from Pandora's Box out of the safe and just… stared at it.

Apart from the array of crystals embedded in the handle, a kaleidoscope of colors standing out against the otherwise gold dagger, there's nothing at all that hints at what this thing may be able to do and whether it's an offensive or defensive object. I don't think dropping it like the Professor's harmonica will do anything, and if it's something to do with the tip, I don't want to try it on myself or ask anyone for advice.

I sigh, confusion twisting me up inside as a knock sounds at my door. Rising from the bed, I quickly place the dagger back in the safe to secure it. When I swing the door open, I come face to face with Harmonia, who is dressed in a floral strappy summer dress that somehow looks brighter against her white hair.

She smiles. "Hey, are you ready to do this at my place? Thalia and Cassandra are waiting at the portal in the main building, and I thought you might want to help get them here," she says as I step out of my room and let the door fall closed behind me.

"For sure," I say, falling into step beside her. Earlier this week, we made the decision to extend the offer of girls' night to the twins too, who immediately said yes, and for the first time in as long as I can remember, I was excited to hang out with friends.

That should be embarrassing at my age, but fuck it, it makes me happy. I'd rather have found friends later than never at all.

I caved earlier in the week, spilling the truth over what happened on Monday without missing a single detail, to Harmonia while we ate lunch. Her level of mad was way higher than I expected, and I had to make her promise to play it cool. Her pupils seemed to darken, the usual light pink hues deepening to a magenta shade. She was a little frightening to look at.

I remember the exact words I said to her, and I stand by them fully.

I'll get my revenge when they least expect it. I don't want to fuck it all up over one hot headed moment.

As we get to the bottom of the stairs, my brows crease as I look from the portal to Harmonia. "How exactly do we get the portal to allow Cassandra and Thalia to come to Agion?" I ask. Even though I may have been forced to go through the process, I have no idea how they made it happen. I just went along for the unfortunate ride.

"It's simple really. We just have to be touching them, while stepping through the portal first," Harmonia explains, just before we step through the black fog to find the twins chatting on the other side.

That makes sense; I remember the hand on my arm, but how they managed to be slipping through the portal just before I was, is completely crazy to me. I hadn't realized someone was walking that close to me.

"Hey," Cassandra calls out excitedly, while Thalia offers a short wave and a smile, remaining as quiet as ever. I think that's why I'm more naturally drawn to her in comparison to Cassandra.

Cassandra is in a white summer dress, while Thalia is rocking denim shorts and a band tee, clearly demonstrating the difference between the sisters.

"Ready to go?" Harmonia asks, and the girls smile as they move to stand in front of the portal.

I watch what Harmonia does, linking Thalia's arm with mine as I step through the billowing smoke. Just as she said, we appear in Agion when I place my foot back down on the floor.

Smiling wide, pleased that it worked, we move just behind Cassandra and Harmonia as they step through. I start to head for the stairs, when one of the dorm doors opens on the left, making my steps falter as Khaos, Xander, Adonis, and Zen step out.

My breath catches in my throat, the Elites demanding all of my attention against my will as I look them over from head to toe.

They're all wearing jeans, Xander in denim blue, Zen in light blue, while Adonis and Khaos wear black. Their t-shirts however, are vastly different.

Zen wears a linen shirt with long sleeves that fits his body perfectly. The top few buttons open revealing golden tanned skin beneath.

Khaos dons a white tee with a thick leather jacket over it, giving him the bad boy vibe I know he can certainly live up to. The mere memory of that night in the woods sends a shiver down my spine as my throat practically begs for his attention again.

Xander has a muscle-fit band tee on, one I'm familiar with from back home, and I can't deny that I agree with his taste of music. Along with the choice of clothing since it accentuates his muscular arms.

Adonis on the other hand, has a fitted black, silk shirt on, the top button undone and the sleeves stopping at his biceps. With the hem only slightly tucked into his waistband, he looks hot as hell. Annoyingly. As always.

"Ladies," Adonis says with his usual purr, pulling me from my thoughts as I swallow past the lump in my throat.

"Adonis," Harmonia replies, a bored undertone, telling me she's nowhere near as affected by them as I am. That fact filling me with more relief than I care to admit to, but also confusing me at the same time because I'm not sure *why* I'm so enamored with them.

Out of the corner of my eye, I look at the twins too, who seem a little nervous standing before the guys, but not all doe-eyed and swoon-worthy, which only makes me like them even more. Then I remember Khaos saying they were his cousins.

"What's going on here?" The man himself asks, ruffling his jet black hair, but still letting it fall drastically over his green eyes. It should be a sin to look as good as these four do.

"We're having a girls' night, Khaos, don't be a dick," Thalia says with a grunt, making my eyes widen in surprise, and I have to bite back the chuckle desperate to pass from my lips. I was not expecting words like that to fall from the mouth of this typically quiet girl.

Khaos glares at her and Cassandra, who doesn't even attempt to hold her laugh in as Xander steps forward, eyes on me. "Will there be pillow fights? *Please* tell me there will be pillow fights," he asks, a cheeky grin on his face that catches me by surprise. He's usually gruff, expressionless and far too growly, but right now he seems carefree, happy even. His comment has thrown me for a loop because it doesn't seem like something he would say.

"You wish," Harmonia retorts, flicking her hair over her shoulder as she links her arm through mine and starts to move us toward the stairs.

"Maybe I do," he responds quietly, his eyes widening slightly like his words surprised him too, but what catches me more off guard is the fact that he doesn't pull his gaze from mine. Not even when one of the guys snorts a chuckle behind him. If anything, it's like he's trying to dig deeper into my soul, and I struggle to even blink, never mind look away.

Harmonia continues to pull me along, the twins right behind us, and I almost trip up the first step which finally releases me from his stare. No one else utters a word, the guys seemingly leaving as we all pile into Harmonia's room.

The layout is exactly like mine, only the walls are a pale dusky pink with gray touches. It suits her perfectly. She has an abundance of throw pillows across her bed, which makes me smirk because of Xander's comment, with a variety of snacks covering the surface of her desk.

"Have we decided on a movie?" I ask, and Cassandra claps her hands in excitement.

"The latest George Freeman movie just went live on Flix, I vote we watch that. I want all the action, hotness, and overall drool worthy scenes, which we know are a sure thing whenever he's in a movie," she says, and I nod in agreement.

It's strange how comfortable it is to be here with them, relaxing and letting my guard down a little as we fall into random conversations, bonding over the movie. The film surprisingly holds my interest as the girls mumble while simultaneously stuffing their faces with popcorn and candy.

"What's everyone's plans for Christmas?" Harmonia asks, tossing popcorn in her mouth without lifting her gaze from the television.

"Christmas? That feels like ages away," I state. It's only just the beginning of November now.

"Yeah, but you *have* to have plans. My parents mentioned taking me to the god-made ski resort this year. My older sister and her partner are going and they want to enjoy some family time before we all start to drift apart with our own lives," she explains. That sounds amazing, to have a family to care for you like that. To *want* to make memories, no matter what they look like.

"We're just going home. Our extended family is huge, so everyone gathers to celebrate before the new year begins," Cassandra explains, and another mention of family has me recoiling inside.

Three sets of eyes glimpse at me, waiting for me to divulge my plans. Clearing my throat, I uncross and recross my legs as I lace my fingers together in my lap. "I'm going to stay here," I state casually, watching as horror washes over each of their faces. A rock forms in the pit of my stomach. Even though I'm not ashamed to not have family, it's always an uncomfortable conversation.

"No way, you can come with me," they all call out, pleading expressions on their faces that say *we won't abandon you here*, and I smile the most natural one I think I ever have.

"Honestly, that's sweet, you guys, but I really do prefer to be alone. Especially at the minute, my life has changed so much. I think it would be good for me to stay while everyone else goes on break, give myself a rest from peopling," I state, ready for them to push back again, but to my surprise, they all nod in understanding

"Whatever you want, girl, we're here to support you," Cassandra says, tucking her hair behind her ear before turning back to the television, and I release a breath of relief when the subject is dropped, making me even more certain that I chose the best group of friends for me. It's comforting not being judged for wanting to be alone. I always find it is rare to find people who let *you* just be *you*.

"Are we going to talk about the eyes Xander was clearly giving our girl," Thalia murmurs, grinning as she glances at me from the corner of her eyes, and I fake glare at her as the others smirk.

"Just Xander? The rest too. Those boys have been trying to help her with anything and everything all week, and all she has done is knock them back time and time again. *Miss Independent* over here don't need no man, am I right?" Harmonia says with a sassy click of her fingers, and the rest of us fall back with laughter.

"Listen, I know they're hot, fuck, hotter than hot, but I literally walked in on my boyfriend fucking another woman days before I came here," I state, watching their jaws drop as I continue. "I wasn't as sad over it as I probably should have been, but I slashed his tires, only to later find out he had lied to me about who he was." Rubbing my lips together, I sigh. "I just need a minute to be me, and find what my happiness looks like, wherever that may be. If we were playing a game of fuck, marry, kill right now, all four of them would fight for the fuck spot for sure, but I have to see these guys around the Academy and in my living space for the next three years. I've made enough mistakes in my past, I don't need to make anymore if I can help it."

Silence falls over us for a beat, each of my new friends searching my gaze as I just spewed all my emotional baggage at them. Before I can even question if I unloaded too much, Thalia is the one to clap her hands this time, matching her sister's usual kind of spirit.

"Oh my Godddds, I want to play fuck, marry, kill," she announces, my shoulders relaxing at her change in subject.

"I'm in," the remainder of us say at once, making me chuckle as I nestle back against the cushions behind me.

Fuck, if the only thing I gain from Saints Academy is these girls as my friends, then I already fucking made it.

FOURTEEN

XANDER

My lunch appears before me on the table, the sound of the other students in the dining hall drifting away as I focus on my immediate surroundings. I'm too lost in my own mind today to even hear the sounds of the clattering plates and cutlery.

Fuck.

I'm quite sure that if a girl lay before me with no clothes on, her pussy on full display and willing to let me do anything to her, I would still be wearing the same disinterested look on my face as I am now. Unless it was one girl in particular.

Rhea Harrington.

Treat the new girl like she doesn't exist.

Sure. That's what I convinced Adonis and the others to agree to when the woman in question first made an appearance.

The words I said, burning like acid on my tongue.

You really think she's going to be any different? A girl from Phoenix Valley, likely desperate to fit in? She'll cling to anyone and everyone she can, just like she has done with Harmonia.

Hell, it's like she heard the damn words slip from my mouth and decided to prove me wrong in every way imaginable. I hate to admit when I'm wrong, but as I sit beside Zen in the dining hall, with Khaos and Adonis across from us, I can't stop my gaze from flickering to where she sits in the far corner of the room, separating herself from everyone except for the three females who've welcomed her.

Harmonia sits across from her, but the twins, Cassandra and Thalia, now join them too. The moment the pair joined Rhea's little friendship circle, I was sure it was a ploy to slip in with Khaos, but again, I was wrong.

I watch as she tucks a piece of her brown hair behind her ear, a small smile gracing her lips as she looks at Harmonia, who just so happens to glance my way.

Fuck.

I quickly avert my gaze, hating the feeling of being caught, but when I refocus on my closest friends at my table, my brothers, I realize they too have similar looks on their faces. Even Zen.

It seems I'm not the only one captivated and intrigued by the earthling. None of us are willing to admit it after the agreement we came to a few weeks ago.

Although, I feel like all that changed after she was attacked, or did it happen before?

She was only attacked because of the Halloween party. I'm sure of it. which indirectly made it our fault.

Zen was able to pry that piece of information from her, or had her confirm who she thought had attacked at least, and that's the only logical conclusion.

Halloween.

When Khaos… well, when he let his natural vampire instincts take control, and I can't deny how fucking envious that made me.

Zen clears his throat, cutting off my train of thought so I focus on the food set before me. The cheeseburger and onion rings look like heaven, but my brain still wills me to look back over at the mysterious woman who won't stop infiltrating my mind. No one has ever gained interest from the four of us, and something in my gut tells me she's different.

"What did everyone's parents say about Christmas break?" Zen asks, cutting into the steak on his plate as he glances around at the rest of us.

"My parents are beyond pissed, but they haven't forbidden it," I grumble, taking a bite of my burger before I continue. My parents aren't strict, they just have traditions that they like to be followed. Especially ones that charge the shifter soul within us. The variations of shifters in Paradise Heights is unreal, so to be the second born child of the Alpha wolf, leader of the Bishop pack, almost feels anti-climatic. But nonetheless, my parents love to gather alphas, betas, and omegas to share the love on special holidays. "Just one less body on the puppy cuddle pile, they'll get over it," I add with a shrug, forcing myself not to fall down that rabbit hole in my mind.

"My parents won't even notice," Adonis mumbles with a huff, as he does every time his family is brought up. To have as many siblings as he does, I'm not surprised he was raised by nannies, and as much as my family's traditions might annoy the fuck out of me, it still beats the alternative. *His* alternative.

My eyes trail to Khaos, waiting for his response, but I find his gaze fixed on Rhea again. Zen must kick him under the table because the sound of a bang is quickly followed by a grunt from Khaos' lips, and a glare thrown his way.

"They weren't happy, but I gave them some bullshit excuse and it pacified them. Definitely helps that the extended family are all getting together this year too. It'll keep them occupied," he grumbles, rubbing a hand over his jaw before swiping a hand down his neck.

The move reminds me of the final remnants of his moment with Rhea in the woods. I only caught the way he stood over her, chest heaving as they stared into each other's eyes, and that was enough to leave me surprised.

Out of all of us, Khaos was the hardest to break, the one on the straight path to his fate. No distractions, no pointless bullshit as he likes to put it, yet there he was, just as enraptured as the rest of us.

"Thank you," Zen finally says, his voice much calmer now as he offers an appreciative smile around the table. The second he said his parents were still going to be out of town this Christmas, we made the necessary arrangements to all be here together with him.

No questions asked.

No separating our circle of trust.

Just the four of us, with some peace and fucking quiet, and I'm so here for it.

"Don't mention it," I reply, squeezing his shoulder in comfort, before returning to my food.

The table settles into silence, but it doesn't stop the glances from other students coming our way. From Selene, who is our public enemy number one, desperate to be the center of our group, to Hector *fucking* Ariti who wants to be a part of us.

It's annoying as fuck, and embarrassing on their part, but it's the joys that come with being one of the Elites. My brothers and I have been stuck like glue to each other for as long as I can remember and we have the kind of bond that means we will never let anyone infiltrate our group.

The normal life of a supernatural being is to be sent to boarding schools for other people to train and aid us until we're twenty-one, and I've never cared to moan about it since I found my unwavering friendship with the guys who sit at the table with me.

After the war, that's when the unit situation became more of a thing, when men outweighed the women. Most of our parents are in monogamous relationships, and even they don't really understand the level of trust the four of us have together. It's not something they ever needed.

Everyone wants a piece of us, though, all except the one woman who I thought would.

Rhea.

It's beyond clear I was wrong about her, and the four weeks that have passed since she arrived have only proved that to be true. Now it's hard to deny how pissed I am with myself.

Finishing my burger, I swipe my napkin across my mouth as my eyes cross the dining hall to her again. Nope. She's still not looking over here. An indescribable emotion swirls through me.

It doesn't help that her back is to us, but it's beside the fucking point. I don't know what I want from her, not really, but I want to catch her looking our way, just like she does to us.

My hands clench at my sides, the shifter inside of me warring to be released and stalk across the room to her. It feels like needles pricking my skin, desperate to feel her touch.

I haven't mentioned it to the guys, the war battling inside of me ever since Halloween, when my wolf somehow managed to get a sniff of her as she walked away from the drama Selene was causing.

My wolf shouldn't be making an appearance yet, not to the outside world at least, but I've felt my connection with him for the past two years, slowly learning and adjusting to having what feels like two sides of the same person. It's a sensation that I can't describe, yet it makes total sense to my body at the same time.

"Are we going to address the elephant in the room?" Zen asks calmly, slouching back in his chair as he looks at each of us. He has that knowing look in his eyes, all wise beyond his years, and it catches me by surprise.

I frown, squinting at him as I respond. "What's the elephant?" I stretch my arms back behind my head as I wait for him to answer, forcing myself not to glance to the corner again.

"He means the fact that we all keep looking at the new girl," Khaos grumbles in response, raising an eyebrow at Zen, who simply nods, rubbing his lips together as he fights the need to glance at her once more.

"She did nothing but decline our attempts to help last week. Repeatedly," Zen grouches, his hands clenching on the table as he scrambles to understand that fact alone.

It was bizarre to all of us. We were so used to people taking from us, that we simply expected her to do the same, but she never did, which only entices me more. We aren't used to rejection either, which stings in its own way, but I'll never admit it out loud.

Seeing her beaten and discouraged did something inside

of me, which I think caused my wolf to stir, and now I'm left gaping at her like a fucking puppy, no pun intended, desperate for attention.

"I didn't even manage to catch a glimpse of her," Adonis adds, folding his arms over his chest. "I thought for sure I would be able to talk to her, but she keeps managing to elude me in the adjoined bathroom too. She started to lock the fucking door." The pout that appears on his face is comical.

It's confusing, seeing us like this, all twisted up over a *girl*.

None of it makes any sense at all.

"Is there anything you want to do about it?" Zen asks, his question far more complex than the nine words hint at. He means *her* as a whole.

Rhea Harrington is more than just the new girl. He's hinting at Rhea Harrington being an open interest among us.

My heart pounds twice as fast in my chest, my mind and body flooded with the need to nod immediately, but I refuse to get my wolf's hopes up if no one else even agrees.

The thought flits through my mind that everything I'm feeling is because of my wolf and not me, but the way my gut clenches immediately dismisses the idea.

"That depends on what the entire group has to say," Khaos says, his eyes piercing the three of us as he waits for our response, leaning forward and bracing his elbows on the table.

My eyes widen slightly in surprise, watching as he runs

his tongue over his bottom lip. He wants this, wants her. I have no idea what led him into the woods after her on Halloween, but it seems capturing a little taste of her essence wasn't enough for the blood hungry asshole across from me.

"I'm in," I blurt, watching as the others glance at me in surprise.

I lean back in my chair, squeezing my lips together so I can't say another word without at least fucking processing them first.

"Good. Me too, there's just something... about her that makes me want to drain every ounce of her lust for myself," Adonis murmurs, his voice dropping an octave or two as he peers across at her.

"Then it's agreed," Zen says with a smile, rising to his full height in his seat, making me scoff.

"You say that like she's even willing to talk to us," I grumble in response, refusing to get my hopes up when it looks so bleak in reality. Even when we weren't trying to pursue her she denied us.

"She might be if no one else is here," Zen replies, tugging nervously on the collar of his shirt.

"What's *that* supposed to mean?" Khaos asks, suspicion dancing in his eyes as he searches Zen's for an answer.

He casts his gaze to the far corner of the room once more, and I can't help but follow his line of sight too, sighing when I watch Rhea rise to her feet with her friends and slowly begin to exit the dining hall. It must almost be time for the next class to start, but that doesn't force me to my feet. Even though I want to chase after her, demand she let us take care of her, even though she doesn't need us to right now, I force myself to remain seated, too intrigued by what Zen has to say next.

"It means… she's the reason we're staying at Christmas."

Well, fuck.

FIFTEEN

RHEA

I step through the portal leading from Agion hall to the Academy building, but when I reach the bottom of the grand staircase, I opt to head outside for a minute before I go to the dining hall. A minute of peace and some fresh air was needed.

The moment I do, the sun beats down on my face, a gentle breeze swaying the trees that frame the pathway, and I remember the day I arrived. How foreign it all looked, and even now it still feels strange. I guess it's because I lock myself away in my room a lot, instead of making the most of the outdoors.

Once Christmas is over and we're heading into the new year, I'm going to make it my New Year's resolution. To be outside more. All this portal business makes traveling from one place to another really easy, but it also makes me lazy since it completely strips away enjoying the beautiful, scenic journey.

Turning on my heel I head back inside, expecting the usual hustle and bustle, but there's not a soul in sight, and I relish in the moment of reprieve.

Everyone left for the Christmas break yesterday evening. So for the first time since I arrived, the hallways are quiet, and I'm not checking over my shoulder for some supreme bitch and her cowardly friends to come at me.

My stomach grumbles, making me pick up speed and head toward the dining hall as my mind drifts to the past few weeks since I was attacked.

Very little has happened, because I've acted how my attackers wanted me to, which is annoying as fuck since I really haven't done that on purpose. I've just chosen to keep my head down and stay focused, biding my time before I get my revenge and make them pay for what they did to me. But to them, I was letting them walk all over me.

All because of the Elites. It's ridiculous. The four men in question have taken the hint and given me the space I demanded when they kept attempting to help me carry my bag, escort me anywhere I wanted to go, or whatever else they reeled off. But that hasn't stopped me from feeling their gazes or their movement as soon as they walk into a room, my body highly aware of theirs at any given moment.

A fun fact Harmonia likes to point out, chuckling under her breath before murmuring about them looking in my direction.

Any other circumstance and I guess I would be jumping all over them, desperate to find a release, but with everything else going on, I've had to put my needs to the back of my mind.

The doors to the dining hall are thankfully open, and when I step into the room, a grin spreads across my face that there's no one else here, and classic Christmas songs play in the background. A cute christmas tree is decorated in the opposite corner of the room, but otherwise nothing else is different.

Making my way to my usual table in the corner, sans Harmonia and the twins, my steps slow a little when I realize which song is playing, and the memory that comes with it.

Last Christmas Eve I met Dante, which feels like a lifetime ago, a very far off distant memory. It's strange how there's no worthy emotion inside me when I think of him now, not even anger, just relief. The sex was decent enough, but everything else was… a disaster. Even without the cheating and the lies he apparently told.

Everything happens for a reason, and my life began to change the day I slashed his tires. I'd do it again in a heartbeat. The memory of flinging my arm out with force, blade in hand, reminds me of the strength and power I wield in my soul so I need to channel that feeling now.

It instantly makes me question why I haven't retaliated for the attack because it's out of character for me to wait, but I have to remind myself that I'm living in a new world, where people have fucking *powers*. I am completely out of my element and that makes the playing field a little uneven, at least for now.

I opt to take Harmonia's usual seat which has a view of the dining hall and the tree, as opposed to giving my back to the room like I usually do. The tablet immediately appears before me as I sit, and I quickly opt for a soda and a chicken supreme pizza.

As the tablet disappears before me, I freeze in place, hearing the sound of someone laughing drifting in from outside the room.

Shit. Shit. Shit. Shit. Shit.

I'm not alone.

That's not an issue though, it's the fact I fucking know who that laugh belongs to.

As if sensing my internal panic, the Elites step into the hall, eyes searching me out right away before the laughter and conversation they were having fades away.

Silence descends over the room, each of their facial expressions becoming more stoic as they meet my gaze.

I try to swallow past the lump forming in my throat, watching as they take one predatory step after another. I'm about to release the breath I've been holding as they approach their table, anxiety waiting to be released with the exhale, only for them to continue moving directly toward me.

Fuck.

I'm so screwed.

What are they even doing here? They should be

off campus doing whatever it is the Elite families do for the holidays, not interrupting my peace and quiet. The very least they could do is sit at their own table.

With the width of the aisles between tables, they walk two in front and two slightly behind. Adonis is, of course, up front, in a pair of black painted on jeans and a white polo top. His circular glasses are perched on the bridge of his nose, with his blond hair swept back off his face, making him look hot as hell with his piercing blue eyes shining with mischief.

Xander is beside him, his wide shoulders covered in a plain navy tee with a pair of worn-in jeans covering his thick thighs. He moves with purpose, silently observing and calculating as his eyes travel over me from head to toe. My thighs clench together, imagining what it would be like to be wrapped in his arms. He has the ability to make you look and feel petite beside him, and it's intriguing and desirable as fuck.

Glancing behind him, my eyes fall to Zen, with his blond hair longer than it was when I first arrived, curling behind his ear, wearing an off-white button down henley shirt, the top three buttons undone and the sleeves rolled back revealing his forearms, with a pair of chino pants. His hazel eyes are enticing, like he's full of wisdom and joy, while also calming your soul like a balm, the feeling seeping into your very being. He's poetic.

That leaves Khaos. Just thinking his name makes me desperate to lift my hand and stroke over my neck where he teased me, but I manage to refrain. I don't need to encourage his alphaness or give me any more unnecessary attention. His black hair falls over his stunning green eyes as his facial expression remains stoic. In a leather jacket, with a black tee underneath and matching pants, he looks every inch the villain, just like he's going for. And fuck me if I don't care. A villain has never looked more enticing.

Before they reach me, I glance down at myself, only to realize I opted for a girly outfit since I thought I would be here alone. Gone are my usual oversized pants and shirts, and in their place is a floral, strappy dress that floats around my thighs and offers a glimpse of my slim figure.

I don't miss Adonis swiping his tongue over his bottom lip before dropping down into the seat directly across from me. Zen takes the spot beside him, Khaos following, while Xander slowly walks around the table and takes the seat next to me.

I really can't fucking breathe.

"Who knew you looked so pretty in a dress," Adonis starts, abandoning any form of greeting as they take over my peaceful space and overwhelm my senses. Well, except for taste, but if my body had any say over the situation, my mouth would be stimulated too.

My eyes narrow as I finally remember who I am and find my voice. "What are you doing here?" I ask, folding my arms over my chest.

"Eating," Khaos grumbles in response, raising his eyebrows at me in challenge, but I simply shake my head.

Asshole.

"I mean on campus. It's Christmas break. I assumed I would have the place to myself," I reply, casting my gaze at all of them, who are staring at me intently. I could feel the relief I had at the prospect of being alone slowly disappear and in its wake, a mixture of anger and disappointment floods my chest.

Xander leans his elbow on the table before him, placing the side of his head on his fist as he stares intently at me. "Well it's a good thing we aren't. Otherwise you'd be all alone, and we can't have that now, can we," he practically purrs, my mouth drying up as my thighs tighten. The rasp of his voice vibrating through my body on its own accord.

"I mean, we can, that's the whole reason I—"

"We wanted to get you alone," Adonis states casually, then winks, interrupting my response to Xander, leaving me to gape at him in surprise.

Is this a joke? Why would they want to get me alone?

I know I shouldn't engage in this discussion because I'm getting sucked in every second they're here but fuck if I'm not curious to know more.

All the questions run through my mind, but what catches me off guard is the fact that they're being open and honest about it. My brain can't seem to compute and all I can come up with to say out loud is, "Why?"

"Because you've been avoiding us," Khaos cuts in, pulling my gaze to his and my pulse quickens. It's like he can fucking sense it when the smallest smirk graces his lips. Fucker.

"I've been avoiding *everyone*, not just you," I murmur, relieved as my drink appears in front of me, and I take a quick sip, praying my food will come soon too, so I can ignore them and eat.

"Well I don't like it, or should I say, *we* don't like it." That comes from Zen, catching me completely off guard as my jaw drops in surprise.

What am I even supposed to say to that?

I really am fucking screwed.

Supreme bitch and her drama be damned.

"Thanks for your concern, but what specifically don't you like about me avoiding everyone?" I ask, clenching my hands together in my lap, my lips rubbing together as I search each of their eyes for an answer.

"The distance. We want it to evaporate. Not for everyone though, just us," Adonis answers simply with a shrug, and I frown in confusion, but before I can respond, Xander interjects, continuing their point.

"I know you feel it, Rhea. We're man enough to admit it. So that just leaves me to question where you're at with it too." His voice is gruff yet soft at the same time, his deep tone almost soothing, but I can imagine in other circumstances it could cut you to shreds.

"Feel what?" I mutter, captivated by his brown eyes, and he grins, like he knows he's won because my words do sound like a weak attempt at denial.

"Don't pretend there isn't something in the air when the five of us are together. Fuck, it was definitely there in the woods that night," Khaos states, pulling my gaze to his green eyes, a stark reminder of the night in question, and I almost shiver at the thought.

Pull yourself together, Rhea.

"That's irrelevant. I've honestly spent enough of my time here fighting off guys who want to chase me for being *nothing*, and I'm over it. I have no interest in—"

"You're not fucking *nothing*," Zen grunts, his usual calm and collected demeanor slipping away for a moment as his eyes drill into mine and he leans forward, bracing his elbows on the table. "You can't be placed in Agion hall by the portal *and* be nothing, it's impossible. We never thought you were nothing, ever, don't insult my awareness," he adds, glaring at me until I offer a slight nod in acknowledgement.

I've officially been chastised for assuming the worst in them, all because of my insecurities and the way other students have been treating me too. Although I can feel whatever it is they're feeling, I'm not convinced I should act on it. I still don't even know who I am. The thought causes a twinge of pain to ricochet in my chest, but for now, I'll humor them.

"Then what do you want?" The words slip from my lips before I can think better of it, and as all of their eyes seem to darken, my head dives into the pits of desire I feel whenever I'm around them.

"To get to know you," Adonis states, finding his voice again. I almost like the fact that he isn't so attention seeking and dominating the conversation when his friends are here like you would expect. His words seem earnest and true, but my entire relationship history leaves me hesitant.

Do I risk getting to know them only to be dropped and hurt, *again*? I've felt enough of that already in my life. *But* it doesn't really have to be more than simply hanging out, and that thought alone seems to settle the pull inside of me.

I can do that, easily. I think.

"What would that entail exactly?" I ask, rubbing my lips together just as my pizza appears in front of me. Xander groans, reaching for a slice, but I slap his hand away at the last minute, offering him a glare, only to find puppy dog eyes pleading back at me.

The huge, gruff, asshole, looks like a wounded puppy, desperate to get what he wants, and just like that, I'm rolling my eyes and offering him a slice. He is going to be trouble.

"Thank you," he whispers softly, leaning forward and kissing my cheek before taking it from my hand and biting half of it down in one go.

The touch leaves me shaken, goosebumps rising in his wake as I stare at him.

Completely blindsided, it's too little too late for me to do anything about it when I realize the others have all stolen a slice too.

Motherfuckers can't keep their hands to themselves.

I sit gaping at them, and it's Zen who meets my eyes first, flicking his gaze between Xander and me with a slight smile and a shrug. "Don't mind him, his beast makes him all touchy," he states so matter of factly that I think I might fall off my seat.

His beast?

The fuck?

My round eyes trail back to the guy in question, who smiles around the pizza in his mouth, not offering any further information. I search his features looking for a hint at what beast Zen is referring to but find nothing out of the norm.

What is this alternate universe I seem to have fallen into?

"Let's have a makeshift Christmas Eve party," Adonis suggests, gliding his fingers through his hair as he nods in agreement with himself like it's the best idea he's ever had.

"Good idea," Zen murmurs as Khaos shrugs.

"Whatever you want." His words sound casual, but the way he looks at me through his jet black hair is not so gentle. If anything, I feel like he's tearing my body apart to find my soul. Which is both arousing and intriguing at the same time.

"I'll pass." I offer a tight smile as I glance down at my single slice of pizza, avoiding all of their stares. Being this close to them, for this long, feels suffocating, and the only way I'll catch another breath is if I steal it from one of them.

It's a slippery slope of desire, need, and I can't explain the strength of the feelings that are running through my body right now. Not a single ounce.

"It wasn't an option," Khaos retorts, glaring at me as I whip my eyes to his.

I remember that harsh tongue, the tip of his nose as he dragged it over my throat, and a whimper begs to pass my lips. My body and my brain aren't on the same page right now, like, at all, which is another huge sign that I need to grab what's left of my pizza, which isn't much, and run from the four of them, hiding away in my sanctuary aka my room.

Before I can even take a breath to give Khaos a piece of my mind, Zen waves his hand in front of us, trying to break the rising tension.

"Have you ever seen snow?" His words catch me off guard, pulling my attention from the asshole beside him, and my wide eyes must be answer enough as Zen chuckles under his breath. "Would you like to?"

I nibble on my bottom lip, my fingers twisting in my lap. Agreeing would mean spending more time with them, and I just told myself how much of a bad idea that was, but I still find myself nodding against my better judgment. I don't know which I should be pissed at more, my mind or my body.

I just have to see the snow and get the hell out of there, then at least one of my dreams can come true. My others involve orgasms and a lot of sweat, and I can't give into those.

There has to be a reason why they're suddenly acting like this, and I can't deny that I'm intrigued to find out.

"Lead the way, oh calm one."

SIXTEEN

ZEN

It's hard to keep the pleased smirk off my face as Rhea walks beside me. We've waited patiently, biding our time until the right moment when she wasn't so overwhelmed by the Academy as a whole, so we could make our move.

The Halloween party, and what ensued after that, feels like a lifetime ago at this point, but it will be worth it, I just know it. I still can't explain what it is that has us all pulling toward her like a magnetic field, but I'm more than happy to be dragged the distance to her.

We had stepped into the dining hall with a plan, but it seems we took one step through the doorway and forgot it completely. I could see in her eyes she was getting skittish, ready to pounce to her feet and run, and I couldn't let that happen.

Adonis had been quieter than usual, likely trying to

watch his tongue so he didn't piss her off, while Xander had completely relaxed at her side. The moment he cut the distance between them and planted his lips on her cheek, I had inhaled sharply, worried his naturally touchy personality had burst the bubble, but it somehow hadn't. She seemed okay which completely surprised me. A testament that this *could* work.

She didn't even cower under Khaos' blunt tone like most others do. If anything, she sat a little straighter, squared her shoulders some more, and prepared for a stand-off with him. If this works out, he may have met his match with the feisty beauty.

Excitement buzzed through my body from head to toe. This was all new for me, this attraction and desire to be near someone. Whenever the four of us have tried to date the same person, I'm usually the one to feel absolutely nothing and ruin it for everyone else, struggling to feel an emotional connection with anyone.

We've always known it would be a business transaction, but the four of us made a pact early on that there had to be at least… something. Which feels too mild of a word now for what I feel just looking in Rhea's direction. Fuck.

I wet my lips, glancing at her out of the corner of my eye as her silky brown hair floats around in the light breeze, brushing against the exposed skin on her shoulders as the dress she chose for today grazes against her thighs.

Her full lips, sapphire blue eyes, and petite nose almost

make her look soft, gentle, demure. Until the anger brewing under the surface and the telltale trust issues rise to the forefront, making her seem far more lost than I like the idea of. The sense of protectiveness I feel for this woman is unfathomable, catching me completely off guard.

As we head through the grounds of Saints Academy, toward the woods, just like we did on Halloween, I catch her glancing at me with a raised eyebrow. I know my brothers are here too. Khaos, beside me, with Adonis and Xander to Rhea's left, but my entire focus is on her.

All the bruising has gone from her face since the attack, which we narrowed down to Selene and Hector after Rhea subtly glanced their way when I had asked.

Hector got a shocking surprise a few weeks later when he was least expecting it, finding himself at the mercy of his own attackers, aka the Elite. Fucker squealed, ratting out Selene as he sobbed like a little bitch. I just wish we could have warned him against even looking at Rhea in the future, but it would have only made the situation more difficult, so a blind attack it was. Though, that doesn't mean we're not watching him like hawks to make sure the prick doesn't step out of line.

Selene on the other hand, seems to be getting worse in her attempts to pursue us, not taking no for an answer, and it's exhausting. Borderline stalkerish too. On the surface, she may look beautiful, but that bitch is rotten to the core, and we all know what a relationship with her would look like. Her pining over Adonis the entire time and not giving two shits about the rest of us. That's not the strong and powerful foundation we want. Not at all.

"I feel like an idiot for letting you lure me into the woods. Those old fairytales rarely ended well for those who put total trust in others," Rhea grumbles beside me, folding her arms over her chest and pushing her cleavage up, making my cock twitch as she pouts.

"I thought you enjoyed it the last time," Khaos says from beside me, a knowing smirk on his lips as he glances in her direction, and she rolls her eyes.

The fact that she doesn't immediately respond, defending herself against his statement, only seems to please all of us. It almost feels like a chink in her armor. She holds the attention of the Elite four, and is completely oblivious to the fact which gives an ample amount of time for her to adjust to us being around. That way, when she does realize we're all about her, she can't disagree and say it's not real.

Girls older than us in their second and third year even fight like catty bitches, vying for our attention, just like the guys do for Rhea, who ridiculously believes she is nothing. It's embarrassing, but this is what our society has done to people. Image is everything, and I can't fucking stand it.

Shaking my head, I clench and unclench my hands as I focus on the here and now with Rhea. She has to get to know us, and to do that, she can't run at the first sight when we approach her. I've waited almost two months for this, watching her from a distance, like fuck is that all going to be for nothing.

I pull my phone from my pocket, sending a quick text to my older sister, Serenity, as we step through the woods to the opening on the other side. The lake shimmers under the sun, the grassy area slowly darkening with the sign of a cloud passing overhead, and I come to a stop in the center of the field.

Looking up, I spot the clouds suddenly appearing in the otherwise clear skies, rolling to a stop above where we are. "Are you ready?" I ask, looking down at Rhea, who glances back at me with surprisingly wide eyes.

"Yeah," she whispers, like she can't believe this is going to happen, and it startles me that I managed to find something we could offer her a glimpse of, to make her stick around. We just need her to agree to spend the rest of the day with us and hopefully this is a good start.

"So you really haven't seen snow before?" Adonis asks, breaking the silence we've mostly carried with us, not wanting to spook her and send her running for her dorm.

"Only in old movies," she says in response, nibbling her bottom lip nervously.

Before any of us can say another word, I watch as her mouth widens. Jaw hitting the floor in surprise as she gapes up at the sky. I know what has her attention, a tiny snowflake flutters through the air, heading downward. I can feel the shift in the air and the temperature drop, but I can't pull my eyes from her, mesmerized by the sheer awe dancing across her face.

Her blue eyes glisten as I feel a few drops land on my forearms, and I watch as she shivers.

Fuck. I didn't consider that part.

Before a solution can even come to me, movement behind Rhea catches my attention, and I turn to find Xander stepping up to her, his front to her back as he wraps his arms around her.

I freeze, fearing we've burst the trust bubble, but to my surprise, she's too caught up in the snow falling from the sky to worry as Xander's natural body heat wraps around her.

"She could have had my jacket," Khaos grunts under his breath, making me smirk as I turn my focus to the sky.

"You were too slow, but don't say anything else about it, we don't want to ruin this," I whisper to him, hoping Rhea didn't hear our conversation.

Thousands and thousands of snowflakes fall, coating the grass and icing the lake with the temperature drop, all while we stand and pay witness to the beautiful show. The silence nature provides enhances the ambiance and I can't deny how important this moment is.

"How are you making this happen?" Rhea asks after a while, peering over at me, and I shrug.

"My family are angels, we each have a weather type that we are drawn to, this is my sister's," I answer honestly, watching as she wets her lips, tilting her head back to look up at the snow again. Xander somehow manages to wrap her even tighter in his hold, leaving me desperate to be near her.

It's like magic has been cast upon us or something, leaving us off kilter and confused by our own actions as we fall deeper and deeper under her spell without any real reason why.

I look down at my phone after a while, noticing the time and realizing we've been out here for almost an hour. As much as Xander's hold is warming Rhea, her lips are still starting to turn blue.

My eyes meet Adonis', and he must sense my desire to get her inside now, because in the next moment, he's standing before Rhea, drawing her attention down from the sky.

"So, about that party," he murmurs, making me turn to face them fully as Xander remains at her back, and I feel Khaos leave my side, slowly prowling around them to come to a stop on their other side, boxing her in.

"I don't—" Her response is cut short as Adonis reaches out, tucking a loose tendril of her soft brown hair behind her ear. She gapes at him for a moment, before finally finding her tongue again. "I'm not soft and pliant you know," she mumbles, making me frown.

"If we thought you were, we wouldn't be here," Khaos interjects, rolling his eyes before giving her a pointed look when she shifts her gaze his way, and she shakes her head.

"*Why* are you here?" she asks, still not seeing how we all just naturally gravitate toward her.

"Because we want to be," Xander mumbles against her ear, making her shiver as she lifts her hands to grip his biceps. I don't even think she realizes she's seeking him out on her own.

"That makes no sense," she retorts, focusing back on Adonis before her as he grins.

"No one said it had to, because we're not even sure ourselves," I state softly, extending a hand for her to take.

We all wait on bated breath as she eyes the arms around her, Khaos and Adonis who stand close, before fixating on my hand.

It feels like an eternity passes before her fingers release Xander's arm and slowly slip over my outstretched hand.

Mine.

My heart thunders in my chest as she steps out of Xander's hold, following my lead as I steer her back through the woods, causing a shift inside me that I can't quite explain. We've barely taken a dozen steps when a leather jacket slips over her shoulders, and she glances at Khaos, but he's focused straight ahead, not uttering a word.

I don't want to get lost in the silence again this time, fearful she'll get trapped in her own mind and come up with a hundred reasons why she has to run away from us when we get back to Agion.

"So, you know nothing about yourself and the magic you come from, huh?" Adonis blurts, falling into step on her left side, and she shakes her head nervously. I almost want to strangle him for being so damn nosey, her story hasn't changed.

"Nothing at all," she breathes. My brain struggles to imagine what that must feel like as I stroke my thumb across her long, delicate fingers.

"What did the Box give you?" Khaos asks, glancing back over his shoulder as he slows his steps and falls into line with everyone at my side.

Rhea eyes him for a moment, before quirking an eyebrow at him. I can't tell if she's pissed, annoyed, or curious. "Why do I feel like that's a personal question?"

"Because it is," Xander states, glaring from the other end of our line to stare Khaos down, but he doesn't acknowledge it as he waits for Rhea to respond.

She rubs her lips together as we make our way up the Academy steps, before looking at me. "Is it like asking someone what they are?"

Her question catches me by surprise. It's hard to remember or even imagine what it must be like to have no idea about this entire part of the world, lifestyle, and even yourself like she does. Just the thought makes my skin crawl.

"It's worse," Khaos responds before I can, being completely honest with her. "But since you don't know what you are, I thought I might try my luck," he offers with a wry grin that has a small chuckle slipping past Rhea's lips.

"You're some ballsy assholes," she grumbles, not offering them anything beyond that, and it makes my lips tilt up at the side, watching her stand her ground with them.

No one utters a word as we head for the portal to Agion. As we appear in the usual hallway, we all immediately turn to the first door on the left; Xander's room. It's bigger than the rest, for when he starts to garner his powers and shifts unexpectedly, so it tends to be our main hangout.

Plus, I didn't want to give Rhea the chance to be near her room. She would definitely give us the slip then.

Xander places his palm against the wood, letting the door fall open, and my hand instinctively tightens around Rhea's. I'm acting like a damn child, but fuck if I care, there's something here that I can't put my finger on, and I'm desperate to explore more of it, with her.

I pull her into the room beside me, watching as her eyes dance around the gray and cream colored walls, but before she can take anything in properly, Xander speaks.

"I'm a shifter, expected to be a wolf, and my parents are the alphas of the Bishop pack." The words fall from his lips without care as his brown eyes fixate on her piercing blues, and it takes a second for me to understand what he's doing.

We admitted it was a personal question to ask someone what they are, and he's offering that information up to her freely, the knowledge shining in her eyes as she offers a simple nod in response.

"You know what I am," Adonis says with a wink, dropping down on Xander's bed as Rhea rolls her eyes at him in response.

"And I know what you are," she murmurs brazenly, eyes moving to Khaos with a knowing glint, and he flashes her a wide smile in response, the memory of Halloween clearly still fresh in both of their minds.

"I'm an angel," I remind her, before any awkward silence can consume us, and her eyes widen as she turns to look at me, fingers still interlocked as I offer a small smile.

"Of course you are," she replies, like it really is that obvious. "Please tell me you have snacks somewhere because a bunch of greedy assholes ate most of my pizza before taking me out into the freezing cold. I'm hangry," she states, slipping her hand from mine and offering us all a pointed stare.

Fuck, she has fire in her belly, and I love it.

Don't get me wrong, I'm glad we were able to get her here. The urge to know more about her is desperate inside of me, but she's not like other girls, not one bit.

And I approve.

Anyone else would be falling over themselves to be whoever we wanted them to be, but she seems unapologetically herself, and it's definitely part of her charm.

"A few of us can head down to the cafeteria to—"

"All of you go, except Rhea," Xander says, his voice dropping in tone as he looks at the girl in question, and it makes me frown until his eyes flash to mine.

They're almost amber, a clear sign his wolf is playing

havoc on his body right now, and something tells me this has everything to do with the girl present.

"Are you sure that's a good—"

"It's fine," Rhea says just loud enough for us all to hear. "I'm fine," she adds quickly, her gaze searching Xander's. She can clearly see the difference in him, and whatever it is, she doesn't feel unsafe and she's willing to accept it. If anything, Rhea's felt more comfortable around Xander and I'm sure she's curious to learn more about him.

For someone who grew up as an earthling, her reaction is extraordinary.

With a simple nod I move to the door, Adonis grumbling behind me as Khaos follows suit.

"Take your fucking time," Xander adds, and when the others meet me in the hallway, I turn to look at him one last time, but before I can meet his gaze the door slams shut in our faces.

Fuck.

SEVENTEEN

RHEA

My mind races at a mile a minute, but I remain rooted to the spot, watching as Xander paces across the room.

Back and forth. Back and forth. Turning to glance at me. Then back and forth. Back and forth.

Repeat.

What in the hell is going on with these guys?

I almost feel like they're acting out of character, like there's an agenda I haven't figured out, but in reality, I've barely spent any time with them to know if that's true or not. So the reality may be that they're acting differently than I *assumed* they would.

There's a pull, something drawing me closer and closer to them and it feels uncontrollable, inevitable, and as I watched the snowflakes fall from the sky in a mesmerizing dance, I basked in their presence. It was comforting.

Xander wrapped his strong arms around me, keeping the chill off my exposed skin, and I couldn't bring myself to pull away. Zen made it snow for me. Like actual snow. Well, his sister did, but that's beside the point.

Something so small, so inconsequential, warmed my soul to the point I thought it might set on fire. I was so caught up in the moment, that when Adonis brushed a lock of hair behind my ear, I felt nothing but the desire to give into him, even against my better judgment.

Adding to the fact that I could feel Khaos' eyes boring into mine as Zen extended his hand, my body moved toward him before my brain could even catch up.

Now, I'm standing in Xander's room, his eyes no longer the brown I remember as they shine amber. He seems restless, like something is clawing at his insides, begging for release, and as much as I said I was fine to stay with him, unafraid and curious, I don't know how to help him.

And for some reason, I *have* to.

Rubbing my lips together, I glance around his gray room, aware of the slight differences to my own dorm. The bathroom and walk-in closet are to the right, with the large window on the back wall. There's a huge bed in here, almost twice the size of my own, with nightstands, a desk, and a chest of drawers in white. The main difference is the four beanbags that scatter the floor in the corner to my right.

My gut tells me it has something to do with him being a shifter, but my brain doesn't actually understand the reason why.

I focus my attention back on the prowling man before me, only to find his eyes on mine as he stands by the bathroom door with his arms folded over his chest. I'm still standing in the same spot by the beanbags from when he slammed the door in the other guys' faces. The hard tone of his voice as he pretty much kicked them out, caught me off guard. He didn't sound like *him*.

Maybe I was stupid to be left alone with him, especially with him in such an agitated state, but it doesn't leave me feeling uneasy, which is confusing the hell out of me. Usually, I would at least feel defensive, but right now, only curiosity and concern thrum through my veins.

Fuck, my emotions are giving me whiplash.

"Is everything okay?" I ask, relaxing my shoulders back and letting my hands fall to my sides to try and ease my posture.

"Nope." He pops the p with sass, but his tone is short and gruff. Even still, a slight chuckle falls from my lips in disbelief. He stands with his hands clenched at his sides, his jaw tight, and his shoulders tense, not seeing the funny side.

"Is there anything I can do? Or do you need me to get the guys—"

"You're twisting my insides up," he grunts, taking a step toward me, the raw confession has my feet planted in place. It sounds like he's lost between anger, confusion, and exasperation, but he's looking at me like I'm going to help ease his rolling emotions and make it all go away.

"I'm… what?" My brows knit together as I stare at him. With confusing sentences in the form of riddles, I'm never going to be able to help him, and what's even stranger, is the fact that I fucking want to. The desire to do something is too hard to resist.

Without a word, he puts one foot in front of the other again, cutting the distance between us, and he doesn't stop until we're toe to toe. The press of the wall behind me makes me jump as I realize I stepped back when he stepped forward, leaving myself with no room to run.

I don't let my uncertainty show as I look up at him, his wide frame caging me in as he plants one hand on either side of my face. My pulse rings in my ears, arousal rising through my body, adrenaline coursing through me as I wet my lips.

He doesn't utter a word, his eyes seeming even lighter and brighter this close, and before I even realize it, my finger runs along the side of his face by his eyes. "How are they a completely different color right now?" The question slips from my lips before I can stop it, and it seems to catch Xander off guard too.

"You're making my wolf rise to the surface," he states in response, like it explains everything. Clearing his throat, he continues as my fingers remain against his temple. "Ninety-nine percent of the female population piss me off, fuck, most of this entire society is full of fake bullshit that I fucking despise. Everything is always about what people stand to gain, no one ever just wants to… be." His chest pounds faster with each breath he takes as his eyes burn into mine. "Then there's you."

Every word that falls from his mouth is intoxicating, drawing me further into his hold as I try to take a full breath, but it's far too difficult with him this close and I don't even care.

"Then there's me," I finally reply, unashamed of how his words twist something new inside of me. A yearning, a need. I try to search his eyes for some kind of understanding, his woodsy scent floating around me as my body moves on its own accord.

Rising up on my tiptoes, I keep my eyes fixed on his as my hands move to his shoulders. His hands immediately drop from the wall, landing on my waist as he takes another step closer so we're chest to chest.

All I see is Xander.

All I feel is him

All I smell is him.

Then, all at once, he's all I taste as our lips crash together.

The undercurrent floating between us pulls us together in a frenzy, our mouths fighting for dominance as I drag a hand up into his hair, while his deathly grip on my waist will undoubtedly leave bruises that'll last a lifetime.

I knew I would give in to one of them, and it didn't matter to me which one because I felt drawn to all of the Elites, but fuck if I care now. Maybe getting lost in all of this desire and need will help calm me.

With my back pressed against the wall, Xander moves one hand to cup my face as he devours my mouth, winning the battle of dominance as his other hand drags over my thigh, leaving goosebumps in his wake.

It's like his touch on my bare skin burns, he's that hot, that primal against me, and I'm desperate for more. I want him to burn me from the inside out, and I need it to happen now.

He pulls his lips from mine, and I inhale as if my life depends on it, which only serves to fill my senses even more with his woodsy essence. The scent is so *him*.

It takes me a moment to pry my eyes open since I hadn't even realized they'd closed, but the second I do, they slam shut again as Xander trails his mouth over my throat, before dusting kisses over my collarbone. A moan elicits from my lips, rippling in my chest.

His lips are gentle, while his hands are rough and coarse against my skin, but as his fingertips reach the apex of my thighs under my dress, I find my hips tilting off the wall, desperate to feel more.

"You're flooding my brain," he growls against my skin. "All I can smell is your fire and sweetness all at once," he adds, and I groan as his finger strokes along the edge of my panties.

"You're doing the same to me," I bite back, before his lips crash to mine again, just as his finger slips under my lace panties, and finds my tight nub desperate for attention.

A low groan of desire falls from my lips, which makes him growl in response, his teeth nipping at my bottom lip as my back arches, close to drawing blood.

Fuck.

What is he doing to me?

Every move he makes is carnal, and it leaves my brain short circuiting as I wonder if that's because of him or the fact that he's a wolf shifter, but a part of me knows it's got to be a mixture of the two.

I am here for all of it.

Another moan falls from my lips as he runs his finger through my folds, seeking my entrance as my nails bite into the skin at his neck.

"Fuck, I can't stop," he hisses, circling my core as he breathes against my lips.

"If you stop right now I'll fucking kill you," I shout, prying my eyes open to look up at him. The first thing I see are his glowing amber eyes searing into mine, a vein at his temple throbbing as he seems to try and contain himself, and I quickly shake my head. All this built up tension, it's been there since Halloween, if not longer, and now… now we deserve a taste.

"Stop holding back, Xander."

Those three words seem to snap something inside of Xander, another side of him taking over like I never could have prepared for, and I simply gape at him with pure ecstasy coursing through my veins, ready to explode.

"Don't fucking move," he grunts, tilting my chin up so my head falls to the wall. I manage the smallest of nods, before he takes a step back, marching to the nightstand before quickly returning with a condom in his hand. "You're lucky my wolf hasn't taken over completely because he wants me bare inside of you," he adds, before grabbing the back of the neck on his tee and pulling it over his head.

His ripped abs and chiseled chest come into view, leaving my body even more desperate than before. Thankfully, he doesn't keep me waiting as he crowds me again, condom slipping into his pocket as he presses himself against me.

Knees bent so his cock lines with my core, he stands with his thighs on either side of mine, trapping me in with his huge frame. Without a word he grips the sweetheart neckline of my dress and pulls, tearing the material down to my belly button to reveal my breasts.

"Fuck," I breathe, the word falling from my lips in desperation as he brings his mouth down on my left nipple, sucking and nipping as I cry out with pleasure.

My thighs rub together, desperate for friction and release, as if sensing my need, Xander moves back just enough to slip his hand between us. His mouth doesn't stop as he runs his fingers up the inside of my thighs again, only this time he snags the lace and pulls, feeling a bite of pain as the fabric cuts into my hips letting the material scatter to the floor, exposing my center, before thrusting his finger deep inside of me.

"You're so fucking wet," he groans, quickly adding a second finger as he peers up at me, but all I can do is stare back, lost in the heat of the moment. My pussy tightens around his thick fingers, but as soon as it does he retreats, leaving a sob to fall from my lips. "You come on my cock or not at all," he grinds out, unbuckling his jeans and revealing his thick length between us.

"Holy fuck," I gasp, staring down at his dick in awe as he rolls the condom over his length with precision.

My skin is prickled with goosebumps from head to toe, my body tingling with an undercurrent of almost painful need to feel him inside of me, and when he looks up, determination shining in his eyes, I feel a sense of connection to him like I've never felt before. Something clicking into place that I can't explain, yet it fits together like a perfectly matched jigsaw piece.

Xander grabs me by the back of my thighs, keeping me pressed against the wall behind me as he rolls the remainder of my dress up, and lines his cock up at my entrance. The cords in his neck tighten as he stares me down, desperation clear in his eyes. "Don't make me stop now," he mutters, the words barely audible.

"Do it," I plead, and his hips snap forward at my words, his thick length hitting all the way inside of me as pleasure zips through every inch of my body. We stare at each other with wide eyes, my chest heaving with every breath as my body burns beneath the surface, desperate for more.

What the fuck is he doing to me?

Slowly retreating, he pulls out until only his tip remains, his eyes still fixed on mine before he thrusts deep inside of me again, a cry falling from my lips.

He's rough. He's careless. He's almost fucking feral as he fucks me into the wall again and again, and I love every goddamn minute of it.

This is next level compared to any experience I've ever had before. I don't know what it is, we've barely interacted, yet the connection is incomparable.

His amber eyes burn brighter somehow, his pupils dilating rapidly before me as he places his forehead on mine.

"More."

The single word slips past my lips before I can catch it, but I have no control, it's like my body has taken over. I have no idea what more means, what else I need from this moment, but it seems Xander does.

I can feel my climax bubbling beneath the surface, ready to shatter me into a million pieces with or without my consent, but it's like my body refuses to give into the pleasure until it gets exactly what it wants.

"I have to. I have to. I have to," he chants, holding me in place with one hand as he slips from my core, grabs the condom with the other hand and tears it off, before slamming straight back into my pussy.

"Ahh, fuck." Tears prick my eyes as my brain and body battle. Electricity zings through every fiber of my being, pleasure and relief washing over me as he pounds into me time and time again with nothing between us. While my brain screams for the protection.

Every ridge, every vein, every inch of his cock drags along the walls of my pussy as I frown at him, my mind momentarily takes over and overrules my body. "Condom."

He shakes his head furiously, his jaw tight as he grips my thighs enough to mark and fucks me even harder. "No. Nothing. This is exactly what was missing," he growls, staring deep into my eyes, and I can't find the voice within me to argue back, because my body is singing because of his touch. My mind, body, and soul agreeing with his statement when my words betray me.

The moment my mind accepts the rawness of this moment, my body gives in to the ecstasy clawing at me, and just like that, I shatter. My pussy clenches around him as my arms suddenly fly out to my sides, flat against the wall as I scream. In my sex-induced brain it almost looks like the light flickers above us, mere seconds later it shatters, scattering glass around the room.

"Fuck," Xander practically roars, his eyes almost yellow as his movements stutter and he climaxes along with me.

Panting for breath, his cock still twitching inside of me, I feel like every molecule in my body is on fire, burning for him just as bright as I was a moment ago when I screamed with pleasure.

"Your eyes," he murmurs, sweat dripping between us as I frown at him.

"What about them?" I ask, blinking a few times, but I feel okay.

"They're red."

He says the words so matter of factly, that I imagine it's exactly what I would say if I told him his were amber. "No, my eyes are blue," I reply, still trying to catch my breath, when the sound of fists pounding on wood catches my attention. "What the hell?"

"Xander? Open the fucking door! Xander!"

The guys' voices filter in, almost out of breath and filled with desperation, and it seems to kick us both into motion. Slowly lowering me to the floor, I stand on wobbly legs as Xander places a gentle kiss to my forehead, before zipping his jeans up and heading for the door.

Knowing the others are going to step in at any moment, I remember the state of my dress and quickly try to cover my breasts the best I can. I knew I should have worn a fucking bra today.

Xander turns to look at me once more with his amber eyes, and a soft, calm, smile on his lips, before he turns the handle, and the door swings wide open, forcing him to jump back a step.

Adonis, Khaos, and Zen storm the room, eyes searching as they flick between Xander and me. It's clear what we were doing, and I'm not ashamed of it, but the way they're looking at us right now is like we were having more than just sex.

"What the fuck was that?" Khaos barks, making my defenses rise as they step further into the room, leaving the door wide open, and I slowly start to shuffle toward the exit as they glance at Xander.

"I don't know what you're talking about," he retorts with a sigh, raking his fingers through his hair as his eyes seem to soften again to the usual brown. It happens so quickly that I almost question if I even saw them any other way.

"Like fuck you don't," Adonis grunts, hands on hips as he turns to look at me too. "Are her eyes red?" he adds, moving to take a step toward me, and I lift my hand defensively, encouraging him to stop where he is, which he thankfully does.

"Adonis, calm the fuck down, you're pushing her in the wrong direction," Zen says calmly, trying to ease the situation, but that's two people now who have said my eyes are red and I'm freaking the fuck out.

"Me? Calm down? I'm not the one fucking Rhea the minute everybody else disappears," he throws back, glaring at Xander, who to my surprise smiles wide and proud at his friend.

"It wasn't fucking," Xander says with a shake of his head before turning his attention to me. "It was more than that," he adds, making my stomach clench as his cum trails down my legs, making me squirm, and he immediately catches sight of it.

He moves to take a step toward me, ignoring his friends behind me as I still stand before them like a deer caught in the headlights.

Get a fucking grip, Rhea.

"Why's there glass all over the floor?" Khaos asks, and it's my turn to shake my head at Xander as he continues toward me, ignoring my silent plea.

I'm not explaining any of that. I can't. I literally fucking can't.

There's too many people wanting to know too much I can't explain, and I'm at my limit.

"I'm leaving. Don't try and follow me," I say firmly, using both hands to hold my dress together as all four of them shake their heads in sync.

"Like fuck—"

"I said, I'm. Leaving. Don't. Fucking. Follow. Me."

My voice is low, lower than I've ever heard it before as every hair on the back of my neck stands on end. The Elites look over at me with surprise in their eyes, none of them arguing, yet not agreeing either as I edge to the door.

"Her eyes are definitely fucking red," Khaos mumbles under his breath, Zen nodding in agreement, but I don't stick around for anything else, quickly fleeing the room and racing upstairs with Xander's fucking cum coating my thighs.

I don't stop until I'm in my bedroom, with the door to

the bathroom locked as I swing open the walk-in closet door to reveal the floor length mirror. Raking my eyes over my body, and my torn dress, my hair is a mess, and my skins all blotchy, I can tell I've been well and truly fucked, that's for sure.

But what causes me the most concern, leaves me the most questions, and just as lost as ever, are the deep red pupils looking back at me.

What the actual fuck just happened?

EIGHTEEN

XANDER

I stare at my bedroom door that slammed shut behind her, trying to figure out how the fuck that happened when she didn't touch it, but I'm still riding the waves of bliss after getting up close and personal with Rhea.

Fuck.

I can't explain the need that burned inside of me for her. With every passing second, my wolf neared the surface and there was little I could do about it. I felt like a passenger in my own body. He's done that a few times, made his presence known, but in Rhea's presence it only escalates.

Wetting my lips, I recall the entire moment in my mind as I glance at the wall beside the door. She felt like everything in my hands. Weightless and soft as she begged for more. She didn't shy away from my rough tendencies. If anything, she encouraged them, which only pleased my wolf.

Rhea fucking Harrington.

It's safe to say I have never fucked anyone like that before, and I don't ever want to again; only her.

The moment I ripped the condom off and thrust deep inside her stirred my soul, every inch of my body burning for her even brighter, and as she shattered in my arms, her tits bouncing with every thrust, I followed straight after her. Something shifted inside of me, my body seeming to align with Gods knows what, but I feel indescribable.

I feel light headed, and I don't know whether it's from the drain of my climax or because she's gone, but I'm considering running after her to find out.

"Fucking focus, Xander!" I blink, and blink again, before glancing toward Adonis who glares at me. His perfect hair is slightly messy as he rakes his fingers through it once more. Khaos stands beside him, looking at me through slits so small I can't even tell his eye color right now. While Zen taps his fingers on his mouth, deep in thought. "Something happened here and we need to know what," Adonis adds, expecting me to have all the answers.

I swipe a hand down my face as I sigh. "I don't know what."

That instantly earns me a scoff from Khaos. "Don't be an idiot, Xander. Her eyes were fucking red. Red. There's a broken light bulb shattered in the room," he continues, waving his hand at the debris on the floor. "And the lights in the hallway flickered so much I thought they were ready to go too."

"That doesn't mean I know why," I retort with a bored look as I move to my closet and grab a fresh t-shirt, instantly feeling guilty that I didn't offer one to Rhea before she high-tailed it out of my room.

"We were banging on the door for five minutes straight and you acted like we didn't exist. Explain," Adonis hisses, and when I turn to look at him, agitation all over his face, I almost consider the fact that he might be jealous that I got to feel Rhea first, but the concern and surprise in his blue eyes tells me otherwise.

I flick my gaze to Zen, who remains noticeably quiet, before I walk around them and take a seat on my bed, bracing my forearms on my knees as I think.

"I don't really know how to explain it if I'm honest," I start, running my tongue over my teeth. They know I'm not really the best with words, that's why I always leave them to do the talking. I even consider getting Rhea back in here to do it, but think better of it. "I just *had* to have her, feel her, taste her, smell her. All of it."

"You've got to give me more than that," Khaos grunts, but when I look at him, there's an understanding of my words in his eyes, he's felt the *same* thing.

"Having her in my space seemed to escalate everything I was feeling. My wolf was screaming for her, and when she didn't put a stop to it, I gave in to the need burning inside of me." I try to keep my face straight, but the memory of being inside of her makes a small smile gloss over my lips in delight.

"Why is there a condom on the floor?" Adonis asks, pointing down at the discarded latex, and I shrug like it's the most unimportant question to ask out of this whole ordeal.

"It was in the way."

He rears his head back in surprise at my words, his eyes rounding as he takes in what I said.

"Condoms are *never* in the way, Xander. They're there for a fucking reason," he gasps in response, but I still don't care. The wolf inside me seems to smile, all fucking proud of himself, liking the consequences of what could happen without protection, but I beat that shit down because that'll only cause more trouble.

Zen claps suddenly, before placing his hands on his hips and turning to me. "How do you feel now?"

I squint at him a moment, considering his question as I take stock of myself. Listening to the rhythm of my heart, the sense of content from my wolf, and the euphoria dancing through my body. "Honestly? I feel fantastic. For the first time in forever, I feel… whole. No voice in my head from my wolf trying to overwhelm me, no stress or anxiety, no anything, except the need to hunt her the fuck down and declare her as mine again and again." I rise from the bed, ready to do just that, when Zen places a hand on my shoulder, halting me in place.

"It was right to let her run, Xander," he states, dropping his hand as I frown. I don't understand what he's saying, but it seems to make perfect sense to him.

"Why?"

"Because whatever happened between you two triggered something inside of her to change her eyes, and create the energy that seemed to surge around her as she left. The tone of her voice was off, her general energy seemed different, and not to mention the fucking door shut without her touching it," he explains, *almost* supporting his case.

"Let's not forget Xander's eyes were amber before we even left the room," Adonis adds, and I'm taken aback in surprise with the knowledge. I know it happened a time or two when my wolf was close to the surface, but no one else has ever mentioned it.

"So it's as if they were both encouraging some kind of energy between each other?" Khaos asks, leaning on the wall right where I took Rhea as Zen agrees.

"Yes, I think so."

"That could explain a lot," Khaos mumbles in response, while the three of us wait expectantly for him to continue. As if sensing the questions in the air, he sighs, his eyebrows knitting together as he thinks. "Halloween. I felt like I was fighting the vampire blood inside of me, the hunger burning deep in my soul, which had me desperate to sink my teeth into her skin and fucking change her into a vampire already."

Shock radiates through my body at his revelation.

"But the suppressors in place mean vampires and shifters can't turn others until they're twenty-five," Adonis murmurs with a frown, and Khaos scoffs again. The suppressor stops it from being possible to change someone, while also dulling the need, but apparently not in this case.

"I fucking know that, but I just didn't care. Then you guys showed up and broke the moment. I've been fighting the urge to get her right back where I want her ever since." The way he says it, I can't decide if he's happy with that fact or not, his jaw ticking.

Adonis looks from me to Zen, then Khaos to Zen, and back to me and Zen. His brows knitting closer together with every sweep of his eyes, before he settles his gaze on Zen, a flicker of enlightenment twinkles in his eyes. "You don't think…"

"I'm not sure," Zen whispers back, rubbing his jaw as he seems to think and assess us. "But if they just did what he said they just did…"

He doesn't finish his sentence, which only serves to piss me off, but before I can say anything, Adonis continues like Khaos and I aren't even here. It's like a private conversation between Adonis and Zen and we're eavesdropping.

"How do we find out?" His voice is firm, determination flashing on his face as he regards me.

"Find out what?" I blurt, swinging my arms out wide.

I hate being left in the dark, and they're ruining my fucking afterglow bliss with all this vague bullshit. "Just fucking spit it out."

"Adonis," Zen warns as Adonis cuts the distance between us, but he pays him no attention as he comes to a stop right in front of me. Toe to toe, we're so close our noses could touch.

"Rhea Harrington is *mine*," he declares, the glint in his eyes says he's goading me, my wolf immediately rising to the surface as I glare at him.

"You don't get to fucking say that. Not yet, not like me," I find myself hissing back without thought, my hands clenching at my side. My heart is racing with anticipation, my wolf making his presence known beneath the surface. All sense of calmness I felt moments ago completely obliterated.

"I can say and do whatever the fuck I want, asshole, and I say, Rhea. Is. Mine."

My hands lift, pushing at his chest for him to step back, and he does, eyes wide in surprise as my strength seems to increase, but I need the distance between us.

Where the fuck did that sense of power come from?

Lifting my hands to my face, I try to take a calming breath, but it's pointless. This fucker has angered my beast, my soul, and I can't control the fury swirling inside of me. It's a losing battle trying to control my emotions.

"Adonis, what the fuck, you idiot? Xander, you need to

calm down," Zen orders.

"His eyes are amber again," Khaos almost sings like he's enjoying the drama unfolding before him. He's just as stupid as the demon for pushing me.

"Fuck off, Zen. I mean it. Rhea. Is. Mine." The smirk that immediately graces his lips after he claims her, has my wolf begging to be released and eliminate the competition.

My mind, body, and soul can't take those words from his mouth again. "Stop fucking pushing," I bite out through gritted teeth, but he repeats it again, the words heavy in my mind as I *finally* snap.

Pain radiates through every inch of my body as I crouch, and an almighty growl burns up my throat and rips past my lips. The pounding in my ears is excruciating as I squeeze my eyes shut.

Anger.

Rage.

Fury.

All the same, but they're all I can feel.

Trying to blink past the crimson red that fogs my vision, I pause when I hear Zen speak.

"Holy fuck."

But when I open my eyes, that's all I can seem to do. I can't feel anything, not my hands on my face, not the ground beneath my feet. Nothing. I just see the mixture of surprise and fear on my brothers' faces as three words pass Khaos' lips, changing my life forever.

"He fucking shifted."

NINETEEN

RHEA

I step out of the shower, my sensitive flesh burning from the high temperature of the water, but it still does little to alleviate the stress bubbling beneath the surface of my skin. As I wrap my fluffy cream towel around my waist, I catch a glimpse of myself in the mirror again, and the biggest problem I'm dealing with stares right back at me.

Red.

My eyes are still fucking red. It's never a good color to wear, and for me, it's even worse because my blue irises have been replaced with crimson. Why can't they be a less aggressive color? Maybe gold or amber like Xander's.

Fuck.

I swipe a hand down my face in exasperation as I march back into my room, making sure to lock the bathroom door behind me just in case Adonis attempts to make an appearance. I don't need to deal with any of the drama he might bring so I move straight to the closet, eyeing my options, before I settle on a plum colored two-piece lounge set.

There's no denying I feel different. I just don't know why or how, apart from my eyes, there's nothing else physical to go on. Just the bliss still coursing through my body.

I check my body over once more as I slip into the yoga pants and thin, long-sleeved tee, before running the towel through my hair, still coming up with nothing different inside of me.

The stark reality is that I need to talk to someone about what happened, and my options are limited. I have Harmonia, Thalia, Cassandra, or in these desperate times, I could always reach out to Dante, but I haven't spoken to him since I got angry at him on my first day here. Besides, I don't really want to have to explain how this happened with him either way.

Harmonia it is.

I don't want to spoil her holiday plans, but fuck it, this conversation is not one that can wait until she returns. I need her help right now.

Flopping back on my bed, I grab my phone off the nightstand and quickly hit her number before I change my mind. The phone barely rings three times before her voice filters through the room.

"Hello?"

"Hey, how's your break going?" I ask, not wanting to blurt my crazy shit at her straight away.

"It's been fun so far, although I've definitely missed you being around," she replies, when my phone buzzes, and the buttons flash up for me to accept her face time call. I stall a moment considering if I want her to see my eyes. "Girl, you're randomly calling me so I want to see with my own two eyes that you're okay. Besides, you hate small talk, and you literally opened the conversation with it. What's wrong?"

I gape in surprise at the phone, caught off guard by her correct analysis of my semi antisocial behavior, before I hit the accept button, rolling on to my front as her face fills the screen. It looks like she's sitting on a bed, white hair framing her face as she gives me a pointed look, until the moment she sees my eyes, hers going wide in shock.

"Rhea. What the fuck?" she says with a gasp, hand rising to cover her mouth and I cringe, squeezing my eyes shut as I take a deep breath before blinking them open and refocusing on the phone. I look down at the small screen to still see my irises are still red. I sigh.

"They're that obvious, huh?" I try not to let the hopelessness I've been feeling creep into my tone, but I'm just dumbfounded and have no idea what the fuck this means.

"Just a little," she replies with a gulp, wetting her lips before clearing her throat, a failed attempt at trying to smother the shock on her face. "I've barely been gone five minutes, and you got into trouble already. What on earth has happened?"

There's no way I can explain without giving her *all* of the details, so with a heavy inhale and a rough exhale, I do just that, spilling the past couple of hours to her without stopping for breath. I try to process what felt like a sudden change in the Elites, the attentiveness from Zen, the truth easily slipping from Adonis' lips, the hint of need and overall less angry vibe from Khaos, before *everything* with Xander.

I went from barely saying two words to the guy, to feeling my body shatter around him. It was like a magnetic force, pulling us toward one another, uncontrollably, and all consuming. I don't regret it, not a single ounce. It felt right being with him. I just couldn't stay in that room with them for one more minute as they stared at my glaringly different eyes. Their reactions made me feel like a science project, trying without words to decipher my heritage.

Coming up for air, I realize I'm almost panting as I wait for Harmonia to respond. It takes a moment for her to lift her jaw up off the floor, but when she still says nothing, nerves start to get the better of me.

"What the fuck is wrong with me?" I blurt, hand clenched in my lap as I grip the phone with the other, desperate to get straight to the point and figure this out.

"I don't think you're ready for my honest answer, Rhea," she murmurs, brushing her hair back off her face, before rising to her feet, searching for something and dropping back down to the bed with a book in her hand.

It looks old, worn, and tattered, like it has the answers to all of life's problems and is used far too much for the sacred details it holds.

Fuck, this can't be good if she needs reference materials to explain what's going on.

"You're not filling me with confidence, Harm," I grumble, swiping my damp hair back off my face. "Are my eyes likely to go back to normal or not?" I ask, just as much to myself as Harmonia.

"Honestly, I'm not sure, but everything you've described sounds like you have sealed your souls together or something," she mutters, flicking through the pages before coming to an abrupt stop.

"What the fuck is that? Sealed souls? You mentioned it the other week and never expanded," I state, moving to sit up as concern burns my chest, and as much as I try to rub the ache away, it does nothing but intensify.

"Don't worry about it. It can't be that, you would have used protection, and the barrier condoms provide stops it from happening," she says passively as my entire body freezes.

Fuck.

Fuck. Fuck. Fuck. Fuck. Fuck.

The blood drains from my face as my pulse rings in my ears, fingers trembling all while my brain short circuits.

"It says here—"

"Harm…"

"That if you—"

"Harm!" I shout, louder this time so she stops reading the book and looks up at me, confusion flashing in her pink eyes as I shake my head. "He… I… uh, he took it off, the condom, I mean," I mumble, watching as her eyes widen and she gapes at me in shock, while I try not to cringe.

Apparently, I *did* leave a part out after all.

"Were you not taught about practicing safe sex down in Phoenix Valley, Rhea?" she hisses, her face reddening as she gives me a pointed look, and I shield my eyes with my free hand, squeezing my temples as I try to remain calm. Even though she's trying to help, I don't need a fucking lecture about using condoms.

"I was, Harm, I really was. But we were in the midst of it all, and when he slipped it off and thrust back inside of me, it was *exactly* what I needed. Besides, I had to have the angel dust injection when I was fourteen. It's mandatory for humans, forcing us to not procreate outside of marriage," I add with an eye roll, another of The Hex's rules that we, *earthlings*, must adhere to.

"I thought that was a myth," Harmonia responds in surprise, and I simply shrug, not wanting to get into the details right now.

For population control, once a woman turns fourteen in Phoenix Valley, every girl has to have the angel dust injection which essentially acts as magical pregnancy protection, and can be reversed once you have a marriage certificate.

It's a load of bullshit if you ask me, but for moments like now, I'm thankful as fuck.

"Don't worry about that right now, we're getting off track. I had sex, Harmonia, that's all. There was definitely no sealing of souls or any of that shit. I would have felt *something*," I state, raising my eyebrows at her, but the tight smile she offers back tells me I'm incorrect.

Fucking hell.

"It's so rare, Rhea. To the point that people even gave up on it before the war. Everyone started arranged marriages for power and all of that crap, hoping that would give them the strength to grow, but let me make this clear. Nothing, and I mean *nothing*, compares to sealed souls."

The conviction in her words do nothing to calm my racing heart as I try to swallow past the lump in my throat.

She's not hearing me. She can't be.

It was just sex.

"Harm, I think we're digging too much into—"

"What color were his eyes?" she asks, interrupting my excuses, my tone starting to sound borderline frantic, and I frown at the random question.

"They were like an amber shade, but they were almost yellow at one point," I answer honestly, and she nods, scanning through her book, but the way she looks up through her lashes at the phone, with certainty in her eyes, I know I'm fucking screwed.

"Gods, I'm such an idiot. What does this mean for me, Harmonia?" Desperation is clearly causing the tremor in my voice, her mouth is open as she starts to speak but her response is halted when a pounding sounds from the other side of my door.

It can only be one of four people, and I don't want to see any of them right now. I'm going to ignore the fuck out of them once they stop hitting the door like they're trying to punch a hole through it.

I get more annoyed with every knock when they don't stop, cringing at the phone as I glance back at Harmonia. "Find out everything you can from that book, Harm. I'll call you back," I state before ending the call and tossing my phone down on the bed.

The knocking on the door seems to stop, giving me the false sense of relief that whoever has been being an obnoxious asshole has left. Closing my eyes, I scrub my hands down my face trying to digest the two words Harmonia said.

Sealed souls.

"Rhea, come the fuck out, it's urgent." Khaos. Huh, not at all who I was expecting. Maybe that's why they sent him because he didn't really look at me in utter shock. "I can knock all day if you like, but we *really* fucking need your help right now."

Nibbling on my bottom lip, I consider my options, my mind wanting to stay exactly where I am, but it's like my body has a mind of its own, moving with the same unexplainable pull as earlier until I wrap my hand around the door handle and swing it open.

Khaos' hair is mostly swept back off his face with a few strands still dropping over his eyes, like he's been stressfully raking his fingers through it repeatedly.

Welcome to the fucking club.

Standing tall, his eyes squint as he stares at me, my red eyes clearly confusing him, but he doesn't utter another word as he takes a step back and indicates with his hand for me to follow him.

He doesn't keep a slow pace, leaving me to chase after him in bare feet, my damp hair falling down my back as I slow to a stop outside of Xander's room.

Khaos himself pauses too, looking back over his shoulder at me, a hint of concern and uncertainty flashing in his emerald green eyes, before he seems to push it down, focusing on the situation at hand.

I want to ask what's wrong before I step inside, but it literally feels like my soul is magnetized to something on the other side of the wall, and before I can acknowledge Khaos' emotions, I'm pushing past him through the already open door and moving inside. Any concern about feeling uncomfortable being back here so soon is nonexistent. Not with what visual comes into view.

"What the fuck?" My mouth falls open, gaping at the scene before me. I can sense Adonis and Zen over by Xander's bed, trying not to startle the animal pacing and growling on the other side of the room.

Not just any animal; a wolf.

And if I'm correct, it's not just any wolf either. It's Xander.

What the hell happened here?

I remain frozen in place, rooted to the spot with surprise and concern as I look him over. His fur is pure black, from head to tail, except for a red mark on his right side, but I can't get a good view of it yet. When I focus on his eyes, shining the same amber as earlier, I know I'm right. He's fucking beautiful.

As soon as his gaze hits mine full on, he freezes, and in the next second, the growling stops too.

"Oh my gods," I whisper, shock still running through my veins as I take a step forward, only to have a hand grip my forearm to stop me. I don't turn. I don't look away from the pleading in Xander's eyes as I speak to whoever has a hold on me. "Let go of me. Now."

My voice has dropped again, my anger clear as the hand immediately drops, followed by a scoff, which tells me it was Adonis, but I don't turn to clarify. Instead, I take another two steps toward Xander, before dropping to my knees in front of him. My back is ramrod straight as I try to remain calm yet strong before Xander.

In the same breath, it's like I have no idea what I'm doing, yet I do, all at once. It's confusing as fuck so I just let my soul take the lead. But I know he's confused and needs me, so here I am.

"Hey," I whisper lamely, not really sure what else to say, but needing him to hear my voice, and it's thankfully not deep and dangerous like it was moments ago. If anything, it sounds softer, gentler.

The wolf takes one cautious step toward me, then another, and I reach my hand out, letting him sniff my palm as I wait with bated breath for his next move. His soft fur glides over the tips of my fingers as he leans into my touch, a whine falling from his lips before he moves closer.

I shift to my butt, crossing my legs as silence continues to fall heavily over the room, letting him explore me in this form. Once he's walked around me twice, rubbing against my side as he captures my scent, he comes to a stop right in front of me, so close our noses could touch. Out of nowhere, his tongue whips out, gliding across my cheek, once, twice, three times, before I manage to lean back.

"Don't fucking push it," I say with a chuckle, shivering at the wetness on my cheek, and to my surprise the fucking wolf's tail *wags*.

A hum of laughter filters from behind me, telling me the other Elites caught our exchange too. A calmness washes over the room and through my body, and as Xander paws at his eyes, he quickly lies down flat on his belly, but I jump with shock as I move to stroke him, only to connect with skin.

"Oh, shit," I gasp as a naked Xander fills my vision, a lucid smile on his face as exhaustion seems to trickle through his body.

"Thank Gods," Zen mutters as someone throws a pair of boxers over my head for Xander, but he doesn't pull his soft gaze from mine.

"Are you okay?" I ask, heart pounding in my chest, and I realize I'm far more concerned for him than I thought. He nods in response, and my body relaxes. "Good," I add, and his hand reaches for mine. I let him take it, squeezing for a moment, before I pull my hand away and rise to my feet.

Wetting my lips, I finally glance at the other three, who watch us with an almost concerning amount of curiosity, before I clear my throat. There is so much unsaid in this room right now, but I only have one question, which is not easy to ask, and not that simple to answer I imagine, but it has to be said.

"So, who's going to explain sealed souls to me?"

TWENTY

KHAOS

The five of us, my brothers, Rhea, and I, step through the portal and head toward the dining hall. Today has been exhausting for all of us. How the fuck has it only been one day?

The snow.

The audible sex between Rhea and Xander.

The shift.

Now, the mess.

If I'm expected to handle any of this, then I need some fucking food to fuel me. My desperation for a drop of blood also runs high, but right now doesn't seem like an acceptable time to venture down that path.

As we cut through the main building, my gaze falls to Rhea, who walks slightly in front with Zen at her side. Adonis is to my left, Xander to my right, and if the growls that are slowly releasing from his chest are anything to go by, I would guess his wolf isn't all too happy about not being right beside Rhea.

Fuck.

I hate complications.

I had run up to her room and pounded like crazy until she appeared in the doorway. In a relaxed outfit, that somehow accentuated every inch of her curves, I couldn't find my tongue to speak to her. I was too busy fighting my internal need to pin her to the wall and lay claim too.

What the fuck is wrong with me?

Then, when we got to Xander's door, I paused, almost wanting to protect her from the beast on the other side, completely doubting what I had gone to get her for in the first place. But to my complete shock, she stepped into that room and… was *everything*.

She didn't shy away from the jet black wolf that growled as it paced, unhinged and unpredictable. Instead, she dropped to her knees and fucking *soothed* him.

Crazy. As. Fuck.

With a quick glance over her shoulder, she manages to run her gaze over Adonis, Xander, and me, before focusing back ahead. Her eyes are dimming, the red slowly seeping back to her beautiful blue irises. Which leads to far more questions than we have answers, but the main one being the words that passed her lips when she spoke them back in Xander's room.

Sealed souls.

She was right in her assumption, but where had she gotten it from? It was exactly what we had thought too, which was beyond crazy, because that kind of shit just didn't happen anymore.

I could sense the unease in Zen, him feeling out of control since it's not a subject we are well versed in. Adonis seemed to still be in shock over Xander letting his walls down so freely with someone, magic involved or not, while Xander himself literally looked like a love sick puppy, pining for Rhea's attention.

While I… am in complete fucking awe of her.

Usually, Adonis is the easiest for a woman to lure in, while Xander and I are the hardest, for no other reason than we don't let our guard down with people. Vulnerability is not in our DNA. Yet here we both are fighting an internal war within ourselves over how to act around the stunning brunette who has waltzed into our lives, leaving us gasping for breath.

And apparently, she is the catalyst for bringing back sealed souls.

Stepping into the dining hall, we move toward the center table, the spot unofficially reserved for us, and before Rhea can attempt to move to her usual corner spot, Zen drapes his arms around her shoulder and steers her along with us.

Xander's breathing becomes shallow as he clenches his fists at his sides, not liking Zen's hands on her. I almost chuckle at his show of jealousy, but I manage to refrain, since the little green goblin is perched perfectly on my shoulder too.

Zen holds out the middle chair for Rhea, and she slips into the seat with a short thanks, before he takes the spot to her right, and Xander quickly drops to her left, leaving Adonis and me to sit facing them.

Nobody speaks as we browse through the menu. I settle on the steak, rare, and a soda before relaxing back in my seat. Everyone quickly follows, ordering their food and turning their attention to Rhea and Xander, the pair of them glancing at each other out of the corner of their eyes. It's almost sickening, it's so sweet.

"So, what are the rumors on sealed souls?" Rhea asks, and I grin, liking that she doesn't shy away from the situation. She seems to face it head on, just as I would, and it draws me into her energy even more.

"Your eyes are less red," Adonis states, clearing his throat as he glances at her. I watch her eyes widen in surprise, relief slowly rolling off her in waves. Her worry is understandable since she still doesn't know who or what she is yet, and the red eyes only served as a reminder.

"Thank Gods," she mumbles in response, brushing her damp brown hair back off her face as she waits for someone to explain. She doesn't look at just one Elite for answers, her gaze sweeps over all of us.

"Sealed souls aren't common anymore. They're taught to us as myths these days because it just doesn't happen," Zen says, and I nod in agreement, which only seems to make Rhea frown as her eyebrows pinch together.

"So you don't think that's what happened here?" she asks, a hint of hope in her voice. But before anyone can say a word, Xander slams his fist onto the table, making the whole thing fucking rattle with his anger.

"It's exactly what happened here," he bites, slipping his arm over the back of Rhea's chair as he glares at everyone but her, like we were the ones to ask the question. When his gaze meets hers, he wets his lips, before lowering his face to hers so their noses brush, and to my surprise, even with his burst of rage, she doesn't back away. "It's exactly what happened, Rhea, I know it," he repeats, much calmer this time, like he's talking to his delicate, most-prized possession.

She stares into his eyes for what feels like an eternity, before she nods. "I think so too," she mutters, barely more than a whisper, her eyes falling closed at the admission. It's hard to read and understand where her head is at, but this is all a mess, so I can't imagine being in her shoes.

Adrenalin courses through my veins, the unpredictability and uncertainty of the future wars inside of me.

Xander tilts his head, pressing his lips against her forehead in one of the gentlest moves I have ever seen, before sitting back in his seat with a pleased, relaxed grin on his face.

It takes a moment before Rhea blinks her eyes open again, and I can't be sure, but the red seems more evident again.

Fuck.

I don't utter a word about it, and if Adonis notices, he manages to keep his mouth shut too, while Zen continues to explain the limited information we know. I don't want to spook her, and send her running for the hills again.

"Sealed souls are bonded by passion, sex, and desire which are known to become uncontrollable, consuming the body," he states, and the way Rhea and Xander look at one another, it seems like that's *exactly* what happened. "Mentally, it tethers you together for all of eternity."

"The how it happens seems quite apparent, especially since the condom was peeled off and tossed aside, and that's when everything was heightened," Rhea advises, not concerned about discussing her sex life at the table, and it leaves me even more intrigued to find out more about this woman from Phoenix Valley. "What I mainly need to know now is how this will affect us going forward," she adds, somehow sitting taller in her seat as she laces her fingers together on the table. She's not afraid to show how serious she's taking this.

"Have you learned that there are usually multiple men to one woman?" Adonis asks cautiously, and she immediately nods.

"Yeah, Harmonia explained it to me, and that it's usually arranged for power and status gain," she replies with an eye roll, clearly not liking the reasoning behind it, which only makes me want to lean closer to her, but in that exact moment our food appears before us.

I lick my lips as I look down at my steak and mashed potatoes, noticing she ordered the exact same meal as me, even the steak cooked the same way.

Why the fuck do I care? She shouldn't be consuming me like this.

As Zen twirls the pasta on his plate, he continues. "That's exactly right, and if it's not for those purposes, it's simply a case of settling among each other, never really love or feelings, and certainly not sealed souls."

"Sealing your souls together can enhance your powers and strengths as a supernatural among those sealed. Which in some cases, can lead to powers activating earlier than usual. Like Xander and his shifting," Adonis states casually, grabbing a slice of his pizza, but my focus is on Rhea's wide eyes as he explains what could have happened to them.

It would make sense that Xander shifted, and her eyes changed color. Fuck, the door slammed behind her earlier without her even touching it. If anything though, that only seems to help narrow down her species.

Sensing the question in her eyes, I swallow down the steak in my mouth, unable to look away. "It'll still be difficult to decipher what you are between an angel, a demon, or even a God, but with the way your eyes glowed and the energy you gave off, you're definitely *not* a vampire or shifter," I say, watching as she swallows nervously.

"But I could have activated my powers?" she asks for clarification, and this time Zen beats me with his response.

"Both yes and no. For a male, like Xander, it can fully activate his, because he will only ever be bonded to you. While with the female, because she can be bonded to more than one person, you won't fully activate your powers after sealing your soul with just one person. If you don't find the true members of your soul before the third year, you'll simply wait until then for them to activate."

It's all a lot to take in, but it's crazy as fuck to know that Xander is now a fully confirmed shifter. We spend what feels like a lifetime waiting to find out for sure who we are in the supernatural world, for him to simply find out so early after fucking Rhea unprotected against the wall.

Wetting her lips, Rhea glances around the table, almost nodding to herself as she takes all the facts in. "And going forward?"

The question is simple, yet complicated all at once. "If people know you've sealed your soul, you'll become an even hotter target than being classified as nothing," I state honestly, watching her brows knit together in confusion as she waits for me to expand. "It'll go from people wanting to charm and lock you into an arranged marriage, to people wanting to test if they can seal to you too," I add, and the way she cringes tells me I wasn't so subtle and calm in my choice of words, but fuck, I'm not sugar coating it anymore. Rhea needs to hear the brutal truth, the brutal *reality* of the situation. The likelihood of people going as far as rape to check is fucking high.

"If anyone fucking touches me, I'll kill them with my bare hands," Rhea grinds out, stabbing at her food in anger as Xander grips her chin, forcing her to look at him.

"No one will fucking touch you. Ever." His words are dark, harsh, and true. A promise to be kept. I can see it in his eyes, the invisible connection between the two of them already. His loyalty to her, just like he has for us. "Understand?" he says, raising an eyebrow at her when she doesn't respond immediately, and she wets her lips.

"I told you once before that I'm not soft and pliant, I *can* handle myself. It was how I lived before I came here," she states, determination flashing in her eyes as Xander's grip seems to tighten and his face lowers to hers again.

It's like electricity crackles around them, both of their eyes changing color as Rhea's reds are met with the shining ambers from Xander. The stare off makes the entire table freeze, the energy seeming to change around us as they silently battle for dominance over the conversation.

Shattering glass makes the entire table jump as I look up to see the bulb hovering above the next table burst out of nowhere, glass raining from the ceiling as we all gape in surprise.

"*Why* does that keep happening?" Rhea asks, frustrated, and Adonis scoffs as I turn to glance back at them.

"You tell us, you're the one doing it," he retorts, a

quirked eyebrow aimed her way as she glares back at him. He quickly covers his mouth as a smile teases at his lips.

"If I am, I don't know how I'm doing it," she bites, and Zen reaches over to squeeze her shoulder in reassurance.

"Your magic will be off balance and volatile for a while. It tends to be like that anyway when we're going into the second year, but you're going to experience it sooner than others now," Zen explains, the concern in his eyes is visible, but yet he's trying to reassure her. She shakes her head, not liking the explanation he provided.

"And alone apparently, since I can't let anyone know what's happened here today," she replies, clearly stressed out with the situation.

"Xander wasn't able to control his shift either, Rhea. We provoked him to prove our theory," I explain, and when she glances at Xander, he nods in response.

"My fucking soul couldn't settle either until I saw you, then it was easier, my head calmer, and the entire transition nowhere near as scary," he murmurs, stroking a finger down her cheek.

"How was it?" she asks, turning her full attention to him. "To shift I mean. Did it hurt? How were you mentally?" Her hand lands on top of his as she looks at him in worry, asking questions no one else has yet considered, and I see the hint of guilt in Zen's eyes. He's always our caregiver, but in all honesty, we've been too caught up in Rhea and her feelings instead of asking Xander how he felt about shifting.

A gentle smile touches Xander's lips at her thoughtfulness. "It was strange at first, like I could see through my eyes but my control was barely there, like I'd literally changed places with my wolf," he explains, running a hand through his hair as he tries to find the right words. "It all happened so fast that the pain didn't register if there was any, but now I feel a little achy."

I think he's in just as much of a daze about the situation as the rest of us are. I'm sure with more time and thought about it, he'll have more to say, but for now he simply shrugs before clearing his throat.

"Are you nervous to learn what you are?" he asks quietly, but we all still hear him.

Rhea rubs her lips together, and I don't know how I can tell, but it's not because she's considering her answer, she already knows it, it's more to do with how honest she wants to be with us. Fuck. That.

"You sealed your soul to our brother's, we're all in this together now, there's no point in keeping secrets," I gripe, the anger evident in my voice and likely written all over my face. If my harshness offends her, so be it.

"I have been alone for twenty-two fucking years, Khaos, excuse me if it takes me a minute to learn how to *not* just handle everything alone," she retorts, and I frown, glancing back at her from my food. Any other girl in this fucking place, and I'd say it was fake, forced, and all in her damn plans, but with Rhea, what you see is what you get. It's as easy as that.

Adonis places his hand on my shoulder and applies pressure, not in reassurance, but to shut me the fuck up as he glosses over the situation. "We all know Khaos doesn't have manners, Rhea. What he *means* to say is whatever is going through your mind, we're all a team and we can help."

She eyes him for a moment before releasing a long sigh. "No, I'm not scared or nervous over what I might be, but I really don't like being out of control, and this is just… this whole situation is just… fucked up," she states, swiping a hand down her face in defeat. Or is it more in surrendering to the inevitable?

"For an earthling, you're handling this better than expected," Zen says with a casual smile, and the death glare she gives him makes my fucking balls shrivel.

"Call me that one more time, I fucking dare you," she hisses, eyes fiery, and he quickly lifts his hands in surrender.

Doesn't like the generalized nicknames for humans. Noted.

"We need to research this more, but are we agreed that for now at least, it stays between the five of us?" Xander asks, glancing at each of us, and we all immediately nod in sync, well except Rhea.

"Us and Harmonia," she adjusts, folding her arms over her chest like it'll create a barrier between us. I guess she needs someone to speak to outside of us, but—

"That's fine, but no one else," Zen agrees, cutting off

my internal debate, and I roll my eyes at how easily he gives in to her demands. Asshole.

Silence descends on the room again, everyone eating, when Rhea suddenly drops her fork to her plate, round eyes flicking to Xander as she seems to realize something. "When you were in wolf form, you had like a, uh, a red mark on your side. It's not going to be there when you're a human, is it?" she asks, her fingers twitching to lift up his tee to check for herself, but he saves her the trouble and does it anyway.

"Fuck."

Gasps and curses fill the table as the stark red mark remains on Xander's ribcage.

I'd had no idea what she was talking about before, because I was too busy looking into his wolf's eyes to notice anything on his fur, but it's unmistakable now.

It looks like a symbol of some kind. A large 'Z' with a line through the bottom, connecting it to an 'O' beneath.

"I didn't see one on my side when I showered," Rhea murmurs, lifting her t-shirt in the same spot to reveal her silky soft skin. The same skin I had my hands on a few weeks ago, the memory begging to be recalled.

"Did you check everywhere?" Adonis asks, a knowing smirk teasing his lips as he wags his eyebrows at her.

"I wasn't exactly looking," she grumbles in response, before rising to her feet and lifting her t-shirt up behind her to reveal her back. "Is there anything there?"

Holy. Fucking. Shit.

There, taking up the bottom half of her back is a huge 'O', just like the bottom of Xander's but without all the extra parts.

"I'm going to take it by the looks on your faces there's something there," she prods when no one responds, trying to glance over her shoulder or twist her body with no luck.

"We'll head back now and show you, but it seems to only be the circle of Xander's, but on a much bigger scale, like much bigger," Adonis explains as I rise to my feet, happy to remain silent as my cock strains after the brief glimpse of her bare skin.

"It looks like you guys are going to have to make sure these marks stay covered at all times," Zen explains as we all fall into step and head for the exit.

"That won't be a problem," Xander replies, nudging Adonis out of the way to be beside Rhea. "I'm sure it would be much harder if it was Adonis trying to conceal it," he adds with a smirk, and I chuckle under my breath. Rhea looks at me like the sound surprised her. Have I not laughed in her presence yet?

The look in her eyes holds me captive for a second, rooting me to the spot, before Zen breaks the moment and encourages us all to carry on walking with a slight shove against my back. I hadn't even realized we'd stopped.

She's under my skin, there's no denying it. I both hate it and love it all at once. The foreign feeling wreaking havoc on my body. A tightness in my chest causing mayhem internally. Which only leaves one question in my mind.

The pull that I feel toward her, is that what the others feel… what Xander felt? I don't know, I'm too much of a fucking pussy to ask it out loud just yet, but boy do I want to find out.

TWENTY ONE

RHEA

After the most bizarre Christmas Eve that ever existed, I made the mature decision to avoid the Elite yesterday, hiding away in my room as I absorbed all the crazy this world has thrown at me already.

Not even six months ago, I was living a normal *human* life. A cheating ex, a shitty diner job, and a tiny apartment in a run down building. Now, that all seems so distant it barely feels real, but it serves to keep me grounded, because since then, well, everything has been flipped upside down. The challenging part to deal with is how none of what's happened is in my control. It's *supernatural* and I'm being forced to hold on for the wild ride.

I thought finding out I had some kind of magical gift was crazy enough. Now I've managed to finally move on from my life back in Phoenix Valley, fuck someone for the first time here, and somehow manage to seal my goddamn soul to his.

Xander.

Fuck.

As a wolf he was… stunning. Fierce, but beautiful.

Everything about those moments were a frenzy, *more* than just need and desire, and his words were true when he said it was more than just fucking, but I'm not really ready to admit that yet, because developing a deeper connection with someone is *not* what I signed up for.

Now he has a mark taking up his right ribcage, while I have a thick red circle covering the bottom of my back, and I'm quite sure they aren't going to rub off. Ever. It feels just like the skin around my back, no raised scar tissue, nothing, like it is just simply a part of me.

I'm so screwed.

As if juggling this new world wasn't enough, between classes, magical objects I have no clue how to use, and motherfuckers trying to jump me, this is the last thing I need. But something seems to tell me this is a gift from the fates, offering a stability in my life like I've never been given before.

I told Harmonia and the twins only weeks ago that delving into a relationship of any kind with anyone was not on the agenda, but the picture Harm sent me last night offered me a stark reality check.

The magic of two souls sealed is all consuming.
You'll breathe better as one.
Stronger together.
United as one.
The magic of more souls sealed is incomparable.
A memory of what was once possible for a loved one.
Cherished, true, and pure.
Love will prevail with no cure.

What the actual fuck does any of that mean?

I don't really know, and I'm far too put off by the entire thing to find out more, because if my gut is right, it means I'm expected to be with him, except there is the possibility of adding in a *them*, for the rest of my life.

I've only just arrived here. Do I find them attractive? Fuck yeah, I'm not blind. Did I find being in their company the other day a different experience than I originally thought? Yes. They somehow managed to get past my walls, forcing me to spend time with them, and to my surprise, they weren't as assholey as I had originally thought.

But do I want to say I love them and commit myself to them? I don't know what love is, and as much as I'm not saddened by Dante's bullshit, it's still left me a little tainted. Fuck, these guys are supernaturals. If sex with Xander is anything to go by, everything is going to feel ten times stronger, and hurt one hundred times worse if this ends badly. And with my stellar track record, *everything* ends badly.

I swipe a hand down my face, knowing full well I need to get the fuck up and go find the library if I want any sort of answers, but I don't want to open my eyes, not yet. Keeping them closed means I can avoid the day and the worries that seem to constantly swirl in my mind like a tornado. It's wreaking havoc on my mind, body, and soul.

I've wallowed enough, I know I have, and wallowing isn't me.

Fuck it.

Blinking my eyes open, I stretch my arms above my head and point my toes as every inch of my body groans in protest. Reaching for my phone on the nightstand, I notice it's just past ten in the morning.

Everyone will be back from their break tomorrow, so if I want to get over myself and go and do some research without anyone gossiping about it, today is the day. With that in mind, I throw my covers off, swinging my legs over the side of the bed before heading to the bathroom.

My stomach grumbles, a stark reminder that I foolishly didn't eat yesterday except for breakfast, the rest of the time was spent under my sheets. I don't like Christmas anyway, so the drama of the day before was almost soothing in comparison to the realization that I was alone yet again. No fond memories of being a happy and loved child. Nothing.

Quickly turning the shower on, I let the spray warm up

as I strip out of my panties and oversized tee, discarding them onto the floor without care, before the warm water hits my skin. My eyes fall closed, my mouth open, my chest releasing a silent sigh, as I let the water beat against me, washing all my troubles away for at least a few minutes.

I'm so lost in the mundane task of running the shower gel over every inch of my body, I don't realize there's someone else in the bathroom until I go to place the bottle back, and a screech slips from my lips in surprise.

"What the fuck, Xander?" My heart pounds in my chest as I try to catch my breath, but if my tone is too harsh, you wouldn't know it, not based on the casual shrug he offers as he eyes every inch of my body.

In loose-fitted jeans, and a checkered black and gray shirt, he looks hot as fuck, his brown hair messy and unkempt as he gives me a pointed stare, while he leans against the vanity. "You've been avoiding me."

It's not a question, but a statement, one that passes his lips as he casts his gaze over my body again from head to toe. I don't shy away though, that's not who I am. Besides, he had the pleasure of seeing beneath my clothes the other day. I have the mark on my back, along with a few fingertip bruises on my thighs to prove it.

"What do you want, Xander?" I ask, matching his stare with my own, refusing to be the one to break first.

"Do you want my honest answer to that right now?" he

retorts, quirking his full eyebrow at me expectantly as he drags his tongue over his bottom lip, and I fucking shudder at what he's insinuating.

It feels far too tempting, I mean, what could possibly go wrong after the other day anyway? I wish I would have asked myself that question a few days ago but here we are. We're already deep in this together, but I need to understand more of what it means for us before I continue to venture down whatever this path is with him.

His brown eyes seem to sparkle with a hint of amber flicking in his pupils, a reminder of the beautiful beast beneath the surface, and it almost makes me smile. Almost.

Shaking my head, I'm about to tell him to get out, when he prowls toward me. One foot in front of the other, he cuts the distance between us before I can interrupt.

My pulse thunders in my ears as he steps into the shower without concern, his hands finding my hips before he pushes me back into the tiled wall. My back hits the cool surface and I peer up at him, watching as the water cascades over his fully clothed body, but before I can even scramble over something to say to him, his lips descend on mine. Rough, demanding, yet tender.

In the heat of the moment, I rise up on my tiptoes, attempting to meet him halfway, clearly just as desperate as he is for the contact, but his grip tightens at my hips, forcing me back in place. Xander runs his nose over the length of mine, his touch a complete contrast to the grip at my waist as water runs through his hair, down his face, and seeps into his clothing.

"I'm trying to give you some space, Rhea. I want you to be okay with this, but more and more of my senses are changing, my body absorbing the supernatural abilities that come with being a shifter." He pauses, waiting for me to understand that little bit of information before continuing. "One of those things is my sense of hearing. I know you've been in your room the entire time, hiding and not eating, and I refuse to let you treat yourself like that." I gape at him, too consumed with his close proximity to actually understand what the hell he's saying as he looks me dead in the eye. "You're mine now, Rhea. *Mine* to care for, *mine* to cherish, and *mine* to fucking correct if you do something stupid or reckless, and that includes starving yourself so you don't have to run into my brothers and me."

My protest is on my lips, ready to throw some excuse at him, but it's lost when he finally brings his full lips to mine, electricity zapping through my body as he presses against me. My hands lift to his shoulders, running up his neck before finding his hair and raking my fingers over his scalp as I pull him closer, desperate for more.

It seems I have zero control with this man, and right now, I don't give a fuck.

Being this close to him all of a sudden completely obliterates all of the issues I had swarming my mind earlier. At this moment, nothing matters but his touch.

As if sensing my thought, Xander deepens the kiss,

running his tongue over my bottom lip, before he pulls back, shutting the shower off without removing his gaze from mine.

I watch as his chest rises with every breath, his body just as affected as mine, and I revel in it. Until he opens his goddamn fucking mouth.

"Eat or I'll make you," he grunts, releasing his hold on my hips and storming from the shower all of a sudden. He leaves through Adonis' door, and I'm not even able to pull myself off the tiled wall before he's back in the room with a tray loaded with food. He places it on the vanity, before turning his stare to me again. "Now," he adds, pointing at the meal, and I scoff.

Who the fuck does this guy think he is?

Anger coats my skin, my hands falling to my hips as I glare at him. "Let me fucking tell you, asshole," I start, ready to bring this man to his knees as I walk toward him. "I'll do what I fucking want. It has nothing to do with you. Not an ounce. I'm not going to deny that I need to eat, but continue to tell me what to do. Please. I *dare* you, let's see how far you actually get."

My face warms with fury as I stare him down, ready for his growly comment, but his eyes seem to have traveled to my breasts, my taut nipples now distracting his grizzly attitude.

Of fucking course.

I offer an eye roll, which he doesn't see as I step past him, not wanting to hear anything else he has to say, but as I move, I make sure to grab the tray of food. The chocolate topped pancakes look delicious, and regardless if he's an asshole or not,

I really fucking want them.

He doesn't try to stop me, or even utter a word until I'm just about to slam my bathroom door shut. "I know I might seem like a pain in the ass, Rhea. But I'm not sorry. In my family line, I'm set to be the alpha, and now my wolf and I are one, I will do anything and everything in my power to protect what's mine."

I understand what he's saying, I do, but the bit I'm struggling with is where he claims me as *his*. "I'm Rhea Harrington, I belong to *no one. It'd be better for you in the long run if you learn this lesson now*," I grunt, my jaw tightening as he remains against the vanity, wet through to the bone without a care in the world.

"You keep telling yourself that, but I know the truth. I feel it in my bones. I've never felt anything like it in my life, and you know it too," he states, lifting a hand to his chest as my body freezes. I keep my face neutral, refusing to give anything away, but my subconscious knows exactly what he's talking about. What I refuse to accept. "You're mine, Rhea, like it or not. Now go and eat, before I really claim you."

With a heavy sigh I discard the book in my hand, tossing it to the side on the table as I drag another in front of me. I've seen so many pages that I'm worried they're going to start blending together, especially since none of them seem to have any of the crucial details that I want.

I'm on a mission that involves diving into every book that seems worthwhile, hoping to understand more about this whole sealed souls business, while also hoping to find out what I might be with my damn red eyes.

I almost miss them now that they're gone, the flare disappearing just as soon as it came, but I guess it's for the best as we want to keep the information hidden.

Rubbing my lips together, I glance over the title of the book before me, called '*Loving a Supernatural*'. It doesn't exactly scream anything more than some lighthearted fiction, but it's worth a shot. Flipping through the pages, my mind can't help but wander back to this morning when Xander caught me off guard.

My body still begs for him and his attention, while my mind knows better. Sure, I took the food, I'm not stupid, but he can't go around thinking he can claim me or boss me around. I've learned how things work around here, multiple men to one woman, which I am completely for, but does that mean I just accept the Elites? I got to know them some more this week, but it doesn't mean I should be diving into anything head first.

I can imagine other girls in my position at this school would be tripping over themselves to fall into their laps, but I'm not like other people. It's completely alien to me that people marry by arrangement because I wasn't aware this was a thing down in Phoenix Valley. I'm fine on my own if that's the case,

I just need the sex, and maybe some skin on skin contact from time to time, but there's no way in hell I'm signing myself over to a group of guys for the sake of it. For the sake of my independence.

One thing I have lacked in my life is love. From a parent, a sibling, a friend, or even a partner, and as cold-hearted and stubborn as I can be sometimes, I know it's what I crave more than anything else in the fucking world.

I want to feel the intensity I feel with Xander, I can't deny it, the feel of his hot skin against mine, his hard muscles beneath my touch. But my mind also goes back to the way Khaos' breath felt against my neck, intoxicating me as he spoke into my ear.

Fuck.

I need to stop now.

Get my fucking head on straight.

They mentioned the other day that people would use me to break their powers free, does that include them? Am I expected to sleep with all of them to see if they're sealed to me too? Because fuck that, I'm not a whore, and I'm not here for them to use me like that. I guess it's the whole *unit* situation that continues to catch me off guard, scrambling my brain and leaving my mind to run wild.

All of this uncertainty really isn't helping me.

Second guessing people's motives on top of trying to learn more about the entire situation is hard work, but trust has never come easy to me, and it shouldn't.

I spent twenty-two years living my life as a human, to learn it was all a lie. Someone from this crazy supernatural life tossed me aside, left me to fend for myself in Phoenix Valley without a single care. Now, when others have their families to guide them and assist them through this learning curve, I'm left to fend for myself. As always.

Brushing my hair back off my face, I groan in frustration at myself as my fist tightens in the ends of my brown locks. Why can't there just be a godsdamn fucking catalog listing all of this supernatural shit in it? I could do with figuring out the answer sooner rather than later because my patience is running thin.

I breeze through the pages in the book, glancing at the title headers that flash up, but nothing sticks out to me at all. Not even a glossed over poem about sealed souls. Fuck, even if it was something completely made up, I would still devour every fucking word of it.

Dumping the useless read on the discarded pile, I look around the library, thousands upon thousands of book spines staring back at me, but not a single one jumps out screaming 'pick me, pick me.' There are wall to wall books, and a handful of tables in the middle of the room, with the empty librarian's desk at the far end. It's surprisingly open and airy, with the glass roof offering all of the natural light through the stained windows.

I take the handful of books that have offered me nothing, and place them in the book cart as I glance around at the shelves once more, this time focusing on what my powers could mean instead of the deep red circle marked on my back and the reason it's there.

What could I be?

What could I be?

What could I be?

Tapping my lip as I walk the length of the book stacks way to the left, searching in the species books, I'm hoping for one that gives the features of every type of supernatural in one book. Apparently this isn't going to come easily to me, but at least Khaos narrowed down the fact that I'm not a shifter or vampire. Small victories.

Running my fingers over the spines of a series labeled '*Supernaturals'*, with different books in different colors based on species, I sigh, reaching for the orange demons book and the white angels book. My fingers hover over the red God's book for a moment, but that seems the most extreme, so I decide to settle on the two I have.

Just as my ass is about to hit the cushion of my chair, the door swings open with a resounding thud, drawing my attention in that direction, to watch Adonis stroll in like he owns the fucking place.

Every inch of him screams Elite, from the way he carries himself, to the knowing smirk permanently on his lips. Today he's got his round glasses in place, his blond hair swept back off his face, and a button gray shirt with a pair of charcoal pants.

No man should be this put together and hot all at once. It's worse because he *knows* it. Arrogant prick.

His eyes settle on mine, the corners of his mouth twitching when he takes me in, and I force myself not to squirm under his gaze. In a simple black tank top and a pair of pale denim shorts, I'm a stark contrast to him, a reminder that we're very different people, from very different places.

He doesn't utter a word as he makes his way toward me, pulling his phone out and tapping the screen for a moment, before pocketing it again. "Don't mind me, I was just letting the guys know that I won," he explains, running his tongue over his teeth as he slowly drags the chair out across from me and takes a seat.

Like a fool, my curiosity gets the better of me and I take his bait. "What did you win?"

He doesn't bother answering me with words, instead he simply points a finger in my direction, making me scoff as I roll my eyes at his bullshit.

"I wasn't put up as a prize," I retort, making his grin spread wider as he shrugs his shoulders at me.

"I wasn't looking for one either, yet here we are. You. Me. My brothers. One new happy family. Who would have thought, huh?" He steeples his fingers on the wooden desk as he looks me over, and with every passing second, my eyes turn into slits as I glare back at him.

It's hard to tell when Adonis is being serious or sarcastic. It's like he has this whole other personality sometimes, like a mask he fits perfectly in place as a defense mechanism, but I see right through it. Right now is one of those times and his words leave me confused.

"You don't fool me, Adonis. Your fake smile and forced sarcasm is bullshit and we both know it. If anything, it only serves to piss me off more. Now, why are you here? I'm busy and the library doesn't look like your usual stomping ground," I state, folding my arms over my chest.

I don't miss the way his smile falters ever so slightly, dropping at the sides, like the forced edge he always offers falls away as he squints at me, clearly processing my observation.

"I'm here because I want to be. Why are you here?"

Fuck his bullshit.

"I'm not talking around in circles with you. I have too much going on in my fucking head already for you to swoop in here and make things harder by playing games," I bite, grabbing the demons book and pulling it toward me. I flip the hardback cover open, reading through the index as I try to see if this holds anything I might find useful.

Maybe I could use it to assess the asshole in front of me.

Adonis doesn't respond for a moment, remaining eerily quiet to the point I think he might have vanished altogether, but my body is far too aware of his presence as always.

"We agreed as a group that we should split up and come

looking for you. Try to be supportive and all that," he says with a wave of his hand. "It was actually Zen's idea. Although, the way Xander was grumbling about your eating again, I think that might have triggered it."

I look up through my lashes at him, my lips twisting to the side as I think. His shoulders are relaxed, his face smooth of any strain or concern, and it's more like his eyes are smiling than his actual mouth. I can't help but feel he's being genuine. *Him.*

Just like that, a bit of silence on my behalf has Adonis dropping his facade and letting me see the real him underneath it all. It's not much, just a piece of truth without a hint of sarcasm or a joke—a cover for who he is. It's only the reason why he's here, but it's something. A million times better than the bullshit I was getting from him a minute ago.

Wetting my lips, I sit back in my seat, hand still paused on the page of the book as I eye him cautiously. "If you think we're fucking so you can see if we are sealed, then you're wrong and should leave."

The words blurt out of my mouth before I can even stop them, but I don't take them back, even if I have just let my insecurity show. To my surprise he doesn't make note of that or try to sweet talk me, instead he leans forward, bracing his elbows on the table as he reaches for the angel book and pulls it toward him.

"Rhea, when I want to fuck you, you'll know," he states

cooly, enunciating the *when* and not *if*, before flipping the book open. "Now, we have fifteen minutes, twenty tops before the guys get here. I can spend that time pissing you off by simply breathing, or help figure out what it is exactly that you're looking for."

I nod instantly, appreciating it when he talks straight to me like that, before I sit tall in my seat. "I'm trying to find details on what I could be with the whole red eyes and light bulb bursting shit, or at least try to understand what sealing my soul means for me individually, not just now, but in the future, and where that's expected to leave me with Xander in the grand scheme of things."

If he's actually going to help, I may as well be honest with him. I really don't want to waste any more time. I almost think he hasn't heard me when he immediately closes the book before him, before reaching over and doing the same with mine.

"Honestly? You're not going to truly know until the time comes. The line between demons, angels, and Gods, is touchy at this stage. The red eyes and the glass shattering could link to all three in some way, but especially angels and Gods. Each individual has their own traits, some can cross over, but there will be distinct features in your magic that no one else has." He offers a soft smile that reaches his eyes as I nod in understanding. Fuck, his response was not what I wanted to hear.

That completely rules that out for me then. *Great*. "Is

there any insight here on sealed souls then?" I ask, trying to keep the hopefulness out of my voice as I lace my fingers together on the table in front of me, and he shakes his head.

"No, not really. When sealed souls seemed to stop existing, they slowly dwindled down the information on it, turning it into nothing more than a myth instead of history, which is what I truly believed it to be until I saw you and Xander," he admits, fixing the glasses on his nose.

"What are the general rumors about it?" I fiddle with my fingers nervously, desperately hoping for him to give me some kind of hint at my future because at this point, I *need* something to grasp onto.

"That the love is almighty, all consuming, powerful, protective, and sometimes destructive." Wow. "You're supposed to be able to feel where that person is, find yourself drawn to them no matter the circumstances. It's inevitable. Written in the stars, or however people want to fluff up the situation with roses and niceties." My heart thunders in my chest at the rawness in his tone, like it's something people only dream of. But does that include him?

"So is it a good thing or a bad thing?" I ask, my voice thick with vulnerability as his pouty lips flick up at the corners with a genuine smile.

"It's *everything*."

TWENTY TWO

RHEA

I step out of my dorm room, letting the door click shut behind me, only to have an arm lace through mine immediately, and I startle at the touch, until a glint of white hair flutters in front of my eyes.

"Long time no see, my friend," Harmonia says with a smile as she looks me over from head to toe. A natural smile transforms my face, my pure delight at her being back is far too embarrassing, but I don't give a shit. I just need a face to face chat, no phones or distance between us.

"It felt like forever," I reply, falling into step with her as we head for the stairs. The last time I saw her was when I was having a meltdown on the phone over my red eyes and my entire situation with the Elites. Now, the holidays are over and we're dressed in our Academy uniforms ready to head to class. Life at

Saints Academy has semi returned to normal.

So much happened over the break, I don't even know how to explain any of it, but now isn't the right time anyway. But soon, definitely soon. I need to get this shit off my chest.

"Girl, don't tell me you didn't have *any* entertainment in the shape of four hot guys who shall not be named but are also known as the Elites," she says with a wink as we reach the bottom of the stairs and move straight toward the portal. I can't help but roll my eyes at her utter ridiculousness.

Now that she mentions them, I'm surprised we haven't run into one of the guys, but we are leaving a little later than everyone else since we're not heading for breakfast. On my last trip, I made sure to stock up on some protein bars, and now I have a good collection in the drawer back in my room, along with an excellent excuse if Xander tries to give me any shit over my eating, or *lack thereof*, again.

"I don't think entertainment would be the right choice of words," I explain, rubbing my lips together as the portal's black fog coats my skin, and my foot lands down in the main building of the Academy.

Every. Fucking. Time.

I don't think I'm ever going to get used to it.

Students fill the hallway, trying to get ready for their first class or hurry for food as we keep to the outside of the large hall, following the trail around until we're at the portal that leads to Combat.

With all the noise and buzz around us, we pause our conversation, heading through the billowing smoke once more until the doorways to the Combat center stand before us.

Still. Weird.

Admittedly, Combat is one of my favorite classes. I'm sure next year, once I know what I am and what I need training for, I'll feel differently about the other classes, but in here, we all train the same. Defensive. Offensive. Aggressive. Exhausting. Repeat.

It's a hands-on, exhilarating class where we learn different types of martial arts, weaponry, and defensive techniques so I'm not left out on the sidelines. While in others, when the lessons are more specific to each supernatural species, I stand by idly and watch because no one knows where I fit in.

"We have so much catching up to do, especially since your eyes are…" she assesses me, pointing a finger between her own pink pools to indicate what she means, and I nod, a sigh falling from my lips.

I still haven't figured out the best way to explain it to her, but I don't think blurting out that they're only red when magic flows within me is the best idea. Especially when it's supposed to be a secret, and with the unwanted attention I'm already experiencing, I'll never know who's listening in.

"Soon, I swear, Harmonia, but everything is very hush hush right now and it has to stay that way," I murmur, shuffling my satchel over my shoulder as we step out into the huge space.

It still catches me off guard that the ground itself is split into four sections of Earth's natural materials of grass, water, sand, and burned foliage.

Although, as first years, we haven't left the grass yet, and I can't say I'm disappointed about it. Especially when I can't fucking swim. A shudder runs down my spine at the thought, but I shake my head, pushing it to the back of my mind for a future me to worry about, as Harmonia and I head toward the circle of students already here.

I drop my bag by the edge of the field along with everyone else's, brushing my hair back off my face and securing it in place with the hair tie off my wrist.

"That makes total sense, and I swear I haven't mentioned anything to anyone," Harmonia says, moving to stand beside me as we continue toward the line of students surrounding Professor Riva.

He hasn't really spoken a word in my direction since the first day when he told me he was from Phoenix Valley too. There hasn't been very much to say, but his eyes always assess me like they're trying to check if I'm handling Academy life okay.

Looking past him, I see the units holding medium sized daggers, similar to the one I was gifted by Pandora's Box, but black and silver in comparison to my rich gold.

Please tell me I get to use one of those on Hector or Selene today, that would bring me so much joy.

I don't think I'm joking either which is unsurprising at this point. The stares from Selene and the attack I know links back to her pisses me off so much I wouldn't be sad to see her go. Would anyone? And Hector, fuck, if he tries to corner me one more time I'm likely to cut his fucking balls off, shove them in his mouth and enjoy doing it.

My glare is trained on the asshole in question, and the supreme bitch beside him. My body stiffens from head to toe, the hairs on the back of my neck stand on end, and my body feels like it might explode into a million pieces.

I already know why before my eyes pull to the left, watching as the Elites stroll out onto the grass with far too much swagger. It's like a scene from an old movie, watching them head toward us in slow motion, and I can practically hear every single person's heart rate increase as they take them in. Especially the women. *Especially* fucking Selene.

My hands clench at my sides as I worry about her being an even bigger issue, which is ridiculous since the current dynamic with Xander, Khaos, Adonis, and Zen, is *them* chasing *me*, and me freaking the fuck out.

I wet my lips, my pulse pounding in my ears as time stands still, unable to move until I know they're close, and the smug as fuck grin on Xander's face catches me by surprise. It's the kind of look I would usually get from Adonis, if any of them, but with Xander… it's like he knows a secret that no one else does.

And he does. They *all* do. My muscles start to twitch uncomfortably as worry fills my mind that someone might recognize the intensity of our connection.

Xander holds his bag out for Zen to take, which he does, and as the other three drift to the side to discard their satchels, Xander keeps his strides clear as he makes his way toward the group, or more specifically, me.

Every nerve-ending in my body simmers beneath the surface, and when he comes to stand beside me, our arms brushing ever so slightly, I hear a deep chuckle rumble from his chest. I hate that relief rushes my body.

How is he laughing right now when I can barely fucking breathe?

Asshole.

"What's so damn funny, Xander?" I snap, trying to keep my voice low as I glare at him, and he simply shrugs in response.

"Nothing," he says with a knowing smile, and I call bullshit, my blood pressure increasing as his smile grows.

"Don't lie to me, we have to trust each other, *remember*?" I retort, throwing their words back at him, and he glances at me out of the corner of his eye, his smirk unwavering as he leans in to whisper in my ear.

"Rhea, do you know what some of the abilities and strengths are of a wolf? Because if you've forgotten, your sweet little pussy made me shift, and now I'm harboring them all." His lips brush against my ear with each word, my eyes slamming shut as I try to hide my emotions from appearing on my face, but it's obvious I'm doing a poor fucking job of it.

Trying to swallow past the lump in my throat, I squeeze my thighs together as need and desire pulses inside of me. I scramble to remember anything at all about shifters, and more specifically, wolves, but my mind comes up blank. Goodbye logical thinking.

"What does that have to do with anything?" I grunt back, trying to act unfazed as I blink my eyes open, and tilt my head up high, avoiding eye contact with everyone as his chuckle blows against my skin. I fold my arms over my chest, trying to enforce an invisible barrier, but it's useless.

"My sense of hearing is heightened, so I could hear your heart rate kick up a notch or two as we walked in, and your pulse throbbing in your neck as you watched us approach." A shiver slips down my spine uncontrollably, giving my body's reaction away without him even needing to hear it, but he continues. "My sense of smell is also more intense, which means I know that if I slip my hands between your thighs, my fingers will come back… wet," he enunciates, an almost purr on the tip of his tongue.

Motherfucker.

Is what he's saying real? Can he really sense *all* of *that*?

Before I can think of a smart and snarky response to tell him to fuck off so my steel walls can be firmly planted between us again, Professor Riva claps his hands together, gaining everyone's attention as Zen, Adonis, and Khaos appear to the side of Xander.

I can feel their eyes on me, watching my narrowed, pissed off eyes battle against Xander's satisfied grin, clearly trying to read the situation between us, when I hear Adonis murmur under his breath. "Why the fuck is she mad now?"

My jaw tightens with agitation as Xander stands back to his full height, making a show of adjusting himself under his shorts as he offers me a wink. "She's just pissy because I know how much she's denying herself by avoiding us. Isn't that right, Rhea," he says confidently, and I have no response. Not a single retort to bring him to his knees, because ultimately… he's fucking right, and I hate it.

I catch Zen's eyes widening in surprise, but Professor Riva begins to address the class, and I force myself to focus on him instead. Not reading any further into the Elites' facial expressions.

The class stands around him in a makeshift circle, watching as he moves to stand by the weapons. "Good morning, everyone. We're going to cut straight to the point this morning, pun intended," he adds, pointing to the bottom of one of the daggers, and a resounding groan filters around us at his bad joke, but he doesn't seem to mind. "We've got a solid two hours to learn and practice how to wield these daggers. We'll do some individual training, before moving onto sparring in pairs. So, pay close attention because I don't mind sending anyone to the medical center with injuries if they were caused by not listening," he advises, and that's all I need to block the Elites from my mind and focus on the class.

No one here is injuring me, although I would love to send someone else there. Or a few someones if I want to get revenge on my attackers.

"This is going to be fun," Harmonia mutters under her breath, and I nod in agreement.

"Hell yeah," I whisper back, a gleeful smile touching my lips as Riva continues.

"I'm going to hand out the blades. I want you to get comfortable with their weight. The more you learn the balance, the better you'll be able to wield the heavy metal," he explains, picking up two at a time and slowly handing them out to everyone. "Any questions?" he adds, extending a dagger to me and Harmonia at the same time, tips in his hand and handles in our direction, and I shake my head in response.

No questions, no worries, no uncertainty in my physical ability. I'm here to learn.

I take a small step back, feeling Xander's eyes on me as I do, but I don't meet his gaze, my sole focus is on the blade in my hands. It's not as heavy as my own, and there's no intricate carvings or embellishments, which makes a huge difference to the control I have. Holding my palm out, I play with the weight of the twelve inch blade in my hand, trying to maintain the balance as I twirl the handle, before wrapping my fist around the twisted leather.

Making sure I have plenty of space away from my flesh, I swing my hand to the side, letting the sharp edge cut through the air, and the slight swoosh is like electricity, giving me a zap of excitement as I do it again. Nothing else around me matters. I don't care if people are watching me making a fool of myself, if I'm doing it wrong, or if anyone else is even doing the same as me. Wielding the weapon is my priority, and getting to explore the motions with it is completely exhilarating. I struggle to swipe the smile from my face.

I twist the handle in my hand again, but this time, I jab the dagger forward, connecting with thin air still, but testing how much strength needs to go behind the movement to create enough force to damage a target.

Time flies as I relax into my movements more and more, finally noticing that everyone else is doing similar things around me. Some seem to grasp the exercise easier than others, while some can't even hold the handle properly. *Noobs*. I play back and forth with both hands, until Professor Riva approaches.

"Your form is excellent, Rhea," Riva says, catching me off guard as he comes into view, but still maintains his distance for a moment to be sure I don't swing out and catch him.

"Thanks," I mumble in response, lowering the dagger to my side as I catch my breath. I hadn't even realized I was so worked up. Sweat trickles down my temple, and my tee sticks to me slightly, but I take it all as a good sign.

"Does it feel different?" he asks, and I frown, brows knitting together as I look up at him inching closer, clearly seeing the confusion on my face. He doesn't speak again until we're side by side, and even then, it still takes a moment for his cryptic words to sink in. "No one has ever received one from Pandora's Box before, not since the original gifts." I rear my head back, ice coursing through my veins as I search his gaze, but I have no idea what I expected to see. Betrayal? There are a million questions running through my mind, desperate to know how the fuck he knows what I got from Pandora's Box, but he answers the unspoken question for me without prompting. "Everyone's gifts from Pandora's Box are registered when received, and a record is kept for professors to understand what we're working with."

I wet my lips, uncertainty settling through my bones as I eye him suspiciously. "I don't really want to talk about it," I state, hoping to put a pin in the conversation, and he nods.

"Understandable," he says, swinging his arms out at his side slightly in an attempt to lower my guard. "But if you need any guidance, or a safe place to figure it out, I can help."

I don't know how to respond to that, but the chance is squashed when an arm lands heavily around my shoulder, pulling me tight into their side. The woodsy scent screams Xander, and my eyes immediately widen. I remember his mention of enhanced hearing, and my panic increases.

"Everything okay?" he asks, not speaking to me, but

Professor Riva, who nods, offering a forced smile as he takes another step back away from me.

"Of course," he says, his eyes holding mine for a moment, before he claps, gaining everyone's attention, and moving to the center of the space again.

I try to fight it, but my gaze lifts to Xander who looks down at me expectantly, his jaw tight as he looks me over, which tells me he heard my conversation with the professor, but I can't deal with his thoughts or opinions intruding on the situation. Professor Riva's comments are something I have to manage on my own since it involves my gift.

Shaking out of his hold, I move to join Harmonia, who raises her perfectly shaped eyebrow at me, and I roll my eyes in response. Apparently everything I do right now is a public show for everyone to observe, and I fucking hate it. Between the intense gazes of Riva and Xander, I need a break.

I push my shoulders back, seeing a hint of concern in Harmonia's eyes as Riva addresses the class. "When I call out names, I want you to pair off, find a space on the grass and attempt to spar. Then I can come around and assess what you can improve on, or point out what works well for you." I feel Khaos come to a stop at my side, his smoky scent enveloping me, but I keep my attention forward, waiting for my name to be called.

"Selene and Xander… Hector and Adonis… Khaos and Zen… Rhea and Harmonia…"

Fuck, I hate the thought of Xander paired with Selene, but he's a grown ass man, he can handle her. I hope.

I drown the rest out, looking to my friend with a smile to find her staring at me already. In sync we step away from the group again as I methodically spin the blade in my hand, loving how comfortable it feels in my grasp. I'm a little disappointed I'm not training with someone I would actually like to sink the end of this steel into, but at least with Harmonia I can get a good feel for positioning and strength against an opponent.

"Hell, I was watching you practice, Rhea, is it too soon to hold my hands in the air and call it quits already? I will surrender to you," she says with a giggle, and I shake my head with a chuckle too.

"You can't let me down like that, Harm, especially when I don't get the joy of taunting the supreme bitch with my dagger," I say with a grin, wiggling the blade in my hand. It's hard facing the knowledge that Riva and all of the Academy professors know what my gift from Pandora's Box is, when it's supposed to be a huge, private, personal secret.

"Fine, but you have to go a little easy on me, otherwise I'll bypass the medical center and go straight for the morgue," she replies, a shudder running through her as she comes to a stop, turning to face me, and I immediately plant my feet, shoulder-width apart. She slowly copies my stance but looks uncomfortable holding the weapon.

We both lift our blades, the tips touching before we

begin, and Harmonia immediately takes a step back, but as I swing my blade toward her, she lifts hers to block my move, with more strength than I think she realizes she has.

A grin spreads across my face with a hint of excitement at just how fun this is actually going to be. Our blades clang in harmony between us repeatedly as we dance around in a circle, both attacking and defending as Harmonia swings for me once more, but as I block this time, I twist my blade, forcing her grip to loosen, and her blade falls to the floor.

Pointing the tip of mine toward her, a wry grin spreads over her face as she raises her hands in surrender, chuckling as we pant for breath.

"This is too fucking fun, Rhea," she states, swiping her damp hair back off her face as I drop my blade too, the tip slicing into the grass perfectly, before I brace my hands on my knees, trying to catch my breath.

"Agreed," I reply, enjoying it far too much, when a shout from behind me catches my attention. I hadn't realized how much we had separated from the group until now. We're closer to the edge where the sand starts. Lost in the movements and the intense practicing, we drifted away from the sparring crowd.

Searching for where the noise is coming from, it takes me a moment, until I hear Zen call out my name. Uncertainty spikes my veins, and I find myself reaching down and grabbing my dagger before taking off in his direction. I have a feeling I'm not going to like what I see when I reach him.

"What's going on?" Harmonia hollers from behind me, but I'm too focused on what has him drawing my attention to answer her. Besides, I have no fucking clue either.

I notice everyone else has stopped, watching whatever is happening, and a few glance in my direction too, presumably because they're intrigued why Zen called me specifically.

"Calm the fuck down, Xander. It's not my fault you don't like what I have to say about that little whore. Get over yourself." Selene's voice carries all the way to me, and it's then that I spot Xander standing ramrod straight, hands clenched at his sides and the muscles in his back bunched together as a low growl purrs from his lips.

Fuck.

Someone's upset the big guy. *My* big guy.

My footsteps quicken as I move faster, trying to get to him before their standoff can escalate any further. My hand tightens around the hilt of my dagger, ready to slit this bitch's throat. Not for saying something about me, I'm the only one she refers to as whore and it goes right over my head, but for getting him riled up like this.

Someone moves to my side, and I quickly glance over, to catch a glimpse of floppy black hair cascading over emerald green eyes. Khaos. "His eyes are flaring amber, Rhea. We can't let him lose it in front of all these people," he whispers, squeezing my arm in some attempt at support, and I nod in understanding.

Noise comes from Adonis and Hector to my right, tension running high between them as they drop their daggers and push at each other, ready for some kind of fucking brawl, but I keep my eyes trained on the more pressing matter at this exact moment in time. Xander. Once I have him calmed down, I can figure what the hell is going on over there.

"Shut. Your. Fucking. Mouth. Bitch," Xander bites, his breathing becoming more labored, followed quickly by Selene's cackling dancing around us. It grates on my fucking nerves.

"It's not my fault you're too busy watching her to notice what's right in front of you. I've been here this entire time. Adonis had me. I want this arrangement, Xander, and you'll fucking give it to me!" she screams, all whiny like the world owes her everything, but I force myself to block her out as I barge through the few people circling around them, and plant myself firmly in front of Xander.

With my dagger in one hand, aimed down at the ground, I place the other on his shoulder. I rub slightly as I look up into his eyes that have lost nearly all their flecks of brown, glowing more and more amber as I begin to panic. Not. Fucking. Good.

"Hey," I murmur, keeping my voice low as I ignore the screeching bitch behind me. "Focus on me," I add softly, and he thankfully, between my touch and voice, seems to loosen up a little, though his teeth are grinding together so hard I think he might snap his own damn jaw.

"She just—"

"I don't care," I interrupt, moving my hand to his chest, above his heart as it thunders beneath my touch. "Fuck everyone else, Xander, and just focus on me." I use every ounce of self-control to calm my breathing, making myself relax even though I'm strung the fuck out. "Match my breathing," I whisper, watching as his brows knit together, but I nod, encouraging him as his gaze fixes on mine.

"Excuse me," Selene shrieks from behind me, and I cut my gaze to hers over my shoulder, extending my arm and pointing my blade in her direction as I glare.

"I will slit your fucking throat if you don't shut the fuck up," I growl, my voice husky, deeper, as I notice the slight change inside of me, my core reaction of anger igniting my own powers within me.

Fuck.

This is not helping at all.

I'm only going to make this worse when I cut her up for causing him such distress.

"Professor Riva, I will not stand for some lowly whore speaking to me like this," the supreme bitch squeals. He doesn't respond to her as everyone quickly moves around us, heading toward the new drama unfolding between Hector and Adonis as the latter swings his fist into the side of Hector's face, and everyone gasps as he falls to the floor.

What the actual fuck?

Does he not see the fucking situation his so-called

brother is in right now? How the hell is this helping?

As if sensing my internal madness with him and his poorly timed antics, he turns his attention in our direction, before mouthing one simple word which explains it all.

"Go."

Holy fuck. Is he causing a distraction on purpose? Protecting both Xander *and* me?

Before I can think on it any more, Khaos appears at our side, a hand on each of our shoulders as he looks between us. "Let's go, now, before this crazy bitch has you both destroying the entire center in anger," he mumbles, shifting us toward the exit, and I discard my blade, not caring how it falls as I quickly follow after him. When I don't sense Xander doing the same, I pause, looking back over my shoulder for him.

I have no idea where Zen or Harmonia are right now, but priority number one is to get Xander out of here before he fucking shifts and I break shit… or faces.

He's still in place, standing directly across from Selene who stares at him with wide eyes, body trembling as she feebly nods. It looks like Xander is talking, but whatever he's saying isn't filling her with joy, instead it looks like *fear*.

"Rhea!" Khaos calls out to get my attention, and when I look at him he cringes. "Your eyes." Fuck. "Keep going, I have a feeling Xander will chase after you," he adds, and I nod lamely, my brain completely unfocused and lost on all the craziness happening around us.

Rushing for my satchel, I toss it over my shoulder and head for the exit, mumbling my thanks to Khaos as I go. The look in his eyes almost makes me pause. A hint of awe, a splash of pride, and the sparkling of desire.

It's so out of place on him, that I think I imagined it. I likely did, or my red eyes make me see made up shit. Either way, I don't stick around to find out for sure.

I need to hide my eyes.

TWENTY THREE

ADONIS

I flex my hands, relishing the burn and bite from the cuts across my knuckles, and a satisfied smile spreads across my lips. If anyone's paying close attention to me as I take my seat in the dining hall, they'll likely be bewildered by the manic gleam in my eyes as the dried blood makes my skin tight and my muscles ache. It's a nice feeling.

Hector fucking Ariti.

I've been longing for a reason to beat the shit out of his face, long before his part in Rhea's attack, and today offered the perfect opportunity when everything went to shit in Combat between Xander and Selene and then Rhea. I needed to get them out of there for their own protection.

Motherfucker has had it coming for far too long. I'm only sad I didn't manage to do worse, but a broken nose and two black eyes, along with a cracked rib or two will have to do for now.

It's the only time I wish we were truly human, living without the ability of someone healing us with their magic, but I have to settle for what I can get. At least he had to walk around in public to get to the medical center so he had no choice but to wear his wounds. I'm sure the rumors will spread like wildfire about what happened, but again, the fucker deserved it and he's lucky that's all the beating he received. So far.

Relaxing back into my seat at our usual table in the dining hall, Zen sits across from me with Khaos at his side. I wet my dry lips, feeling the slight cut Hector left behind when he managed to land a punch to my chin, but otherwise I'm completely unscathed. Not injured enough to take a trip to the healer anyway.

Embarrassing. For him.

The thought makes my smile grow bigger since this will tarnish his tough guy reputation, and I was more than happy to knock his ass down a few pegs.

No one at the table addresses the mess our first class of the day caused. It wasn't brought up in our last class either, not even when Xander and Rhea didn't show. I sigh, scrubbing a hand down my face as I mindlessly select the ribeye steak and loaded baked potato for my lunch, completely starved after the unexpected, yet cathartic, workout earlier.

I run the scene through my head once more, but it's not

really necessary. It's clear what happened, and as always, the drama leads straight back to Selene.

Whatever she said to instigate the situation clearly pissed Xander off, but the subject was obvious; Rhea. The second his eyes started to flash amber, I knew shit wasn't going to calm down, *he* wasn't going to calm down, and I assessed the situation immediately, attempting to draw attention to Hector and me as quickly as possible. Shoving him the first time was nowhere near enough to gather a crowd, which is why I enjoyed pummeling my fist into his face and stomach, but what caught me by surprise the most, was the way Rhea dropped everything to race to Xander's side without even knowing what happened.

The sheer panic on her face for him was evident. The way she stroked at his chest soothingly, getting him to focus his gaze on her, to get him to control his breathing, was almost poetic, until she tilted her head and her deep red eyes flashed in my direction, causing my heart to sink with worry.

So much for attempting to keep a low profile.

I quickly upped the tempo with Hector, even dragging Professor Riva away as Selene whined loud enough for everyone to hear just how desperate she was for some Elite dick, even though she's been denied multiple times. If I wasn't so preoccupied with the asshole before me, I would have rolled my eyes at her pathetic shit.

Once I was sure both Xander and Rhea were safely out of sight, I finally listened to Professor Riva and relented my onslaught on Hector. I was satisfied with my quick work but disappointed I couldn't continue.

"Knock it the fuck off. You're both dismissed. Get the hell out of my sight." His growl was exactly what I needed to hear as I stalked out of the class, not looking back as no further punishment was offered. The sound of Hector coughing and spluttering filled my ears as I walked away with a pleased smile, everyone giving me a wide berth, and I was more than happy with it.

Now we were all silent on the matter, because none of us had a goddamn fucking clue on how we were going to handle the pair of eye flashing, sealed soul idiots that couldn't seem to handle a little taunting.

"You really don't have to look so pleased with yourself you know," Zen grumbles, eyeing me over the rim of his water bottle as he takes a sip, and I widen my eyes in fake surprise at his words.

"Who, me? I would never," I reply quickly, placing a hand over my heart, and Khaos scoffs, dismissing my bullshit instantly.

"Of course you wouldn't," Zen retorts with an eye roll as his pasta dish appears in front of him on the table, and he digs in while still offering me a pointed stare. "Obviously they both seem very protective of one another at the moment, so we need to be careful of every situation that could possibly trigger that reaction, and no more crap from you, will help." He continues to look at me, all while I continue to feign innocence.

I know what he's saying without spelling it out, I do, but what pisses me off the most is the fact that I can't argue with him, or worse, I don't want to. Because he's right.

Rhea Harrington is a hot mess. One I was more than happy to stick my dick in way back when she first arrived, but everything changed quickly, and I knew it was safer, I was safer, to keep her at arm's length. Not that I would compare the situation to Selene. If anything, it was on the complete opposite scale. Rhea isn't needy or desperate for my attention, which only drew my body closer to her without conscious thought.

After today, and what she did for my brother, I am almost in awe of her. She didn't have to do what she did, sealed soul or not, and I feel myself consumed with an overwhelming need to repay her.

I don't mention this to Zen or Khaos, instead I simply shrug. "Whatever you say."

Neither of them respond as Khaos' burger appears at the same time as my steak and potato. The conversation pauses for a moment so we can eat, just as I catch sight of Xander entering the dining hall.

He's not with Rhea, which both pleases and concerns me, but I push it all to the back of my mind as he wordlessly drops down into the seat beside me, leaving a space between us. It's our usual practice when we don't want anyone to join us unexpectedly. No one wants to take the seat between Xander and me, it's far too intimidating for most to handle, which is just how we like it.

Murmurs seem to pick up from the table beside us after Xander sits down. Selene and her friends clearly have something to say among themselves, but I don't even glance in their direction, not willing to offer them unnecessary attention because it'll only open up a can of worms.

Xander places his food order before he sighs, glancing around the table at the three of us with a shrug as he offers a tight smile. At least his eyes are their usual color now. Not even a fleck of amber in sight. I release a small, thankful breath that he was able to calm down.

"How bad is it?" he finally asks, a slight frown marring his forehead as he braces his elbows on the table waiting for the bad news, and Zen quickly shakes his head.

"Not as bad as you think. Adonis and Hector's fight on the other hand? On the tip of everyone's tongue with minimal mention of yours and Rhea's situation," he states, trying to relax Xander immediately as I smile wide at my brother.

"You're welcome," I add, before taking another bite of my food, and even Khaos shakes his head at me, trying to hide the smile teasing his lips.

Xander offers me a knowing grin as he flips me the bird. "You've wanted a good excuse to beat the fuck out of him for ages. You should be thanking me," he says with a raised eyebrow, and I smile wider, unable to argue with that. The man isn't wrong. Clearing his throat, he glances around the room, and I immediately know what he's looking for, or more specifically, *who*, but Khaos speaks before I get a chance.

"Sorry. She hasn't made an appearance, not since she ran from Combat like I told her to, but I was kind of expecting her to be with you," he states, saying what we were all clearly thinking, but the way Xander shakes his head tells me we were far from being right.

"No. I chased after her, and she soothed my fucking wolf enough to stop me from growling, my anger diffusing almost immediately, but by the time we reached Agion, her eyes were still red. I almost… nevermind. Then we got to my door, but before I could even open it, Harmonia appeared through the portal and the pair of them ran off to do damage control on her eyes."

I just stare at him, confused with every word that falls from his mouth as I try to keep up, nodding along like I have a fucking clue. My brain scrambles to ask a question or two to make sense of it all when a flash of brunette catches my attention as they enter the hall, and everything else falls away except the sight of her.

I'm not sure if the others see her too, but the silence that descends over the table tells me they have. The four of us watching every move Rhea makes as she walks through the tables with Harmonia at her side. She's hypnotizing.

Her eyes are no longer red, her blue pools of sapphire

glistening before us as she tucks a loose tendril of hair behind her ear. It's clear she's beelining for their usual table in the far corner, where Khaos' cousins are already sitting, and away from us.

The obnoxious sound of Xander's chair scraping across the floor jolts me from my thoughts, but it doesn't pull my gaze, it only makes hers involuntarily shift our way, and that's all I need.

Raising my hand I crook my finger, beckoning her near, and I see the hesitation clear on her face. Her mouth twists to the side as she glances from her table to ours repeatedly, her steps slowing.

I don't look at the others, I don't even blink, offering her my full attention as she debates her options, challenging her. I'm sure she's about to flick her hair over her shoulder and dismiss me without a backward glance, but to my utter surprise, Harmonia whispers something in her ear, and a moment later she's confidently heading our way.

It shouldn't be seductive, the way she subtly moves her hips as she puts one foot in front of the other, but it's fucking mesmerizing. As she gets within hearing range, I relax back in my seat, finally lowering my hand to the table as I offer her a casual smile.

"Choose a seat, Rhea," I murmur, dragging my tongue over my bottom lip as I continue to assess her. I expect her to glare at me or use that smart mouth to put me in my place, but yet again she surprises me when she drops her satchel from her shoulder, and slowly makes her way to the seat between Xander and me.

But what stuns me more than anything, is the way her gaze doesn't leave mine. She's clearly intrigued, willing to play my little game, and I have no idea why, but I can't deny the fact that the way she is looking at me now has me fascinated.

Rhea's arm grazes mine as she takes a seat, dropping her bag by the chair as she runs her tongue over her teeth, finally pulling her gaze from mine as she looks around at each of us.

I watch how every one of my brothers eye her too, desperate to see what truly lies beneath the surface of the girl before us. The mystery of her red eyes and all.

Red eyes are only ever connected with vampires, but Khaos is adamant she isn't one, and the crazy shit that seems to happen sporadically when her power seems to bloom inside of her, only makes us more confused as to what she is. Nothing is adding up or making sense when it comes to trying to identify what Rhea might be.

"How are you?" she finally asks, turning to Xander at her other side, who offers her a soft smile in response. It blows my mind how tall she sits in her seat between us, unfazed, and completely blowing our usual seating strategy out of the water. She is not intimidated at all.

"I'm fine. You?" Xander responds gruffly, swiping a hand over his mouth as he traces his eyes over every inch of her face, and she nods in response.

Silence descends over the table for the moment, so much uncertainty and questions in the air around us, none of which we can answer. Not that we could ask here out in the open anyway.

As if sensing the same, Khaos rises, offering us his back as he whistles loud and sharp, gaining the attention of everyone here, including his cousins and Harmonia. One swift swipe of his hand in their direction has the three of them rising from their seats and heading in our direction in no time.

Thalia and Cassandra drop down on the other side of Khaos, while Harmonia tentatively takes the seat across from them next to Xander. "Whistle at me like I'm a dog again and I'll rip every tooth from your mouth and shove them so far up your ass—"

Thalia's words are cut off as Cassandra dramatically claps a hand over her mouth, making the rest of the table chuckle except Khaos, who seems to shiver with the thought of her threat.

The way Rhea chuckles behind her hand, trying not to laugh so openly at his pain, she looks almost carefree; it's a strange sight to see. All I've observed of her since she arrived is trouble, confusion, and anger. The walls that surround her are hard to penetrate, and there's clearly a reason for that. I just don't know if I care enough to find out what's behind them, or if I'm happy to live in blissful ignorance.

We all have walls, every single one of us, they're just made out of different materials, and purposeful for different reasons. The thought of my own has me shaking my head and focusing on the conversation that's taken over the table.

"The supreme bitch is glaring so hard at the side of my face right now it might explode. Does she know we're related, Khaos, or does she think I'm trying to get in your pants?" Cassandra asks with a quirk of her eyebrow, followed by a scrunch of her nose in disgust and Rhea tenses beside me.

One glance to the left, and I instantly piece together who the supreme bitch is, and scoff at their choice of nickname for Selene. It's far too fitting yet doesn't do her personality justice.

Before I even realize it, my hand is reaching over to Rhea's thigh, grazing the soft skin above her knee as I squeeze in comfort. The move is foreign, even to myself, but I roll with it when she doesn't immediately jerk away, instead turning her full attention to me with her eyebrow quirked, matching Cassandra's.

Did she do that before she got here, or is that a trait she's picked up from the twins?

Why the fuck am I intrigued to find out?

The conversation continues to buzz around us as I pay no mind to anyone, except Rhea, and the way her skin lights up with goosebumps in the wake of my touch.

Interesting. I could have sworn she would pull away.

"What are you doing?" she murmurs, her eyes focused

on mine as I continue to run my thumb lightly across her skin, and I shrug in response.

My body is desperate to touch hers, more so than usual, to the point that I can't control it. And if she thinks this is confusing to her, she has no idea what it feels like for me. She's holding me captive, my body making my decisions as she lures me in.

I know where this all stems from though; I'm not stupid. The moment she stepped forward and placed herself between Xander and Selene only solidified her unspoken loyalty to figuring this all out with him. *Us*. Potentially. And I am here for it.

Watching as she lost control of her own power rising within, in an attempt to calm Xander down, filled me with an emotion I can't fully comprehend, and I don't think I want to either. All I do know is I want to thank her for it, show my appreciation for how she treated him, but this is me. Words aren't enough and there's only one way I can think to do that.

"Don't mention that stupid bitch around me," Xander grunts, reminding me Selene is still the topic at the table, but I have no interest in rehashing what happened earlier. It's played out in my head enough times already. I'm focused on a completely different subject.

Rhea continues to stare at me, the noise at the table sinking into the background as I inch my hand slightly higher up her thigh, watching her face for any tell or sign that she wants me to stop, but nothing comes.

She seems tense, and I can help work that out of her.

Just this once.

I keep my touch gentle, grazing her skin as I dismiss my food and brace my elbow on the table, palm against my cheek as I smile at her lazily.

Her Academy skirt is loose enough around her thighs for me to slip underneath, moving higher and higher, and to my utter disbelief, her legs part, challenging me to go higher as her pupils dilate.

It's like she's beckoning me forward, expecting me to back down before I reach the apex of her thighs. The way she smirks ever so slightly, tells me she doesn't believe I will do anything more than tease. The mirth in her eyes seems to think I won't go any further in such a public setting, but she doesn't fucking know me.

I don't glance to see if we have anyone's attention, happy to bask in the bubble we seem to have created as neither of us say a word. There's no need to. Not one. And when the pad of my finger runs over the lace of her panties, I almost groan, my cock jolting in my pants.

Her teeth dig into her bottom lip, her cheeks dusting a pale pink, but otherwise she doesn't stop me, doesn't close her legs, and doesn't push me away.

No is a word I'm aware of. Fuck, I'm happy to take it as a full sentence without question on my end, but she's not giving it to me.

Slipping under the lace, my mind desperate to know the color, I run my finger over her folds, surprised to feel how wet she is already. How long has she been needy? Does it link to her powers bursting inside of her earlier?

I rub my own lips together as I circle her clit. Once, twice, three times. I watch as her throat bobs when she swallows, the moan trapped there pleading to release as she holds still. I'm not at the best angle with my left hand, trying to remain discreet, but I can make it work. It'll be worth it.

Trailing down to her core, I tease her entrance, and again her thighs part wider, her knee brushing mine, and I wonder if her other is touching Xander. Sinking two fingers inside her, she gasps, ever so softly, unable to contain it fully, and I grin, swirling my fingers inside of her. The walls of her pussy tighten, silently begging for more, and I'm happy to oblige.

I can sense eyes on us, coming from Zen, Khaos possibly too, but I'm too deep in the desire to please her to let them interrupt now. Pulling my fingers from her pussy, I brace my glistening hand on the back of her chair as I lean in, dropping my right hand to her knee and following the same path I took moments ago, only quicker this time.

Leaning in close, my breath blowing against her ear as I yank the lace blocking my ease of access, hearing the material tear as it rips along the seam. I don't even glance to see if anyone else hears, too intoxicated by her as the remaining material still hangs off her waist.

A grin spreads across my face as her eyes somehow manage to widen even more, but I don't utter a word, instead, sinking my fingers back into her core.

"I didn't realize we had a little exhibitionist on our hands," I mutter against her ear, feeling her shiver before me as I fuck her with my hand, grinding my palm against her clit. Rhea can't seem to stop herself from rolling her hips against my hand, wanting more, and it only seems to strain my cock.

"There's a lot you don't know about me. Sexual preferences included," she mumbles back, catching me off guard, and I grin, loving the bite on her tongue as always.

"I'll know the taste of your honey," I reply, bringing my free hand to my mouth and running my fingertips over my bottom lip. I hear the intake of breath at my brazen act, and it leaves me wanting to wrap my hand around my dick, her juices coating my tip as I jerk off to her scent alone. But this isn't about me, this is my thanks to *her*.

Rhea's hand moves, clenching around my arm, desperate to contain her body's reaction to my touch, but it's difficult. To watch her fall apart at the seams, in a crowded room, enemies and friends alike surrounding us, it's a sight I'm suddenly desperate for.

"Come for me, little earthling, show me how much you appreciate my thanks," I whisper, watching as her brows knit together in confusion. Likely unsure of what I'm thanking her for, but she's too lost in the ecstasy rising within her as she leans in to hide her face from the rest of the table, bringing her lips to my ear this time.

"Don't. Fucking. Call. Me. That," she bites, grinding out each word in time with my thrusts, but I hear the way her breath catches, and just as I circle my fingers deep in her core, I feel Xander place his hand on her left thigh, squeezing tight.

The combination of both of our touches sends her over the edge, her breath stuttering in my ear as her pussy clamps down around my fingers, dragging every ounce of pleasure from my touch. When she eventually sags against me, completely wrung out, I can't wipe the salacious grin from my lips.

Pleased with myself, I reluctantly pull my fingers from her cunt, making a show of adjusting myself as Rhea falls back in her seat, watching my every move.

The room slowly begins to filter in, the noise, the smells, the eyes.

Looking across the table, I find Zen staring straight at me, eyes full of questions as Khaos grins, distracting the girls as they ramble about something I have no desire to get involved in.

It takes Rhea a moment to catch her breath, and when she does, she leans forward, placing her food order like nothing happened, before finally turning her gaze back to mine.

"What do I need to say you're welcome for?" she asks casually, and it makes my grin spread wider.

"For stepping in to help me," Xander replies before I

can, and I offer a simple nod in response. Frown lines crease her forehead, but I don't offer any other words as I reach for my bottle of water, unscrewing the lid to swirl my wet fingers around the rim.

Khaos chuckles under his breath as Rhea's eyes widen, jaw dropping as she watches me bring the bottle to my lips and swallow it down in a few gulps.

"You take care of us, we take care of you," I finally state, a shit eating grin on my face as I stretch my legs out in front. "In more ways than one," I add with a wink.

"We do have things to discuss though," Xander adds quietly, and she nods, tearing her gaze from everyone as she focuses on anything but our faces.

There's plenty to discuss, but there's a time and a place for a heavy conversation.

Orgasms however, must be seized whenever the moment strikes.

Like now.

TWENTY FOUR

RHEA

I take a deep breath, inhaling the fresh air with every move as I bask in the evening sun. It feels like an eternity since I've been able to do something so casual, normal. I definitely haven't found a minute since I arrived at Saints Academy, but after the mess of today, I had to quit my bullshit excuses and make it happen. For my own sanity more than anything.

Twisting my torso, I stretch my arms out to the side, my knee dipping as I extend the Warrior II position. I take another long, deep breath, checking in with each part of my body as I let the familiarity of my favorite yoga move wash over me.

Back in Phoenix Valley I would always go to the nearby park for free classes. It was run down, nowhere near as green as I imagine it once was, but it offered far more room than my shoebox apartment did. Which is why I find myself outside again.

After all the classes had finished for the day, I made my way back to Agion with Harmonia, before changing into a set of Academy issued shorts and t-shirt and heading down toward the lake.

I haven't been down here since Zen showed me snow. It still left me speechless and awe inspired as I remembered the soft and delicate snowflakes falling from the sky so easily. Now, it's back to its luscious green grass, pale blue waters, and cherry blossom trees, which were surprising for the time of year, but I guess anything goes in Paradise Heights.

Raising my hands above my head, I inhale slowly before bending in half to touch my fingers to my toes. Today has been a complete fucking mess. Utterly disastrous, no matter which way you looked at it.

It feels like too much has happened in one single day for it to even be real, but here I am, standing in the aftermath of my actions, and trying to wash it all away with some yoga.

From everything that happened in our Combat class with Xander, my own eyes glowing red in reaction to his amber orbs, and my uncontrollable flecks of magic desperate to rise to the surface at his anger and rage, I'm drowning in the secrets.

It was instinctive to intervene, even if the Elite called me into the drama too, it was natural to do so. The need to protect him, to protect what is… mine, was confusing as fuck. I've never felt that way toward anyone before.

I've gone from being intrigued by the hot Elites to being entirely consumed by them, and there is nothing I can do about it. It's like the magic inside of me knows what is best. Fuck my thoughts and life choices, right?

A sigh falls from my lips and I squeeze my eyes shut for a moment, desperate to not lose the rhythm and solace I had managed to find out here, so I attempt to think of something else. But I don't know whether it's better or worse when my mind immediately shifts to the other colossal mess of today.

Adonis.

Or more importantly, his goddamn magical fucking fingers.

I'd walked into the dining hall, head held high, thankful my eyes were no longer shining red, but when my eyes met his and he crooked his finger at me, I'd faltered.

"If you don't go over there and swim in some big dick energy, Rhea, someone else will," Harmonia had murmured with a chuckle, and I instantly found myself in an internal battle.

Part of me wanted to remind them I wasn't a puppet on a string for them to beckon closer, only for me to follow blindly into the darkness, while the other part of me was jealous as fuck. Which is exactly why I found myself putting one foot in front of the other and heading toward him without a second thought.

I'd seen the challenge in his eyes when he told me to take a seat. The one beside Khaos seemed like the safer option, a bigger space with less proximity to all of that big dick energy

Harmonia had murmured about. But it was like my body had a mind of its own again when I dropped down between Adonis and Xander. I surprised him too, I could see it flash in his eyes, and it's not like I sought his approval because of where I sat, but my chest blossomed with victory at managing to catch him off guard.

Fast forward to him 'thanking me', and I almost fucking blush again as I remember the way I fell apart at the fucking dining table with his fingers learning every groove of my pussy. Shattering into a million pieces in silence as Xander's hand clamped down hard on my thigh, my pent up energy exploding at their combined touch.

Watching him taste me afterwards had my pussy clenching all over again, leaving me a wanton, needy little whore, desperate for round two. I've avoided them ever since, confused with the way things seem to be transpiring between us at lightning speed. I still can't seem to align my mind and body; one thinking rationally about all the reasons why it's a bad idea, while the other seems to be driven by desire and does what it wants.

I place my fingertips down on the grass before me, slowly and calmly moving down into the cobra as I control my breathing, stretching the move a few more times before I fall into my meditating position.

Crossing my legs and bracing my palms on my knees, I keep my back straight and continue to control my breathing. It's so fucking refreshing to find a minute of calm among all of this crazy. I hadn't realized how much I needed this until my feet touched the ground but it feels short lived as I sense someone taking a seat beside me.

It's safe to assume that they're not a threat, since they could have attacked me with my eyes closed and they haven't, but it still doesn't stop my body from tensing in response to being caught off guard.

Happy to let whoever it is stew for a moment, I take a few more breaths, before I peer to my left. I'm not at all surprised to find a man sitting in the same position as me, a linen shirt covering his chest and a pair of loose shorts stopping at the knee. His feet are bare, just like mine, connecting with the earth beneath us as he rakes his fingers through his messy blond hair and offers me a calm smile.

Zen.

"I didn't know yoga was your thing," he finally says, turning his gaze to look out over the lake as the sky begins to shift in color, offering a glimmer of reds, pinks, and oranges as the sun sets.

"I didn't realize you knew me at all," I retort, quirking an eyebrow then instantly annoyed at myself for getting defensive for no reason, but he doesn't seem to acknowledge it, which is a relief.

"I haven't seen anyone do yoga without a mat before though," he adds, peering back at me, and I shrug. I don't respond, not wanting to admit it's because I could never afford one back home, and I still hadn't made my way down to the on-site shops here at Saints Academy to look. I refused to tempt myself with fanciful items when I know the bill would go straight back to fucking Dante. I'd rather make do with what I've got because, so far, that's been working. "I could use a partner, if this is something you enjoy. I don't know anyone else who does, and I find it calming," he states, making me wet my lips as I observe him.

Of course he's the yoga and meditating type, it's written all over him. I pause as I contemplate his question. Having someone to enjoy this peacefulness with sounds appealing but he could also distract me. "I'll think about it," I reply evenly, which earns me a nod in response.

Rising to my feet, I grab my bottle of water, taking a few gulps before reaching for my phone, ready to head back. Zen stands too, observing me without a word until I turn to him with a raised eyebrow.

I know he knows what Adonis did at lunch, I felt his eyes burning me as I shattered, and I know that also played a part in the intensity of it all, but neither of us have mentioned it since, and I'm quite happy to keep it that way.

"I'll walk you back," he finally murmurs, making me squint in confusion as I turn to head through the woods with him right beside me.

"You don't need to," I grumble in response, eyeing him,

but he doesn't seem to falter.

"I insist," he says with a soft smile, which only seems to make my brows knit together in confusion. It always feels so hot and cold with these guys, but I can't decide if that's my own doing or theirs. Maybe both? Are they always trying to be this attentive, and it's me who allows certain things over others, unsure of their intentions and putting up my guard?

Fuck if I know. But it definitely doesn't help that I can't pinpoint how they view me as a person. Which is exactly why the next words stumble from my lips as I keep pace.

"Do I *look* like a damsel in distress to you?" His eyes round in surprise, but he immediately shakes his head.

"No."

"Do I *act* like a damsel in distress to you?" I continue, and I don't think his head stops shaking as he replies again.

"No."

"Do I *cry out for help* like a damsel in distress to you?" I ask, angrier, annoyed that he's not engaging with me.

"No," he replies soothingly, and it's my turn to shake my head this time.

"Then stop making me fucking feel like one," I grumble, turning my gaze from his as I step through the last line of trees, the gothic Academy building coming into view.

He remains silent for a moment, and I almost think he isn't going to utter another word as we climb the steps and enter the main building, leaving me with the peace and quiet in my mind, but I'm wrong, oh so fucking wrong.

There's no one around, which is surprising. As we near the portal to take us to Agion, his hand grips my wrist, tugging me toward him as he slips inside a nearby empty office.

I gape at him in surprise as he tilts me back against the wall, shutting the door behind us. I don't see a thing around me, my eyes locked on his as they shimmer with a mixture of emotions I can't quite decipher. And right now, I don't have the energy to question it.

"Do not mistake my calmness and protectiveness for something it's not, Rhea. It isn't about me underestimating you, viewing you as a damsel, or any other bullshit like that. It's about me wanting to discuss who or what we all are to each other, because this all means something to me. Whatever it actually is that's going on."

My jaw only slackens further as I scramble to find something, anything to say in response as heat crawls up my neck, desperate to consume me.

"If this is about the sealed souls bullshit then—"

He cuts me off with a finger to my lips, shaking his head at me as he interrupts. "It's not bullshit, and it's more than that and you know it. It was more than that when it happened, and it's more than that now, but it's there too, strengthening every inch of this thing between us all and you know it. You just won't admit it."

Do I though? Do I really? Because I don't fucking think

I do.

He inches closer, his nose almost close enough to brush mine, and I shiver under his intense gaze. I can practically see him internally trying to piece together how he can word it so it gets through my thick skull. "If anything, Rhea, it may help with making everyone else back off if we're announced as being in a committed relationship," he states, my frown deepening, my eyes zoning in on his lips as they explain.

"I can't Not now, not yet," I whisper, unable to tear my gaze from his full lush lips as he slowly trails his tongue over them.

I can feel his need to push back and state his full argument in the way he somehow manages to step closer, his waist sweeping against mine as his hand tightens on my wrist, but whatever words were about to stumble out of his mouth are cut short when the sound of a door slamming makes us both jolt.

Zen takes a step back, eyes darting to the door looking for the intruder, but there's no one there, the noise is coming from the side door to my right that must lead into another office. Low mutterings filter through, the topic of conversation seemingly intense as two people shuffle around.

We don't move another inch, planted in place so we don't get caught for being in here, but my pulse begins to ring in my ears when their words finally become loud enough for us to hear.

"Can you believe the vision she just foretold?" a woman

asks, shock and surprise etched into her voice, and Zen's fingers flex around my wrist as he steps back toward me, almost trying to shield me as we both listen.

"I didn't think it was possible," someone else responds with a sigh, and I twist my lips to the side, intrigued to know what has the administration staff so worked up.

"How are we supposed to go through all that again? I can't handle the mere thought of it, nevermind the actual first-hand experience," the first lady cries out, tension radiating through the wall as the other seems to try and comfort her.

"What has me most concerned is the fact it will be at the hands of a student at this very Academy. You and I both know Zellus will not allow it. Never again."

Allow what? I frown, glancing to Zen to see if he can piece together more than I can from what they're saying, but he offers me a subtle shake of his head in response.

The gossiping women don't leave us in suspense for long though, the fear that's sparked within them falling from their tongue so freely.

"The darkness is coming. Again."

TWENTY FIVE

RHEA

I step into the huge hall for my Skills class with Professor Fury, catching the side profile of his constant scowl as I drop my satchel down beside Harmonia's, who offers me an apologetic smile before bouncing over to the group of angels in the far right corner of the room.

Shaking my head at her sympathy, I feel Zen's gaze from where he stands near Harmonia, under the same umbrella of magic skills since they're both descendants of angels. I refuse to meet his eyes, instead, observing the room before me.

After what I overheard yesterday with Zen, I can't help but cast my gaze over every single person in here, wondering if they're the one from the vision the women were talking about. The one who will bring back the darkness. But it all confuses the hell out of me.

The plain cream walls behind me separate the room from the rest of the main building, but otherwise the entire space is surrounded by stained glass, like an atrium. Yellows, blues, greens, and reds splatter the glass, some in random marks, others in intricate details of Gods that have passed. Hecate, Apollo, and even Zeus is there, but he's still among us.

I'm surprised the rest of the members of the Hex aren't up there with him, but who am I to question the decorative choices of the Academy?

Flooded with natural light, the room practically glows. It's a pity it's my worst class with such a beautiful setting. Since everything in here is skills based, I'm practically useless until we know which species I descend from. The angels take the far right, demons beside them straight ahead, leaving the Gods to take the far left. This then puts the vampires directly to my left and the shifters to my right. And me… floating somewhere in between.

After all of the conversations with the Elites, they seem certain I'm not a wolf or a vampire with the little bursts of power we've seen, so I'm ultimately wasting my time when I have to watch their areas. It's not like I can mention our findings to Professor Fury though. That's completely pointless and I don't really think he'd give a shit about our theories.

As everyone else separates off, I step toward the man in question, watching as he taps away on his laptop for a moment, propped on the only piece of furniture in the room; his desk.

He doesn't meet my gaze, not right away, completely inconvenienced by the sight of me, but I don't care if he likes me or not, and I don't care if he doesn't appreciate me floating between groups. It's not like it was my choice, but the way he glares at me tells me he feels different.

Asshole.

His brown hair stops just below his ear, brushed back off his face like he constantly has a reason to run his fingers through it. With his chiseled jawline and piercing mint green eyes, you could almost say he's attractive, but his permanent scowl ruins the entire thing.

With my sports shorts and tee on, I fold my arms over my chest, my hair swept back in a loose ponytail, I glance around once more while waiting for him to call the class to order.

Who had a vision that could predict the future?

Who would bring the darkness back? And why?

It was a part of the war no one talks about, fear rendering them mute, so I have no idea what it was actually about, but the uncertainty easily slips through your bones as you hear a tremble in the voices of those who experienced it. Once Nyx died, so did the darkness.

What had me more intrigued was whether this knowledge would go public. My gut said no, but it also wouldn't surprise me if Zeus wants to look like a hero in front of the world as always. The guy is delusional. Or from my perspective he is at least.

Like we should thank him for his existence since he laid Nyx to rest and 'saved the world'. Gag. The man has no hint of humbleness about him, and watching his desperation to receive that recognition was cringeworthy.

"Something on your mind, Miss Harrington?" Professor Fury asks, a hint of a snarl on his lips like my mere pondering in his presence is an insult to his entire existence.

"Nothing for you to concern yourself with," I retort back, quirking a brow in challenge, but he simply scoffs, rising from his hunched position over his laptop and walking around me to address the class.

I don't move, happy to stare at the back of his head while he speaks. It sure as fuck beats looking at him. He claps his hands once, the room falling into silence as he captures everyone's attention.

It doesn't even make sense to me why we would have this class before our magic comes through. I mean, what fucking skills are we training and perfecting if nothing has developed? Even if I had a group to slot into, it all seems pointless to me, yet here we were.

"Today we're going to go through where each magical being garners their magic from. Shifters, demons, and vampires, each pull magic the same way. While angels and Gods can pull from one source or multiple, it's never known until the time comes," Professor Fury explains. "We're going to delve deeper into the details, with the leaders of each house offering expert knowledge and advice as we take a closer look at what the future looks like for you." He places his hands on his hips, nodding at the house leaders who hover by the door, and they slip into the room, each heading toward a different group. "Any questions, ask them. It's going to be important for you to understand every aspect of magic before you reach your full potential," he adds, before waving his hand and dismissing the class, returning their focus back to the assignment.

Murmurs pick up again as everyone chats in small groups, while I continue to hover around Fury as always.

I notice Sky, the pretty blonde who is the head of Agion, over with the Gods. I've never spoken to her before, only seeing her in passing a few times, but I think a lot of that is because third years oddly don't seem to be around that much. Unless I'm just not looking hard enough.

The other leaders though, I have no idea who they are, but I'm sure I'm about to find out.

"Keep up," Fury barks, not bothering to look back over his shoulder as he heads towards the vampire group, Khaos catching my eye instantly.

No one should be that fucking hot with messy, uncut hair that dangles in front of their eyes, but here he is, melting my panties without a single word. His piercing green eyes find mine as we near, but he doesn't say anything, which isn't out of character for him, but the way his eyes rake over me tells me everything I need to know.

Khaos is the most confusing out of the Elites, or is it Adonis? Xander? Zen? Fuck… all of them are, but Khaos somehow manages to get under my skin in a way I can't even begin to explain.

He shakes his head to brush his hair from his eyes, but as soon as he finishes shaking it, it returns to its previous position, and he doesn't attempt to correct it again. A slight tug at the corner of his lips tells me he can clearly feel me watching him, and I quickly clear my throat, diverting my gaze as I get a grip on my goddamn hormones.

"Hi, for those of you that don't know me, my name is Marco, and I'm the head of Aeras," the tall guy in the middle of the group states, a casual smile on his lips as he glances around at everyone. "Since we're all descendants of vampires here it's safe to assume that we'll all gain the same skill sets, which will all manifest from the same source. Can anyone tell me what that is?"

I look around the group, waiting for someone to shout the answer, but to my surprise, a few of them side glance at each other, seemingly unsure of what to say. But what shocks me even more, is the eye roll Khaos gives, before planting his hands on his hips and answering in a bored tone.

"The magic comes from within us, but it will deplete if not replenished," he states, and a few nod in a mixture of agreement and understanding.

"That's correct, and what replenishes us?" Marco asks,

cocking a brow as he glances for someone else to answer, but his eyes settle on me with a hint of interest.

In an instant, his fangs extend as his mouth widens and he's before me in a flash, my wrist poised at his lips as his eyes flash red. Not the same as mine. Bright, yet harsher. Almost dangerous.

Before I can fully process what he's about to even do, a fist connects with the side of his face, snapping his head to the side. It startles the both of us as he releases his grip on me to turn to the person behind the fist. My heart is racing like crazy in my chest as my arm continues to hang in the air with the utter surprise of everything transpiring, freezing me in place, only to find Marco and Khaos standing toe to toe in a stare off.

What the ever loving fuck just happened?

"Blood," Khaos spits, anger deepening the green of his eyes as he glares at Marco. "We need blood to replenish us, and we take it from whoever and whatever we please. Except. Her."

I can feel eyes looking between me and the pair in the center, but I don't pull mine from Khaos. The anger that radiates from him is indescribable, yet Marco simply chuckles, his teeth retracting as he swipes his hair back off his face, playing everything off like it was a big joke.

I want to find the words to defend myself, tell this fucker not to lay hands on me ever again, but it feels stupid and irrelevant now since Khaos already has. The other vampires stare at him in a mixture of shock and worry.

Khaos doesn't move an inch as Marco shakes it off, until his eyes wander back to me. "Do you fucking hear me, Marco?" he grinds out, but before Marco can respond, Professor Fury steps in to split them up.

"How about you two calm down and go through the skills a vampire inherits while I escort Miss Harrington to a different group," he hisses, fists clenched at his side in distaste as he offers me a disapproving look.

Of course this is my fault. Dick.

I can't help but roll my eyes at the back of his head as he takes off, but before I step away, I take one final look at Khaos, wanting to make sure he's alright, but he waves me off without a word, reminding me just how much he can get under my skin.

Trailing after Professor Fury, I catch sight of Zen staring between Khaos and me, a questioning look in his gaze like he wants to make sure everything's okay, but I can't give him an answer to that because I honestly don't know, so I focus on the shifter group Fury leads me toward instead.

As we come to a stop beside the group, the girl standing in the center stutters slightly under Professor Fury's intense gaze. "Please, continue, Farrah," Fury states with a wave of his hand, and she quickly clears her throat, glancing at me with a small smile.

I don't offer one in response, my attention slipping to the guy behind her as he stares intently at me. Fuck, any other time and I'd be putty in Xander's hands, but after Khaos' little show, I feel like my head is spinning with it all.

His brown eyes trail over me, a cocky grin playing on his lips as Farrah continues with what she was talking about. "One of the important parts of being a shifter, no matter which form you take, is the mating process." I immediately want to die at the topic of conversation, and from the way Xander's lips turn up even more, he can sense the truth in that thought too. Asshole. "Does anyone know why?"

"Because males only choose one mate, and even for females, it is a sacred connection," someone answers. Xander wets his lips as he continues to stare at me, and I balk at the statement, turning to the redhead who spouted off the information as Farrah hums in agreement.

"That's right. The mating process is something uncontrollable, our shifters take over as they claim what we believe is ours," Farrah adds, a ripple of noise flowing through the group as I frown in confusion.

"But, like, what if your mate dies or something?" I ask, not considering if it's insensitive or not, but it's too late to retract it now. My brain is locked onto the fact that Xander and I sealed souls, and I can only assume that links to this whole mating bullshit too. Fuck my life.

"There's no one else for us. Ever." Those words come from Xander himself in a commanding and final tone, one-hundred percent certainty in his eyes as he speaks, leaving my mouth dry as I process what he's saying.

"That's right. A shifter's mating ceremony is practically a wedding. Til death do we part," Farrah explains, and I feel a flush wash over me.

Is she saying I'm fucking married to Xander? What the hell. Of all the times to join this group, it had to be now. I can't handle this.

Please for all that is good in the world, let Professor Fury continue our walk around the species world.

As if answering my prayers, Fury simply begins to walk away, and I waste no time following behind him as quickly as possible.

He surprisingly doesn't pause near the demons, moving straight toward the Gods section, but I manage to overhear a little bit of what the woman is explaining.

"We all know where our magic comes from guys, am I right?" she says with a waggle of her eyebrows, and it instantly whirls me back to the first time I met Adonis in our adjoined bathroom.

Sex.

They draw magic from sex.

Of course they do.

Adonis catches my eyes, offering me a wink as I pass, and I manage to hold back the eye roll I want to give him. The memory of yesterday, the way he played my body so perfectly, has my thighs clenching as I walk.

Is this class over yet? I need a cold fucking shower or

maybe four.

As we approach the Gods group, we find Sky in the middle of answering a question, and she doesn't falter or bother to acknowledge our arrival as she offers the group her full attention. I don't know what it is about her, but she always gives off a badass, confident vibe, and I'm here for it. The supernatural world of Paradise Heights feels daunting to me. Maybe that's because I arrived twenty-two years late and she simply takes it all in stride. Like she was born for this.

"Every God, no matter which line of descendants they are from, pulls an endless supply of power from within themselves. We don't require replenishing, we can never lose our powers, we are rare as I'm sure you can see, our group is much smaller than the others," she says with a smile before flicking her gaze over to the demon group. "The only member of the school here today that is a direct descendant of a God is Adonis. Child of Persephone and Hades, who, because of his lineage, will flourish at the top of the demon's power structure," she says, almost in awe as she eyes him.

My body jolts with a surprising burst of anger, unhappy that she's looking at him, but I bite my tongue, the taste of copper evident in my mouth. He's not mine. It's not my concern, but why the fuck am I mad about it?

He literally is the child of Hades and Persephone.

Hades and fucking *Persephone.*

What the fuck?

No wonder he's an Elite with half of the student population dancing around him, never mind the fact that he'll grow into his incubus powers and fucking glow with strength under all of the sexual tension he creates.

My Gods.

Literally.

Finally turning her glance to Professor Fury and me, Sky offers us a dismissive tight smile. "Really, Professor? I think it's almost irrelevant for her to be present here. If she was a God, she wouldn't have been living among the earthlings for so many years," she states blindly, instantly making my back stiffen.

Her clear sneer at me, and the use of that damn fucking nickname pisses me off.

I'm prepared for Fury to nod in agreement and shuffle me along, but to my surprise he quirks an eyebrow at her. "This is my class, Sky, you'll do well to remember that," he retorts, folding his arms over his chest in challenge as he nods for her to continue.

With a pout of her lips and a roll of her eyes, she turns her back to us and continues to address the group.

And to think I thought this bitch was cool a minute ago. Is she related to Selene? She has that supreme bitch vibe about her. Speaking of the cunt, I spy her in my peripheral vision with a grin on her lips as she nods along with Sky as she speaks.

"As rare as we may be, there's a hierarchy among the

Gods which exceeds all else. Zeus, our gracious leader, who you will begin to spend more time with as you come into your third year, sits at the top." The pride in her voice is sickening, but it's intriguing to learn that they actually spend time with members of the Hex the closer they get to leaving the Academy. "He earned his rightful place overseeing the Hex and the Gods when he brought the Goddess Nyx to her knees, wiping the darkness away with her and all of her descendents."

"Her descendents?" someone asks, a frown on their face matching mine, and Sky gleams with pride as she turns to answer her.

"Yes. Her descendents. We couldn't have her children remaining when she left. The risk of them manifesting the same powers and bringing the darkness back was too high of a risk," she states casually, like she's explaining why rain is… wet.

But what she doesn't realize is she's just added another piece to the puzzle of what Zen and I heard yesterday in the office.

The darkness is coming. Again.

Does that link to what she's saying?

My gaze moves to Zen's on instinct, my brain considering whether I should mention it to him or not, but I don't truly know how much I can lean on him, or any of them for that matter. Maybe I need to catch Harmonia up on the gossip swarming the staff at the moment.

"Come," Fury grunts, turning his back to the Gods as he

trudges away, and I reluctantly follow. I want to stay and learn more about what she's saying, even though she's a bitch.

His long legs cut the distance to the angels quicker than I expect, and I have to rush to keep up, avoiding Adonis' smirk again as we head for the far right of the room, only to have Zen shuffle to my side the moment I stop at the edge of their circle. I literally can't escape them.

The woman in the middle of the group offers me a gentle smile as I approach, but my focus is on the hot blonde beside me with his hazel eyes trying to search mine.

"Thank you for joining us, my name is Athena. We were just discussing where angels pull their magic from," she says directly to me before turning back to the group. "I know we just mentioned it, but to recap and make sure you were all listening," she says with a soft chuckle, "Can you tell me where we pull our magic from?"

Zen inches closer, his knuckles brushing against mine he's that close, as Harmonia smiles wide and answers Athena's question confidently. "Either from the earth, water, air, or fire."

"That's correct. Angels can pull magic from one of the elements, or multiple, but it's also what makes us the most compassionate species. We're softer, calmer, and more caring than the others, but we shouldn't be overlooked, because we are just as fierce when angry. Am I right?"

The group chuckles as I feel Zen lean in even closer. After we overheard the conversation yesterday, I slipped from between his fingers and didn't look back, but it seems now I have no way out. I should have known it was coming. If Zen is anything, he's persistent.

"Would you agree, firecracker? Or are you going to run off again before you can find out?" he whispers against my ear, making me shiver.

"I don't know what you're talking about," I murmur, not turning to glance at him as I spy Harmonia looking between the two of us with a grin. She loves watching me fight my truth about the Elites.

Maybe it's denial, but it's comforting right now and it's the only thing I seem to have control over.

"You don't? I told you what would help settle the tension and you ran. Do I have to run damage control alone, or are you willing to cooperate?" he asks, his fingers grazing my waist as he somehow manages to inch even closer.

What on earth is he actually talking about?

This class has been a complete information overload, and this is toppling me over the edge. If anything, I thought he would be the calmest of the four of them, but right now, that seems to be Adonis. Who would have thought?

I have a vampire laying claim to me so that no one takes my blood, which I won't argue against, but what the fuck?

A werewolf telling me he will only ever have one mate, *after* sealing souls with me.

An incubus happy to use me to recharge his powers

when they come into effect. Public or not.

And an angel who… is not calm and collected right now like I expected him to be.

Turning to face Zen, my brain mush from the past hour of revelations, I find a determined look in his eyes as he peers into mine, seemingly touching my soul with his gaze. I squint at him, a hint of confusion burning under my skin.

"Actions first, explanations after," he says, almost like a promise as his breath blows over my lips, and in the next second, his lips touch mine.

TWENTY SIX

ZEN

Her lips mold to mine perfectly, her eyes fluttering closed as she gives into the kiss, any objection that was about to fall from her mouth cut short.

It's not how I expected our first intimate moment to be as I brought my lips to hers, but she left me no choice, and I had to do something to rectify the situation. Hopefully now, after this, she will damn well listen while I explain my actions.

Rhea's body tilts toward mine, facing me head on as I run my tongue over her parted lips, my hand falling to her waist as I pull her closer, my throbbing cock nestling against her stomach.

I kissed her because someone was watching our interaction and I had to move fast, but now, it's like no one is in this room, fuck, no one in the universe exists except us.

Her mouth is an addiction alone, I can't imagine what the rest of her body would do to me.

Teasing my lips against hers slower now, I cup her jaw, tilting her head to the perfect angle to deepen the kiss, when Professor Fury interrupts us, clearing his throat loudly enough to wake the dead. I apply pressure once more before I reluctantly force my mouth from hers.

Panting for breath, I watch as she does the same. With rosy cheeks and a heaving chest, Rhea's eyes slowly blink open, her lashes flutter as she withdraws out of a daze, before her bright blue orbs peer up at me.

A pleased smile uncontrollably takes over my face as I look down at her, my mind sure I did the right thing, when she seems to realize where we are and takes a step back. I let her, dropping my hands to my sides as she folds her arms over her chest in an act of total disbelief. But she's not embarrassed at having the attention of everyone in the room.

"What the fuck, Zen?" she whisper-yells under her breath, glancing at the group from the corner of her eyes, but I don't stray my eyes from her, not even when Professor Fury finally opens his mouth.

"Care to keep public displays *out* of my classroom, Miss Harrington?" he grumbles, Rhea's cheeks tinting deeper as I bite back a smirk. "You know what? We're done for the day. You're all dismissed. Get out," he barks, his words angry and choppy as his disapproving tone fills the room.

Thank the Gods.

Now I can take Rhea somewhere private and explain myself, but before I can even mutter a single word, she takes off. I stand and watch in surprise as her feet carry her toward the door, mingling between the students who are all more than happy about an early finish. She manages to grab her satchel without even pausing or waiting for Harmonia, while I just gape in surprise.

Fuck.

I thought after everything at Christmas, the time we got to spend together, and the connection that suddenly formed between her and Xander, that we'd fall into some kind of communication much easier, but she's making it more difficult than I care to admit.

Yesterday, after I watched her fall apart at the dining table with muted gasps and ecstasy at Adonis' touch, I thought there may have been progress, but when I ran into her later in the day, I was wrong again. Rhea Harrington is a conundrum.

Getting back to the main Academy building, I couldn't take another step without almost forcing her to listen, but when I pinned her against the wall, all I could think about and focus on was her lips. Then we were interrupted by the administration staff and their concerns over some vision about the darkness. Rhea was able to use that moment to slip away from me, just like now.

Double fuck.

I drag my hand down my face, my mind scrambling to think of a way to get her to hear me out, when Adonis appears at my side. The rest of the class heads for the doors after Rhea, while I continue to stand and stare at the exit she just took. I'm almost positive if I chase after her, it would only push her farther away.

I'd tried to approach the subject calmly yesterday, but that did me no good. Which leads to today, and *them* watching, which is what forced my hand, I just hope she can forgive me. But if that kiss is anything to go by and her physical reaction, I'm hoping there's nothing to forgive at all.

Xander and Khaos appear simultaneously before Adonis can even speak, each of them looking at me expectantly, when Harmonia appears in front of me with a shake of her head. With her white hair tied back off her face and her pink eyes darkening as she glares at me with a twist to her lips, I know she has something to say. And I know she won't hold back.

"Honestly, I don't know what the fuck is wrong with you guys. I've never known anyone, let alone a group of four, who fuck up as often as you lot, and you're supposed to be Elite," she says with a sarcastic tone and a roll of her eyes. "Get your shit together, or instead of encouraging my friend to explore whatever *this* is, I'll be pushing her to run for the goddamn hills, like I did when she first caught your gaze," she adds, her teeth snapping together in anger, and I offer a single nod in response while the others remain silent, watching her with a hint of surprise.

Harmonia has always just been… Harmonia. We crossed paths for sure, especially since we live in the same hall, but never really had a conversation or deeper interactions, until Rhea made an appearance. But I heed her warning well, because just like Athena said, we are as fierce as we are calm.

As she retreats, storming out after her friend, I turn to my own, all of whom have a mixture of emotions on their faces, silently communicating with their eyes that I need to hurry up and explain my actions.

"What the fuck just happened?" Xander asks, rubbing the back of his neck as he stares me down and I shrug, wetting my lips as I try to take a calming breath. It's not that I regret my actions, but now all I feel is frustration. Knowing she's run off only adds to my stress.

I don't respond at first, just flicking my eyes in the direction I know *they're* still standing in, and the three of them offer no hint of saying any more. I shake my head as I brush past Khaos and Xander and walk toward my own bag.

I'm not having the rest of the conversation here, there's too many people around, and you never know who might be listening in, intended or not. I can vouch for that after yesterday with Rhea.

Sensing the three of them falling into step behind me, I swipe my bag up off the floor and head for the exit. The few people that remain in the room step out of my way quickly as

I march past, raking my hand through my hair as I hurry to the portal.

I find myself back in Agion all too quickly, but of course she's nowhere in sight. She could have gone to the dining hall, but my gut tells me she's here hiding. I just need to have a firm conversation with my brothers first, before I fucking ruin things for *all* of us.

Stopping by Xander's door, he appears at my side moments later, palm flat to the wood as it clicks open, and I don't wait for him to invite me in, moving straight past him and flopping down on his bed with a sigh.

"Zen Elias, what the actual fuck is going on?" Khaos asks this time as Adonis shuts the door behind the three of them, and I give him my own pointed look for using my full name. Dick.

He fucking knows what's going on, we all do, but there's so much, we don't even know where to begin. We need to make sense of where we stand with regards to Rhea and figure it all out.

"What are your thoughts on Rhea, like for real, everyone's thoughts?" I ask, watching as the three of them stand taller at the mention of her name, even though she's exactly what we've been dancing around this entire time. We've had light conversation, but not enough.

"We all know what my thoughts are," Xander grumbles, pacing slightly in front of me with his hands out at his side.

"She's mine. Sealed souls, forever mate, all of that shit. I just need her to fucking see it like I do." He rolls his shoulders back, turning to face the three of us as Adonis sits on the bed beside me. "The class today didn't help when Farrah was talking about a shifter's mate and what that all means," he adds, hands on his hips as he hangs his head, and I nod in understanding. Although it's amazing for Xander that he's found his mate, Rhea is a different story.

Yeah, I can't imagine that going down well. She's far too skittish to truly understand what it all means, but that's about to change.

"That wasn't a good addition after Khaos went all growly on Marco," Adonis adds, a grin on his lips as he looks at the straight faced vampire before us. Khaos' eyes squint at being blatantly called out, but he shrugs like his actions made total sense.

"Marco was about to fucking bite her to prove a point for his little talk. I wasn't about to let that fucking happen. *No one* tastes her blood. Except me." He says it so matter of factly, but hearing the words drop from *Khaos'* mouth is far more surreal than he's letting on. He's been the quietest when it comes to the girl at the center of our attention.

Turning my focus back to Adonis, the others must do the same because his eyes widen as he raises his hand. "What? They didn't stop by my group today," he says quickly, before his lips spread into a wide grin. He's like a fucking cheshire cat.

"She just overheard Varna explaining where we get our power replenishment from."

I roll my eyes, watching as he beams with enjoyment, but my cock stiffens with the memory of yesterday all over again.

Fuck, I need to get a grip.

"And none of us have a clue what happened when she was over with the Gods," I state, but Xander scoffs.

"Maybe you can explain what happened with the angels, asshole," he states with a deadpan expression. Khaos and Adonis hum in agreement, and I swipe a hand down my face.

Right.

Me.

What did I do to tip her over the edge? Apart from the obvious. They know why I did it, which is why we're having this conversation now.

"Nothing. But we can't carry on with this weird as fuck hot and cold shit we have going on with her. We need to decide what's going to happen now, and make her see one way or another," I say, determination in every word as I look at my brothers. Xander nods in agreement, while Adonis and Khaos are a little more unreadable.

"To be clear, you mean you want us to admit we feel something for her so we can pursue her and claim Rhea as ours in front of everyone," Khaos surmises like he's reading my mind, hitting the nail on the head as I nod.

"Yeah, that."

Silence descends over us as the reality of the situation drenches the room. A mixture of hope and anxiety forming around us.

Resting my palms on my knees, I look at each of my brothers. I know we're all on the same page, every last one of us, but the difficulty here is the fact that some of them aren't ready to admit it. Which makes this all the more fun.

Besides, time is running out.

"We all know where I stand," Xander repeats again, which only seems to set Khaos' mouth in a harder line.

"That's because you got your fucking powers early. The girl could literally have a tight pussy with teeth that bites your dick off, and you're still going to think she hung the moon," Adonis says with a dramatic roll of his eyes. I hold back the smirk that's begging to cross my lips because he's right.

Xander cuts the distance between them lightning fast, his eyes flaring, bits of amber visible in his irises, as he crouches down so he's eye level with Adonis. "If you ever get the chance to seal your fucking soul, come talk to me, until then, keep your damn mouth shut because you know nothing about it," he growls, hands clenching as he stands tall and forces himself to take a step back.

Adonis glares back at him, but surprisingly keeps his mouth shut. Well, that's a first.

"I'm assuming after your public make out session, you're happy to be all in with her?" Khaos asks after a moment, rubbing the back of his neck as he eyes me, and I nod firmly, confident in my decision. "You need to say it out loud."

I always assumed it was because I'm an angel that I'm so in tune with my emotions, but who knows. All I know is I'm intrigued by Rhea, yet unsure of her all at once. But I can't step away now.

"Yes, I am." The surety in my tone leaves no room for doubt.

Adonis sighs as my knee starts to bounce a little, nerves getting the better of me as I wait for either of them to speak. We're split down the middle right now because Khaos and Adonis refuse to admit shit even though their actions speak loudly, which doesn't work in my favor at all.

"Fine," they both breathe out in sync, kicking my heart rate up as a grin spreads across my lips. Fucking finally.

"Don't sound so happy about it," Xander grumbles, folding his arms over his chest, but his eyes are the normal shade of brown so I'm not worried he's about to beat the shit out of one of them.

"We all need to consider the fact that even though *your* soul is sealed with hers, that doesn't guarantee all of ours will be as well," Khaos states, making total sense, but my gut tells me that fact is irrelevant anyway.

As long as I have my brothers and Rhea, I'm happy to

explore this.

"What will be, will be, but I'm completely on board to find out," I reply, rising to my feet.

The time is up on giving Rhea space. Our fate has been drawn without our say so, and we have to roll with it. Since Xander's outburst in our Combat class the other day, a lot has happened. A lot that she isn't yet privy too, but that's about to change.

Doing this will protect her and us at the same time, while letting us see where our feelings may take us.

"Do you want to head up there now?" Xander asks, and I nod, eyeing the other two who nod in agreement.

"I feel like I need a shot of something strong first," Adonis grumbles, opening the door and stepping out into the hallway.

"It's not going to be that bad," I say with a pointed stare, which he matches with one of his own.

"Of course not. Rhea Harrington seems like the quiet and pliant type who will agree to all of this shit without putting up a fight. My bad," he retorts with a humorless laugh, and I sigh.

Fuck.

He's right.

She's the most defiant, independent woman I've ever met in my life. She won't agree easily, but it'll only make it more fun when she's truly mine. *Ours.*

We already know enough about her to be sure, but I'm going to enjoy learning every piece possible. I'm hooked.

"Let the fun begin."

TWENTY SEVEN

RHEA

This stupid motherfucking Academy has done nothing but cause me stress. How am I supposed to push through and survive this place and learn all of the things I desperately need to know about this world, when there's drama at every turn, especially when it's not my fault?

Annoyingly, it's unavoidable drama too. Or it seems that way at least. I didn't initially instigate anything with Selene, the supreme bitch, yet I've felt her constant disdain and the brunt of her attack ever since the four guys started paying attention to me. Then there's the Elites. I never asked to be put in their path, but somehow I manage to find myself there anyway. I'm cursed at this school.

Scrubbing a hand down my face, I sigh, pulling my uniform from the closet as I discard my Academy issued shorts and t-shirt.

What irritates me more than anything, is how I fucking felt when Zen's lips unexpectedly touched mine. Euphoric. *Fucking ecstasy*. Just like every encounter I've had with the others. So as much as I may pretend I am nothing but physically attracted to them, there's something *more* there. Something I don't want to admit. Not even to myself.

It's hard with Xander. Fuck, with him, everything is out of control on an entirely different level. I might not know him, but it's as if my soul does. Like they were torn apart, and now we're here, finally joining them back together again.

But the intensity of it all doesn't make it any easier. If anything, it only fucks with my head more, and it makes me wonder if those emotions are bleeding into how I'm feeling about the others.

I'm lucky he hasn't smothered me, but whenever we're in the same room, I feel his eyes track my every move, his beast thrumming beneath the surface, and gods-fucking-dammit, it makes my thighs clench.

It seems like I have no say in the matter, but at the core of it all, even if I did, would I say anything different? The truthful answer to that question refuses to come to fruition in my thoughts as I tamper it back down and step into my school skirt.

I don't have long until the next class, but the feel of Zen's lips crushing against mine, in a way that's totally him, has my movements more sluggish than usual as I replay it over and over again in my mind.

Why?

Why would he do that? And in the middle of class?

Deep down I'm not complaining. Fuck, his lips were soft, full, and all-consuming, but it felt like he was making a statement, and cut of all the Elites, he seemed like the one least likely to do something in that manner. But that only made my temperature rise even more.

Fuck.

A knock booming from my door interrupts my internal turmoil, and I take one step toward it before pausing in place. No way in hell is that Harmonia, not with a knock like that. Which can only mean one thing.

The Elites.

Nope. No way. Not answering it.

I can't even consider facing them right now. I'll likely crumble before them like a fool, desperate to take the euphoria to another level.

A moment later, the rap of someone's knuckles gets even louder on the wood, rattling the door a bit, and I scoff, shaking my head as I busy myself with my Academy shirt. Slipping my arms into the sleeves, I begin to button it up from the bottom in time with the incessant pounding that is now joined by their deep, raspy voices.

"Rhea. Open the fucking door, we know you're in there." Xander's voice makes me pause, but I push past the instant pull

I feel toward him and shake my head. No they fucking don't know. They're just guessing. As if sensing my thoughts, a low chuckle seeps from his lips as he talks quieter, but still loud enough for me to hear. "I can smell your scent, little red riding hood. Or did you forget what you did to me."

Fuck.

Fuck. Fuck. Fuck. Fuck. Fuck.

I still don't utter a word in response as I continue buttoning up my shirt, turning my back to the door, like that will make a difference. Just as I'm nearing the last few buttons, the sound of a throat clearing makes me freeze.

Fuck. Fuck. Fuck. Fuck. Fuck.

Apparently it's my favorite word of the day but it's the only way I can seem to express thoughts about my current situation.

There's no way in hell that came from the other side of the door. I was too caught up in ignoring them to consider the other point of entry.

"If it isn't my favorite sweet treat. Fancy seeing you here, Rhea."

Adonis.

My hands clench at my sides, shirt forgotten as I turn to glare at him. "What the fuck, Adonis? Get the fuck out," I bark, pointing at the door right behind him, but he just smirks at my feeble attempt.

Leaning against the open door frame, he quirks an

eyebrow at me as he looks me over from head to toe, paying far too much attention to my breasts. I know there will be at least a hint of my bra revealed right now, but I refuse to shrink and hide under his gaze. I'm stronger, thicker skinned than that. He knows it too.

"Nah, I fingered you, honey, but I'm down for fucking too if you'd like?" His crude words turn my veins molten, not cutting me like glass, like they would if they came from someone else outside of the Elites. But what the fuck was with that nickname? As if sensing my internal question, he licks his lips, a reminder of what he did yesterday, and it makes sense immediately.

Rolling my eyes, I fold my arms over my chest, realizing my mistake far too late, but unable to rectify it now, instead I stare him down. "You're a dick."

That's all I've got? Get a grip, Rhea.

"You want to see my dick? Is that what I heard?" he retorts, leaning up off the doorframe to thrust his crotch in my direction a few times, before he reaches for the waistline of his shorts. Adonis has officially lost his mind.

I don't get a second to respond when a hand appears from behind him and shoves his head forward, knocking him off balance, and he stumbles a step or two. Like the damn fucking fool I am, I immediately stretch my arms out to catch him, but it's not necessary. I *know* it's not necessary. Although it doesn't stop him from moving straight into my embrace.

"Look what you did," I grumble, shoving him back hard as Xander, Khaos, and Zen slip into the room too.

My room.

My personal space.

My sanctuary.

Fuckers.

Xander's heated gaze is fixed on me. Khaos is trying to smother a dark laugh at Adonis who straightens himself and reluctantly takes a step back from me. While Zen casts his eyes around my room. A slight frown marring his forehead as he does, before settling his eyes on me.

"Can you all fuck off now?" I hiss, brushing my hair back off my face, using the hair tie on my wrist to pull it up into a high ponytail. My annoyed glare doesn't seem to concern any of them as Adonis flops down on my bed, getting comfortable as Khaos perches at the bottom, leg crossed over the other as he watches me. There is intensity and insinuation with every move they make.

It's like there's a challenge in their actions, their eyes, which only pisses me off more. Annoyance, frustration, and a hint of desperation oozes through me, sending more warmth through my veins and I want to scream.

"We need to talk," Zen says calmly, ruffling his messy blond hair as he remains in place, while Xander inches toward me, but still keeping enough distance away, like he knows what will and won't cause me to explode right now.

Test the waters with me, buddy, I dare you. Now isn't the time.

As much as I think it, my tongue won't move to let the words pass, like there's something stopping me, and I want to scream at that too.

"There's nothing to talk about," I manage to say, wanting to hurry this along so they'll fuck off and I can get to class, but Zen just shakes his head while giving me a heated, yet expectant look.

"You wouldn't listen yesterday, so I had to take action today." He says it so matter of factly, so simply, that I gape at him.

"Is that so?" I reply sarcastically, planting my hands on my hips as I match his stare with one of my own, but he doesn't falter at my attempt to look intimidating.

"Yes." The determination is clear in his tone, and I shake my head at his approach.

"And here I was thinking you're the calm, rational, and collected one of the group. Joke's on me," I state with a scoff, and he simply shrugs.

"Oh, I am." Fucker. I dread to imagine what the others would be like then if they were the ones to lead this conversation. I even catch a glimpse of Xander nodding in agreement with his friend slightly, which doesn't help.

Casting my gaze over Khaos and Adonis who continue to relax on my bed, I decide we need to move this along. I can't handle them in my space, not like this. It's too personal. I feel… consumed by them, all my rational thoughts ready to jump out the window into the mid morning sun so I can join them on my clean sheets. Tempting but not happening.

I clear my throat, stiffening my spine as I get a grip on myself and turn to face Zen. "What's so important it couldn't wait, and had you practically claiming me with your mouth in the middle of class?"

Zen's eyes darken at the mere mention of what happened, his tongue dragging ever so slow along his bottom lip as he stares at my mouth. I almost think he's going to cut the distance between us and do it again, but he manages to release a sigh and begins to explain. "Xander's eyes didn't go completely unnoticed yesterday, Rhea," he says calmly, and a frown instantly mars my face.

"Wait, what? By who? Have they said anything?" The words come out of my mouth in short, quick bursts as I glance over at Xander. All I see from him is a muted smile and I know why that is instantly. I'm showing my fucking hand, unable to smother the fact that I am indeed concerned about him, but I don't give a shit. His safety is paramount to me, whether I like it or not, and as I continue to stare at him, waiting for the answer, his grin only spreads wider.

Pulling my gaze from him, I glance at the others, and it angers me to no end to see matching smirks on their faces too. I fell right into their damn trap.

Fucking hell.

"Who do you think?" Khaos finally asks, a quirk of his eyebrow, and my veins instantly turn to ice.

"Selene," I breathe out, worry rattling through my tone. Fuck. This is worse than I thought.

"Ding. Ding. Ding," Adonis chimes in, propping his face on his hand as he looks at me. Why isn't he angry, concerned, and ready to tear everything to hell like I am?

"We can brush it off. I'll beat her within an inch of her life if I have to. She fucking deserves it anyway after what she tried to do to me. Fuck, she will use this to her advantage and expose Xander," I growl, my body dripping with anger, finding an excellent excuse to do just that, like her attacking me alone wasn't a good enough one.

"Right now, your red eyes make me believe you," Khaos says, calmly, almost softly, and when I look into his piercing green pools I can't read what emotions are crossing through them.

Fuck.

These goddamn eyes.

Turning my back on the four of them, I try to take a few calming breaths, but it does little to help when I can feel all of their eyes burning into the back of me.

"Please, someone talk. Tell me what we do or what I need to do," I mumble, rubbing at my closed lids to no avail, no solutions coming to mind, but I stop when Zen speaks.

"Well, that's the reason I had to take action today," he explains, making me pause. Maybe he should stop talking instead. I can't imagine my eyes dimming back down to my usual blues if this links back to his lips crushing against mine. When I don't respond, a hand on my arm pivots me on the spot to face them again. I trail my eyes up the arm that belongs to Xander, my gaze settling on his as they flash amber around the edges.

Without a single word from him, I feel every ounce of reassurance he's sending my way, and with a deep breath, I nod, focusing back on Zen to continue.

"I came to speak to you yesterday because Selene has been devising a plan for herself," he states, making my jaw clench and my eyes turn to slits as I wait for him to continue. I fucking knew it.

"What?" I bite, eager to know what the sly bitch has been up to, but nothing prepares me for the words that fall from Zen's mouth next.

"She told Zellus that she believes her soul is sealed to Xander's."

If anyone else adds anything to the conversation, I don't hear it over the sound of my heart thundering in my chest and my pulse ringing in my ears. My vision clouds over and all I can visualize is killing her.

My hands lift to my head, fingers lacing as I squeeze my eyes shut and try to contain the rage burning within me. I bet they're loving the sight of this right now, me breaking down over something that involves them, when it's so far from what I want.

"Like fuck," I hiss, letting the rage consume me. That bitch. That stupid, motherfucking, supreme bitch. "Over my dead fucking body," I add, my chest heaving as Adonis' chuckle filters through my mind. I cut him a glare, but he doesn't stop, his grin spreading wider at my dismay. He is loving my reaction, and part of me wants to rip his balls off.

Zen clears his throat, drawing my attention back to him as he takes a step closer, his hands raised in surrender. He considers taking another step, but to my surprise, Xander's arm swings out and halts him in his tracks.

I wet my lips, unable to turn and glance at him in fear of what emotions I might see in his eyes, and thankfully, Zen continues talking. "We needed to show that our unit has already chosen someone else so what she's saying can't be possible."

I release a breath of relief. That makes sense. That's a totally on-point explanation. Except…

"So you chose me."

"So we chose you."

The words are heated as they fall from Zen's lips, and I turn to Xander to see the confirmation on his face too. The longing smolder makes my body zing with electricity, knowing full well our bodies claimed each other, the pair of us unable to stop it.

I love it and hate it all at once.

I don't want to be forced into this situation, yet the thought of them choosing anyone else fills me with an embarrassing level of fury… and even pain.

Clenching and unclenching my hands, I drag in another long breath through my nose, and exhale through my mouth, trying to calm myself as I look at the situation objectively.

"Okay. So what does that mean for me? For us?" I ask, placing my hands on my hips as I make eye contact with the four of them. Adonis, to Khaos, to Zen, and ending with Xander.

"It means you are ours and we are yours to everyone around us," Adonis states simply, like it is the easiest equation, making my brows crinkle in confusion as I look back at him still casually taking up my bed.

"You want to *fake date* me?" I clarify, confusion swarming me as I try to decipher how I feel about that, but I don't get far before Xander cuts in.

"No, we actually want this to work. We voted and it was unanimous," he states, a soothing tone to his voice, but his choice of words make my back stiffen.

"Oh, you voted. I'm so glad deciding my relationships is a democracy," I say with a scoff, defensively folding my arms back over my chest. I don't know what to do with my fucking hands. I feel open, exposed… vulnerable, and I don't fucking like it. The standoffish approach I've been taking toward them is slowly beginning to crumble.

"It wasn't like that and it won't be like that," Zen adds, trying to soften the situation, but I just offer him a glare in response. "There's no half-assing this. We have to be all in or not at all, Rhea," he adds, and I purse my lips.

"Does that rule apply for all of us, or just the four of you? I'm trying to figure out if I get a say or not because you're not giving me a straight answer," I mutter, confused with the emotions swirling around in my head. Today has been a complete fucking overload of information and I'm ready for it to be over, my mind can't handle much more.

Xander moves across the short distance that remains between us, standing toe to toe with me so I have to tilt my head up to look at him, the move alone irritating me. I'm expecting a power move, a show of dominance, but the softness in his eyes as I look at him doesn't match the stance, which helps me relax.

Lifting his hand to cup my cheek, I gaze up at him, scrambling the badass, independent woman I always am, yet in his hold, it's hard not to lean toward him. A move I'm not familiar with, but it seems whatever magic lives inside of me is more than happy to let him support us so my mind won't complain.

"This is everything to me, to us. Zen kissed you publicly because *Zellus* was watching in on the lesson, likely wanting to watch Selene and me, how we interact, which he was never going to see. So Zen did what I'm sure he's been wanting to do since you first walked through the doors of Saints Academy."

I'm lost to every word that falls from his lips. He moves his other hand to my waist as he consumes me, and my hands fall to his chest, clutching at the material of his shirt. "He claimed you. For himself, for me, for us, and for you. Don't be so stubborn to deny what is right here in front of you, Rhea. What's actually been here for a while. I feel it, you feel it, fuck, even if he doesn't want to admit it, Khaos feels it too."

I can't pull my gaze from his to look at the others in confirmation, but I feel all eyes on us. My mouth opens a few times, scrambling to find the right words, fuck, *any* words, but I seem to come up short.

"This is still your choice to agree but say yes, Rhea. Please just say yes, and we'll figure this out. Together."

Without any further thought or consideration, a piece of my soul settles and I'm no longer rendered speechless for the sake of one word. One word that will change the course of my future forever. I know it. I can feel it in my bones.

"Yes."

TWENTY EIGHT

RHEA

I have no idea what the fuck I've just agreed to, none at all. And as I look around at the four of them standing before me in their uniforms, ties and all, I can't seem to retract my decision. And do I even want to?

I'm out of my depth, that's for sure, but I want to figure this out. Together. Just like Xander said.

I wet my lips, wrapping my hand around the door handle, ready to leave, as Xander strokes his hand over the small of my back. Apparently uttering the word yes to him has led to small, intentional delicate touches that send shivers down my spine.

Fuck.

Zen continues to smile at me with the gentleness he always seems to exude, while Khaos and Adonis act exactly the same; aware of my presence but nothing more.

"We need to leave now, before the next class starts," I explain, and Zen nods in agreement as Adonis slowly pulls himself up from my bed, the spot he's clearly claimed as his own. Khaos ruffles his hair, teasing me with a full glimpse at his green eyes, but I force myself to clear my throat and turn back to the door. Otherwise I'll be finding an excuse to convince them to stay here with me so we can learn each other's bodies. Together.

Get a grip, Rhea.

Swinging the door open, I'm too busy scolding myself that it takes me a second to see Harmonia waiting for me. Her eyes bug out of her head as she watches every single one of the Elite's trail after me, and before I can offer any form of explanation, Xander laces his fingers through mine, like it's the most natural thing in the world, and I roll with it. Enjoying the feel of his hand around mine.

His calloused fingers against mine makes my pulse pound in my ears. The public show of affection is something I'm completely unfamiliar with, but I relax into his hold because even though I may not admit it out loud, it feels almost… nice?

I hear my door click shut behind the guys, but my focus is on Harmonia's gaze as she too looks down at our joined hands. "Is this a two of you thing or are you all…"

Her words trail off as Zen places his hand at the base of my spine, encouraging me toward the stairs in a show of Gods fucking knows what, and the grin on her lips slowly spreads as we begin to move.

"Altogether. Understood. Don't make me castrate any of you," she states, flicking her white hair over her shoulder with a hint of sass as she steps around us to be in front. Offering a pointed glare at all four of them, none of them utter a word in response, and I can't decide if it's because they don't want to piss her off or don't care about her threat.

My gut tells me the latter. These assholes do whatever they please, and since I've already committed and said yes, I don't think there's much Harmonia can do. But I bite my tongue and say nothing, too busy feeling the heat coming from everyone's bodies, Khaos and Adonis included as they walk behind us.

In a flash, we're down the wooden staircase and a few feet away from the billowing black smoke of the portal, when Xander's hand squeezes mine, gaining my attention as my steps slow. He pulls me to a halt as Harmonia steps through the portal first, giving me no time to tell her, but the way Xander grips my chin between his finger and thumb leaves me speechless anyway.

Gazes locked, his brown eyes swirling with desire, I swallow past the lump lodged in my throat as he adjusts us so we're standing chest to chest. This close, his presence is all-consuming, with his height, wide shoulders, and intense gaze. If it was anyone else, my protective instincts would kick in, fighting to get away, but with him, it's my fucking primal ones instead. Like the connection our souls now seem to have beckoned me closer, setting me on fire from the inside.

"Before we step out there and feel the eyes of everyone watching, I need you to know this isn't just a public show for their benefit or to prove Selene and I don't have sealed souls," he explains, my eyes rounding in surprise as I rake my teeth over my bottom lip.

"It's not?" I ask with a quirk of my brow, and he scoffs while Zen's hand at my back adds more pressure.

"It's not," he responds, repeating my words at me but in confirmation, and before I can utter anything else, his lips descend down on mine.

Gentle.

Soft.

Everything you *wouldn't* expect from a growly fucking shifter, yet for me, he somehow manages to offer a glimpse of him no one else gets to see. And I am so here for it. Learning them feels like I'm also learning myself too. It's exciting yet daunting, but I like it.

My hands slowly glide up his chest to circle around his neck, bringing him closer, his kiss deepening as he continues to hold my chin in place, tilting my head back so he has complete control. The part of him that screams alpha dominating shifter.

I fucking love it.

All too soon he pulls his mouth from mine, our chests

heaving with each breath as I pry open my eyelids I hadn't even realized had closed.

Fuck. He literally consumed me from the inside out.

Xander reluctantly loosens his grip on my chin, and the second he does, I'm spun on the spot, my chest colliding with Zen's as his mouth finds mine in an instant.

Holy fuck.

I've barely recovered from Xander's touch, so falling into Zen's is seamless as he cups my neck with one hand and grips my hip with the other. His tongue drags along my bottom lip, making a shiver run down my spine as he makes my body hum with desire.

Where Xander was dominating and consuming, Zen is taking my breath away with his slow pace and attention to detail, and he fucking knows it. My fingers find their way into his hair, but no sooner do I tug on the ends does he release me from his hold.

Blinking up at him, a shit eating grin spreads across his face as he makes a surprising show of readjusting himself beneath his Academy issued pants, and my thighs clench together with need.

Pleased with himself, he takes a step back, not uttering a single word as my vision is suddenly filled with the heated gaze of Adonis. Silently, he lifts his hand to my face, stroking his finger down my cheek as he inches closer, before running the tip of his finger over my lips, making them tingle as he smirks.

"I felt the need to stroke these lips since I'm already well acquainted with the others," he says with a hint of mischief flicking in his eyes, and I scoff.

"Fuck you. I'm—"

My retort is cut short when he replaces his finger with his lips, stunning me as I freeze in place. His mouth is firm, demanding, and hot as fuck pressed against mine. After a moment, my irritation at his choice of words is long forgotten as I mold my mouth to his. One brush, two brush, three, and he steps back with a heated gaze and a tense jawline. He's either mad for kissing me or because he had to stop, but my guess is he fucking liked it more than he cares to admit.

And the only reason that is my guess is because… well, I feel the fucking same.

My hands clench and unclench at my sides as I take calming breaths, but my body is high on desire now, desperate to take more from them, but we have classes to get to, people to be around, a show to put on, and I can't damn well start dry humping one of them in public. Can I? I can. But I won't.

Scrubbing a hand down my face as I release a heavy sigh, I jolt when a hand grabs my wrist, pulling it away from my body. Peering up, my eyes widen when I find Khaos standing toe to toe with me, and I'm instantly reminded of the night at the Halloween party. His body pressed up against mine as the bark from the tree was rough against my skin. And the kiss that accompanied the touch has done nothing to cool the burning need inside of me. Combined with the heated moment earlier when he defended me against Marco, and I'm left gaping at him in surprise.

Khaos is unpredictable.

When Xander and Zen pressed their lips to mine, deep in my gut I'd felt a hint of disappointment knowing not all of them would claim me like that, but I would accept us for what we are. Which for Khaos, was far too hard to read.

His emerald green eyes darken before me, highly charged as he continues to hold my wrist, and my heart gallops in my chest, waiting to see what it is he plans on doing to me.

"You don't have to kiss me because the others did," I manage to state far too quietly and unsure for my liking, but I blame it on the fried brain I've got from making out with the others. I want him to know it's okay, he has a choice in the matter too.

He doesn't utter a word in response as he looms above me, chest brushing against mine, catching my hardened nipples through the fabric of my shirt *and* my blazer. His lip tilts ever so slightly at the right corner, but it's gone again before I can be sure.

With every passing second my breath hitches more and more, until I think I might pass out from lack of oxygen.

"Fuck, what's taking you guys so… oh." The sound of Harmonia's voice swarms around us, but it doesn't seem to be enough to break the intense stare off between Khaos and me.

"This looks like an… awesome moment, but uh, classes have been canceled before lunch for a last minute assembly, and we're going to be late."

My brows crinkle at that last minute change in plans, but I still don't move an inch or pull my gaze from Khaos. I can't. Not even if I wanted to. And to my surprise, none of the guys utter a word either, almost like they're captivated by the pair of us too, but I can't turn to check.

His face inches closer, slowly, his eyes searching mine as his nostrils flare, when he places the smallest, gentlest kiss to the corner of my lips, before stepping back.

I'm left gasping for air, my brain short circuiting as my pulse rings loudly in my ears. What the fuck was *that*? And how am I so affected by a single touch? I feel like I'm trembling, riding a high like never before as I clear my throat and turn to face Harmonia, who is staring at me with a wide and knowing smile on her face. I know there's going to be so many questions she's going to want answers to but thankfully, that all has to wait.

"Assembly?" I finally mumble, running my hands down my skirt as I try to process who I am and what the *fuck* just happened, and she nods in response.

"Yes, and the buzz around the main building definitely has something to do with whatever it's for, so let's go," she says, turning on her heels and heading back through the portal, and this time, I'm sure to follow her.

The weird feeling I always get going through the portal, doesn't override the energy already flowing through my body like I hoped, and when Xander is right behind me, fingers back to lacing with mine, I immediately want to turn on the spot and head back to Agion and say fuck it to the assembly, consequences be damned.

Looking back over my shoulder, I see Khaos staring off into the distance ahead, trying to get a read on the situation, as is Zen, yet Adonis is glaring at me with a knowing grin and a waggle of his eyebrows, like he knows *exactly* what I'm thinking.

My lips twist to the side, considering whether or not he would take me up on the offer of retreating back to… explore, but Zen's words cut off my train of thought, sobering me up with just a few short words.

"I have a feeling this somehow links back to us."

It's like a bucket of cold water has been dropped over my head, and I quickly turn back around to see if there's something happening that makes him specifically say that, but I come up short.

"What makes you say that?" I ask, and he peers back over his shoulder to look at me.

"Because we vowed to never offer any public declaration of affection during school hours, unless we had found *the* one."

Wait what?

My pulse spikes, but for an entirely different reason this

time, and I stand taller. Why the hell would that make them call an assembly? What am I missing?

"Then let's find out."

TWENTY NINE

XANDER

With Rhea's hand in my grasp, I walk ahead, a rare move from me, tugging her along as Zen keeps pace beside Rhea, and Harmonia holds up the rear with Khaos and Adonis.

No one speaks, each of us casually strolling into the assembly hall with our heads held high and posture relaxed. Well, the Elites are at least, myself included. Rhea and Harmonia, on the other hand, are confused by the attention we seem to have garnered by simply walking through the doors.

Only this time, it feels different, even to me. The atmosphere feels charged, ready to burst at the pull of a trigger, yet I have no idea what the target is.

I usually let the others walk up front, since we get attention no matter where we go, but I can feel everyone's eyes burning at the point where my hand is locked with Rhea's. It seems the rumors of Zen claiming her lips in class circled faster than we thought.

Good.

My wolf is far too fucking pleased with that fact. The rumble in my chest is barely containable like he wants to howl for hours. Contentment mixed with excitement courses through me at the prospect of moving forward with Rhea.

It's not like I could have taken no for an answer anyway, my wolf wouldn't have allowed it. I would have just had to repeat the process, explain everything again and again, until she realized what was between us, what links us together.

I can't see past the future I want. Not a single thing. It makes it all worthwhile. Holding in my wolf was harder than it sounded, but I know I have to, to protect us as a whole, but fuck she makes it easier.

Squeezing her fingers tighter on instinct, I feel her gaze shift to me, but I keep my focus set ahead. Walking between the pews, the sunlight gleaming in through the multitude of patterned stained glass that adorns the ceiling and walls, I watch as each house turns their attention our way. Rhea stiffens, but keeps moving.

My smirk is barely manageable with each step I take, until we come to a stop at the very front of the assembly hall and my eyes land on Selene. This stupid bitch thought she could play us to get what she wanted, like that would make us magically fall in love with her, promising her everything and anything, when it's never been further from the truth.

All it has done is make us despise her more than ever. A fact that won't ever change. And now we get to show her once and for all.

My wolf begs me to lift Rhea's hand to my lips, publicly displaying my dedication to her, just to make sure there is no mistaking how I feel, but I manage to stop myself. Barely. Stalking down the wooden pew, I take the end seat, keeping Rhea to my left. Harmonia snags the spot beside her, much to Zen's displeasure who sits beside her, while Adonis and Khaos fill the row.

I can feel Rhea twitching beside me, nervous under the intense scrutiny of the other students, and I get it. We're used to this, among the communities we grew up in, and the hierarchy here at Saints Academy. We've always been held with high regard, with even higher expectations, based on each of our families heritage.

But for her, this must be bewildering. I can imagine once upon a time, she may have been a wallflower, hiding from anything and anyone, but it was inevitable that her natural beauty and presence would make it impossible to continue down that path. That then only led to her defending and protecting herself from anyone with the chance of caring.

Now that ends.

Here.

With me.

Us.

I relax back in my seat, pleased with that thought as I sense Rhea stiffen beside me. I frown at first, my brows knitting together in confusion as I turn to glance at her, and it takes me a second before I hear what seems to have her troubled.

"I mean… are you shocked? Of course they would want to go after the girl at the bottom of the pecking order. She's a nothing, a no one, and that will only work in their favor when it comes to the dynamics of their unit." The gossiping girl's voice behind us does little to shield her tone or harsh words as she digs into the woman beside me, and anger rises inside my chest.

Are people actually this oblivious to life?

Clearing my throat, I release her hand, watching as she looks in my direction with a hint of confusion in her gaze, but it quickly disappears when I sling my arm around the back of her seat, leaning in to brush my lips against her temple.

A pale pink blush dusts her cheeks as I lean back, speaking loud enough for the bitch behind us to hear too. "Imagine thinking someone was a nobody when the portal chose them to be placed in a higher hall than you," I say with a smirk. "Imagine gossiping about someone else when a unit still hasn't chosen you?" I add, my own catty side making an appearance, and I hear Harmonia chuckle on the other side of Rhea.

"Imagine, being the girl who stole Khaos' bracelet from a party at the beginning of the school year so she could pretend he gave it to her when anyone asked where she got it?"

Harmonia says with a gasp, widening her eyes as she flicks her gaze over her shoulder.

"The fuck?" the man in question grunts, a glare being thrown around by him, but I focus on Rhea instead of encouraging any further digs. With the inhale of breath and increased heart rate coming from behind me, I know for sure this girl is about to piss her pants with fear if the glare on Rhea's face is anything to go by.

To my surprise, at the mention of Harmonia's words, Rhea sits tall and turns to face the girl behind her. I don't really recognize her. With wispy blonde hair and a button nose, she seems like… well, any other girl that doesn't hold my interest. I watch as she audibly swallows as Rhea leans back over the pew, angry eyes fixed on hers

Rhea's pulse is pounding like crazy at her neck, anger coating her from head to toe, and it's moments like this that I love the new heightened senses I've got. I'm able to go on the emotional and physical rollercoaster with her and get to enjoy the ride.

Touch.

Scent.

Sound.

Everything.

I can read my girl better than she can read herself.

"I want it. Now," she bites, making the girl frown in confusion as a few other people in the row glance to see what's going on, but Rhea doesn't bat an eyelash, continuing to give this girl the death stare.

"W-w-what?" The girl stammers, but I catch the movement of her gripping her wrist protectively, and I understand what's being asked. Fuck, I'm proud of this girl.

"You heard me. He's *mine*, and I want it. Now," Rhea repeats, cocking her brow as she leans even closer. "You don't want to know what I learned to do as an *earthling* when people didn't do as I ask," she spits out, her obvious distaste for the nickname evident. "But if you want to find out, I'm more than willing to show you."

Rhea cracks her neck from side to side, before moving as though she's going to stand, but the girl gives in immediately, pulling the sleeve of her blazer up to reveal a black, leather braided bracelet which definitely belongs to my brother.

"That's fucking mine," Khaos grunts, angry that some random girl has something that belongs to him, but Rhea scoffs, cutting him off before he can grumble anymore.

"Wrong. Now, it's mine," she corrects him, holding her hand out toward the girl as she offers a sweet smile in Khaos' direction, and to my utter surprise he doesn't correct her.

Instead, he snatches the item from the bitch's hands, leaning around Zen and Harmonia as Adonis chuckles, and makes a show of wrapping it around Rhea's wrist gently, placing a small kiss at the clasp when he secures it in place. Rhea's eyes flash with desire, before she shutters her expression.

A smile creeps over my face, pleased with him accepting her a little more, but the beast inside of me is desperate to rip from my body and show everyone she's mine too. I'm willing to share, my brain understands, but it doesn't mean I can't be a jealous fuck on occasion.

"Take care of it," Khaos murmurs, before releasing his hold on Rhea and turning back to the front, just as Zellus begins walking into the hall with his two assistants on either side of him.

The hall breaks into a hushed quiet, silence sweeping through everyone as he slowly makes his way to the podium, gaining everyone's attention as he goes. It doesn't surprise me, he's an attention whore. Just like Zeus, but there's nothing we can do or say. We just have to accept his fucking presence and get on with our education. For the next three years at least.

After that I won't have to watch him make a dramatic display every time he enters into a public space. Well, except this morning when he didn't want to be seen, yet I had heard him anyway, and pointed Zen's attention in his direction.

The thing is with a man like this, him saying nothing at all, says more than he'd actually like. It gives him away. Showing his hand as he attempted to observe us in class, trying to read between the lines to see something that shouldn't be visible to his eyes.

Motherfucker.

I hate that we had to make a statement the way we did,

but I don't regret it, not when my girl is tucked in beside me.

Zellus' eyes scan the room, his fake smile plastered in place as he takes everyone in, but his pace immediately slows as he reaches the Agion pew, his eyes raking over each and every one of us at the front as he takes in Rhea's positioning among us. It probably would have served us well to have Zen right next to Rhea instead of Harmonia, but there's nothing we can do about that now. Besides, he saw Zen's claim earlier. There is no denying his intent.

I'm expecting a phone call from my parents later this evening for sure. The gossip mill will go through the roof with buzz at the Elites completing their unit. Some will be mad, especially those who don't have a brain and consider Rhea to be a no one, but I don't care.

Not. One. Bit.

"Good morning, students. Thank you for gathering at such short notice," he begins, straightening the lapels on his blazer, black eyes still fixed on Rhea, who doesn't flinch under his gaze at all. "After some curious and… surprising news we received earlier today," he continues, eyebrows raised as he clearly draws everyone's attention to us. "We have decided to bring forward the Solstice ball to this coming weekend."

Gasps ring out around us, excitement and squeals coming from all angles as a buzz fills the air, but I see right through it all, understanding his intentions.

I pull my gaze from his, looking around Rhea to see Zen

who shares the same knowing expression.

Fuck.

Zellus continues to mumble on, talking about shit I have no further care for as the reality of what he's put in motion sets in.

The Solstice event is for the Hex, the students of Saints Academy, *and* their families to gather together in a show of unionship, but all I'm hearing is the fact that he's clearly unhappy with our choice in woman, and he thinks bringing our families in will change that.

Well, fuck him. He gets no say whatsoever.

We're not quiet, follow-the-rules types. Being a supernatural puts enough expectations on our shoulders, we don't require any more. When we became friends, Zen, Adonis, Khaos, and I, we made a pact to be united on all fronts. That meant no internal disagreements, yet with the ability to speak our minds.

Our communication is open, our irritation is usually high with each other, but these men are my brothers, and sending in our parents to right a situation you feel is incorrect is not going to end well for him. Not when we're fucking adults in our own right, but this is typical of the supernaturals in charge. Believing they can control every aspect of our lives in one way or another.

Not at all.

Rhea remains quiet beside me, completely oblivious to the bigger picture since she's not aware of the customs, while I scramble to think about how each of our parents may react. Not that I truly care what the reactions will be, but I need to prepare in advance so I can counteract any arguments, and change their minds before they get ahead of themselves with their opinions.

Zellus pats the podium, calling the assembly to a close, and I realize I've listened to nothing further from him. Shit. Hopefully someone else did, because otherwise, that's not going to help me.

"Girl, I will take you dress shopping, no stress," Harmonia says with a smile, also oblivious to everything going on as she nudges Rhea with her shoulder.

"I can't, I refuse to use the money set up for me," Rhea explains with a sigh, making me frown as I silently listen to the girls interact.

"What? Why? The trusts are set up for you to be able to get everything you require to attend Saints Academy, Rhea, and that includes clothing," Harmonia says, her brows also knitted together as she looks at her friend, but Rhea just shakes her head strongly.

"I get that, but I can't, Harm. Not when I found out my ex is the goddamn human representative in the Hex."

I gape in surprise, and I'm not the only one when Adonis suddenly rises to his feet, glaring at Rhea. "What the fuck?"

What the fuck indeed.

THIRTY

RHEA

With Zen's hand at the base of my spine, nudging me along, I take a seat at the Elites' table at the center of the dining hall. My bottom lip feels sensitive because of the way I've been raking my teeth over it, but when I'd been talking with Harmonia, I was naïve enough to think they wouldn't hear. Especially since I know Xander's hearing is more sensitive now that he's shifted.

Fuck was I wrong about the others though.

The second my butt touches the seat, I come face to face with a grim stare from Xander across from me, almost matching the one on Adonis' face as he sits to his left, leaving Khaos to look at me curiously from his right.

Nobody makes a sound at first, not even Harmonia as she sits to my right, while Zen takes the spot to my left, continuing to stroke circles on my back, the delicate touch noticeable to me, even through my blazer.

I can sense the fifty questions hanging on the tips of their tongues, the expectation of an explanation gleaming in their eyes, but I pretend none of it exists as I let the hum and chatter of the room swarm me. This isn't going to be a fun conversation. Not even a little bit.

If I thought I was the center of attention before as the new kid, I was wrong, I had been practically invisible in comparison to now. It seems the Elites held everyone captive with their mere presence, not just me. I can't help but find the unhappy faces in the crowd as I glance around.

Guilt isn't an emotion I'm all that familiar with, so I'm not going to back out of this, my body and soul wants these guys more than words can express, but it doesn't mean I won't grumble about everyone's scrutiny of our relationship. It's none of their fucking business.

Focusing on the tablet that appears in front of me, I scroll through the menu for the day, taking my sweet ass time so I don't have to explain anything, opting for the pot roast, a roll, and a bottle of water.

When I tilt my head up, I notice the three Elites across from me haven't moved an inch, all staring at me, wanting a response, and I bristle under their glare. Swiping a hand down my face, I offer each of them a pointed look as I sigh. I guess it's time to get this shit over with or else they won't stop staring.

"What do you want me to say?" I grumble, aware of how dumb I'm playing it, but fuck, this isn't really a conversation I expected to be having anytime soon, let alone today. But, here we are.

Not only is there a ball I refuse to buy an outfit for with Dante's money, but he is also going to be in attendance since the Hex are among those invited. I need to find out what the expectations are about students attending, because maybe I could get out of it that way. Otherwise, I'm going to have to fake being sick or something.

"Explain how you forgot to mention that Dante fucking James is your ex," Xander says, hands clenched on the table as he continues to stare at me unblinking, and Adonis nods along eagerly, encouraging him.

When I don't answer immediately, even Harmonia slips in as she clears her throat. It's awkward in sound, almost appearing fake, which means what she's about to say is going to be unpleasant. "They have got a point, Rhea. No member of the Hex would sleep with a Saints Academy student, it's just not a thing."

"I wasn't a student here at the time, and I didn't even realize who he fucking was until my first full day here when they had to arrange the finances for me," I say with a roll of my eyes. They shouldn't have assumed I had dated him while being here.

"How is he your *ex*? What did he do wrong, Rhea?"

Zen asks, thumb still circling. "I just want clarification for when I kill him," he adds casually, and I gape at him in surprise. Part of me can't tell if he's being serious or not because if there's anything I've learned recently about Zen, it's that he's just as fierce and fiery as he is calm and collected.

"None of that matters. I ended it. I'm not pining over him, for fuck's sake, so can we just drop it? Please?" Even I can sense the pleading in my voice, but the way Adonis immediately shakes his head tells me I'm not getting out of this any time soon.

Perfect.

"You fucked him." The words leave Adonis' lips as a statement, not a question, and I just stare at him blankly, not needing to clarify with him, but the anger that swims in his eyes leaves me surprised. Is he fucking for real?

"I never claimed to be a virgin, Adonis," I bite, sarcasm dripping heavily in my tone, squeezing my hands together in my lap as I imagine them wrapped around his throat for the disdained look that takes over his face.

He rolls his eyes dramatically at me. "That's not what I said, honey."

"Why did you leave him?" Xander asks, shifting the direction of conversation back to the topic Zen was addressing before Adonis and I continue to argue, rewording the same goddamn question again, and I sigh. Answering him seems like an easier battle than Adonis right now.

"Does it really matter?" I ask, knowing full well I'm not in the wrong, but I don't want this man's death on my hands, do I? "It should be enough that there is nothing between us anymore. That's my answer, take it or leave it."

"So there was something between you?" Adonis hisses, pushing for more information and I throw my hands up in frustration.

"Of course there was, douchebag, otherwise I wouldn't have called him my *ex*, I would have just said someone I *slept with*," I grumble in response, desperately pleading in my head for my food to arrive so all this bullshit jealousy can stop.

"So you fucked him on multiple occasions?" Xander asks for clarification, and I want to scream. What the fuck is with these two? I look to Khaos, hopeful he's the reasonable one of the group since he's remained quiet so far, but when I turn to him for help, he simply shrugs his shoulders before folding his arms over his chest and leaning back in his seat. He's taking their side and waiting for my answer.

Asshole.

They all are.

"Zen…" I start, tilting my head in his direction, but the tight smile and wide-eyed expression on his face tells me he's not willing to stand next to my side, and I practically growl as I try to take a calming breath. "Yes I fucked him. Multiple times, and he was good at it," I add, purposely twisting the knife like a bitch in annoyance with having to explain myself. They wanted the gritty details so fuck it, they're going to get them. "Until he decided to put his dick to other uses, inside another woman on my birthday." My chest heaves with agitation, the familiar burn of disappointment crawling up my throat as I glare at Xander and Adonis. "Is that what you wanted to hear? *Does it make you feel better?*"

Do you like seeing me wrecked? Trodden and discarded?

I stop myself shy of adding the other line that plays in my head, but I refuse to let them see my weakness. Only, the way Xander looks back at me, makes me think he can see right through me, feeling every bit of my emotions with me. Fucking wolf abilities.

The table falls into silence as I catch my breath, and I glance around the room to make sure no one heard my outburst. I can feel a couple of people looking my way, clearly still the hot topic of the day, but it seems my words were just quiet enough to not cause a scene.

Thank the Gods.

I wet my lips, considering whether I should get up from the table and leave or not, when my food appears in front of me, and as much as my appetite has suddenly vanished, I busy myself with stuffing my face and avoid everyone's gaze. I have nothing left to say about the situation anyway.

I don't know how long passes, a minute, two, ten? But when Xander finally breaks the silence around us, it does nothing to calm my racing heart because he *knows*. "You're not heartbroken over it, you never were. Why is that?"

I pause mid-chew, looking up through my lashes at him as he eyes me curiously, and I quickly swallow the mashed potatoes and vegetables to reply. "I don't fall in love with anyone. Ever."

My response is as simple as that, always has been, always will be. Although, there's a pinch in my chest that tells me I'm not being truly honest on the matter anymore, but I rub it away with my hand balled in a fist.

"Is that why you're more disappointed that you weren't enough for him?"

It's a good thing there's no fucking food in my mouth because I'd damn well choke on it at Zen's words. Glaring at him, he simply raises his eyebrows in challenge as Harmonia's hand squeezes my arm in comfort.

How can he read my fucking mind? I literally trampled down that thought moments ago, and here he is reading me so easily.

"I don't know what you're talking about," I murmur, my voice monotone and void of emotion as I turn back to my food. "So, if we've all got that inquisition off our chests, can we discuss this so-called ball and how I can get myself out of it?" I add, swiftly hoping to change the conversation as I turn my attention to Harmonia.

I steel my spine, ready for whatever comeback they're about to throw at me to continue the conversation, but to my surprise, it's Khaos who speaks next. "We can put a pin in it, for now," he states, his voice husky as he offers me a lifeline, and I sag in relief. I'll fucking take what I can get at this point.

I don't bother to correct his sentence to say *forever* instead of just *for now*, instead I take the opportunity to shove more food in my mouth as I wait for someone to actually answer my question about the ball.

"The ball is like a supernatural tradition, that is usually fun. Food, drinks, pretty dresses, and hot guys in suits, but I have a feeling it might look a little different for you this year," Harmonia says with a tight smile, her gaze flicking between me and the Elites. "You can't back out on me though, Rhea. We need to go dress shopping, shoe shopping, accessory shopping..."

I wave my hand, her words trailing off as I shake my head. "That's far too much shopping for me. Besides, I don't want to go. It's as simple as that," I state, and she cringes immediately, looking to one of the guys who explains for her.

"You don't get a choice. *Everyone* at Saints Academy has to attend. Even if you get sick, they have a healer on hand to take it all away," Xander explains, eyes boring into the side of my head as I keep my gaze fixed on Harmonia for a moment.

Shit. I was really hoping I would be able to get out of this and the guys would help me figure out a way to do so, but clearly it's not possible.

Swiping a hand down my face, Zen places his palm on my thigh, my back immediately missing the gentle swirls, but the second he continues the same pattern on my leg, I relax again.

"What do you mean, it's going to be different for me?" I ask, recalling her words, but she shakes her head this time, nodding to the guys again, and I reluctantly turn my head to cast my gaze over each of theirs. There's clearly something I'm missing, not privy to, and it instantly has me defensive. "Someone just spit it out. You made me talk, now it's *your* turn," I mumble, not wanting to waste unnecessary time over someone not knowing what words to use.

"They brought the day forward the same day we confirmed our unit to you," Xander says slowly, a twitch in his eyes as they beg to flash amber instead of the deep chocolate looking back at me.

My brows raise as I try to piece the invisible jigsaw together, but it still means nothing to me. "I'm a newbie here, remember? You have to spell things out for me because I can't read between your cryptic lines," I deadpan.

"It means they don't like our decision," Adonis says, just as pizza and a soda appears in front of him, and he takes a huge bite out of the gooey pepperoni goodness as I crinkle my eyes in confusion, the immediate reminder that I'm not good enough swarming in my head.

"Why does it matter?" I ask, my voice losing some of its confidence as I brace myself for the reality check he's about to hand deliver on a silver platter.

"Everything around here matters, Rhea, you know that,"

Adonis replies between bites. "Everyone wants to align their families, and in your case… Well, you don't have one."

That makes sense, but…

"Shut your fucking mouth, asshole. Don't say shit like that to her," Xander growls, hands clenched and shoulders bunched together as he glares at his friend. Before I even realize what I'm doing, I reach my arm across the table, squeezing his hand with my own as I interrupt.

"It's okay, he's not wrong," I mutter, and he turns to look at me like I've got five heads.

"He doesn't get to say shitty things about your life, Rhea, true or not. None of that matters now anyway," he says with a shake of his head, his gaze turning heated as he stares me straight in the eye. "We're your family now."

My mouth dries as I gape at him in surprise, too shocked for words as I simply blink at him.

Family?

It takes me a moment to regain myself, letting go of his hand as I sit back in my seat, Zen's hand now gripping my thigh in a silent show of support.

"But your families are going to think their line is wasted on me, aren't they?" I state, not replying to his words of family as I look at everyone, including Harmonia, who is the only one to actually nod in agreement with me. Her eyes shine with empathy because the situation isn't as simple as it sounds.

"Don't put it like that," Zen mumbles, a pained look in

his eyes as I turn to him.

"It's the truth. If we're going to figure this out, then that's what we're going to need to deal with; truth, facts, and whatever other bullshit people may throw at us," I reply, my voice even as the worry of being enough thrums through my veins once more. But I'm right, this is the way it has to be.

I close my eyes, only for a second, and my defensive armor is back in place. To anyone else it would look like a long blink, an exaggerated effort with the topics flying around, but really it's my way of tucking my insecurities firmly away again.

"Why the fuck am I stressed out about everything but the damn magic itself?" I grumble under my breath, scooping the remaining pot roast onto my fork and popping it into my mouth with a sigh. My internal dialogue with myself seems to have slipped from my lips.

"You need some down time, girl, this is all draining as hell," Harmonia states, and I nod in agreement.

"No shopping," I quickly add, and she chuckles because she knows it'll happen regardless if I want it to or not. "Not yet at least."

"That's not down time for you, that's down time for me," she replies with a wink. "I've got you covered, no stress."

Before I can even ask what that means, it's Xander's turn to lean over the table, hand reaching for mine which I accept instantly, and he smiles.

"I have something in mind. Are you free now?"

THIRTY ONE

RHEA

With my fingers laced with Xander's again, I take the steps two at a time to keep up as we leave the main building and head toward the woods. The same direction as when I saw snow.

My curiosity is piqued as I feel a hint of excitement buzz beneath the surface of my skin. When he asked me if I was free, I was expecting it to lead to something sexual, and I wasn't opposed to it, but out in the woods in the middle of the day isn't exactly what I had in mind. Although, Khaos, Adonis, and Zen as an audience leaves me intrigued.

Wait. Been there, done that. I internally smirk at the memory.

Glancing at the side of Xander's face, I can't help but sense a mixture of determination and nervousness floating within him. I want to ask what it is, what has him tight-lipped and kinda on edge, but I know he's in his head right now and will tell me when he's ready. Or I hope so at least.

Since our next class was a study hall session, I don't feel bad for skipping out. There's nothing for me to be catching up on at the minute since the last class was canceled, so the extra break won't leave me worried later.

Khaos and Adonis talk quietly behind us as they stroll along, Zen to my other side as we step through the trees toward the clearing by the lake. It's not lost on me that this is the only place I've been on campus that isn't in the main building or Agion, and I make a silent agreement with myself to venture out more. There are plenty of things on site for me to explore. Gods, even a trip to the library again might be both fun and insightful.

I did promise Harmonia a trip to the on site little town they have, with coffee houses and clothes shops among other things. She ducked out to go to the study hall without even considering or asking to come with us, and I appreciate her respecting my time with the Elite.

This is all strange, between the guys and me. There's something here, something worth chasing, other than the pull and sexual tension that burns between us. I want to know more about them.

I want to know what makes Khaos tick, what could put a genuine smile on his stunning face. I want to see Adonis behind his front, where he's just him, without pretenses or any of the other bullshit, I want to know *that* version of him.

My eyes want to feast on Zen as he does yoga and meditates across from me. I want him to show me how he seems to be so calm and collected… most of the time. And Xander, I want to see more of the soft and gentle side of him.

I just want it all, and it's surprising how true that is, even to my own ears.

The mention of Dante earlier was a stark reminder of the difference between the two situations. I wanted an occasional friend, a person who would sit across the table with me at a restaurant so I wasn't always alone, and his dick, but other than that, I didn't really care who or what he was.

This is different. This *feels* different.

Frighteningly different, but it's exciting too.

Coming to a stop in the middle of the lush green field, the sun blazing overhead and a gentle breeze blowing around us, I take a deep breath as I relax in my surroundings. There's something about nature that just soothes me so no matter what Xander has planned, I'm appreciative for this moment.

Definitely not something sexual then.

I notice Khaos and Adonis have gone quiet when I turn on the spot to see everyone, and my eyes settle on Xander who releases my hand and scrubs his fingers in his cropped brown hair.

"What are we doing out here?" I ask, a small smile playing at the corner of my mouth as I tighten my ponytail. When

Xander doesn't answer immediately, I glance at the others, none of them seem to want to share with me what the purpose of the field trip is, but it's clear they know.

Focusing on each of them, I look to Adonis first, his heated and knowing gaze tracking mine as he adjusts his circular glasses on his face. I really need to know why he wears them because they're not always perched there, and he seems to get around just fine without them, unless he lives in contacts? That's a question for another time.

I rub my lips together, moving my gaze to Zen. He stands with his hands in his Academy pants pockets, a gentle and serene grin on his lips as he quite happily stares at me, but I don't miss the way he flicks his eyes to Xander a time or two as well. Hmm.

Turning to Khaos, he's already looking at me with his piercing green eyes boring into my soul, his dark hair hanging over his face as he quirks a brow at me and nods his head in Xander's direction.

So I'm apparently supposed to draw the information out of him. Awesome. Surely one of them could help me, but it seems like today isn't the day for that. Lack of communication sucks dick.

It's on the tip of my tongue to threaten the quiet vampire-to-be with something devious from his cousins, Thalia and Cassandra, but I refrain, pulling on my big girl panties and turning my full attention back to Xander.

"Are we going to stand around for the next hour, or was there something specific you had in mind?" I ask, swinging my arms at my sides instead of planting them on my hips like I want to. I need to show I'm open to the conversation instead of letting my frustration get the better of me.

He takes one step, then another, followed swiftly with another as he begins to pace before me. "I want to try something." Turn. "It's been driving me insane." Turn. "But I really don't want to do it without you around." Turn. "But he's literally going crazy," he rambles, rubbing at his temples as he continues to pace, and I wave my hand in the air to get his attention.

Whatever it is has him rambling like a madman, and it's not helping my own stress levels all of a sudden. "I need you to spit it out because my entire body is reacting to your tension and that's not going to go well for anyone," I state, clenching my hands as I place them at my side.

A hint of guilt washes over his face as he turns to face me head on, feet planted shoulder width apart as he stares straight into my goddamn soul. "I want to shift. No, I *need* to shift, Rhea."

My head rears back in shock at his words, surprise coloring my face as I immediately take a step toward him. "You haven't shifted since..." my words trail off as he shakes his head, and it's my turn to feel guilty this time. "You should have told me sooner. I know things have changed quicker for you than me," I state, my hand instantly reaching out to his side where I know his mark is now; my mark.

"It's not your fault," he replies, shaking his head dismissively as he cuts the remaining distance between us so we're chest to chest. "Everything else I've gained from kick-starting my powers early can be over sensitizing sometimes, all the new scents, sounds, and the fucking speed. I can't tell you how hard it is to not move as fast as I know my body can now," he adds, a buzz of excitement zinging in his now amber eyes, and I smile. "But he's going crazy up in here," he states, tapping his temple as I tilt my head back to keep eye contact with him.

"We're not sure if his shifting might also calm that for him too," Zen adds from behind me, and I nod in understanding.

Gods, the last time he shifted, it was… magnificent. Beyond any words, and I can't deny that I'm eager to see it again.

"Are we safe out here?" I ask, not wanting to be the bearer of bad news or the one dousing us in negativity, but my heart, my soul, my magic, believes that keeping him safe is paramount over everything else right now.

"We just have to hope we are," Khaos states, a hint of uncertainty in his voice too, but I don't look away from Xander to get a sense if there's any hesitation from his perspective. "We can keep watch while he does, and you're here to calm him if needed."

I can do that. I can *definitely* do that.

"We couldn't ask someone to put a ward up to shield us away from everyone, they would have wanted to know why, and it's not a risk worth taking. Not yet, at least," Zen explains, which makes my eyes widen, offering me a reminder that I am no way accustomed to the fucking supernatural world and the abilities within it because I didn't even consider the option of a ward to be a thing.

I have a lot to fucking learn, but yet I'm an unwilling participant in Academy drama.

Xander's Adam's apple bobs a few times as he swallows past the lump in his throat, and I watch his pulse throbbing at his neck.

He needs this, and he needs us to be here for it, me included, and who the fuck am I to deny him a moment to find peace within himself?

Leaning up on my tiptoes, I place a gentle kiss on the corner of his mouth before taking a reluctant step back. "Do it, Xander," I breathe, my chest tightening with a mixture of excitement and trepidation at the unknown. "I'll be right here with you."

As if those words were the soothing balm he needed, he offers me a panty-melting smile from ear to ear, before taking a step back himself. Slipping out of his blazer, he undoes the first few buttons on his shirt, before reaching back over his shoulder to pull it off in one swift motion, revealing his marked ribs, chiseled abs, and buff chest.

Hot. As. Fuck.

And all mine.

I shake my head, berating myself for not focusing on what's important, when he kicks his shoes off and drops his pants, leaving him in only his boxers. My teeth sink into my bottom lip, my thighs clenching together as I stare in awe at him, but to my disappointment, he doesn't slip his hands inside the waistband of his boxers. No, instead, he transforms before my very eyes.

I didn't blink and I still feel like I missed it.

"Holy fuck," I say with a gasp, feeling someone place their hand on my back as they move to stand beside me, almost protectively, but Xander's not going to hurt me, no matter which form he's in.

Gaping in utter astonishment, I look at the jet black wolf before me, red marking still on his side, a stark sign to anyone and everyone that he's mine, and I fucking love it.

Gone is the buff man, and in his place stands a four-legged growly beast. I don't know what I expect his first move to be, but when he stretches out his front paws, tilting his tail up in the air, I almost fucking pass out with how cute he is. It's on the tip of my tongue to squeal 'big stretch' at him, but I manage to hold it together. He turns on the spot and takes off at a crazy pace, racing around the edge of the woods and around the lake.

The four of us stand in complete silence, and I turn to see Adonis at my side, but I don't speak a word. Zen has moved closer, all of our eyes tracking every move Xander makes, and I feel tears prick my eyes.

Watching him, like this, free, happy, and leaping through the air, I want him to feel this way forever. Yet I somehow get the feeling there's a lot coming our way before we can have that. A lot of which will be issues with them choosing me to complete their family unit.

I try to force that thought to the back of my mind, concentrating on the moment. "I swear to the fucking Gods, I hope I'm this happy when my magic kicks in," Adonis murmurs, almost to himself, but it makes me smile because, Gods, do I fucking agree.

Xander laps us a few more times, until he barrels toward me, panting. His tongue is sticking out and his face looks so calm, it's hard to believe it's the same person from a few moments ago. He comes to a stop before me, and I drop to my knees without thought, the feel of the grass against my skin as I hold my hand out again like last time.

He moves into my touch immediately, his soft coat brushing against my palm as he nuzzles into me. Nose to nose, he doesn't move, but there's a lot said between us without a single word being spoken.

He's got my back, and I've got his.

No matter what.

And the determination to make this work is overwhelming as I stare into his amber eyes. It feels hard, whatever may develop between the five of us, but nothing worth having ever comes easy.

The wolf leans in, brushing his tongue over my collarbone and making me jolt back with a giggle, before he moves back to his pile of clothes. Lying down on the grass with pride shining in his eyes, before he shifts back.

Watching as the fur dissolves into the air, leaving my hot and broody man behind, I slowly rise to my feet with the help of Adonis.

"Feeling better?" Zen asks, grabbing Xander's blazer off the ground, and he smiles wide with a nod in response.

"I feel good." He pauses, his nose twitching for a moment as his brows slightly crinkle, but he quickly straightens, tugging his shirt back on.

"What is it?" Khaos asks, but he waves him off.

"Nothing, I just thought I could smell something, but it must be the transition throwing me off a little." I nod like it makes total sense, but definitely add another research trip to the library to my to-do list, because I'm still not up to speed on this whole supernatural way of life.

"Everyone ready to head back for a while before dinner?" Adonis asks, swinging his arm over my shoulders as he steers me toward the path that leads back to the main building, and everyone hums in agreement.

Nerves course through me at his embrace, which is completely out of character for him, but I roll with it, my body in tune with every inch of his as the others fall into step with us. His touches are always intentional, premeditated, and this almost feels casual. A word I wasn't sure if Adonis was familiar with.

Xander answers the questions we throw at him as we make our way back through the main building and the portal to Agion, attempting to explain the rush and feelings he felt in his wolf form. None of us would ever truly understand. But living it through his eyes was more than enough anyway. It was truly magical.

He strokes a hand down my cheek as he slips into his room, Khaos offering a subtle nod as he does the same, and Zen offers me a calm and wide smile as he follows suit, leaving Adonis and I to take the stairs together.

Silence descends over us, but it's surprisingly not awkward as he keeps his arm perched on my shoulders. As we reach the top, I expect him to release me to head for his door, but instead, he continues toward mine.

Rubbing my lips together, I turn to face him, my door behind me as he refuses to give me any space, crowding me in as he leans close.

"What is it about you, Rhea Harrington, that makes me want to tear every fiber of your clothing off and feast on you for days?" he asks, my blood heating at his words as I stare up at him.

"That's nothing to do with me, and everything to do

with the incubus magic inside you," I retort, trying to tamper down the sexual tension rising between us, but he doesn't let me, shaking his head as he somehow moves closer, pressing me into the door.

My hands rise to his chest, not to push him away, but to feel him beneath my skin. It's like we're frozen in position, locked in each other's grasp as our lips collide. A moan breaks past my lips, my body igniting at his touch as his hands find my hips, squeezing as he pins me against the door.

He consumes me effortlessly, every ounce of me desperate for more as I reach a hand down between us, running it over his crotch, groaning at the material separating us. The growl that tears from his lips surprises me, and he quickly pulls my hand away, breathing against my lips. "You're going to make me blow like I'm not a fucking God at this," he grumbles, and I chuckle at the irony of his words as he pins my hands at my side, crashing his mouth to mine again.

But in slow motion, my world fucking tilts.

I don't fight his hold on my wrists, letting him pin them to the door behind me, palms first, but it suddenly swings open at the simple touch.

"Ahh," I squeak against his lips as we crash to the floor, but he somehow manages to wrap his arms around me and turn us so he takes the brunt of the fall, hitting the floor with a thud and I land on top of him.

I gape down in surprise at him, my hair falling loose

from my ponytail, framing my face as I try to catch my breath.

His eyes are blown, need coursing through them, they match my own as we stare intimately at each other. I don't want this to end, I don't want this fall to break the moment, and to my relief, it doesn't.

"I'm done dancing around us. I need you, and I need you now, tell me to stop or I'm slamming that door shut and laying you on your bed to do with as I please." His voice is husky, dripping in desire, and I don't even consider my answer before it falls from my lips.

"That better not be an empty threat."

He laughs, running his tongue over his bottom lip as his pupils somehow get smaller. "You're about to find out I don't make threats, Rhea. I make promises."

THIRTY TWO

ADONIS

It's impossible to fight this feeling any longer, this clear pull I feel toward Rhea with little effort on her part. Fuck, I don't even have enhanced senses like Xander, and yet I can smell her everywhere. But right now, with her sprawled over me, pushing me to take control of the situation, she is fucking intoxicating.

With one hand cupping her chin, and the other at her waist, she keeps her hands against my chest as I roll us over on the carpet. We're still in her doorway, and anyone could walk by, but I just can't bring myself to give a shit.

None.

But the thought of someone other than my brothers or me seeing her naked sends a boost of anger coursing through my body, and immediately has me rising to my feet. Holding my hand out to her, she slips her fingers in mine and I lift her up, kicking her bedroom door shut behind me as I stare into her sparkling blue eyes.

I've been a total goner for her since the moment she slipped into the bathroom, watching as I jerked off. I should have known then. It took me far longer than I care to admit that I feel something for her, but it's easy to see how I've known all along, or hinted to those around me, that I felt something more for her.

As Zen so kindly pointed out earlier, murmuring in my ear a question that I haven't been able to stop thinking about since. *"Since she arrived, Adonis. How many women have you slept with?"*

None.

Fucking none.

I've gotten all too familiar with the palm of my hand, coming at the thought of her, and now I'm going to take her as mine.

Finally.

Standing so close, our breaths mingling together between us as our chests heave in sync, I tighten my hold on her hand and pull her toward our adjoining bathroom. She moves seamlessly with me, but there's a slight pull of tension in her arm.

"We don't have to go to your room, my bed's right…" her words trail off as I draw us to a stop in the bathroom, placing her back against the vanity and peering into her eyes.

"I've wanted to feel you shatter around my cock since the first time I saw you. Tell me where that was, Rhea," I murmur, brushing a loose tendril of hair back from her face, before I take my glasses off and place them down behind her.

"In here, we first saw each other in here," she says breathlessly, and I grin, trailing a finger down the side of her cheek, continuing down her neck until I reach the top button of her shirt.

She leans back, bracing her hands on the granite vanity behind her, knuckles turning white as she watches my every move.

"That's right," I state, leaning in closer so my mouth is at her ear before I continue, my voice husky even to my own ears. "I was jerking off to nothing, just enjoying the tight grip on my dick until you stepped in. Since then, that's all I've been able to see. Until you gave me a glimpse of what being close to you could feel like. Watching you shatter in the dining hall almost had me nutting like an inexperienced teenager, Rhea," I admonish, my cock straining to come out and play as my words make her shiver before me.

Leaning back, I grab the lapels of her blazer, eyes fixed on hers as I undo the one button she has fastened, and slowly drag it down her arms. She lets me discard it easily, and I toss it to the side uncaringly, before moving back to the buttons of her shirt.

One by one, the buttons pop open and it takes everything

in me not to just tear at the fabric to have this over and done with quicker, but watching her chest rise and fall with my slow approach is far too enjoyable. For her and for me.

I lift the hem of her shirt out of her skirt, undoing the buttons before letting the material fall completely open, to reveal a white cotton bra. It feels almost innocent, but I know she's far from it. I want to see her in lace… silk… satin, but a reminder of why she refuses to use her money plays in my mind, and I make an internal note to rectify that situation as soon as possible.

I'll buy her whatever she needs, fuck, I'd even buy her poison to unalive me if that's what she wanted, I don't care. I'd rather that over her using money from her *ex*, someone who is familiar with her body in a way I'm desperate to be. That will soon be rectified, and I will never take advantage or be ungrateful for what she's offering me.

Shaking my head, I focus on the beauty that is before me, leaning down to gently graze my lips over the swell of her breasts as she gasps. I sense her kick her shoes off as I slip my fingers into the waistline of her skirt, letting the material pool at her feet so she's only in her panties and bra.

I take a step back so I can get a full view of her, my cock bulging in my pants in bliss at the sight of her pale skin against the innocently white lingerie set.

"You better be joining me," she purrs, hinting at the fact that I'm still fully dressed as she runs her finger from her collarbone, down between her breasts, trailing over her stomach and down to where I'm desperate to be. "Otherwise, you don't get to continue," she adds, and I'm shaking my blazer off before she can even finish her sentence.

Undoing the top five buttons on my shirt, I reach back and slip it off over my head. I watch as she visibly gulps at the sight of my chest and abs, and it does a whole lot of good for my ego as I kick my shoes off and slowly unfasten my pants, discarding them along with the rest.

The tip of my cock is sticking out of the top of my waistband, begging for attention, and to my surprise, Rhea slips off the vanity and drops to her knees before me, hands on my thighs as she looks up at me with a sex induced haze already in her sapphire eyes.

"I've been wanting to return the favor," she murmurs, looking up at me through her long lashes as her hands inch closer to my throbbing cock. My pulse thrums in my ears, desperate to feel her touch as a smirk spreads across my face.

"I'm never going to stop you," I reply, dropping the remaining material that stands between us, and my cock instantly juts out in her direction. I shiver as her breath sweeps over the sensitive skin, one hand stroking ever so gently over my balls, while the other circles my cock.

She licks from the base to the tip slowly, before blowing her breath over the wet trail, and my head falls back on an exhale in pure delight. My excitement has me looking away too soon, because in the next breath, her lips are wrapping around the tip of my cock as she swallows me straight down to the back of her throat.

"Holy fuck," I groan, grabbing her shoulder for balance as I look down at her. The way she cups my balls and takes me so deep to the back of her throat, without needing to work herself on to the long length, has me ready to fucking come all over her pretty tits.

Expecting her to gag and choke, I almost fucking whimper when she moans around my cock instead, the vibrations from her hum only bringing me closer to the edge.

I catch sight of us in the large mirror before me, letting it capture the perfect view of us as she works my cock like a queen. My muscles clench, the impending feeling of my orgasm ready to wash over me taking form, and I can't stop it.

"You're going to swallow my cum if you don't stop now," I manage to bite out through gritted teeth, but she doesn't stop. No. She looks up at me through her lashes, cheeks pink as she tightens her lips around me, determination in her eyes and I explode, hitting the back of her throat over and over again as I find my release.

When she's wrung every drop out of me, I almost sag forward, but I manage to keep it together. Slowly rising to her feet, she keeps her gaze fixed between my legs, watching as I stay hard and throbbing.

"You didn't think you could fully bring me to my knees like that, did you?" I ask, cupping her cheek before grabbing for her waist and placing her ass back on the vanity behind her.

"I have high expectations for you, incubus," she says, her voice a little raw from the slamming of my cock down her throat, and it only turns me on more. Hearing her call me by my supernatural being too only makes my heart pound faster for her.

"Hmm, I like high expectations. But first, I'm hungry," I say, licking my lips as I reach behind her and unclasp her bra, discarding it over my shoulder before I move my attention to the material covering her pussy that begs for my touch.

I'm careless this time as I rip at the side of the cotton, before doing the same on the other side, and tossing the scrap of material away. "You owe me new underwear," she states, and I smirk.

"Oh, I fucking plan on it, don't you worry," I reply quickly, placing a gentle kiss to both of her taut nipples, before dropping down to my own knees this time.

Her core clenches in anticipation as I reach out and stroke my finger through her folds, remembering every inch of her skin from the last time I had the pleasure of touching her, only this time, I get to taste her sweetness directly from the source.

I nudge her thighs further apart as I drag my tongue from her entrance to her clit, before blowing my breath gently over the skin, just as she did to me, and she shivers, clenching the vanity so tight her knuckles are white.

I'm desperate to be inside her, but I've wanted to taste her properly for too long. I'm not going to drag this out and take my time though, I want to watch her face when she comes without the public setting around us. I want to hear how she cries out in pleasure when she's not muted.

I want it all. Now.

Sucking and nipping at her clit, she gasps and moans, writhing with every stroke as I bring two fingers to her center, my cock jutting out in her direction with how wet she is for me already. Rhea parts her legs even further as I sink inside of her, a long groan falling from her lips as her tight little nub pulses under my tongue.

"Fuck, Adonis," she cries out, her head thrown back as I work her core with precision. I want to demand her eyes come back to me so she can watch me doing this to her, but the way her pussy clenches around my fingers tells me she's already there.

Holy shit.

Keeping my pace as I fuck her with my fingers, I graze my teeth over her clit once more, and she climaxes around me, my name a cry on her lips. I lap at her juices, tasting every drop of her honey, before I force myself to rise to my feet.

I find her eyes closed, her chest dusted pink, and her pulse throbbing at her neck as I drag my fingers across her bottom lip, and without even opening her eyes she peeks her tongue out, tasting herself on my skin.

"You're hot as fuck, Rhea Harrington," I murmur, a clear obsession with how her full name rolls off my tongue, and a slight grin appears at the corner of her mouth.

"Right back at you," she whispers, blinking her eyes open as I crush my lips to hers. Our mouths are sloppy and languid, and I fucking love it. I let my hands trail over her slight curves as I kiss her, my cock nudging at her entrance before she freezes.

"Condom," she mutters against my lips, and I nod, blindly reaching into the drawer to my right to find one.

Quickly dragging it over my hard length, I grab Rhea's waist and turn her around in my arms before placing her down on her feet. With her back to my chest, I can see her full body on display in the mirror, and so can she. It almost makes her stand taller, more certain in herself, compared to the expectation of her shying away, which only makes me harder.

Her confidence is on another level, and it's fucking stunning to watch.

Bracing my hands on her waist, I line up my cock with her core and snap my hips, surging deep inside of her in one swift move, and we both groan together.

"Fuck," I grind out, marveling in how wet and tight she is at the same time. Every inch of my body is on fire, desperate to chase this feeling with her. I pull out until only the tip remains, before surging forward once more.

My pulse rings in my ears, my brain fogging as lust,

desire, and need consume me.

Fuck. It's never felt like this before.

"Oh my Gods, Adonis," Rhea cries out, a hint of panic in her voice as I meet her gaze in the mirror, only to find red pools of surprise flashing in her eyes. My movements slow, my pace slowing as concern fills me, but she shakes her head frantically. "Adonis, fuck… has it… has it ever felt like this before?" she bites out, her body trembling with pleasure along with mine, and I take a second to answer her honestly, but when I almost come to a stop, Rhea growls. "Don't. Fucking. Stop. Just answer me," she pleads, sweat trickling down the side of her face as I thrust into her hard and fast once, twice, three times as I think.

My heart feels like it's about to beat out of my chest, my skin feels like electricity is coursing through the veins beneath, my body burning with an insatiable need. "No, no it hasn't," I admit truthfully, and she curses again.

"Holy fuck it's going to happen again," she murmurs, a delirious yet curious tone to her voice, and I frown in confusion, refusing to stop my thrusts, my grip tightening on her waist enough that it'll leave bruises.

"What is?"

She doesn't respond right away, the sound of our skin slapping together the only noise to fill the room. But when she does finally speak, her words leave me breathless.

"This is how it felt with *Xander*, Adonis," she says with a gasp, her eyes flaring red. It takes a moment for me to understand what she's saying, my body roaring to life as I stare at her in disbelief. "If we carry on, you're going to take that condom off and…" she doesn't need to say the rest, I already know where it will lead.

Holy. Fucking. Shit.

My movements halt altogether, and she growls at me through thin lips. "I didn't fucking say to stop," she hisses, her chest heaving rapidly as she glares at me through the mirror. "Shit, I'm sorry, this is hard for me," she adds, a whimper playing at the corner of her mouth as she tries to take a deep breath.

Gaping at her, I try to find the right words to say, the right questions to ask, but I come up blank. As if my body has a mind of its own, it retreats from her body, my hands dragging the latex from my cock, and I slam back inside her without a single word.

"Oh, Gods," she screams as I look down at where we're joined, my body trembling with the new sensations washing over me. It's almost like relief, yet euphoric all at once.

I can't stop chasing the need, the desire, everything with her, when I hear her call my name.

"Oh my Gods, Adonis. Adonis!"

I look up to meet her gaze in the mirror and falter when my own eyes capture my attention.

Lilac.

My eyes are fucking lilac.

THIRTY THREE

RHEA

Every fiber of my body is set to detonate with his touch. It's like I'm watching this thing between us from the outside in third person. I've been through this once before, I didn't even consider it would happen again, but that's my own fault for burying it at the back of my mind for the most part, not wanting to venture into what ifs.

But now here we are, sweat clinging to us as we gape at Adonis' lilac colored eyes, unable to stop fucking hard and fast against the vanity as our magic takes over, leaving no room for anything else.

My heart lurches as he leans closer, his fingertips burning into my molten skin as he reaches around to pinch my clit, and I explode. My body heaves with relief, exhaustion, and raw emotion as wave after wave of pleasure flutters through me, but as my feelings heighten, the next wave of ecstasy releases a scream from my lips, and the mirror shatters before us.

Thousands, maybe millions of shards dance around us, and I hiss as a few graze my skin, but it does nothing to dilute the pleasure that Adonis gives me. His moves become jagged, his hips slamming into me without caution, before he lets out an almighty roar in my ear, and my pussy clenches again in response to his cock spasming.

"Fuck, Rhea. Fuck," he groans with a gasp, the entire situation feeling unreal as we slowly climb down from our high.

Panting, with my palms splayed out wide on the vanity, I scramble to piece everything together. I can't see Adonis properly, not now that the glass is everywhere but on the wall, and I'm desperate to get a look at his stunning lilac eyes once more.

We did that. Our connection brought his magic to the forefront, leaving me utterly slayed at the sheer beauty of this man. I'm screwed, so beyond screwed that I can't even comprehend how this is even my life.

Down the road, we'll declare that we should have been more cautious, taken more time to consider things, especially since we have already seen the beginning of this with Xander, but right now, none of that even matters. Not one bit.

Our magic took from one another, claiming what was theirs, and now we get to bask in the afterglow before reality sets in.

I feel Adonis' hand brush against my spine as he leans forward, bracing his forehead against me, and I take a calming breath as his cock still somehow manages to spasm inside of me.

"Adonis," I finally murmur, a tingle running down my spine at a sudden chill in the air, but before he can respond, the door leading to my room is swung open, splintering into pieces as it ricochets off the wall, shocking us both at the intrusion.

What the fuck?

I blink repeatedly, confused and stunned at the sight of Zellus before us. I stare into his black eyes, too shocked to acknowledge anything else as Adonis remains inside of me, holding me to his chest as he attempts to shield me from view.

"What the fuck is going on here?" Adonis growls. "Get the fuck out," he spits, not seeming to care who he's speaking to, and I mentally pat him on the fucking back because I have no words. This goddamn supernatural world seems to keep leaving me stunned silent, and I can't stand it. For now, I'll let Adonis handle Zellus.

Attempting to take a calming breath, I brush the damp, loose hair back off my face, but before I can try and repeat Adonis' words, with a little less growl, Zellus fully steps into the room, with two guards on either side of him.

"Separate them," he says, disgust heavy in his tone as he glares at me. "And take her," he adds, pointing a manicured finger in my direction, and I shake my head immediately as

Adonis scoffs.

"Fuck off. You can't just storm in here and do this. I don't care who you think you are but you are not taking her," he grunts, taking a step back with me, but the guards continue forward as the sound of a door slamming booms from behind us too.

Looking back over my shoulder, all too late I see another two guards approaching, completely unfazed by our level of undress, and if I wasn't so angry, I'd be dying of embarrassment right about now.

With my arms pinned at my side beneath Adonis', I feel helpless, but as one of the guards coming toward us gets close, I kick my leg out, connecting my foot with his shin, I wince as I seem to cause myself more damage than him.

"I've got you, Rhea," Adonis murmurs in my ear, but whatever plan he has, I don't get to bear witness to it as out of nowhere, a blue powder is blown in my face by a guard, and then… I see nothing but darkness.

"What is so important, Zellus, that you deem it suitable to force us all into attendance?" The man's voice sounds distant, yet right by my ear all at once.

My throat is dry, my eyelids are heavy, and my head is pounding.

What the fuck is going on?

I try to pry my eyes open, but it's harder than I expect, and I rack my brain to remember how I even got myself into this situation but concentrating is hard with all of these people talking.

"I have something that may be of interest to you all." I recognize that as Zellus this time, and the twist in my stomach tells me it links back to me as the memories flood me.

Adonis.

Me.

A beautiful moment destroyed and shattered by the arrival of Zellus and his men. But I still don't understand why. It doesn't make any sense.

"Then get on with it, Zellus, I have places to be," a woman says with a sniff, clearly inconvenienced.

Trying to feel my surroundings, I attempt to wiggle my fingers and toes, but it's impossible. A sickly feeling drips down my throat as dread threatens to consume me.

With a deep breath, using all my strength I force my eyes open, blinking rapidly as the bright light burns my fucking skull. After a few moments I'm able to adjust, but being able to see doesn't fill me with relief. No, it makes everything worse.

I'm suspended, in the fucking air, arms out wide at my side and my legs together, feet straight, my toes are even pointing down like a dancer, while an audience looks up at me with curiosity.

Zellus.

Three men.

Two women.

And Zeus.

They're all standing, in what looks like a sacred room in the main building. The high ceilings no longer glisten in an array of colors as darkness covers the night sky.

I need to get myself out of this, and I need to do it fast. But how?

I'm completely outmatched. Any hint of magic I have shown has been uncontrollable and not used consciously. Considering whether or not I should call out feels futile, my life is in their hands, and it doesn't seem like any of them are eager to help a girl out. They're too busy being inconvenienced by Zellus.

At least someone managed to put a robe on me, but the thought of someone fucking touching me while I was unconscious pisses me off.

"We've had word from a student that a few of our other students have seemingly activated their powers early, fighting through the repression we put on everyone as a child, controlling when they receive their powers," Zellus says, walking a few strides in front of me, but his back is to me, and all eyes are on him, so it seems like no one knows I'm awake as I frown at the information he just dropped.

Repressed magic?

Is this a joke? A secret? What?

"How? That's entirely impossible. The only way that could happen was if…"

"*If* they sealed their souls to one another, yes, Mrs. Black, that is indeed correct," Zellus states, cutting her off with a single nod, and I turn my attention to the woman.

Dressed in a crimson red pants suit, with her jet black hair twisted up into a tight bun at the top of her head, she looks equal measures dark and cunning. She purses her lips at Zellus, offering him a look of disdain. "It may be correct, but that hasn't happened in a very long time, we made sure of it."

Before anyone else can respond, the door behind the group bursts open, distracting everyone as a man in brown overalls comes running in with a piece of parchment waving around in his hands.

"I have it here, sir, I have it here," he calls out through heavy breathing, cutting through the crowd to get to Zellus, who wordlessly takes the sheet of paper from his grasp, hiding whatever it details from the others.

Everyone looks at him expectantly as the guy quickly retreats, but the door doesn't shut behind him as Dante saunters into the room like a fucking rockstar. He looks around curiously, his eyes immediately falling to mine as my name slips from his lips. "Rhea?"

One word and all eyes turn to me. Some even look like they had barely registered me there to begin with. Assholes.

I open my mouth to speak, but nothing comes out, and Zellus gives a little chuckle. "Oh, I rendered our little trouble maker silent for a while," he says with a cluck of his tongue, before offering me his back like I don't exist, and turns to look at the group. All of whom keep their gazes fixed on Zellus.

"Get to the point, Zellus," Zeus rumbles, the tension in his neck tightening as he works his jaw in agitation, but instead of speaking, Zellus offers the paper to the God, who gapes in surprise and lets the paper flutter to the floor.

With his slick backed hair and larger than life persona that drifts off him in waves, you could pass him as Zellus' sibling or something.

"It can't be true. It can't be." His words are barely more than a whisper as the Almighty God's face pales, his brows knitting together as he turns a stern gaze my way.

"Can someone fucking explain to me what the hell is going on?" Mrs. Black barks, hands on her hips as the man with blue hair huffs.

"You and I both know they have a flare for the dramatics," a man says dismissively, his gaze flicking back to me for a moment. "But I would like to know why you have my son held in another room, Zellus."

"Do you even know which one it is, *Hades*?" Zellus retorts with a quirk of his eyebrow and a scoff, which Hades doesn't even bother to respond to.

Hades, as in *the* Hades, as in Adonis' *father*?

Shit.

Yeah, that would have something to do with me I think, but I can't tell him that, not with my lead tongue.

"She's a God," Zellus continues, moving away from Zeus as the others look at me in surprise, and my heart about stops in my chest with my own shock.

"A God that was lost to the human world for twenty-two years?" Dante asks in disbelief, seeking clarification for all of us, and Zellus simply shrugs in response.

"I mean, after reading that," Zellus says, pointing at the discarded paper on the floor before continuing, "I would say it all makes a lot of sense, wouldn't you, Zeus?"

My heart rate kicks up, my body pulsing with every throb, but I'm left completely helpless as I'm unable to say or do a single thing.

"It can't be possible," Zeus repeats, and even I want to strangle the pair of them now, and not for my current situation, but because Hades was right; they love the fucking drama.

"We ran a sample of her blood while she was knocked out to determine her heritage without triggering her magic. Not something usually appreciated, but desperate times call for desperate measures," Zellus explains, moving to stand in front of me now as he sweeps his arm out to draw their attention to me. "Ladies and gentleman, fine leaders of the Hex, I give you…"

He pauses for dramatic effect, my eyes widening a fraction as I desperately wait to hear what he has to say too.

I've waited my whole life for this moment, to understand where I came from, who my parents might be, before my magic was even known, and here this man is going to drop it like a gossip bomb.

I still lap it up, every morsel, every word, like a greedy, starved child.

Until the words fall from his mouth.

Uncaring.

Emotionless.

World shattering.

I wish he could take them back.

I wish I had closed my ears somehow, squeezed my eyes shut, and continued to live in unknowing bliss.

But there's no going back from this.

No bright future.

Only darkness.

"The child of… Zeus… and Nyx."

AFTERWORDS

Holy. Motherfucking. Shit. Balls.

How in the ever-loving fuck did I just write my first paranormal/fantasy book?

I'm obsessed with all of the guys, and Rhea herself.

She's fire, a total badass with the love for peen that I'm here for.

Honestly, when I started plotting Featherstone way back when, I truly thought it was going to be paranormal, but the story shifted into exactly what it was supposed to be. Then I stayed safe in the contemporary world.

Until a nightmare.

Literally, I had a nightmare, and when I woke up, for the first time in my author life, I reached out blindly for a piece of paper and a pen, needing to jot down everything I felt before I lost it all. And now here we are.

Thank you, truly thank you, for being here on this journey with me. I'm also showing thanks in what I'm calling a soft cliffhanger, we all know I could do worse, haha!

August isn't too far away… is it?

THANK YOU

Thank you all the world to my husband and children, who as always, support me, encourage me, and protect me. Everything I do in this world is for you. Yet you've somehow taught me to do it for myself too, and I will forever love you for that.

Nicole, Jeni, and Tanya.

No words explain the crazy that is our group chat and alpha comments. You fill me with fire and motivation, and I can't thank you enough!

Michelle, Emma, Monica, Brianna, Kerrie, and Keira. You all rock, thank you for arguing over the guys, showing me when you're ecstatic, angry, and dickmatized, it fills me with all the joy and evil cackles haha!

Kirsty, I wrote this entire book before you officially came onboard, but your daily progress messages kept me on track, and focused, knowing I had an ear to bounce off when needed.

Sloane and Sarah, thank you for prettying my interiors and my words, cos you both know I need it haha. I really appreciate it, thank you.

Thank you to Christian and Laura for literally seeing the visual for this book and bringing it to life in a way I never thought possible.

ABOUT KC KEAN

KC Kean is the sassy half of a match made in heaven. Mummy to two beautiful children, Pokemon Master and Apex Legend world saving gamer.

Starting her adventure in the RH romance world after falling in love with it as a reader, who knows where this crazy train is heading. As long as there is plenty of steam she'll be there.

ALSO BY KC KEAN

Featherstone Academy

(Reverse Harem Contemporary Romance)

My Bloodline

Your Bloodline

Our Bloodline

Red

Freedom

All-Star Series

(Reverse Harem Contemporary Romance)

Toxic Creek

Tainted Creek

Twisted Creek

(Standalone MF)

Burn to Ash

Emerson U Series

(Reverse Harem Contemporary Romance)

Watch Me Fall

Watch Me Rise

Watch Me Reign

Saints Academy

(Reverse Harem Paranormal Romance)

Reckless Souls

Damaged Souls

Printed in Great Britain
by Amazon

11505949R10287